In Antarctica everyone can hear you scream!

Action adventure sci-fi horror set in Antarctica.

The spaceship entombed in the huge iceberg calved from the Pine Island Glacier drifts towards the warmer air and ocean temperatures of the South Atlantic. The race is on to claim the alien technology before the ice melts and releases its hold on the trapped alien vessel.

The mission: Board the spaceship and salvage as much alien technology as possible before the doomed vessel sinks to the bottom of the ocean.

The obstacles: A disintegrating iceberg, a collapsing spaceship, an armed Russian salvage force intent on claiming alien technology for themselves, an approaching storm, and the biggest obstacle of all—the spacecraft's alien inhabitants.

The aliens have another mission—survival—and when opposing species clash, there can be only one victor.

Ice Rift - Salvage is the sequel to **Ice Rift**, which needs to be read first to gain the most enjoyment from the story.

Ben Hammott

ICE RIFT - SALVAGE
Ben Hammott

Author can be contacted at: **benhammott@gmail.com**
Author's website: **www.benhammottbooks.com**

Ice Rift - Salvage is the direct follow on book to Ice Rift, which needs to be read first to get the most enjoyment from this book. Available here or from your Amazon

Acknowledgements

First of all I would like to thank my readers for their continued support of my literary endeavors.

A big thank you goes to the men and women of the British and American coast guards who risk their lives to rescue others and advised me on helicopter performance limitations and capabilities in adverse weather conditions.

I express my thanks to Captain Aristarkh Ivanov for his information on the Russian Mi-26M helicopter (Halo), multi-purpose Russian salvage vessels and the MPSV07 deck plans he gratefully provided, and certain members of a certain special forces team for their information and advice on small team infiltration tactics, weaponry, the merits and limitations of using Night Vision Goggles (NVG) in confined spaces and within the imagined scenario depicted in this book, and the limitations of communications in many-roomed, multi-level metal structures.

As always, any errors or liberties taken with the information provided is entirely my own doing.

CHAPTER 1

Lucy

UNCONTROLLABLE FEAR GRABBED hold of Lucy when the monster outside the room slammed against the door with such force she expected it to burst open. Shaking as much from terror as from the cold due to her near-naked state, she backed away and tried to calm down. Panicking would do her no good. She told herself fear was a reaction and not a threat unless she allowed it to be, so if she could fight her fear, she might be able to fight the cause. The metal door was solid enough to hold the monster at bay, so for the moment she was safe. Her gaze followed the flashlight she swept around the room. Neither picked out the alternative exit she desperately sought. The room that trapped her would become her tomb if someone didn't come and rescue her. She found it difficult to believe Jane or Jack would abandon her. Richard, yes—that she could understand. The man only worried about himself. But not her friends, not unless they were dead, slaughtered by the alien monsters that prowled the spaceship. It could be the only reason for their abandonment. She fought back the tears that threatened to flow and sunk to the floor.

*****

The computer checked its sensors. Though many were not working, those that still functioned indicated a third of the specimens had survived their extended hibernation period and were now loose in the vessel. One species, so dangerous that not even in an emergency was it to be set free, remained firmly imprisoned in its chamber.

Aware the specimens' only chance of survival now was to escape from the doomed vessel before it slipped beneath the sea, she opened every door it still controlled.

*****

Startled by the door opening along the corridor and fearing another species had tracked it scent, the Hunter outside Lucy's room shot a glance at the sound, but relaxed on seeing the doorway absent of any menace. It was surprised again when the doors set in the corridor walls opened one by one, gradually moving towards the door blocking it from its next meal. It had been about to give up and go in search of easier prey, but not now. While it waited for it to open, it screeched in anticipation of the feast it was about to enjoy and stared hungrily at the door as it scraped a claw down it.

*****

Lucy hugged her knees to stop them from shaking when the Hunter outside shrieked and chalkboard screeches from the claws it scraped down the door set her frail nerves on edge. Hope replaced her dread when a different sound filtered into the room. She climbed to her feet and rushed for the door. The faint, but unmistakable rasp of doors opening grew nearer. Someone must be looking for her? They would see the monster, kill it, and set her free. She would be saved.

Confusion banished her hope when the door of the room next to hers opened and still the monster scratched at the door. She backed away. Something was wrong. No one was coming to rescue her. The door opened. The monster peered through the ever-widening gap and snarled at her. Lucy sobbed as she frantically glanced around the room for something she could use as a weapon. When her frightened gaze drifted over the bed chamber, she remembered Jane had opened the one in the dormitory room. She rushed over and pressed the buttons until the door slid open. The monster growled as it stepped through the doorway, but wary there might be more than one of the strange creatures inside, its cruel, hungry eyes searched the room to check. Lucy scrambled into the sleeping pod and stabbed buttons on the interior console. The monster lurched forward when the bed screen began to close, but it wasn't fast enough and found its prey sealed in the bed chamber. Frustrated by its meal's escape, the Hunter struck the transparent view panel and screeched.

Though she had escaped its clutches, Lucy was well aware their kind could open doors; it only had to jab at the buttons like she had until it struck lucky. Fearful the Hunter would be upon her at any moment, she turned away from the horrifying sight and examined the control panel. Perhaps there was a way of locking the door or disabling the outside control. A button she pressed brought a screen to life. Her eyes swept down the list of unintelligible alien words until she spied one in English. She assumed by this that when the spaceship's main computer added the English translation to its database it had gone ship-wide. She silently thanked the computer and pressed the screen. A list of English options appeared and though there was no choice to lock the door, there was another option that might save her.

The pod shuddered and glass splintered when the Hunter struck it again. Lucy jerked her head around to see the cause; spider cracks crept across the window. The Hunter howled and struck it again. The cracks spread. One or two more blows and it would break and the monster would finally get its meal. Lucy re-focused her attention on the screen and selected the eject pod option. Another menu appeared asking her to confirm or cancel the action. Her finger jabbed at the confirmation option. A rasp of metal from the end of the pod outside announced the opening of the hatch she, Jane and Jack had seen previously in one of the ejected pod rooms. The bed chamber lurched and shot forward. Lucy tumbled back and glimpsed the side of the hatch portal passing the cracked window. When it was through, the pod pivoted to the side, giving Lucy an opportunity to glance back into the recently evacuated room. The Hunter's vicious face stared at her until it disappeared when the pod shot forward.

Dim lights set in the sides of the escape chute sped by faster and faster as the pod increased in speed. It was then Lucy realized, in her attempt to escape the monster, she hadn't thought her rash plan through. The spaceship was encased in ice and it would be this she would be ejected into and not open space the pod was designed for. She thought it doubtful, at the speed they were travelling, the escape pod or she would survive the impact. Maybe she could climb out? She pressed the open door button, but it failed to respond, probably because the pod was in motion.

As the pod's speed continued to increase, Lucy snatched up the ends of the restraints she noticed fixed to the pod walls and buckled them around her. The slack was automatically pulled out to hold her snugly, not that it would help when the pod crashed into the ice and crushed them both. Without any warning, the pod tilted on end and threw her against the restraints before it plummeted down an almost vertical chute headfirst and continued to increase in speed. Lucy gazed at the cracked window. The lights flashed by so fast they were a continuous blur.

Refusing to just lie there and hope for the best, Lucy formed an idea, though risky, might be her only chance to survive this journey. She released the harness and slid to the bottom. She righted herself and moved into a position facing the window. Hoping she wouldn't rip her bare feet to shreds when it broke, she kicked at the window. The transparent panel bulged in the middle a little more with each blow and her forth kick dislodged it from the frame; it struck the side of the chute and shattered. She peered out. The chute rushing by was circular with three other rails for more escape pods distributed around its circumference to expedite the evacuation of a doomed ship. Luckily, she was travelling along the bottom rail; it would make her next move slightly easier.

Lucy poked her head out and gazed down at the lights disappearing into its depths that gave no indication how far away the bottom was. It could be one hundred feet away or one thousand. When she climbed out the slipstream whipped her hair around her face and caused her to shiver from the cold that blasted her body. Keeping her body as flat as possible to prevent the wind drag from pulling her off, she climbed onto the top, crawled to the back of the pod and shone the light over the speeding walls. *Okay Lucy, now what are you going to do?*

*****

After the Hunter had watched its prey escape a second time, it had climbed into the empty bedchamber and leapt through the hatch when it began to close. It rushed after the pod and barely paused when it changed direction and disappeared into a tunnel in the floor. It dived in after it and sprinted headfirst down the steeply sloping chute and screeched when its prey appeared a few moments later.

Lucy shot her gaze above. The Hunter bounded towards her at amazing speed. She had swapped one danger for another just as deadly. When it had almost reached the speeding pod, the Hunter leaped. Lucy backed away as it landed on the back end of the pod and swayed unsteadily. She lashed out with a foot, landing a blow to its stomach. It stumbled, fell, and howled in pain when momentum slid it down the chute on its back, scraping gouges in its flesh until it started tumbling.

The Hunter halted its painful tumble and righted itself. A few bounds and it reached the pod again. Saliva dripped from its vicious mouth when it snarled at Lucy, who only had seconds before it would be upon her. Lucy glanced at the walls speeding by and jumped for one of the thick cables that ran between the rails. The flashlight, held precariously in one hand, almost fell from her grasp when her fingers circled the cable. Her momentum tugged her grip free and sent her hurtling back towards the monster that lashed out a claw. She snatched out for another cable, wincing in pain when her arm was almost yanked from its socket. She held on tight. Her life depended on it. She glanced behind at the receding pod and the Hunter riding it. A rasp of metal echoed up the chute when the hull's outer hatch opened. As the Hunter crouched, ready to spring its body off the pod and climb up to its prey, the escape pod struck the ice blocking the opening and crumpled into an unrecognizable shape. The sudden halt slammed the Hunter against the wall. Its body exploded from the impact and sprayed the area with blood and innards.

A sigh of relief escaped from Lucy's lips. That was one problem taken care of. As her pounding heart slowed, she glanced up at the receding lights that seemed to go on forever; she had a long climb ahead of her and one she wasn't confident she could make.

After climbing a short distance, Lucy noticed what seemed to be an access hatch on the opposite side of the shaft. Hoping it might lead to an easier route back up to the engine room level, she scrambled across the steeply sloping tunnel and climbed the wall. A hiss of air escaped when she released the catch and pulled it open. A dark void almost filled with a mass of shiny, black cables that had the appearance of a horrifying monster's tentacles waiting to entangle her in its grasp greeted her. It wasn't a view that inspired confidence climbing inside would be a wise or safe thing to do. She closed the small door and continued her strenuous climb.

The stressed spaceship groaned, creaked and belched distant thumps that sounded like rumbling thunder, and the occasional throaty crack produced by the ice that vibrated through the ship seemed to be amplified by the escape chute's acoustics adding to the ominous soundtrack to Lucy's troubled plight. When she paused to rest for a moment and gazed above to see if the end of the climb was anywhere near, Lucy pressed her body against the cold metal and froze on seeing something entirely different—creatures moving down towards her.

Heads low and their rumps high, the creatures moved on three long fingers attached to each of their four, long, spindly limbs. Their skin, stretched taught over their bony bodies gave them the appearance of plucked chickens. Pimples, like goose bumps, larger and more pronounced on the shoulders and thighs covered their bodies and reinforced the illusion.

Fear threatened to reclaim the confidence Lucy had regained since the death of the Hunter—that she could survive and escape from her metal tomb. She started to shiver as she watched the creatures pale-green, hairless bodies pass through the dim patches of light before entering the gloomy spaces again. Because none of them had so far shown any interest in her, Lucy thought it unlikely they had detected her presence yet. Their eyes, small, round and milky-white, set either side of their short snouts might indicate they were blind or had poor eyesight. Like most of the alien monstrosities Lucy had encountered on board the vessel, their jaws sported sharp teeth.

The eight creatures were attracted by the scent of the Hunter's fresh spilled blood wafting up the shaft, and were seeking out the source. Though they weren't completely blind, their species had been living in darkness for thousands of years and each new generation had experienced diminished sight and heightened senses of smell and hearing.

Trying to make as little noise as possible, Lucy retreated down the chute. Though she suspected the creatures might be blind, and if she remained still they might pass her by without noticing her, they were too vicious and horrifying, and she was too scared to take the risk. The unwelcoming hatch was her only escape. She pulled it open and squeezed inside headfirst. It worried her that the creatures were small enough to crawl inside after her if she left the hatch open, but the narrow area in the center free of cables, left her with no room to turn and close it. She hooked a foot on the door edge and pulled it shut as far as she could. Though she hoped they would pass by the hatch, it wasn't something Lucy was going to rely on. She crawled and slithered through the duct as fast as the cables pressing against her body would allow.

Though seven of the creatures continued towards the appetizing scent of fresh blood, the eighth, slightly smaller than the others, paused and sniffed the air. Its inquisitive face turned towards the wall and followed the scent to the partially open hatch. It forced its snout through the opening and sniffed to confirm the trail continued inside. It glanced in the direction its brethren headed down the chute. It knew unless the dead or wounded creature below was large, not all would manage to sate their hunger. As it was the youngest, it would be last to feed and might not get anything. Deciding it was better it found its own source of food, it pulled the hatch open wider, climbed inside with its long front limbs stretched out ahead and scrambled along the cables towards the sound of something moving.

Lucy, sweating with the effort of forcing her body through the tight passage, paused for a breather. Vibrations sent along the cables were transferred to her body pressed against them. As they weren't there a moment ago, it was an indication something was now in here with her. The flashlight she aimed ahead picked out no threat. Dread swept over her when she realized one of the long-legged chicken creatures might have followed her. She rolled over and aimed the flashlight back the way she had come and stared at the two distant pinpricks of light caught just beyond the farthest reach of the beam. At first, she thought it might be the light reflecting off something, pieces of metal perhaps, but when she noticed the lights blink and move closer, Lucy stifled a sob, twisted onto her stomach and slithered through the shaft as fast as she could.

Realizing its furtive movements through the cramped tunnel were no longer necessary, the creature abandoned its stealthy approach and crawled faster towards its prey.

Though already scared enough because she couldn't see what was coming or how close it was, Lucy's imagination increased her fear as she imagined the thing biting at her feet and legs, devouring her from the toes up. She whimpered as adrenaline coursed through her bloodstream and pushed her onward.

CHAPTER 2

First Incursion

FIGHTING THE GUSTS that blew across the choppy sea, the helicopter swooped towards the colossal iceberg and hovered a foot above the ledge of ice at the end of the tunnel the scientists and Haax had used to escape from the spaceship. A six-man team stepped out with weapons held ready to suppress any threat and formed a defensive position around the tunnel entrance. The seventh team member, who rarely ventured so close to the action and whose thoughts had dwelt on the alien monsters since he had been informed of their presence aboard the spaceship, wasn't so eager to leave the relative safety of the helicopter. He reluctantly stepped onto the ice with his eyes focused on the dark tunnel opening. As the helicopter rose into the air behind him, spraying his back with wind and ice, he knelt behind the defensive team, placed a rigid plastic case on the ground and speedily assembled a small drone. He stepped back and used the control pad to power up its four spinning rotors and watched the drone rise into the air. He moved it forward, spun it around and peered at the small screen attached to the remote control. The high-definition image of the armed men caught in the drone's camera was crystal clear.

Sergeant Vincent Monroe, the battle-hardened squadron leader, glanced at the drone hovering in front of him and then at its operator. "All set, Fitch?"

Fitch nodded, wishing the Sergeant would lower his voice so he didn't draw any monsters that might be close by to them.

Sergeant Monroe spoke into his helmet mic, "Alpha Team leader to Control, are you receiving the feeds?"

The men gathered in the hastily set up control room aboard the container ship, Starlight— charted at great expense by the American military and stationed a short distance from the large iceberg— stared at the screens showing feeds from Alpha Team's helmet-cams and the drone.

Corporal Giles Norton cast his gaze over each screen before answering, "All crisp and clear, Sergeant. Send in the drone."

Every eye in the control room followed the drone's progress through the tunnel. Its bright light reflected off the ice tube it sped along before it reached the spaceship and emerged into the large hangar. The men gasped at the group of spacecraft caught in the drone's light.

Rear Admiral Thaddeus Thomson, the officer in charge of the salvage mission, pointed at the screen showing the drone's feed. "They must be the smaller spaceships the scientists mentioned."

Todd Fleming, NASA's chief science advisor, and Bradley Clines, head of NASA's R&D program, almost salivated as they studied the impressive shuttlecraft the drone focused on. "The technology aboard even one of those crafts could advance us hundreds or even thousands of years," said Fleming. "It's imperative we salvage one."

"Two would be better," added Charles Mason, the British representative, who was determined Britain would not be left empty-handed when the salvage mission was completed and the spoils allocated. The frosty reception he had received from Admiral Thomson when they had first met hinted that sharing alien technology was not high on the man's list of priorities.

"I wonder what propulsion they use," pondered Clines aloud. When he had first been informed of the unbelievable discovery and alien monsters he was certain the scientists had been mistaken and had suffered a group hallucination brought on by gases trapped underground. It was only after he had seen the photographic evidence and satellite scans of the spaceship were his doubts firmly banished. His dream and those of many of his fellow colleagues might now be realized in their lifetime; humans would travel to far-flung planets and perhaps even visit new galaxies, something they had only dreamed of doing before. He almost shook with anticipation of the wonders to be discovered.

"Does it really matter?" said Admiral Thomson, a little irritably. Though he knew the importance of the discovery and its possible benefits to mankind and humans ever constant desire to explore space, he first had to complete the mission assigned to him by the President of the United States of America. If the damn scientists and engineers would just let him be to concentrate and get on with it, there would be plenty of time for them to drool over and play with their new toys later.

"Anything has to be better than strapping two giant fuel-bombs to every shuttle you shoot into space." He found it hard to believe astronauts were prepared to take the risk, especially after the horrific 1983 Challenger disaster.

Mason glanced at the Admiral and felt it provident he reinforced Britain's involvement in the mission in case it failed to go as planned. "If all we manage to salvage is one of the small spacecraft, *our joint mission* will still be a success."

Thomson glared at Mason. He had been against letting the British aboard and had seen no reason to hide the fact from the pompous man. However, the President insisted their English allies be involved, up to a point. He briefly wondered when that point would be reached. If the decision had been his to make it would have already passed. He returned his gaze to the fascinating images relayed from the spaceship and watched the drone fly around one of the larger cargo transport vessels and hover in front of a large door.

Corporal Norton pointed at the screen. "If the power's still on and that door opens, we'll have access to the cargo bay and the hundreds of storage pods the scientists described."

Admiral Thomson's orders included the securing of the Aladdin's cave of alien stores and he was keen to fulfill the mission parameters as soon as possible before something went wrong. The huge spaceship and what lay inside was an unknown he wasn't altogether comfortable dealing with. To add to an already difficult situation, a storm was heading their way.

"Send Alpha Team in to find out if the door opens. If it doesn't, we'll have to cut through it," ordered Thomson. "According to the scientists the cargo bay will be free of monsters, but warn them not to enter the next room until it's been gassed. That's the domain of those alien insects." Even with the firepower each man carried, Thomson knew they wouldn't be much use against thousands of things so small and deadly. A delay so early in the mission would be disastrous to his timetable.

Corporal Norton relayed the Admiral's instructions to the Alpha Team leader.

The drone flew back to the ice tunnel and observed the marines approaching the hangar. Fitch walked slower at the rear as he continued controlling the drone. When a deep-throated shriek pierced the silence, he spun the drone and sped it across the room to seek out the source.

When Monroe halted the team, they stared at the hangar entrance a few yards away and the darkness within.

Garcia glanced at his team mates. "What in hell's name was that?"

Mitchell smiled at his nervous companion and tapped his assault rifle. "Does it matter?"

Garcia shrugged. "Suppose not."

"It could only be one of those alien monsters the scientists encountered," added Cobb, a little nervously.

"I wouldn't worry," said Washington. "Those scientists survived with little more than their wits. With the firepower we're carrying the aliens won't stand a chance."

Monroe directed his gaze ahead. "Keep in formation and your eyes peeled. We're after technology, not live alien specimens, so kill anything that moves that isn't us."

The men in the control room aboard the container ship were staring at the drone's camera feed screen when the shriek rang out. They had reached the same conclusion as Monroe that it had originated from one of the alien monsters. Fascinated to set eyes upon a live one, their heads moved slightly nearer.

Norton shifted his gaze from screen to screen. It was like watching a live horror movie. "I thought the scientists said the hangar was free of monsters."

"That was then," said Fleming. "When the ice broke free it might have caused damage to parts of the ship, allowing the aliens access to areas they couldn't reach before."

Admiral Thomson creased his brow. Whatever the reason, that the creatures had ventured into the hangar was one of the many unknowns that concerned him.

The men concentrated on the screens as Sergeant Monroe turned his head and looked at the drone operator.

"You see anything, Fitch?"

Fitch shook his head. "That doesn't mean something's not in there though."

"Stay here and keep searching and if you see anything, you be sure to let us know."

Fitch, concentrating on controlling the drone via the small display, nodded.

Sergeant Monroe led Alpha Team forward.

The men's cautious footsteps barely made a sound when they entered the hangar and roamed their weapons around the large space they crossed through. The flashlights attached to their weapons followed their amazed expressions wandering over the shuttlecraft they moved between. The groans and creaks of the hull heightened the tense atmosphere and their anxiety.

The men in the control room were glued to the screens.

Sergeant Monroe halted his team with a raised fist when he heard clicks on the metal floor growing steadily louder, nearer. His light focused on the patch of darkness the noise originated from. A monster the size of a large dog entered the beam. It neither glanced at the lights that followed it or halted its slow, menacing stride.

Alpha Team's weapons and gazes, that were an equal combination of fascination and concern, followed the fearsome beast. Though they had seen the scientists' photographs of some of the alien monsters, it did little to prepare them for the creature that had just appeared. It was shocking even for the battle-experienced men.

"I think it's a Space Rat," whispered Mitchell, recognizing it from the description the scientists had given of the ferocious creature.

The vicious rat, as if noticing their presence for the first time, stopped and turned its gaze upon the men. Its eyes reflected their lights and gave it a supernatural appearance.

"Why is no one shooting it?" asked Garcia, his finger poised on the trigger.

"I want to see what it does," Monroe answered. "We might learn something."

Terrifying shrieks rang out from all around them.

The men in the control room stared in horror at the glimpse of monstrous yellow eyes and a mouth choked with sharp teeth from Garcia's camera feed before the image turned to static.

"The lone rat was a distraction," realized Thomson. It hinted they had intelligence and caused him further concern.

Gunfire echoed through the hangar.

Monroe's feed showed Space Rats being riddled with bullets. The dead or wounded were immediately fed upon by others of their kind. Monroe spun when something shrieked close by. A rat leaped at him. Claws ripped at his face. He fell to the ground firing until the weapon fell from his hands when another rat clamped its jaws around his wrist, severing veins and biting to the bone. When the rat perched on his chest ripped out his throat, Monroe's final pain-wracked breaths gurgled blood.

The drone rushed to the team and presented those safe in the control room an aerial view of the attack.

Though many rats lay dead, there were plenty of others eager to take their places.

Mitchell fired a burst of bullets at the one that leaped at him, but his panicked reaction ruined his aim, only grazing its shoulder. The rat collided with his chest and knocked him backwards. He stumbled and tripped over the vermin feeding on Monroe's bloody corpse. He slammed the rifle into the rat about to sink its teeth into his neck, cracking its skull. He pushed it off and rolled to the side but before he could climb to his feet a rat landed on his back. Claws ripped at his clothes and skin, causing equal damage to both. Mitchell's scream was a mixture of pain and fear when he glimpsed others running to join the feast. There would be no escape if they reached him. He struggled to his feet, aimed the rifle over his shoulder at the creature clinging to his back and fired. The rat's head exploded and it fell to the ground. Mitchell sprayed bullets at the alien vermin rushing at him. The weapon clicked on empty. With no time to reload, he used the weapon as a club, smashing rats left and right.

A Space Rat perched on the top of the nearby cargo shuttle observed the carnage taking place below while it bided its time and waited for a chance to feed. The air was filled with the delicious scent of the strange creatures' blood and it salivated at the thought of tasting it. It watched one of the two-legged creatures battling with its brethren and saw its chance. It altered its position so it was directly above its chosen prey and jumped.

When Mitchell sensed a new threat, he turned. Claws and teeth filled his vision. Excruciating pain quickly followed. Claws ripped at his face, slicing through his eyes and skin. Foul carnivorous breath spewed from the jaws that stripped away his flesh. Mitchell stumbled. His screams joined the shrieks that surrounded him. More rats eager to taste his flesh joined the feast, biting and ripping his body to shreds as they each claimed a piece. Blood sprayed. Mitchell died.

Lovell and Washington fared no better. When the Space Rats attacked from all directions, they teamed back to back and had at first managed to defend themselves, but when more rats leaped from the darkness they were soon overpowered. Unable to defend themselves from the multiple savage attacks, the men fell to the ground. The rats fervently feasted and others lapped up the warm blood pooling around the marines' corpses.

Though Fitch was no coward, he had seen enough to recognize the battle had been lost. If he could have helped his teammates he would have, but there were too many Space Rats for their small force to defeat. Alpha Team was beyond his or anyone's help now. He landed the drone heavily on top of a shuttlecraft and ran back along the ice tunnel.

Some of the Space Rats that had yet to satisfy their hunger noticed the fresh source of food's flight to safety and gave chase. Fitch glanced behind at the mass of claws and teeth in pursuit and threw the drone control at them. One of the Space Rats caught it in its mouth and crunched down on it, cutting it in pieces.

"Bring the chopper back, NOW!" Fitch screamed into his mic.

He stared longingly at the end of the tunnel that seemed so far away, but there was no sign of the helicopter. Fitch wondered how long he would survive if he jumped into the freezing sea. Not long, he concluded, a few minutes at most, but it had to be a less painful death than being torn apart and eaten. He shot a glance behind to judge his chances. They weren't good; the rats had gained ground. Fear and adrenalin spurred him on. As he neared the end of the tunnel a rope dropped into view and dangled in the entrance. Fitch would have smiled if he hadn't been so terrified. He leaped from the ice with his arms stretched ready to receive the lifeline. His hands clamped around the rope as he swung out over the sea before the return swing carried him back towards the ice and the rats that poured from the tunnel.

"Go! For fucks sake get me out of here," Fitch screamed at the pilot.

The rats leaped off the ice like lemmings over a cliff. One made contact and dug its claws into Fitch's leg. Fitch screamed and kicked at it with his other foot, pounding its head until it released its grip and splashed into the cold sea. As Fitch began to rise to safety, he slipped the rifle from his shoulder and fired at the leaping rats, though unless they sprouted wings they had no chance of reaching him now. Their blood sprayed the ice.

Realizing their prey was beyond their grasp, some turned on the dead and wounded while others retreated back to the hangar in the hope of feasting on some leftovers.

The shocked men in the control room stared at Alpha Team's corpses being devoured by the Alien Rats in the drone's camera feed and the gruesome close-ups from the dead men's cameras that were still operational.

"Damn!" cursed Thomson. "Prepare another team. Warn them about the rats and send them in. I want that technology and by God I'm going to get it if I have to sacrifice every man aboard this ship."

His eyes fell on Mason who stared at the horror depicted on the screens. Cannon fodder sprung to mind. "Mason. You Brits wanted involvement. Here's your chance. Six of your men can join the next team to go in."

Mason dragged his eyes away from the massacre and glanced at the Rear Admiral. "I'll arrange it."

CHAPTER 3

Publicity

RICHARD STUDIED THE steadily increasing expressions of amazement that appeared on the publicity consultant's face as he flicked through the photographs of the alien spaceship and its ferocious inhabitants. Richard had done his homework. Clinton Smythe was the best in the business and would ensure he received the rich rewards he wanted for his story.

Stunned by what he had just viewed, Clinton placed the last photo on his expansive mahogany desk and looked at the man who had presented them. "This is incredible. I can hardly believe it's real."

"Trust me, it's real. I lived through the nightmare."

Clinton glanced at the photographs spread out before him, calculating their worth and their validity. "But what happened to the spaceship?"

"It's still entombed in the iceberg. As we speak, a salvage operation is underway to save as much of its technology as possible before it slips beneath the sea."

Clinton shook his head in astonishment. It all seemed too fantastical to be true. "As I said, Richard, it's an incredible story. However, our problem is— even with these astounding photos— getting people to believe it. If you'd managed to get some physical evidence there would've been no problem and no limit to the amount you could have made from this fantastical tale."

Richard smiled, slipped a hand into his inside jacket pocket and pulled something out. "Is this evidence enough?"

Clinton's bushy eyebrows almost disappeared over the top of his head at the sight of the tiny creature covered in green velvet fur cupped in Richard's hand. He moved in closer for a better look. It had two small horns on its head, a black nose and large eyes that currently stared at him. It looked more like a cuddly children's toy than an alien creature. He sorted through the photographs and selected the one of Haax holding Lucifer and compared the two. "Is this the same one, as it looks bigger in the photo?"

Richard shook his head. "Not exactly. The one in the photo is the creature that saved my life and which I rescued from the spaceship. This is its offspring, which I've temporarily named Little Lucifer. When I handed its mother back, if indeed there is a male and female of this species, I later found this one in my pocket, which was much smaller then. I believe this species might be asexual. I did some research and we have quite a few Earth life-forms with this ability, sometimes triggered during a decrease in its species resulting in a lack of males. But, of course, I could be totally wrong. What's important is that in my hand I have absolute evidence that alien life forms exist and have visited Earth. What I want you to do, Clinton, is market this alien, my photos and story— and me, of course— in a way that will make me millions before the government and scientists take Little Lucifer from me, as they surely will when they learn of its existence. I want a book deal. I want to sell the movie rights and I want anything else you can think of to wring money out of this. Can you do that, Clinton, or do I need to look elsewhere for someone who can?"

Clinton dragged his eyes away from the cute creature and looked at Richard. He smiled and held out his hand. "I assure you, Richard, I'll make you so much money you'll have trouble spending it."

Richard shook the offered hand. "That's exactly what I wanted to hear." He stroked Little Lucifer while Clinton pressed a button on the intercom and spoke to his secretary.

"Kim, cancel all my appointments for the next month...yes, you heard correctly, the whole month...I don't care, tell her to find someone else, and send Matt in, I need a contract drawn up." He released the button and shared his greedy smile between Richard and the little alien. "You, Richard, have just become my most important client and, I believe, will soon prove to be my most profitable."

Richard grinned. He tickled Little Lucifer under the chin. It purred in delight from the attention. "The kids are going to love you."

Worried that the news of the spaceship story might leak out and ruin them of an exclusive deal, Clinton Smythe wasted no time selling the story to the highest bidder. Two days later, Richard's money-making machine was set in motion and news of what had been discovered in Antarctica swept around the world.

Jane sat up in bed when Jack entered with a breakfast tray. He placed it on a side table, picked up the newspaper and handed it to Jane. "You're not going to believe the headlines."

Slightly bleary eyed, Jane looked at the front page. In large bold letters the headline read:

ALIEN SPACESHIP DISCOVERED IN ANTARCTICA

READ RICHARD WHORLEY'S INCREDIBLE EYEWITNESS TESTIMONY ON HOW HE BATTLED WITH ALIENS IN ANTARTICA TO SAVE HIS FRIENDS AND THE PLANET

Jane shook her head in dismay. "So much for keeping the story under wraps as we were directed. That man would make money out of misery if he could. *'Battled with aliens to save his friends and the planet!'* I've a good mind to tell my version of what really happened."

"What's the point? Richard's not my favorite person, but we all played our part. Let him have his five minutes. Now the genie's been let out of the bottle I'm sure your time will come if you want it. Also Theo, Scott and Pike will get to tell their story now." Jack leaned forward and kissed her.

Jane placed the newspaper on the bedside table. "You're right. We have more important and pleasurable things to occupy our time." She glanced at the tray. "How about you come to bed and help me work up an appetite for breakfast."

"Your wish is my command." Jack slipped into bed.

CHAPTER 4

Second Incursion

THE SECOND TEAM—formed of six Americans and six British military personnel—ordered to board the vessel and secure the hangar, made their way through the ice tunnel. In the hope they would be better equipped to deal with the threat, Bravo Team had been briefed and shown the horrific footage of the Space Rats killing Alpha Team. When the twelve heavily armed men reached the end of the tunnel, Lieutenant James Miller, Bravo Team's commanding officer, halted the men. The lights fixed to the weapons held by those in the frontline swept the dark hangar for the killer vermin, but none were caught in the beams.

Lieutenant Miller turned to the two men beside him. "Light it up."

Flares were struck and thrown into the room in all directions, lighting up the walls, ceiling and the shuttlecraft in their red glow.

Miller turned to Fitch. "Survey the room and let me know what you find."

Fitch, armed with a new remote control, raised the drone from the top of the cargo ship and did a systematic sweep of the hangar. Paying particular attention to the shuttlecrafts, he searched their underneath, sides and tops for concealed Space Rats.

"It seems clear, Lieutenant," declared Fitch, who was far from pleased at being ordered back aboard the alien infested vessel. Though the cuts on his leg had been attended to, they throbbed painfully, a constant reminder of his close encounter with the monsters.

Lieutenant Miller addressed the men, "You've all seen what we're up against, so if you spot anything, don't hesitate to shoot it. Move slow and steady, spread out and move in a line clearing the room as we go. Check the floor, the walls, the ceiling and every object we encounter. We have no idea what other things are aboard this ship, but we can assume most are expert killers. If we are attacked, regroup and retaliate, making sure you focus on what's coming up around you as well as in front."

Every soldier was on edge when the Lieutenant led them aboard the spaceship. When they had first learned of what had occurred, all had found it hard to believe. Spaceships and alien monsters on Earth was something out of a science-fiction movie, not real life. However, the graphic footage of the alien monsters slaughtering their friends and comrades had left them with no doubts they were very real and extremely dangerous. And, if the scientists were to be believed, there were things aboard this vessel that made the Space Rats seem like cute and loveable kittens.

All felt a little relieved when they reached the far side of the hangar without encountering the Space Rats or any other alien creatures. Except for the dark stains on the floor, they had found no evidence of the slaughter that had recently occurred here— no corpses or bones. What they did find was the vicious vermin's point of entry—a hole near the ceiling caused when a support strut had been torn away, probably when the island-sized piece of ice toppled into the ocean. Two men were ordered to guard the hole and shoot anything that made an appearance while the others trained their weapons around the hangar.

Lieutenant Miller spoke into his helmet mic. "Bravo Team to Control, stage one completed. The hangar is secure. Repeat. The hangar is secure."

In the control room, a rare smile formed on Admiral Thomson's lips as he stared at Lieutenant Miller's camera feed. "At last, things were going according to plan." He turned to Norton. "Send in the engineers. I want two shuttlecrafts salvaged today and I won't accept any excuses."

"Yes sir." Norton plucked a phone from the wall. "It's a go. Admiral Thomson wants the scout ship and a cargo vessel moved to the ship today...Those are his orders and he won't accept any excuses. He wants results, so make it happen." He hung up.

The Rear Admiral smiled at Norton. "Engineers giving you lip, were they?"

"Nothing I couldn't handle, sir."

"In my experience engineers are lazy bastards. If you let them they'll take twenty-four hours to do a twelve-hour job. But not on my watch they won't. They fail to carry out my orders and I'll have them hung for treason."

"Err, I'm not sure you can do that, Admiral," said Norton.

Thomson glared at the Corporal. "I'm the highest ranking officer on this ship and I'm acting on the direct orders of the President of the United States. I can do what I damn well please to complete the mission."

"Yes, sir, of course you can, sir."

Thomson pressed a button on the command console. "Lieutenant Miller, the scavenger team is on its way. Proceed to stage two."

"Yes, Admiral. Confirm Bravo Team is proceeding to stage two."

Lieutenant Miller led the team, minus the men guarding the rat hole and the two covering the rest of the hangar, over to the large airlock and peered through one of the transparent panels set in the doors. The door opposite was open and the light he aimed through the window picked out the shapes of the storage crates. He checked the men had spread out with their weapons trained on the door to tackle any surprises and then nodded at Wilcox, who had a hand poised over the door control.

Wilcox pressed the button. Nothing happened. He tried again with the same result. He shrugged at Miller. "Perhaps the power's off, Lieutenant?"

Miller cursed. "Damn! We'll have to cut through it. God knows how long that will take." He was about to make his report to the Admiral, who would not greet the delay kindly, when the doors slid apart. He glanced around at the men. "Be prepared for anything." As the doors opened, he noticed the reason for the delay; the doors opposite were now closed.

When they had checked the airlock was empty, the men stepped inside and Smith closed the hangar door. When it was fully closed the cargo door opened automatically. Flares were thrown across the room, bathing the area in their ethereal red light. Fitch sent the drone in and started surveying the room.

While they waited for Fitch to make his report, the others took a few cautious steps into the room and gazed around at the stacks of storage pods full of unimaginable alien objects.

When the drone had swept the cargo bay and no sign of the Space Rats or any other alien monsters had been detected, the men entered and began a cautious sweep to check for anything the drone might have missed. They had only gone a few steps when the air lock hissed shut behind them.

Miller turned his head and frowned at the closed door. It was their only source of retreat.

"It makes sense it would close automatically," offered Cooper. "It's an airlock."

Miller nodded, but worried it would slow their retreat if they needed a fast exit; he gave one of the men an order, "Sawyer, remain by the door and be ready to open it if we need to make a hasty withdrawal."

"Copy that, Lieutenant." Sawyer took position by the door control.

Lit by the flares hellish glow, the men began their search of the maze of alleys between the container stacks.

On the far side of the room the door between the cargo hold and the insects' domain opened. Mist seeped into the room and concealed within the fog the clatter of tiny claws followed.

CHAPTER 5

Out of the Mist they came...

WHEN THEY REACHED the second block of storage containers, Lieutenant Miller halted the squad and stared at the thick ground-hugging mist emerging from the darkness and rolling towards them.

"That doesn't look good," stated Blake, his nervous gaze searching for anything that might be concealed within the mysterious fog.

Miller had already reached the same conclusion. "Fitch, scout it out."

For a brief, terrifying moment, Fitch thought the Lieutenant meant physically— they had all read the scientists reports about the deadly insects that, in some ways, were more frightening than the larger and easier to shoot monsters— he recovered quickly and sent the drone flying forward a few feet above the mist. He concentrated on the small control screen as he directed the drone through the room. When it reached the far end his already nervous apprehension changed to dread. "The door's open!"

"Why is that a problem?" asked Brody, anxiously.

Fitch stared at the man. "That's where the alien insects live."

The clatter of tiny feet on the floor grew louder as a swarm of insects emerged from the mist's leading edge. Two men fired. Bullets tore into the tiny aliens and ricocheted off the floor. The rest of the men opened fire. Insect blood and body parts flew into the air, but they were too small for the weapons designed for larger prey to have much of an effect upon the thousands that surged towards them.

Egg-laden females peeled off from the pack and climbed onto the stacks of storage crates. One aimed her body at the men below and fired her better designed missiles. The eggs flew towards Blake and Reid. When they hatched in midair, the tiny offspring caught their first glimpse of the world they had been born into. They focused on their first prey and spun their circular rows of teeth like gruesome hole-borers. As soon as the tiny offspring landed on their chosen victims, they burrowed into flesh and tunneled through their bodies, devouring flesh, muscle, organs and bone.

The two men screamed and writhed in agony as their insides were devoured. Blake spun with his weapon still firing. His bullets cut through Reid's head, mercifully ending his pain. The sweep of the weapon continued, peppering O'Toole's legs with bullets. When the well-fed infants exploded in an eruption of blood from the far side of Blake's body, the weapon fell from his corpse and both fell to the floor.

With blood pouring from his leg wounds, O'Toole collapsed to the ground screaming. Oblivious to the pain they had caused, the gorged infants' eyes on yellow stalks picked out the new victims they sailed towards.

Lieutenant Miller glanced at the screaming men and the chaos that had suddenly erupted around him. He aimed at the female on top of the storage container firing small pale eggs into the air. A blast of bullets knocked it into oblivion. He glanced around at the crates. More egg-bearing insects moved into position. "Fall back," he shouted.

Three infant insects landed on Wakoski when he went to help O'Toole. His weapon clattered to the floor as he grabbed at the pain, hoping to free the insects burrowing through his skin. One landed on his hand and burrowed straight through into his body. Wakoski held up the hand and peered through the ragged circular hole at the insects that leaped at him. Others ran up his legs until he was smothered with the vicious, biting creatures. He opened his mouth to scream, but before the sound escaped, an insect entered, bored through his tongue and clawed its way down his throat, muffling his agonized yell. A single shot rang out. Blackness replaced his pain.

Miller lowered the weapon as Wakoski collapsed to the floor. He rushed forward, aiming to grab O'Toole's arm and drag him to the exit, but had to dodge back to avoid the leaping insects. He batted them away with the rifle as he retreated. O'Toole screamed. Miller glanced at the wounded man. So many insects had swarmed over him it looked like a man formed out of insects. O'Toole's agonized screams accompanied his retreat.

The men fell back towards the exit as insects swarmed over their fallen comrades and began feeding. Predicting a fast withdrawal might be in the cards when the first gunshots rang out, Sawyer had opened the door. He was glad he had when he saw some of the men rush towards him followed by a wave of tiny death that flowed ever nearer. Fitch arrived first, nipped inside and maneuvered the drone so it floated near the ceiling. The surviving squad members rushed into the airlock. While the door closed, the men fired at the frontline of insects to prevent them from gaining entry. White pus-like blood spread across the floor and sprayed the air. The last man only stopped firing through the narrowing gap when the door slid into its frame.

The men, their faces creased with shock and fear, panted heavily.

"I never signed up for this hell," complained Brody.

"None of us did." Lieutenant Miller glanced around at the men. Four had died: two American and two British.

Two insects appeared at the window in the door and looked at them. One reached out a claw and scratched at the glass.

Sullivan pressed the barrel of his weapon against the window level with the insect. "Don't tempt me you little alien fucker."

The men turned away when the hangar airlock door opened behind them.

"We need something to block this door so it can't close," said Miller. "If it does and the other one opens like last time, they'll get into the air lock. If they get past this door they'll be upon us again. Something I'm certain none of us wants to happen."

Shocked to silence by that the horror they had all witnessed, everyone present in the control room stared at the gruesome images on the screens.

"Fuck!" cursed Admiral Thomson loudly.

*****

The Scavenger Team formed of NASA and military engineers and mechanics had been previously briefed with descriptions and rough sketches of the two types of shuttlecraft from the scientists. They had worked on the problem of how to transfer the shuttlecraft from the spaceship's hangar, through the ice tunnel and onto the container ship before they had set sail from New Zealand. Materials and the tools they thought they might need had been requested and loaded aboard. They had set up shop in the cavernous rear cargo hold, which proved ideal to construct the sleds they had designed. As the length between each leg of the spacecraft was unknown, it had been designed in separate parts that could be joined together aboard the spaceship.

When the Scavenger Team entered the hangar, they stared in awe at the impressive shuttlecraft. The scientists' descriptions hadn't done them justice.

Corporal Joe McNally, the officer in charge of the Scavenger Team, pointed at the slightly battered, sleek scout ship; it was smaller than the larger cargo shuttle craft and ideal to test out their equipment and plan to remove them. "We'll salvage that one first."

The two motorized carts carrying their tools and equipment were maneuvered over to the scout ship and unloaded.

Corporal McNally glanced back along the tunnel when the thundering roar of the bulldozer, lowered onto the ice ledge by a powerful CH-47F helicopter, echoed into the hangar. While the dozer used its large blade to smooth the tunnel floor, some of the Scavenger Team set about measuring the distances between the legs of the scout ship and relayed the measurements to those making final adjustments to the sled's connecting bars aboard the ship.

While they waited for the sled parts to arrive, men dragged a heavy-lift air bag over to the craft.

McNally glanced over at the footsteps rushing across the hangar.

Cleveland crossed the room and grabbed one the equipment carts. "I need to borrow this."

McNally was about to protest, but the large African American was already heading back across the room with it. "Bring it back when you're done with it."

Cleveland reached the airlock and positioned the cart in the doorway. A few moments later the door slid closed. When it struck the cart, it reversed direction.

Sawyer looked at the Lieutenant. "Now what do we do?"

Miller stared at the insects that had gathered at the windows and scratched annoyingly on the transparent panels. "We kill them all."

Though it was unnecessary, as the sensitive equipment could pick up his voice clearly, Miller tilted his mouth closer to the mic. "Bravo Team leader to Control, send in the insect repellent." He glanced over at the hole the Space Rats had used to enter the hangar and then back at the insects. "We're going on a bug hunt."

CHAPTER 6

Dank and Dangerous

LUCY STOPPED AND shone the flashlight into each
new passage of the crossroad junction she had just arrived
at. The cables thinned out as they split off in two of the three
alternate directions. It was as hot as hell in the passage,
stuffy and claustrophobic; it was time for her to leave before
the creature behind her caught up. The hatch her light rested
on a few yards along the right-hand offshoot might provide
the means for her to do so. She dragged her tired body
around the corner to find out. The hatch's rust-laden hinges
squealed in protest when she pushed it open. Warm, humid
air tinged with the decay of vegetation assaulted her when
she shuffled forward and pierced the gloomy dank chamber
with the flashlight. Though surprised by what the light
picked out, she had seen too many strange things since
setting foot aboard the spaceship to be more than a little
shocked by its latest bizarre revelation. The dim glow that
managed to penetrate the film of green grime covering the
light cells running the length of the subterranean chamber
highlighted a swampy vista. The gloom-shrouded scene

wasn't particularly inviting, but less so than being chewed upon by the alien creature creeping up behind her.

Swampy, algae-rich water lapped against the wall three-yards below; it would be a one-way ticket as she wouldn't be able to climb back up. Ignoring as best she could the sounds of the approaching creature and the urge to leap down, Lucy did a quick recce of the area. Her flashlight probed the edges of the swamp for signs of the monsters she was certain must dwell in the dank habitat. Gnarled trees that wouldn't look out of place in a spooky cemetery film set grew amongst black fingers of rock that arched over the swamp and ended in spear-like points. They had the impression of talons belonging to some immense creature hidden beneath the swamp and surrounding vegetation and if the truth be told, Lucy wouldn't have been surprised if it turned out to be true. Anything seemed possible in this strange alien vessel. She then saw something that instilled hope that entering the swamp chamber might actually prove rewarding. A stone-effect bridge, that was obviously metal by the way its twisted form hung down at a sloping angle into the water, had once formed a high crossing from one end of the room to the other. Something had caused it to break, perhaps when the spaceship crash-landed on Earth. One end remained jutting out from the opposite wall, ending in midair. The other part of the collapsed bridge sloped up to an arch where steps led up into darkness. The escape pod had brought her far below the level of the engine room and the escape hole, so the rising stairs brought Lucy a little comfort they would take her back in the direction she needed to go.

She glanced at the gentle motion of the swamp water. It was further evidence the iceberg the spaceship was entombed in was adrift. She needed to find a way off the ship and the drifting ice before the sea claimed both. Though she had no idea how she would achieve that, or if any of her friends were still alive and trapped on the vessel, as far as she knew the engine room was her only means of escaping the ship. The rest she would worry about later. She also needed some cold weather gear. It would be suicide to climb out onto the ice dressed as she was, practically naked. It was another problem for later. First she had to make her way to the upper levels and avoid the creature in pursuit.

She gripped the open hatch door for support and dragged herself forward until she could hang from the edge and let go. As she dropped she wondered how deep the foul water was and if any creatures waited below the surface. When she splashed into the swamp up to her knees, her feet sunk into its muddy bottom a few inches. As ripples caused by her entry spread out across the thick, floating carpet of algae, Lucy scanned the swamp for signs of movement. A bubble of air plopped to the surface sixty-feet away. A second one emerged a little nearer. When the third one burst even closer, Lucy rushed for the nearest bank. The back of an amphibious creature, adorned with short, thin spikes, rose above the surface when it speeded up its charge. Lucy glanced behind. It had already covered half the distance. An eye on a long, thin stalk, that emitted a beam of blue light, rose out of the water like a submarine periscope and looked at her. Lucy spurted for the edge of the swamp; her feet slipping and sliding on the muddy bottom hampered her progress.

When others of its kind sensed a meal in the offering, six more amphibious horrors converged on the frantic splashing of possible prey.

As Lucy reached the edge, she glanced at the mass of eyes heading straight for her. She grabbed the tree root trailing into the water and climbed the steep bank. She collapsed to the ground at the top and looked down at the creatures that swam in a circle while their eyes constantly turned to keep her in their sight. Perhaps they waited to see if she would be foolish enough to re-enter their domain. If so, they were out of luck, as it wasn't something she planned on doing.

The creature that had followed Lucy appeared at the vent opening, sniffed the air until it detected its prey and stared at her briefly before screeching and leaping into the swamp. It was obvious by its awkward half-walking, half-swimming movements that it wasn't at home in this water-world.

The eyes poking above the water swiveled when something splashed into the swamp behind them. After observing it for a few moments, they headed for the creature and circled it like sharks. Then, as if a silent signal had transpired between them, the submerged creatures converged on their prey. Water splashed and surged as the creature fought for its life. Outnumbered and in its attackers' natural habitat, it fought a battle it could never win and was dragged below the surface to be consumed.

Thankful the creature had been disposed of, Lucy sat for a few moments to rest. She was tired, hungry and thirsty, but assumed it would be a while before any of her cravings would be satisfied. A buzzing sound, similar to that of a mosquito, but louder, turned her head. A small creature covered in pale-grey skin and the size of a pigeon, hovered in the air a short distance away. Its two spindly praying mantis type arms ended in three digits, two shorter than the center one, which ended in a sucker. Its slightly thicker back legs were furnished with three hooked claws. Its tiny bald head was fronted by a face with two small, black, sunken eyes and a vertical mouth that gave it a permanent sad, angry expression.

Observing the strange thing it had happened across, the flying creature flittered from side to side by means of two whirring blades, similar to helicopter rotors, at the end of two arm-like appendages that grew from its shoulder blades.

Lucy watched it tilt its head while it examined her. Though worried by its presence, she didn't experience the fear she would have from a larger ferocious creature. "You don't seem so bad, but if you are sizing me up as a meal, I'd think again. I don't want to hurt you, but attack me and I will." Lucy kept her voice quiet and calm, a distraction from her hand inching towards the short branch she had spied nearby in the purple grass.

The Whirly Bug seemed to lose interest in her, as it emitted a shrill warble and flew away.

Lucy climbed to her feet gripping the short branch. Though probably inadequate against most of the alien monsters she might encounter, it felt good to have some type of weapon. Sensing she had lingered long enough, she moved through the patches of spindly trees and jagged rock formations. Luckily for her bare feet, the ground was covered in a purple, spongy grass-like growth. An increasing drone behind her spun her towards the sound. It seemed the lone Whirly Bug, having sized her up as too large or too strange a prey to tackle on its own, had returned with reinforcements.

Lucy ran.

The Whirly Bug flock gave chase.

When Lucy dodged around the base of a rock finger, she stumbled and came face to face with a group of pig-size beasts covered in long, thick shaggy hair. They were chewing grass and one of them stared at her with disinterest as it munched on a mouthful of purple vegetation. It seemed she had encountered the first species of herbivore since setting foot on this hell ship. Careful she didn't spook them, but with cautious haste, Lucy moved around the edge of the small herd.

On hearing the buzz of the approaching Whirly Bugs, the woolly-trotters raised their flat snouts and directed their large brown eyes at the sound. When the swarm appeared, the hogs' eyes shrunk and glowed red, their long hair stiffened and shot erect, forming thin, sharp spines that covered their bodies like a forest of rapier blades.

Lucy ran when the herd bolted. The bugs gave chase. Hooves thundered on the ground. A fallen tree blocked the path. Lucy and the spiky-hogs leaped over. The alien hog running level with Lucy glanced at her. Though it seemed surprised to see such a strange creature, it saw an opportunity to distract the bugs they obviously feared. It dodged towards her in an attempt to pierce her flesh with its spikes—an offering for the hungry swarm.

Lucy dodged aside to avoid becoming impaled and darted around a tree. The distracted hog crashed into the trunk and tumbled across the ground. Two Whirly Bugs attacked. They landed on the hog's exposed, spike-free underbelly and stabbed their sucker fingers at its skin. The hog screeched, but quickly fell silent when the paralyzing venom injected by its attackers took hold. More bugs joined the first two. Their sucker fingers pulsed as the hog's life-giving fluid was pumped out. Its skin shrunk until it was stretched tightly over its frame like a mummified corpse. Sensing death and a meal, beetle-like insects, all jaws on legs, burrowed out of the grass ready to feed on the hog's carcass when the Whirly Bugs had finished feasting.

The Whirly Bugs unable to find room to feed on the downed hog continued their pursuit of the remaining quarry.

Lucy glimpsed the bridge through the trees and veered away from the hog herd. The Whirly Bugs split their forces between the hogs and Lucy.

When she approached the swamp, Lucy shot a glance behind. The bugs were still after her, though in lesser numbers now, not that it made much of a difference. However apt she was at fighting them off with the makeshift club, they were too fast and maneuverable for her to stop them for long. Only one had to make contact to incapacitate her. She reached the top of the bank, jumped and almost toppled into the stagnant water when she landed in the swamp and slipped on its sludge-layered bottom. She regained her balance and waded for the bridge a few yards away. A disturbance in the water indicated the approach of the amphibian creatures. Eyes looked hungrily at her as they headed for the latest source of food.

Lucy reached the edge of the bridge, scrambled onto it and glanced back. The Whirly Bugs glided towards her. Something erupted from the water. A stalk-eyed fish monster entered the swarm and grabbed a Whirly Bug before splashing into the water with its meal grasped in its jaws. Two more fish monsters leaped and each grabbed a prize. The remaining Whirly Bugs avoided similar fates as their brethren by rising higher than the fish could leap. The un-sated fish plummeted back into the swamp.

The bugs chased Lucy up the bridge. She reached the tunnel entrance and balked at the acrid stench—strong enough to bring tears to her eyes—that assaulted her. She forced herself inside and raced for the steps, tripped on a root grown across the path and fell. She turned as soon as she struck the ground and raised the club ready to fight off her attackers, but was surprised to see the Whirly Bugs had halted at the entrance. They hovered and stared at her, flicking from side to side in an angry, frustrated manner. When a hog screeched in the distance, they turned away and headed for the sound.

Lucy wondered why the bugs hadn't entered the tunnel. Maybe it was the smell? Something splattered on the ground beside her. She looked at the moist, white lump and the wisp of steam rising from it. She balked again when the fresh stench washed over her. A thick, crusty layer interspersed with fresher lumps covered the tunnel floor. She tilted her head back. Creatures hung from claws clamped on the tunnel roof. One of them folded back a wing from its face and stared at her with glowing green eyes.

CHAPTER 7

Oval office

SAMUEL HOPKINS THE President's Chief of Staff, and General Nathanial Colt, the Deputy Assistant to the President and Director of the White House Military Office, entered the Oval office and crossed to the table set off to one side where President Conner cast his astounded gaze over NASA's satellite scans of the spaceship entombed in the drifting iceberg. Made from a collage of smaller images digitally joined together, it showed the full size of the huge vessel.

"It's amazing is it not, Mr. President?" marveled General Colt, sweeping his eyes over the incredible image. "Luckily, whatever was preventing its detection before is no longer operational, giving us the first glimpse of an alien spaceship, or mother ship, as NASA has labeled it. Hopefully, if we can salvage one or more of the smaller spaceships from the hangar, they will have the same cloaking technology we can reverse engineer."

The President glanced at his Deputy Assistant. "But how can something this size be constructed and propelled through space? It must weigh hundreds of thousands or possibly millions of tons. The fuel weight alone would be astronomical."

"If they, the aliens that designed and built this thing, used our type of rocket propulsion, yes, it would," answered Hopkins. "However, according to NASA's experts and what the scientists saw aboard the ship in what they believe to be the engine room, that's extremely unlikely. NASA believes with absolute certainty that the aliens who built it have advanced far beyond combustible fuel and the tubes of green liquid the scientists came across might be a type of extremely efficient or even reusable fuel. Unfortunately, we don't have the time or the resources available, given the short timeframe we have before it's lost, to salvage the main engines. However, if we can salvage one or more of the smaller spacecraft the scientists reported were inside, which probably shares the same or similar propulsion technology, it could advance our efforts to reach farther into space by hundreds if not thousands of years."

"And the military advances are incalculable," added Colt.

"Yes, yes, I've heard all this from NASA repeatedly ever since we learned of the spaceship," stated the President, "but this is a sensitive operation. We have no more jurisdiction in the Antarctic than any other nation and now that British idiot, Richard Whorley, has splashed the spaceship's existence all over the newspapers, this," he swept a hand over the spaceship scan, "is no longer a secret and something they'll all want a piece of."

"Yes, that is most unfortunate," agreed Hopkins. "However, as we speak, steps are being taken to invalidate Mr. Whorley's fantastical story."

President Conner's eyebrows rose. "Another Roswell type cover-up?"

"Not exactly, but..."

President Conner raised a hand. "No, best I remain oblivious of the details."

Hopkins nodded. "As you wish, Mr. President."

President Conner turned his attention back to the spaceship image. "Not that I can imagine how you'll be able to cover up something as large as this. We are not the only nation with satellite technology and I'd be extremely surprised if certain countries don't have theirs aimed directly at the drifting iceberg as we speak."

"I'm sure they have," agreed Hopkins, "but we are fortunate that it's located in such a remote and inhospitable place. The Internet is full of hoaxed spaceship sightings and images; this will just be another. Yes, the conspiracy nut-jobs will have a field day with it, but without any physical evidence, only Whorley's photographs, easily created with graphic software, as were our images that will be posted online shortly. It will capture people's imagination for a while."

The President wasn't convinced. "That's probably what they thought about Roswell, and look how that turned out. However, it's not the general public that causes me the most concern; it's those countries that will want to get their hands on advanced alien technology as badly as us, the Russians and Chinese especially."

"It's lucky that we were able to get our men on site so quickly," said Colt. "We were first on the scene and will be first to claim what we can. The British, already privy to the information, on your orders, will be involved in the salvage operation. The Russians already have a ship heading for the Antarctic, though I'm not certain what they'll do when they arrive as there is only one entrance into the spaceship and we have that well guarded."

"You don't believe they will use force to procure alien technology for themselves?"

General Colt shrugged noncommittally. "This is such an unprecedented discovery, Mr. President, it's hard to predict what the Russians will do. Will they risk starting a war by using force to get aboard the spaceship? I don't believe so. With the British backing us up it will be one nation against two; they wouldn't stand a chance. However, saying that, it's certain they'll have read Richard Whorley's descriptions of the light-beam weapon used by that Haax alien to kill some of the monsters and might think, like us, that there could be other advanced weaponry aboard the spaceship. Given its size it must have at least one armory or weapon store of some nature, and it will be these weapons more than any other technology aboard the spaceship that will be the principle driving factor behind any decisions the Russians might make."

"I agree," said the President. "I've managed to placate the Chinese for a while with promises of sharing the alien technology, but I believe they were only so amenable because they knew by the time they arrived all the best stuff would be gone and the spaceship might be at the bottom of the ocean. The Russians though, it seems, are counting on salvaging something for themselves."

"I would be failing in my duty," said Colt, "if I didn't state firmly enough how important it is that *we* get our hands on any alien weaponry before less responsible nations. Weapons that might be aboard the spaceship could make our nuclear arsenal look like spud guns. If they fall into the wrong hands it's possible the rest of the world could be held to ransom."

"You will get no arguments from me on that score," stated the President.

"I already have a plan in place to do what is necessary to secure and salvage any alien weapons and prevent them from falling into the... wrong hands. I just need your go ahead, Mr. President."

President Conner glanced at the General. "You have it, but it mustn't interfere with the current salvage operation."

"It won't, Mr. President," reassured Colt. "I have a specialized team standing by. They won't fail."

"Nor do I want it to cause an international incident. Though our relationship with the Russians is at best precarious, we've come a long way since the end of the Cold War and I've no intention of revisiting those days on my watch. Is that clear, General?"

The General nodded firmly. "As crystal, Mr. President.

President Conner watched the General leave before turning back to the spaceship scan and frowned as he wondered how all this happening on his watch would affect his political career.

*****

Admiral Thomson entered the room assigned to the NASA technicians and scientists and gazed around at the men and women sat staring at computer monitors and typing on keyboards. He had been asked to find out as much as he could about the internal layout of the ship for a special ops mission to seek out alien armaments. Normally he would have assigned the task to a subordinate, but he wanted to see for himself the satellite scan that had the NASA technicians so excited.

A man he recognized as David Boyd, another NASA lackey, raised a hand at the far side of the room. "Over here, Admiral."

Thomson crossed the room and stared at the large image on the table that was identical to the one the President had been viewing thousands of miles away.

"As you can see, Admiral, we have now pieced together detailed scans of the spaceship."

There wasn't much that surprised the fifty-five year old commander, but what he looked at now qualified. "It's far bigger than I imagined."

"A little over a mile long and half that at its widest point," stated Boyd, his eyes scanning the spacecraft image with obvious excitement. "We have no idea of its depth, but I wouldn't be surprised if some levels are a quarter of a mile from the top."

Thomson walked around the table as he studied the colossal vessel. "It's going to be damn nigh impossible, given the time we have, to find anything aboard that thing. There must be hundreds, perhaps even thousands, of rooms spread out on its various levels."

"I agree," said Boyd. "I'm just glad the shuttlecrafts are right by the entrance. If we get nothing else I'll be happy."

Thomson glared at the NASA technician. "Making you happy is not part of my mission. I've already been informed by President Conner how important this salvage mission is. You worry about what you're good at, and I'll do my part. You want a shuttlecraft or two, you'll get them." The Admiral pointed at the parts of the spacecraft image shaded red. "What are those?"

Apparently unfazed by the man's abruptness, Boyd explained, "The red indicates the parts of the ship the scientists explored. Of course it's not exact given the limited amount of information gathered from the scientists debriefing, and doesn't account for the many lower levels. However, it gives us an idea how much of the ship the scientists didn't explore—more than seventy percent."

The Admiral sighed. "It's all very interesting, but unless you can supply me with a plan of the spaceship's internal layout and the purpose of each room, it's not very helpful. I'd rather not send men in blind with no idea of what direction to head in."

"That is something we have been tasked to assist you with."

The Admiral turned and looked at the man who had joined them. "And who might you be?"

"Wallace, sir. CIA." He handed the Admiral a folder. "If you need someone to help your men find their way around the ship, then this person can be of assistance and will be arriving shortly."

Thomson opened the folder, stared at the photograph and smiled. "Yes, I can see why that might be the case."

CHAPTER 8

Demons

WHEN LUCY CLIMBED to her feet, the bat creature released its grip on the rock, rolled in midair and landed feet first on the floor in a crouched position with its body tucked beneath its wings. As it rose slowly to its full six-foot height, it spread its wings and stood poised like a malevolent demon angel. For a moment it did nothing except stare at her, as if it wondered what she was.

Lucy stared back at the creature that looked as if a bat, a bird and a demon had been morphed into a single terrifying entity, complete with devilish horns on its head. Without turning away she slowly moved a foot up onto the next step.

The creature lunged at her.

Lucy swung the club with a speed that surprised her; her reactions to life-threatening situations had definitely improved.

The Demon Bat's long head that ended in a wicked, pointed beak shot to the side with a crack of bone when the club struck. As it crashed to the ground Lucy dodged out of its path.

When more green eyes appeared in the darkness shrouding the cave roof, Lucy turned and fled up the root-covered steps that did their best to trip her. The flapping of wings from behind indicated the outcome if she stumbled a second time.

The curving steps prevented Lucy from seeing how high they reached or what they led to but she noticed the roots changing the higher she climbed. At the bottom they were relatively sparse, but now they had increased in number and were thicker. A turn around a curve in the staircase revealed they were no longer confined to growing across the steps. Roots now snaked over the walls and were covered in jagged protrusions that poked into the tunnel like the teeth of some strange creature. As she progressed even higher, the spiky tooth-like formations became longer, in more abundance and invaded the space she needed to move through. She shot a glance back when the flapping of wings faded. The abundance of spiky-roots grew too close together for the winged demons to fly through, but they weren't thwarted yet. They landed on the steps and crawled and climbed between, over and under the spiky growths. Lucy worried that if the roots continued to increase in size and number, they would block her progress and the creatures would be upon her. The mass of green eyes coming ever closer was an eerie sight. Except for their claws scraping on the steps, roots and walls, the Demon Bats made no sound.

Sensing danger close by, she turned to face it. A smaller Demon Bat's pointed jaw stabbed at her. Lucy recoiled in fright and swung the club at its head, which exploded when the force smashed it into one of the spiky roots. She continued her climb.

The roots soon invaded the space directly above the steps, causing Lucy to maneuver carefully between their sharp barbs. She couldn't shake the feeling she was moving through a mouth filled with teeth that would snap shut at any moment and impale her. It was a relief when she reached the top without that very thing happening. A glance back down the steps and through the gaps between the jagged protrusions revealed the Demon Bats hadn't given up the chase. Lucy crossed a flat area and passed through a misshapen metal gate hanging askew from one hinge and rushed over to the mass of thick vines blocking the exit. After pulling aside a handful of the sinewy growths, she glanced around the new landscape.

It was hard to believe she was still on the spaceship and hadn't been transported to a far off alien planet. Lucy glimpsed movement and focused upon the creature crouched on what seemed to be a building under a jagged outcrop of rock. Blue lights pulsed along the ribs along the building's sides and the long, thin leg-like appendages that stretched out from the strange construction. Through its transparent walls, small green and red lights could be seen flashing and a spray of sparks erupted intermittently from one section.

The scrape of claw on rock spun her head around. Five Demon Bats crawled towards her. More were close behind. Lucy glanced back at the strange building and noticed the creature never took its eyes off her when it climbed down the side of the building headfirst and raced towards her.

Lucy only had one direction she could go—up. She squeezed through the vines and glanced above. Strange trees leaned out over the rock that formed the tunnel. She grabbed one of the thick vines and climbed. The gnarled, knobby vines were easy to ascend and when Lucy reached the top she cautiously glanced over the edge. The area seemed free of anything that might attack her. Movement rippled through the vines from below. She glanced down. Demon Bats pushed through the vines and leaped into the air. Stretched wings flapped and bore them aloft.

Lucy climbed onto the ledge and ran for the metal wall one hundred feet away, or more specifically, the door set in its base that she prayed would open. A glance back revealed two Demon Bats swooping towards her. She twisted to fight the first off with the club, but stumbled. The Demon Bat soared past above her. The one behind altered its flight and reached out its claws when it prepared to land on its prey. Lucy rolled to the side and swung the club, striking the creature's shoulder. Bones crunched when it struck the ground and tumbled until coming to a rest. It tried to stand, but its injuries were too severe; it would fly no more. Lucy jumped to her feet as two more approached, and ran for the door, bypassing the wounded creature that stabbed its pointed jaw at her in a lackluster attempt its instincts forced it to carry out.

The door was Lucy's only chance to get away. The first Demon Bat that had swooped past her had other plans. It landed in front of the door, cutting off Lucy's escape. She dodged another she sensed coming up behind her by swerving around one of the trees covered in red leaves that grew near the metal wall. She paused amongst the tree trunks when two more Demon Bats landed by the door. She turned as more swooped down to the ground behind her. Wary of the club that had so easily wounded one of its kind, they had chosen another tactic; they would attack in a group from all sides.

Lucy glanced up the trunk of one of the trees. They weren't very high and looked easy to climb, but even if she did seek refuge in its leaf-burdened branches, she doubted it would stop the creatures for very long. There was no other option. To live she had to get through the door before the other demons moved into position. She stared at the three creatures stopping her. The will to live pushed her fear aside and prompted her rush at the three Demon Bats.

Surprised by the sudden attack, for a moment the creatures failed to retaliate and one suffered a broken arm from the club its attacker swung at it. Lucy followed through with a hard kick to the Demon Bat's stomach. It stumbled into the creature beside it and knocked it off balance. The third dodged out of the way and leaped at her. The club caught it a blow around the head. Its neck snapped and hung at an unnatural angle as it staggered about wildly. Lucy searched the handle-absent door for some way of opening it; a concealed panel or something, but there was nothing on the rusty metal wall. She stamped on the Demon Bat's head that had fallen to the ground when it lunged for her ankle. Its eyes bulged when its skull was crushed by the force. The third creature lashed out a claw at Lucy's face. She barely managed to pull her head back in time and felt a whoosh of claw-disturbed air caress her face as her head slammed into the wall. Dazed, she slipped to the ground. Through spinning vision she watched the Demon Bat tower over her and its open, teeth-lined beak snapping together menacingly as it grew nearer. Lucy tried to lift the club, but found it was no longer in her hand, not that it would do her any good, her arms were as heavy as lead. The Demon Bat's warm carnivorous breath washed over her face. All she could see were sharp teeth and a pink throat her flesh would soon be sliding down. Though she willed her body to move and defend itself, it refused; it had had enough. Suddenly, the teeth disappeared, yanked from her view. In a blurred flurry of movement and excited squeals, the Demon Bat landed beside her minus its head.

Lucy stared at the pink, scary face framed with blond hair that filled her vision. Its serial-killer smile revealed blunt teeth stained with fresh blood. Lucy had forgotten about the other creature. As the face edged closer, Lucy drifted into unconsciousness.

CHAPTER 9

Bug Hunt

YOU CAN'T BE SERIOUS, Lieutenant." Cooper stared at the uninviting rathole the stepladder reached to near the ceiling. "That's suicide going in there."

"It's our only option. We have to clear the cargo bay of insects so the containers can be salvaged." Lieutenant Miller checked the five canisters of poisonous gas, the three gasmasks and the other requested items in the backpack and fastened the straps.

"Why not just put the gas in the airlock and close the hangar door?" Patterson asked. "Then, when the cargo bay door opens, the gas will flood the room and kill them."

The Lieutenant looked at Patterson. "Am I to understand that you, Patterson, have just volunteered to wear a gas mask, enter the airlock, open the far door, set off the gas and hope it kills the insects before they reach you?"

"Well, no, Lieutenant. That's definitely not something I'm volunteering for."

"That's why I've chosen this route. The scientists reported the Space Rats were in the same room as the insects, so logically, that opening should lead to that area. The gas should dispose of both species at the same time, leaving the way clear to salvage everything in the cargo bay. However, I can't do it alone. I will need two volunteers. I'll take point, but I need one of you to haul the stuff, another to watch our backs and both to keep guard while I set off the gas."

"Sounds like it might be fun," said Sawyer, with a grin. "Count me in."

Fitch stared at the man. "That confirms my suspicions, Sawyer. You are crazy."

Sawyer shrugged, still grinning. "No one lives forever."

Miller's gaze swept across the remaining men. "I'd rather someone volunteered, but I will choose one of you if no one comes forward."

Fitch sighed. "I'll do it."

Miller looked at the man with surprise. "No, Fitch, we need you to operate the drone when this task is done. Patterson, you're volunteering."

Patterson groaned and nodded.

Miller picked up the rucksack containing the gas and other items they would need, and handed it to Patterson. "Follow me in. Sawyer, you're at the rear."

"Okay, Sarge." Sawyer slapped Patterson playfully on the back. "Don't look so glum. I'll make sure nothing eats you."

Patterson forced a smile. "It's not that I'm worried about so much as crawling through that tight passage with my well-formed arse shoved enticingly in your face."

Sawyer laughed. "I promise to be gentle as it's your first time."

The remaining team members watched the three men enter the rathole. None envied them their task. As soon as Sawyer entered, Cobb climbed the ladder and placed a folded lump of yellow plastic in the opening. A tube fixed to it led to a pressurized air canister on the floor. Cobb nodded to Selby who waited with his hand on the airflow lever and air hissed along the tube. The tough inflatable air bag expanded to fill the contours of the hole. When Cobb was satisfied the hole was sealed and no backwash of gas could escape, the air was turned off.

*****

"Bravo Team leader to Control, we are in the rathole," reported Miller. "The opening led to some kind of access duct."

Admiral Thomson gazed at the image on the monitor lit by Miller's headlamp. The long hexagon passage that stretched into the distance looked spooky as hell, especially knowing the Space Rats or insects might be in there waiting for them. "Take it easy, Lieutenant. I'm counting on you to complete your mission."

Miller fished earplugs from his pocket and inserted them.

Sawyer and Patterson did likewise. If they had to use their weapons in such a confined space the sound would deafen them. Forced into a crouched position by the duct's confines, the Lieutenant led them forward.

A few minutes later Miller brought the small team to a halt. He pointed two fingers at his eyes and then at the intersection ahead before slowly moving forward. When he cautiously glanced down the left-hand turning, a Space Rat surged from the darkness and leaped at him. A spray of bullets dropped it to the ground. Movement to his right alerted Miller to a new attack. Rats with bared teeth spread wide to bite, rushed him from the other direction. Gunfire and squeals of pain echoed through the duct until all fell silent again. The almost empty magazine clattered to the floor when Miller exchanged it for a fresh one.

They moved past the bloody rat corpses and continued along the duct until Miller halted the men again. When Sawyer peered past the lieutenant and glimpsed the end of the passage, he turned, crouched and aimed his weapon and light back along the duct.

After Miller had signaled for the two men to wait, he cautiously approached the opening and poked his head out. What seemed like hundreds of Space Rats stared up at the opening from the room below. He signaled for the others to join him and removed his earplugs. He waited for the two men to remove theirs before speaking softly, "The rats are waiting below. Pass me a canister and put your masks on."

Patterson dished out the masks and handed Miller a gas canister. "How long will it take for the gas to work?"

"I asked the specialists the very same question," Miller replied in a low voice. "I was told with normal subjects in a confined environment, about ten to twenty seconds, but as we are dealing with alien physiology in a large area, they couldn't give me an answer."

Patterson frowned. "So it might not work?"

Miller shrugged. "They breathe oxygen just like us, so there's no reason it shouldn't."

After they had slipped on gasmasks, Miller twisted the knob hard on top of the canister to activate the ten-second delay. An impatient rat poked its head into the opening. A single shot from Sawyer's gun sent it flying back into the room. The men, temporarily deafened by the noise, didn't hear the shrieks that erupted when the corpse fell into the mass of teeth and claws below and was quickly devoured by the lucky few. Miller, his ears still ringing, threw the canister into the vermin throng. A stream of gas fog leaked out when it struck the floor.

Believing food was in the offing, the nearest rats pounced on the can but discarded it when their teeth scraped on its hard, inedible surface. The canister was jostled around the room as it was continually fought over. Fog spewed out and began filling the room. It wasn't long before the gas started taking effect and rats collapsed to the floor never to rise again.

Miller glanced at his watch and then at Patterson. "Forty seconds," his voice muffled and distorted by the mask.

When all movement in the room had ceased, Miller dropped into the gas-shrouded room and Sawyer and Patterson followed him down. There were so many rat corpses it was impossible to avoid treading on them. It was like walking on macabre carpet woven from dead rats. The men stumbled and slid off the bodies more than once as they moved for the exit. Their lights were of little use in the deadly haze that swirled around them; it was like driving through thick fog with lights on full beam. It was instinct that led Miller across to the far side and up the ramp that led to an opening. Though less dense at the top, the deadly gas fog seeped through the doorway and into nearby rooms as it sought out more victims to infect with its lethal breath. The corridor led left to a closed door and right to another opening. Miller led the men to the right, in the direction of the cargo bay.

Wispy trails of gas disturbed by their passing crept ahead of them until it finally dissipated when they reached a high balcony. The three men gazed down at the room below where four bridges led off from a central platform. The turquoise glow emitted by the large liquid-filled tubes revealed the two tall aliens suspended inside and glass shards littering the floor where one of the containers had been smashed. Below the platform and bridges, a ground-hugging mist swirled spookily around the lower level. The three men directed their lights around the lower room but saw no insects or anything else on the prowl.

Lieutenant Miller pointed at the lower, mist-covered level. "That's where the insects live and the door that leads to the cargo bay. I'll toss two canisters down to ensure all are killed in the immediate area before we climb down and head for the cargo bay."

Patterson handed Miller two canisters and while he and Sawyer kept a look out for any surviving Space Rats that might attack, Miller activated the canisters and lobbed them into different areas of the bottom level. The canisters clattered on the floor and rolled noisily. Alerted by the sound, insects converged on the canisters. Their tiny feet clicking on the floor revealed their positions in the fog that shrouded them from view. The lighter death gas seeped through the thicker ground mist, filled the lower level and seeped into the one above.

When five minutes had passed, Miller secured the rope Patterson passed him to the banister and climbed over. He was astonished by the impossibly tall aliens he gazed at when he slid down to the lower level. His light and weapon searched the room below when his feet touched the floor. When he was satisfied, as far as he could judge, the area was clear of danger, he indicated for the two men on the balcony to come down.

Their feet crunched on the insect carcasses littering the floor when they headed for the cargo bay. Their lights and ears continually scanned the fog-cloaked room for signs of insect activity. They reached the cargo bay door and peered into the large chamber. Though a few dead insects were seen around the entrance, when they moved past the first row of crate stacks they saw thousands were still alive. Some crawled over the storage pods and floor, but most were converged around the air lock at the far end of the room where they saw the chance of a meal.

Miller took the last two gas canisters from the bag while Sawyer and Patterson kept watch. He threw one amongst the crates and rolled the other along the floor towards the airlock. Gas spewed out as it rolled and spread throughout the room. The insects turned towards the sound and the nearest converged on the canisters. The alarm was raised when the men were spotted and an army of insects scurried towards them. Sawyer shot three egg-laden females preparing to fire their deadly payload. Patterson dispatched two more with a short burst of bullets at each.

Miller glanced at his watch.

"What shall we do, Lieutenant?" asked Patterson nervously, his weapon sweeping the front edge of the seeping gas that hid the insects. It wasn't so much the dying that scared him, though he would rather not, it was the agonizing death the insects dispatched to their victims that had him so worried.

"Hold your ground," ordered Miller, glancing at his watch. "Another twenty seconds and we're safe."

Patterson forced himself not to retreat a few steps. "What if they reach us in fifteen?"

Sawyer smiled at the worried soldier. "Stamp on them."

"Ten seconds," announced Miller. He glanced at the approaching swarm when they emerged from the gas cloud only fifteen yards away. They had crawled through the gas so they had to be affected. He turned his focus back upon his watch and counted down. "Five. Four. Three. Two..."

The insects continued towards them.

"Lieutenant!" said Patterson, his voice higher than he would have wished. "They're not stopping."

"Back up. It can't be much longer now."

Patterson voiced his worries aloud as he backed away from the insect hoard now only six feet away. "What if it's a dud canister and the gas ain't no good?"

Sawyer squashed the one that spurted forward with a stamp of his boot.

The lieutenant was about to order the retreat when some of the insects stopped. "It's working."

"About bloody time," Patterson sighed.

A wave of death swept over the hoard until they had all succumbed.

Miller scanned the top of the storage crates now hidden by the rising cloud of gas. He detected no movement. "Let's do a sweep of the room to make sure they're all dead before opening the airlock. The gas becomes harmless after exposure to the air for fifteen minutes, so we can't open it until then."

Lieutenant Miller led the two men through the gaps between the storage containers.

CHAPTER 10

An Uneasy Alliance

AS LUCY SLOWLY regained her senses, she became conscious of the throbbing pain in her head and groaned. The second sensation she experienced was something prodding her. Fearing a monster was trying to eat her, her eyes sprung open and she lashed out an arm. The pink creature dodged back and whimpered while it rubbed its arm where it had been struck. When Lucy sat and pressed herself against the wall, she noticed movement in the air. The winged demons circled and watched her, waiting for an opportunity to attack. She glanced around for the club. It was over an arm's length away. With her eyes fixed on the pink creature in case it attacked, she reached for the inadequate weapon.

The creature's eyes followed her groping hand. It picked up the club in one of its elongated hands equipped with three fingers and a thumb tipped with small claws and handed it to Lucy.

Confused by the creature's action, Lucy stared at its expectant smiling face. The blood-tinged smile and its large upward slanted eyes dotted with small red pupils were unnerving. It was like the smile of a murderer about to claim its next victim.

While she pondered her next move, Lucy studied the creature. It had four limbs— two arms and legs attached to powerful hips that jointed at the knee and ankle. Its feet were elongated even more than its hands, and its toes were three small hooves. Even with all its obvious alien differences, including the yard-long tail that swayed snake-like behind it, the creature had a surprising human appearance. This was probably due in part to the smooth, hairless, pink skin that covered its body. Though there was no sign of sexual organs, Lucy had the impression the creature was female and meant her no harm, as it could have easily killed her when she was unconscious.

"Thank you," Lucy said, softly.

The creature tilted its head to one side, brushed back the hair that fell across its face in a surprisingly human motion, and stared at her. It backed away a few cautious steps when Lucy slowly climbed to her feet. She wasn't sure how long she had been unconscious, but she felt a little refreshed and some of her strength had returned. Now, if only she could find something to eat and drink.

Lucy glanced at the gruesome Demon Bat corpses a short distance away and guessed her new friend was responsible and the reason the circling creatures didn't attack. Shredded flesh on one of the corpses indicated Pinky had been snacking while she was out. She turned and faced the door she wanted to enter. A barge with her shoulder failed to move it. Whatever held it closed would require more than her strength to open it.

The creature tugged her arm and beckoned for Lucy to follow. Though reluctant to do so, the creature hadn't shown any sign it meant to harm her thus far so Lucy followed it over to the ledge. The creature moved on all of its four limbs. Hard lumps on its knuckles protected its skin from tearing on the rough rock. It climbed down the vines headfirst, using its tail to grip the vines for extra support. Lucy climbed down in the conventional human manner and followed the creature that kept glancing back to make sure she was coming. Lucy looked across the rocky landscape at the strange building she was being led towards and wondered what the creature's intention was. It seemed to be intelligent; it had known she wanted the club and fetched it for her. It had also saved her from the Demon Bats. She glanced up. The flying creatures followed their progress, but made no attempt to attack; they obviously feared the pink creature, which, in a way, worried Lucy. If it had dispatched five of them so easily, a human armed with a simple wooden club would pose it no problem. She again sought some solace from the fact that the creature hadn't harmed her when she had been unconscious.

The creature headed for an opening in the side of the building and passed through the shower of sparks inside. Lucy followed. The sparks came from a battered control panel. Her gaze swept the interior. It wasn't a building but a giant machine. She crossed to where a series of mechanical metal arms were pressed against the side of the cliff. Hoses and jets were frozen in place from when the machine stopped working. Jets of molten rock, metal or some substance manufactured to mimic the two that had once sprayed out in liquid form from some of the many hoses, had solidified like frozen fountains. The machine was actually building the landscape like some sort of terra-forming machine, perhaps building an ecosystem for some of the creatures the ark spaceship carried.

The creature tugged at her arm again, impatient for her to continue their journey to God-knows-where. Lucy was led past a pool of water lit from below by turquoise light. Stubby, gnarled trees had forced their way through the floor of the machine and stood like strange statues arranged in a museum for public viewing. A large rip in the wall on the far side of the machine revealed a wide tunnel whose floor was covered with bizarre, mushroom-like growths. The tallest was a foot high. Stubby red stalks supported a pointed domed top formed from intertwined tendrils that emitted a soft blue glow and lit up the dark tunnel. The floor was carpeted with a bright orange growth that had a mossy texture. The scene had a magical, fantasyland feeling.

The creature paused at the tunnel entrance and waved Lucy forward with an impatient arm and a creepy beckoning smile. Lucy glanced around the machine; there might be something here she could use as a weapon. If she encountered anymore of the ship's vicious inhabitants, the club wouldn't save her for long. If it weren't for Pinky coming to her rescue the Demon Bats would have feasted on her corpse. Her roaming eyes stopped on a sharp metal shard lying on the ground. She picked it up. It was light, but strong, ideal for her purpose, but the edges were too sharp to grip with her bare hands. She wandered around the room, searching for anything else she could use to fashion a weapon. In one corner she found something that might be useful; a grisly pile of teeth-scarred bones, some of which she thought might be from the Demon Bats. She glanced back at the pink creature, who stared at her. Though the scary smile remained, its expression was one of puzzlement—no doubt wondering what Lucy was doing.

Lucy returned her attention to the bone pile and picked out one of the longest. A glance around revealed the next item she needed, a cluster of thin wires hanging from a rip in the machine wall. She grabbed one strand, pulled it tight and used the metal shard to cut off a long length. Five minutes later, the sharp scrap of metal was secured to the end of the bone. Lucy held up the ad-hoc spear and admired her handiwork. She jabbed it in the air around her, as if fighting an invisible monster, and started when Pinky squealed in what seemed delight at the spear. She relaxed a little and smiled at the creature that understood she had made a weapon.

When Lucy approached the creature, Pinky entered the undergrowth and again turned its head after a few steps to make sure she followed. Though Lucy couldn't shake the feeling she should turn around and seek an alternative route on her own, she entered the mushroom tunnel. When she passed the strange fungi, their tendril tops unfurled and waved in the air, emitting a pleasant, flowery aroma. Lucy was just thinking what a pretty performance it was when hooked barbs sprouted from the tendrils of the nearest one and sprung at her.

Pinky grabbed Lucy's arm and yanked her away from the tendrils grasp before they made contact. It pointed at the vicious mushrooms and shook its head.

Lucy nodded she understood. She wouldn't venture too close to the aggressive plants again. Not for the first time, she wondered how anything had managed to survive on the planet the spaceship and crew originated from with so many things intent on killing and eating its inhabitants, and why they had bothered transporting them to a new world. Taking a wide berth past the hostile fungi, Lucy followed Pinky through the tunnel that didn't seem so magical anymore.

CHAPTER 11

The Offer

JACK GLANCED ADMIRINGLY at Jane's form stretched out on the sunlounger, roamed his appreciative eyes the length of her bikini-clad body and let out a satisfied sigh. This truly was paradise. "Good book?" he asked.

Jane glanced up from the novel, *El Dorado* by Ben Hammott. She had purchased it from a local store and had soon become engrossed in the story set in the Amazon jungle about a search for '*a fabled lost city and a legendary treasure greater than any yet discovered*' as the back cover blurb described it. "Yeah, it's exciting. You should read it when I'm finished."

Something distracted Jack. He raised his sunglasses and examined the man dressed in a dark suit gazing around at people on the beach. He sensed an aura of bad news about the man. "He's a bit overdressed for the beach."

Jane followed the direction of Jack's gaze as the man turned towards them. A look of recognition appeared on his thin face and he headed over. "He seems to be looking for us. I wonder what he wants."

"Nothing good I should think," said Jack.

"Hello, Miss Harper." The suited man stopped at the foot of Jane's sunlounger.

Though his eyes were concealed behind dark glasses, Jane felt them wander over her near-naked body. "Yes. And you are?" She grabbed a thin shawl from the back of the lounger and wrapped it around her.

"Simon Hawthorne. I've been requested to contact you by certain interested parties from the American government. The clerk from your hotel said you were on the beach."

Jack frowned. He had no doubts that 'certain interested parties' included the CIA. "What does the American government want with us? We've already been debriefed."

The man glanced at Jack briefly. "Actually, I've come to see Miss Harper." He looked back at Jane. "They need the services of a glaciologist and I've been informed you are one of the best, but that's not the only reason I have been tasked with seeking you out. It is also because you have first-hand knowledge of the ice in question."

It didn't take a rocket scientist to work out what ice the man alluded to. "The iceberg the spaceship's trapped in," assumed Jane.

Hawthorne nodded. "As you are fully aware, it's now adrift and a salvaging operation is underway to save what they can from the spaceship. However, you won't be involved with that. What we need you to do, as far as it is feasible to do so, is to determine how long they have before the iceberg deteriorates and the alien vessel is lost."

Jack humphed. "If you think we're going back there again, you are very much mistaken, Mr. Hawthorne."

When the man turned his gaze on Jack, his annoyance was hidden behind his sunglasses but not from his voice. "We have no need of a pilot, Mr. Hawkins, as we have plenty of our own. Your services are not sought or required." He refocused back on Jane. "Your services are, though, Miss Harper. You will be well paid for your expertise and time and returned here—or anywhere else in the world you wish—when you have finished your assessment."

Jane stared at the man for a few moments. "As I am sure you are fully aware, Mr. Hawthorne, I have just returned from Antarctica where I, Jack, and the rest of our scientific team suffered a horrendous experience that not all survived. So you can understand my reluctance to return. Sorry, I'm not interested."

"Believe me, Miss Harper, if I had faced those alien monsters I read about from your colleague's newspaper story, I wouldn't want to go back either, but we're not asking you to go aboard the spaceship, only to examine the ice it's entombed in. A crack has formed across a wide section and a few large chunks have broken off, which has caused concern as to the iceberg's stability. NASA scientists and technicians are aboard the craft, as well as American and British engineers and soldiers. Their lives are at risk. This is why they are keen to enlist your help."

"I understand their concern, but I'm sure you can find someone else with more experience connected with the study of icebergs and their rates of deterioration."

"Yes, we probably could, but you are already acquainted with this particular iceberg and what's inside. Bringing in an outsider risks revealing the discovery to another person."

"Surely that's no longer a concern now Richard's splashed the story all over the newspapers?" countered Jack.

"Something I'm confident Richard is now regretting," stated the man, knowingly.

"If you think that, then you've never met him," scoffed Jack.

The man smirked, as if he knew something they didn't.

"I admit his story is sensational, but apart from a few photos and Mr. Whorley's frankly unbelievable account of what happened in Antarctica, he has no actual proof the spaceship or alien monsters exist. The internet is full of faked photographs and alien sightings, and the Pine Ice Glacier is so remote it's almost impossible to go there to verify his story."

"So you'll cover up the discovery?" Jane asked.

The man shrugged. "I am not involved in such decisions. My task is to acquire your services Miss Harper, at any cost. I've been instructed to inform you that you can name your price."

Jane looked at the overdressed man with renewed interest, who she noticed had started to sweat in the heat. "I can pluck a figure from the air and you'll pay it?"

"Not me personally, but yes, that is my understanding. Within reason of course."

"You are not seriously considering going back after all we went through?" said Jack. "We barely survived."

Jane looked at him. "Yes, I think I am. How long is it going to take for me to check out the iceberg? A day—two tops. And I can name my fee? I'll never have an opportunity like this again."

"The clock is ticking, Miss Harper," interrupted Hawthorne.

"If I said I wanted one million pounds, what would you say?"

"I'd say, high, but reasonable, given the circumstances."

"What about three million?"

Jack looked at her in shock.

"Look, Miss Harper, I don't want to seem rude, but time is of the essence here. Just name the price that will get you to Antarctica so we can get things moving."

"Okay, Mr. Hawthorne. I also don't want to seem rude, but this is what I want—three million British pounds: one for me, one for Jack, because he's coming with me or I don't go, and one million to be donated to charities of my choice. That's my price. If it's not acceptable then please leave—you're blocking the sun and ruining our holiday."

Hawthorne sighed. "It's acceptable, but we have to leave now. I have a plane waiting to take you to Antarctica."

Jane was a little surprised by the suddenness. "I'll need certain things to do my job."

"We probably already have what you need, but make a list and I'll see it's taken care of."

Jane turned to Jack, finding he had a stunned look on his face. She smiled. "What's wrong? Isn't a million pounds enough to buy you a new airplane?"

"More than enough, and thanks for the consideration, but it's not that that worries me. I can't believe we're going back."

CHAPTER 12

Scout Ship Salvage

WHEN THE THREE fabricated skids were ready to be pushed into position, the large airbag beneath the front of the spaceship was inflated to slowly lift the sleek scout ship. When it was six-inches off the ground, four men pushed the first skid under the leg and the air let out of the bag. The foot of the spacecraft rested gently on the skid and was then clamped tightly in place so the two could not separate during the journey. The bag was removed, placed beside one of the back legs and the process repeated. After the final skid was in place, they were joined together with lengths of metal bolted on to keep them from twisting or separating.

The roar of the waiting bulldozer echoed through the hangar when its powerful diesel engine roared to life, sending a plume of black exhaust fumes up to the ceiling. The driver drove it into position at the front of the ship and the engineers hitched it to the forward sled. McNally checked everything was secure before giving the signal for the driver to start towing. The skids screeched on the metal floor as the ship slowly moved towards the exit.

The engineers followed it through the ice tunnel and onto the ice ledge. As the bulldozer turned, the ship slewed towards the edge, but stopped after a few heart-stopping moments with half a back skid overhanging the ice. The driver cautiously inched it to safety.

McNally glanced up to make sure the ship had cleared the overhang of ice and told the driver to stop. The ship was unhitched and the dozer pulled clear. McNally glanced up at the helicopter hovering over the cold ocean a short distance away and contacted the pilot with his radio. "It's ready."

The helicopter approached and hovered over the scout ship. Blasted by the downwash whipping up snow and ice, the men grabbed the swinging cables and attached them to the harness they had fitted around the ship. When the skid clamps were released, McNally glanced up at the pilot and gave the lift signal.

The helicopter took the slack out of the cables and strained to lift the weight. After the pilot applied more power to the engines, the spaceship slowly rose from the ice. As soon as it was free of the temporary skids, the helicopter turned towards the ship. The engineers congratulated themselves and watched the impressive alien vessel sway below the helicopter it dwarfed; it was flying for the first time in thousands of years. This was the riskiest part of the operation. If one of the cables snapped, the others wouldn't be able to support the weight and the ship would be lost to the sea.

McNally contacted the ship on the radio. "The scout ship's on its way." He turned to his men. "Well done. Now it's time to tackle the larger cargo shuttlecraft. Hitch the skid trailer to the dozer and bring it into the hangar." He headed back through the tunnel to start preparations for salvaging the second alien vessel.

As the cargo vessel had four legs, the trailer would be dismantled and an extra skid would be connected. Though the cargo ships were larger, no one foresaw any problems.

Admiral Thomson, the scientists from NASA and the crew, watched the spacecraft swinging precariously below the helicopter approach the container ship. Some let out a sigh of relief and others cheered when it was lowered safely onto the ship. Men rushed forward to unhitch the cables and secure the alien vessel to the deck.

Mason walked over and stood beside Thomson. "What we're looking at is probably the most important piece of technology on the planet, so I hope it's not going to disappear into Area 51 like the last one."

Thomson glanced at Mason. "What happens to it when it leaves this ship is not my decision and neither is it yours," he stated, testily.

The NASA scientists and engineers walked over to the amazing spaceship and wandered around it, pointing at certain features and surmising what their functions might be. They couldn't wait to get it back to their workshop and gain access to all of its alien advanced engineering. It should be a simple matter of reverse engineering everything and in a few years they could have a whole fleet of them going into space and traveling farther than they ever thought possible in their lifetime. Mars, Jupiter and beyond, wouldn't be a problem with this ship. The age of true space exploration would soon be upon them. They were reluctantly pushed back when a large cover was pulled over the scout ship to hide it from prying eyes in the sky.

CHAPTER 13

Kidnapped

THE FIRST SENSATION the man experienced when he awoke was the pain behind his eyes. It felt like someone had his head in a vice and was clamping the jaws shut. His eyes blinked open to discover something covered his face, a hood of some kind. His attempts to remove it were foiled by the bindings that secured his hands to the back of the uncomfortable chair he sat on. Through the material he glimpsed a circle of light. Fear washed over him. What the hell was happening? The last thing he remembered was exiting a restaurant with the pretty woman he had impressed with his brave deeds of derring-do aboard the alien spaceship and heading back to his hotel room for a night of drink-fueled passion. When the taxi he had hailed pulled away from the curb he had noticed a hissing sound and then nothing until he had just come around. It was obvious he had been drugged and kidnapped. It was the only explanation. But why and by whom, and what happened to the woman he was with? Fear replaced his confusion when someone walked past the light filtering through the hood, blocking it briefly. He almost screamed when the hood was suddenly pulled from his head and blinked when the bright glare assaulted his eyes.

"Hello, Richard."

Richard's indignation shoved aside his fear as he stared at the hazy owner of the voice concealed behind the bright light. "Who the hell are you and why have you kidnapped me? You won't get away with this."

"But we already have," stated the voice. "Only a select few know of your whereabouts and they won't help you."

The chair the man scraped across the floor was positioned in front of his prisoner. The man sat and looked at his captive, his head haloed by the light behind.

"You have been brought here because we need your help."

Richard snorted. "You drug and kidnap me and then ask for my help. Think again, Buster. You'll get no help from me."

The man ignored Richard and continued, "I have been following the heroic account of your battles and escapes from the alien creatures while you and the other scientists were aboard the spaceship. It makes for a fascinating read."

Suspicion clouded Richard's eyes as he scrutinized the man.

"Someone with your unique experience will be invaluable to the team."

Though Richard suspected the answer, he asked the question, "And what team would that be?"

"The team that searches the alien vessel for advanced technology."

"I'm not interested," replied Richard adamantly. "I'm never setting foot aboard that death-ship again."

The man smiled. "Look around, Richard. You are already onboard."

When the interrogation light was switched off, the darkness that remained was suddenly flooded with light from portable halogen lights set around the room. Richard's eyes roamed over the stacks of storage containers and the large airlock door a short distance away. He was in the spaceship cargo bay. His chair scraped back when he jumped at seeing the hundreds of insects that had been swept into a pile to clear the floor.

"Relax, Richard, they are all dead. We gassed them and the Space Rats. I assure you, you are perfectly safe."

Richard wasn't convinced by the man's reassurance. He had experienced the terrors contained within the ship firsthand. "Nowhere is safe on this floating coffin. There are horrors in here you can't even imagine and all want to kill and eat you."

"That, Richard, is where your experience will come in handy. Also, it's imperative we reach the map room, which, according to your and the other scientists debriefings, you led the scientists to having already visited it previously. You can do the same for our team, as they'd rather not wander around aimlessly in the hope they stumble across it."

"That's your problem, not mine. I've nearly died too many times already on this vessel and it's not an experience I'm willing to repeat. I wish you good luck, but I demand you release me immediately. If you do, and return me to where you abducted me from, I'll say nothing about this."

The man huffed. "Correct me if I'm wrong, Richard, but didn't you give those same assurances about the discovery of the spaceship?"

Richard cringed. Why did things always come back to bite him in the ass? "That was different. You've committed a crime. Release me and I promise I won't say anything."

The man's smile unsettled Richard.

"I'd rather cut a vein, wander through the spaceship and trust one of those alien monsters not to eat me than have any faith in your promises." The man stood. "However, if that's your final word..."

"It is," insisted Richard, obstinately.

"Then I will arrange your removal from this spaceship."

Surprised by the man's sudden and unexpected amicableness, worry creased Richard's brow when he asked, "You'll set me free?"

The man glared at his captive. "Oh, no, Richard, you'll never be free. You seem to forget that I am not the only one that has committed a crime here. Even though it is now in our care, when we searched your home we discovered the alien creature you smuggled out of Antarctica, risking the lives of everyone on the planet if it carries a deadly virus."

Richard snorted. "That's utter nonsense. I've been close to the creature and I'm not ill."

"How can you be sure? There could be deadly parasites or bacteria growing inside you that could affect you in ways we couldn't possibly imagine and which could be very contagious. You have broken so many laws I don't know where to begin. No Richard, you will not go free. When you leave here you'll be taken to a secure facility and kept in quarantine."

Dread now creased Richard's features. "For how long?"

The man shrugged. "For the rest of your life I would imagine."

"You can't do that!"

The man smiled again. "Can't I? Goodbye, Richard." He headed for the airlock.

"Wait! What if I help you?" Richard called out, desperation and fear shrouded his words. "What happens to me then?"

The man stopped and turned. "If you do that, then your future will be very different. The charges against you will be waived and you will be free to carry on with your life."

"If I survive, that is?" said Richard, not confident he would.

"You will be accompanied by well-armed and highly trained professionals who will protect you."

Richard still wasn't convinced. "Trained to fight other soldiers, not the monsters aboard this spaceship."

"If they can be killed, my men will kill them. So, Richard, are you going to join the team?"

Richard sighed. "You leave me no damn choice, but I'm not sure I can remember the route. I was running from monsters at the time and didn't take note of where I was going."

"Then you'll just have to pray your memory returns, because if you can't lead the team to the map room, my men will lead you straight to quarantine where you'll spend the rest of your miserable days—and I assure you, Richard, they will be extremely miserable."

A guard approached and released Richard from the chair.

"Come grab a coffee, Richard. Your teammates should be arriving shortly."

Reluctantly, Richard followed the man from the room. Why did his life have to be so complicated? All he wanted was fame, fortune and all the pleasant things they brought. Was that so much to ask for?

CHAPTER 14

The Russians

THE RADAR OPERATOR aboard the American container ship, Starlight, stared at the image on his scope for a few moments before turning to the large man sipping the strong coffee responsible for the bitter aroma that filled the cabin. "The Russians have arrived, Captain."

Captain Sergio Ramos wasn't surprised. The American commander had already informed him they were on their way.

"Shall I pass the news on to the Americans, Captain?" inquired First Mate Phillip Riesman.

The Captain nodded. "Inform them we're tracking the Russians and they will be alerted if they approach us."

Riesman picked up the internal telephone and did as instructed.

Norton hung up the telephone linked to the bridge and crossed to the Admiral conversing with one of the men from NASA. "The Russians have arrived, sir."

Thomson turned, glanced at Norton and walked across the room. "What are they doing?"

Norton followed his superior. "They have turned on a heading towards the iceberg and the captain will let us know if it changes course towards us."

Thomson paused at the satellite scan laid out on a table to one side of the large room. "I wonder what their plan is. We have the only access to the spaceship covered."

Norton briefly pondered answering, but held his tongue. It was a habit of the Admiral's to speak his thoughts aloud. "Will you contact them, sir?"

Thomson shook his head. "Not yet. We know why they are here, so let's see what they do first."

*****

The Russian ship, Spasatel Kuznetsov, a MPSV07 class, multi-purpose salvage and icebreaking vessel, approached within sight of its destination, the Antarctic iceberg recently set adrift.

Captain Georgy Brusilov, the man tasked with leading the Russian salvage operation, entered the below-deck storage area and glanced around at the men constructing the equipment designed to gain entry to the spaceship. The large metal hull of the cargo barge that had been stripped of everything that wasn't needed for the mission ahead, occupied center stage of the spacious room. Streams of molten-metal sparks flew from around the men busy welding extra plates of steel to the square-nosed platform stretching out slightly proud of the bow. The barge would act as a platform for their plan to gain entry to the spaceship entombed in the ice.

Brusilov crossed to the large boring machine and ran a hand over one of its cutting teeth. Though it wouldn't cut through metal, rock posed it no problem. Because ice was only about ten percent as hard as concrete, the machine would bore through the iceberg as easily as vodka slipping down a thirsty Russian's throat. He turned on hearing footsteps approach. It was Nikolay Rezanov, his chief engineer.

Rezanov nodded. "Captain."

Brusilov returned the greeting, "Chief."

The two men glanced around at the work in progress.

"How long before its ready, Nikolay?"

"We are just adding the final touches. We might have to make a few adjustments once we get started, but I believe what we've designed will be more than capable for the task ahead. The only unknown that causes me any concern is the spaceship's alien metal hull. We have no idea what it's made from, its thickness, or if our equipment will be able to cut through it."

Brusilov glanced over at the store of cutting equipment that included thermic lances. It was the best Russia had and they had some of the best metalworkers in the world. He was confident the hull would yield to the men's expertise, whatever alien metal it was fashioned from. "ETA for reaching the launch position is ten minutes, so before long we'll find out."

"One way or another, we'll get you inside the alien vessel, Captain."

Brusilov smiled at his chief engineer. "I never doubted it for a moment. Mother Russia is relying on our success. We cannot let the Americans and British be the only ones to possess alien technology and, more importantly, alien weaponry. The outcome for Russia if we fail could be catastrophic for our standing as a world power." He slapped his chief engineer on the shoulder. "But of course that will never happen, because we will not fail. Ready the barge to be raised as soon as work is completed so it can be moved to the iceberg. We are against the clock here. The Americans and British might have a head start but we can still ensure we don't leave empty-handed." He climbed the metal staircase and headed back to the bridge.

When Brusilov entered the bridge, Ivan Chersky, his second-in-command, removed the binoculars from his eyes and glanced at the Captain. "The iceberg is dead ahead, Captain. Range, half a mile."

Brusilov glanced out the window and through the driving snow that had started an hour ago and caught his first glimpse of the huge iceberg. He took the binoculars and focused on the approaching behemoth. It looked more like a continent than a floating block of ice. "Have the Americans or British moved position or made contact?"

"Apart from keeping pace with the iceberg's drift, they have made no attempts to intercept or contact us, friendly or otherwise."

Brusilov lowered the binoculars. "They know why we're here, the same reason they are. They are also aware they have no more claim on the iceberg or salvage rights on what's inside than we do."

"Maybe they will leave us alone," suggested Chersky. "The Americans, who I understand were the first soldiers to set foot aboard the drifting spaceship, are hardly likely to risk an international incident by using force to keep us away."

"I agree, but we are all dealing with a unique situation. The Antarctic Treaty states that all knowledge and discoveries are to be shared with all other signed up nations, but I doubt the discovery of an alien spaceship was envisaged when it was drawn up."

Brusilov stared out at the large iceberg.

"Even though I know there's an alien spaceship entombed in the ice and..." he waved a hand at the Russian satellite scan of the spaceship laid out on the chart table three-yards away, "...we have proof that it does, I won't truly believe it until I step foot inside."

"What about the alien monsters the British scientist reported are inside? Won't they be a problem?"

"I have read the newspaper accounts of the man's heroic battle with the aliens and I would be extremely surprised if he hasn't exaggerated them out of all proportions to make himself seem braver. It's a typical trait of Westerners, especially the Americans."

"I'm sure you are right, Captain, but the photographs of the aliens seem formidable."

"I'm confident it's nothing the men and Russian firepower can't handle." Brusilov turned away from the window, crossed to the chart table and roamed his eyes over the impressive spaceship. He regretted the complete vessel wasn't salvageable, but even if every nation joined together they couldn't save it; the vessel was too large and shortly to be at the bottom of the ocean. He concentrated on the markings added to the scan. A tunnel had been drawn where the hull was the closest to the ice. Entry would be through the side of the ship at the opposite end to where the Americans had entered and about half a mile from the front of the ship. They would have to drill a tunnel through the ice a little over one hundred yards long to reach the hull.

He gazed at the helmsman. "Bring us alongside the iceberg's eastern edge at a distance of two hundred yards."

*****

The American salvaging operation was progressing as planned. McNally watched the final piece of the sled dangling beneath the approaching helicopter and glanced around the ice ledge to ensure his men were ready to receive it. If everything went to plan the cargo ship would soon be heading for the Starlight. Like all who had set eyes upon the spacecraft, he wondered what their capabilities were and what impact they would have on humans' thirst to reach out into the unknown and witness the marvels, opportunities and challenges it had to offer. He estimated, depending on the alien vessel's complexity, it could take between five to ten years before the ships were reverse engineered and replicated and scientists worked out how to pilot one.

When the helicopter arrived its downwash battered the men waiting for its payload. When the fourth sled piece was lowered onto the trailer, men rushed forward to unhook the tethers, and the helicopter turned away. McNally signaled to the dozer driver to proceed and the men followed the bulldozer towing the trailer through the ice tunnel.

*****

Brusilov gazed at the iceberg that slid past two hundred yards away. Even from this distance he had to tilt his head back slightly to see its top. It was an awe-inspiring and humbling sight.

"Approaching our point of entry, Captain," reported Chersky.

The two men glanced down on hearing the cargo deck doors open and watched the crane swing into position. The cable was lowered into the hold and a few moments later the barge rose above the deck with two men onboard. They held on to the rail as the barge swung out over the side and was lowered into the water. As soon as it was afloat and the cables went slack, one of the men aboard released the tethers while the other man entered the small wheelhouse at the stern and started the powerful diesel engine, which belched out a thick cloud of black smoke when it chugged to life.

Brusilov was both apprehensive and excited by what they were about to do. As men scurried across the deck attaching cables to the equipment that would be craned onto the barge, he turned his attention back to the iceberg and scrutinized their landing point. It had been chosen not only for its proximity to the spaceship, but also because of the natural ledge of ice that protruded twelve yards from the wall of ice. The borer required a stable platform to begin its task and the ice ledge fulfilled that requirement.

When all the supplies were aboard the barge hugging the ship's hull, the roll of climbing netting was unfurled over the side and the engineers clambered down and boarded the barge.

As the strange vessel headed for the iceberg, the crew in the ship's hold moved the borer in position below the open deck hatch. When the engineers were ready it would be airlifted to the iceberg.

The barge slowed when it approached the ice ledge and two large harpoon cannons were moved to either side of the bow and locked into place. Beside each was a coil of thin, but extremely strong cable, attached to an electric winch. The harpoons had been designed to spin and in front of the barb at the harpoon's tip was a screw thread that would pull it deep into the ice. When two explosions rung out, the spinning harpoons shot through the air and struck the ice above the ledge. The winches were powered up and as the slack was taken out of the cables the barge was pulled closer to the iceberg.

Nikolay moved to the bow and shot his gaze from the harpoons to the approaching ice. If one came free and snapped back, it could maim or kill someone, but they held firm and slowly the barge was drawn nearer the ledge. Nikolay ordered the winch operators, Alexei Vanyushin and Kolya Antonoff, to slow down when it was only a few feet away. The men stumbled to keep their footing when the barge struck the ice with a resounding boom a few moments later. When the cables were taut, the winch drums were locked and motors switched off. The metal platform chaffed against the ice as the waves raised and lowered it.

When he was satisfied the tethers would hold and were locked into position, Nikolay pulled out his radio and communicated with the ship, "Barge is secure, bring the borer."

While four men flipped the wide metal ramp hinged to the bow over from lying flat on the deck to rest on the ice, Nikolay glanced back at the ship and watched the large helicopter lift from the helipad and maneuver above the hold.

The rotors of the large Russian Mi-26M helicopter, known in the West as the Halo, began to spin. It had the load-carrying capability of a C-130 transport plane and a payload capacity of twenty-five tons, making it the world's largest production helicopter. It rose from the helipad and with constant directions from his co-pilot leaning out of the side door, the pilot, Yegor Kristoff, positioned the Halo over the open hold. The co-pilot winched down the cable and when the crew signaled the payload had been attached, he informed Yegor that all was ready.

The pilot applied power to the twin engines and slowly lifted the borer from the hold. As it was drilling through ice and not the rock for which it was originally designed, the borer's frame didn't have to be so strong, so along with any excess weight, some of the frame had been stripped away or replaced with lighter aluminum. Left in its original state the helicopter would have struggled to lift it. After the borer had cleared all obstructions, the Halo turned and headed for the men waiting to receive it on the iceberg.

An overhang of ice prevented the helicopter from hovering directly over the ledge, so it lowered its payload onto the barge. Men grabbed the skids they had added on the bottom and communicated directions to the pilot until the machine faced in the right direction. It clanged onto the deck with a thump that rocked the barge. The lift cable was released and the helicopter swooped away.

Nikolay glanced over at the men on the ice ledge. They had screwed an anchor into the ice and attached a diesel-powered winch. Two men dragged the cable towards the borer and attached it to the front of the machine. The winch was started and slowly the borer slid along the deck. Men positioned around it kept it on course. It reached the top of the gently sloping ramp and when it reached its center of gravity, it tilted forward just as a swell raised the barge a foot. Unable to hold the heavy piece of equipment back, the men released their hold. The borer slid and screeched down the ramp, heading for the winch-operator. The man dived aside a moment before the machine crashed into the winch and the borer skewed to one side before coming to a rest.

Nikolay rushed down the ramp, his view of the winch operator blocked by the borer. When he rounded the machine he saw the man sprawled on the ice. He was about to rush over to check if he was alive, dead or injured, when the man lifted his head and grinned.

A quick inspection of the borer proved it to be undamaged. The same could not be said for the winch that was damaged beyond repair and leaked diesel fuel. Luckily, it had already carried out its task and was no longer needed.

Nikolay glanced at the men who had gathered on the ice ledge. "Babinski and Mikhail, dump the winch into the sea."

While that task was carried out, Nikolay positioned men around the borer, straightened it up and pushed it against the wall of ice. Metal struts were jammed into the ice at the back to keep the drill teeth pressed against the ice until it bit and dragged itself forward.

A power cable wound around a large drum and connected to the generator aboard the barge was unwound and attached to the borer. After Nikolay had checked all the connections, he flipped the ON switch. The control panel showed all green lights. He pressed the starter and disengaged the clutch. Slowly, at first, the borer cutting drum began to turn. Nikolay turned on the pump that normally sprayed a coolant on the rotating drill, which wasn't necessary in this situation and had been replaced with anti-freeze. The jets spluttered before achieving a steady blast of liquid. The ice sheered from the wall as the borer inched forward was collected on the conveyer beneath the machine and disgorged behind; normally a long conveyer belt would remove the spoils, but in this situation it wasn't possible. The men cheered. It was working.

"Okay, comrades, now the hard work begins," warned Nikolay. "Remove the props, grab your shovels and clear the scrapings."

The men shoveled the ice away from the back of the slowly moving borer and tossed it into the sea. When the borer went deeper, freeing up room on the small ice ledge, a mini excavator would be brought from the ship to remove the loosened ice. For the first time in a long while, Nikolay took a moment to relax. There was nothing he could do now until the hull was reached. He lit his pipe and blew a plume of strong-scented smoke into the air. Like the captain, he found it almost impossible to believe they would soon be aboard an alien spaceship. He smiled. You just never knew what surprises the future held in store.

CHAPTER 15

SEAL Team Five

THE ROAR OF the C-130's powerful engines vibrated through the fuselage and the uncomfortable seats occupied by the six men of SEAL Team Five.

"Two minutes to drop," called out the pilot over the radio headsets they all wore.

The men stood as the large rear exit ramp opened and after the routine safety check of examining each other's gear and parachutes had been completed, they walked to the end of the ramp and waited for the red jump light to change.

As one unit the Navy SEALs rushed forward when the jump light turned green and dived out the back. They spread their arms and legs as they plummeted to stretch their wingsuits. Far below the tiny spec of the American salvage ship was dwarfed by their target, the large iceberg. The men spiraled as they swooped down and headed for the entrance at the end of the iceberg lit by bright halogen lights. At five hundred feet they deployed their rapid-release parachutes and glided towards the ice.

The men working around the entrance had been warned of SEAL Team Five's approach and stood to the side as they stared at parachutists gliding expertly towards them.

The SEALs hit the ice running and detached their parachutes without stopping, letting the wind drag the expensive canopies away and toss them into the sea. The six men glanced disinterestedly at their spectators as they unslung the assault rifles from their backs and headed into the tunnel.

Lieutenant Miller turned towards the entrance when hurried footsteps entered the hangar and stepped forward to introduce himself when the SEALs grew near.

When the SEAL team had been brought up to speed on the latest developments, Richard was reluctantly brought forward.

Miller indicated Richard. "This is Richard Whorley, one of the scientists who discovered the spaceship and your guide to the map room."

The six men did nothing to hide their skepticism.

Richard, never one not to defend a slight on his abilities, ran his eyes over the men and their weapons. "Yeah, well I'm not impressed by you either. If you think your weapons and training will protect you against all of the alien monstrosities aboard this spaceship, you are wrong—very, very, wrong."

Commander Nickolas Colbert, the SEAL team officer in charge of the mission, moved forward abruptly, forcing Richard to step back from the invasion of his personal space.

"Let's get this straight, Mr. Whorley, it is not my choice and nor do I want you tagging along with us, but you have mission-critical information we need so come with us you will. You are also an unknown that could put our lives at risk and jeopardize the mission. And make no mistake, if I have to make a choice between my men's safety, the completion of the mission, or you, you will always lose."

Richard smiled nervously at the man in a lame attempt to show he wasn't afraid. "I've heard more inspirational pep talks, but if you think I am here willingly, then you are mistaken. You have been forced upon me as much as I have you, so I suggest we hurry up and do what needs to be done so I can get out of this hellhole and back to civilization. And let's get this straight, Commander Macho," Richard stepped closer to Colbert. "I only look out for number one—me—so if a situation arises that threatens my life I will do anything to save it, even if that means putting you and your dick-waving diehards or the mission at risk."

Colbert smiled at Richard's surprising outburst. It was an indication the man wasn't completely spineless.

"Looks like we got a live one here," commented Stedman.

Ramirez slapped his assault rifle and smiled. "He won't stay that way for long if he keeps talking like that."

Richard leaned to the side to see around the Commander and looked at Ramirez.

"Maybe not, but I bet I survive longer than you."

Miller thought it was advisable to intervene before Richard got himself killed. "Corporal Jenkins and Lance Corporal Talbot will tag along as far as the map room and then return with Richard so he won't be with you for long."

Commander Colbert nodded. "Probably just as well. Are they ready?"

"They are," affirmed Miller.

"Then let's go." Colbert looked at Richard. "Lead on Pathfinder."

Richard pointed at one of the SEALs weapons. "Hey wait a minute, don't I get one of them? I can't go back in there unarmed."

"You're an untrained civilian, Richard, you don't get one," Miller told him.

"And we don't want you shooting us in the back," said Cleveland.

"Don't worry, hero, we'll protect you," said Ramirez.

Richard smirked at Ramirez as he walked past. "But who's going to protect all of you?" He headed for the airlock.

*****

A trail of molten metal that bubbled and dripped down the spaceship's interior hull wall was left in the wake of the jet of intense white light cutting a hole in the alien vessel and lighting up the dark room. When the edges of the glowing door-size hole met, the cutout clanged loudly to the floor. As the clang echoed through the room, the man who had formed the opening raised the dark welding visor and peered through. His excited expression changed to surprised disappointment; it wasn't the advanced technological vision he had pictured. He turned on hearing someone approach; it was Nikolay. He stepped aside to give room for his superior to catch his first glimpse of the spaceship interior.

Because of the threat of alien creatures roaming free inside the ship, the captain had advised no one to enter until armed backup arrived, but Nikolay couldn't resist the temptation to be the first Russian to set foot aboard an alien spacecraft. He pulled out his pistol and stepped inside. His flashlight lit up the bulky metal shelves that lined the walls of what seemed to be a storeroom. Though a few disarrayed objects remained on the shelves, most were strewn across the floor. He cast his eyes over some of the strange pieces of equipment without being able to fathom their use, though he thought they might be spare parts for something in the ship or the ship itself. The top two shelves on one of the racks had all but completely collapsed and hung at an angle. He aimed the light at the open doorway that led into an adjoining room. A two-foot high metal beam had fallen and blocked the lower part. He climbed over, shot a glance at the sagging ceiling and roamed the light and the weapon around the room, highlighting workbenches and machinery. The height of the benches and the machinery's work levels, high for a normal-height human, was the Russian's first hint the crew was taller than humans. Objects, which he was certain were tools, hung from the walls and lay spilled on the floor. He jumped like a frightened girl in a horror movie when someone placed a hand on his shoulder and spoke.

"What do you reckon this place is, Chief?" Yelchin's flashlight searched the objects in the room.

"I think it might be a workshop. The aliens must have had a maintenance crew."

"Makes sense," Yelchin agreed. "A ship this size must have millions of moving parts and if it's anything like our vessels, something must have constantly been breaking down, needing attention or adjustment."

"When I pictured an advanced alien spaceship I imagined everything smooth and sleek, but this..." Nikolay indicated the chunky ribs of metal and the machines and objects stained with what might be grease or oil, "...it's like something we might build, simple and functional."

"Give it chance, Chief, this is just one room and, if it is a maintenance workshop, sleek and smooth ain't needed, is it?"

Nikolay shrugged. "I suppose not."

"I'm sure the rest of the ship will be more impressive and more like the alien spaceship we all imagined."

Some of the other engineers entered and shone flashlights around the room.

"Go no further than this doorway," warned Nikolay, as he walked back to the hole in the hull, stepped out and gazed along the ice tunnel. The borer had done better than expected and had reached the hull after a few hours. He pulled out his radio and contacted the ship. "Captain, we are in. The spaceship is all yours."

"Well done, Nikolay. You and your men's efforts won't be forgotten when we return to the Motherland. I'll be there with the exploration team shortly."

Thirty minutes later, the captain and the exploration team joined Nikolay and his men in the alien workshop. The men were busy collecting anything that looked technologically advanced and was easily portable.

While his men handed out the spare weapons they had brought with them to the salvage engineers, the Captain had a brief word with Nikolay.

"We'll make our way through the ship to the higher levels and mark our passage and any rooms with technology worth salvaging as discussed. Though we'll clear the route of any alien monsters we come across, others might come, so ensure your team keep the weapons with them at all times."

"I will, and good luck, Captain." Nikolay watched the men head for the exit.

Captain Brusilov led his team out through the workshop and shone his light into the corridor the exit opened onto and checked both directions. Two nearby doors revealed another storeroom and what seemed to be, by the screens on the tables and a bank of equipment similar to a large computer terminal along one wall, an office of some sort. He ordered two of his men to notify Nikolay about the computers and then remain in the corridor to protect the engineers while they salvaged the equipment.

At the end of the corridor were a large door that seemed to be an elevator and a metal staircase that led to a higher level. Believing the armory would be on one of the upper levels to be easily accessible if the weapons were needed in an emergency, they headed up the staircase and stepped out into a similar corridor as the one below. Along its length doors stood open to dark rooms where anything could be hiding. Brusilov headed in the direction leading to the center of the colossal vessel. They cautiously checked each room before they passed to ensure nothing was going to jump out at them or come up behind them and marked the rooms containing anything of worth with a spray-painted tick.

When they came to the first closed door—which might indicate something important was stored inside—Brusilov halted the team. He doubted it was the armory, but if it was, the main focus of their mission would soon be completed. Brusilov pressed the door control. Orange light seeped into the corridor as the door rasped open. The ominous squeal that accompanied it sent a shiver through the men. All wore surprised expressions when they peered through the doorway and drifted farther into the room.

*****

Gunfire lit up the darkness and echoed along the corridor. Hunters screeched as bullets tore into them. Richard whimpered and backed away, but found his retreat blocked by the two soldiers ordered to guard their reluctant guide. When the Hunters had appeared, Richard's previous nightmare encounters with the monsters had washed over him. Infected with fear, he slid down the wall and covered his head with his arms, dulling the deafening gunfire and the horrific gut-wrenching screeches.

The gunshots ended as the surviving Hunters retreated when they realized they couldn't survive the onslaught from the humans' deadly weapons.

Talbot looked at the cowering man and shook his head. "The man who saved the world from aliens! My arse he did."

Richard tilted his head and glared at the man. "Your time will come."

"On your feet, hero," ordered Jenkins.

Richard glanced along the corridor at the six members of the SEAL team at its far end. One of them beckoned him. Richard climbed to his feet and reluctantly walked towards the men. His eyes flicked across the mass of Hunter corpses and the SEALs positioned at the T-Junction with their weapons trained along the corridor. Brody stepped up to a writhing creature and shot it in the head, stilling its pain-wracked throes.

While some of his men reloaded, Colbert turned to Richard. "Which way now?"

Richard searched his memory for any recollection of his surroundings. He thought they might be near the staircase where Haax had killed the Clickers, but he had been so scared at the time he had taken little notice of his surroundings or how far they had travelled.

Richard pointed along the corridor. "We go left, and if I'm remembering correctly, a little farther along there should be a short corridor on the right leading to a room with a staircase that leads up to the map room level."

"Okay, men, let's go. Ramirez, Sullivan, take point."

Richard waited until the men had moved off and followed with his guards close behind.

*****

The seven surviving Hunters headed back through the ship and away from the intruders with the weapons that dealt death from afar. When they had sensed something was happening to their now unstable world, their instinct to survive had led them to investigate the drafts of fresh air that intermittently wafted through the spaceship. Turned back by the strange intruders they sought another way to escape. When they had returned to their domain, they rested. When a small lump of ice thudded to the ground, one of the Hunters gazed up at the roof and the large patch of ice it had fallen from. It studied it for a few moments before climbing to its feet. It growled for the others to follow and started climbing the walls.

*****

Though the SEALs had been apprehensive about heading deeper into the spaceship with the monsters and the unknown dangers they were certain to encounter, after the Hunters had proven easy to kill, the men were now confident they had enough effective firepower to handle anything the ship threw at them.

Richard was the only one who knew better. His eyes shifted enviously to the weapon held by the man directly in front. When the first man died he'd make sure he grabbed the dead man's weapon.

The team halted at the bottom of the staircase and looked at the scattered Clicker skeletons that decorated its treads and the floor around its base. Every carcass had been stripped of flesh and was covered in teeth and claw marks. The soldiers showed particular interest in the neat round holes in the ribcages.

Crowe knelt and fingered the smooth cuts around the edges of the ribs before glancing at Richard. "Are these the monsters that Haax alien killed with the light beam weapon?"

Richard nodded. "We named them Clickers. You'll know why if we meet any. The weapon Haax used shot a ball of light, not a beam." He glanced up the staircase. "And he didn't kill them all, so some might still be up there, waiting for us."

Ramirez slapped his weapon. "It might not be alien technology, but it kills aliens just as effectively, whatever species is it."

Richard shook his head. They had no idea and he doubted many would survive. Shadowed by his two babysitters, Richard followed the testosterone-fuelled men up the stairs.

CLICK! CLICK! CLICK!

Two Clickers attacked the first men to reach the top.

Bullets ricocheted harmlessly off the walls as the ambushed soldiers tried to shoot the monsters dragging them along the corridor. Men rushed up the steps. Two short bursts of gunfire dispatched the Clickers. The two captives, still held by their attackers, were pulled to the ground when the dead creatures fell. After Ramirez and Sullivan had untangled themselves from the monsters' dead limbs, they climbed to their feet and backed away.

Colbert ran his eyes over the men. "Are you hurt?"

Surprised they felt no pain, the two men checked their bodies for damage. The only casualties were ripped clothing and damaged pride from being ambushed.

Colbert glanced at Richard. "Clickers?"

Richard nodded.

Each soldier glanced at the Clickers when they passed. All noticed their sharp, vicious teeth, claw-tipped limbs and their frightening eyeless faces. The two men had been lucky.

They passed along the short corridor through a doorway and followed Richard's vague directions through the ship.

CHAPTER 16

A Rescue Mission

WHEN LUCY AND her new companion reached a metal door that blocked the far end of the mushroom tunnel, Pinky peered through the small barred opening set in the door before removing the prop that held it closed. The door squealed slightly when Pinky opened it wide enough for them to slip through. Lucy followed Pinky into a rocky area dotted with trees and thorny, large-leaved bushes. Distant squeals and howls alerted Lucy they were not alone. The presence of other creatures put Lucy's senses on alert and again caused her to wonder if the creature she followed could be trusted. Though she thought it unlikely, it was a carnivore and she couldn't help but worry that she might still end up on Pinky's menu. Her hands gripped the makeshift weapon tighter as she carried on.

She almost tripped over Pinky when the creature stopped without warning. Lucy brushed its tail away from her face and took a step back as Pinky crouched behind a bush and pulled aside a branch. After peering out at something, it whimpered and turned to Lucy.

Even though its permanent killer smile remained, Lucy was surprised by Pinky's sad expression and wondered what had caused it. She knelt beside it and peered through the gap in the foliage. Across the room a creature, the same species as Pinky, though slightly more muscular, was in a cave entrance thirty-feet from the ground, throwing rocks at the vicious six-legged creatures the size of a large wolf attempting to climb up the rock to reach it.

Pinky grabbed Lucy's arm to attract her attention, tapped its chest and then pointed at the trapped creature.

"Is that your mate," asked Lucy, attempting to make sense of Pinky's gestures.

Pinky looked at her curiously and then stood, pointed at the spear Lucy held and mimicked jabbing the air with it.

"You want me to help you rescue your mate." Though Lucy felt sorry for the two creatures, she didn't have the time or the confidence they could succeed. The spaceship would soon slip beneath the sea and the whole vessel would be flooded, killing everything aboard. Rescuing creatures that would soon be dead was pointless. She noticed Pinky staring at her. It seemed to have read her reluctance and pointed at her eyes and then across the room. Lucy gazed in the indicated direction. A metal staircase, all but hidden in shadow, hugged the far wall. It led up to a balcony and in the gloom shrouding the top was an open door. If she could get past the Wolf Monsters it could be her way up to the next level.

Pinky whimpered as she stared at a Wolf Monster climbing unseen by Pinky's mate up the rock to one side of the cave entrance while the others distracted the trapped creature's attention.

Lucy watched, hoping the trapped creature would see it in time. The lone Wolf Monster drew level with the cave and moved along a small ledge. One of its back legs slipped off the edge, sending a rock tumbling noisily down the cliff. Aware it had lost the element of surprise, the Wolf monster rushed at its prey.

Pinky's mate turned and faced the threat. When its attacker leaped, it dodged clear of its claws and smashed a rock at its head. The Wolf Monster hit the ground and rolled. Dazed by the blow, it rose on its legs unsteadily. Pinky's mate gave it no time to recover and rushed at its attacker and shoulder-barged it over the edge. The Wolf Monster struck the rock repeatedly as it tumbled down the cliff, leaving behind a trail of dark blood. Though still alive, as soon as its battered body struck the ground, the pack leaped on it and started feasting.

Lucy studied the ground between her and the staircase. Bushes and rocks would hide her approach over much of the distance. A plan formed in her mind that just might work. She turned to Pinky and even though she knew the creature couldn't understand her words, she hoped her tone and hand movements would hint at her meaning, and whispered, "I will help you." She brandished the spear and pointed at the Wolf Monsters. "I go. You stay here." She pointed at Pinky and then at the ground.

Pinky looked at the ground with a puzzled expression.

Lucy sighed. She could do with a console to plug Pinky into to teach her English. She took a few steps away. Pinky followed. Lucy shook her head, held up a hand and backed away. Pinky remained and watched her go.

Stopping often to glance at the Wolf Monsters preoccupied with eating one of their own, Lucy moved across the room using the rocks and bushes as concealment. When she glanced back she noticed Pinky watching her from behind a bush. Lucy carried on and soon reached the bottom of the staircase. So far her presence had gone unnoticed by the Wolf Monsters, who had now picked the bloody bones of their comrade clean and refocused their attention back on the trapped creature.

Pinky watched the strange intruder cross the room. When she climbed the staircase it became anxious. Why wasn't it attacking the monsters? Pinky snarled when Lucy disappeared through the doorway. It had been tricked. It looked at the pack of vicious creatures between her and her mate. It might be able to kill one, perhaps two, before she was brought down by the more powerful foe, but she would die in the end. It would be a useless death. Her mate would still be trapped.

The Wolf Monsters howled when they realized no more rocks were being thrown at them and their prey had no more to throw. They started climbing.

Pinky turned away. She couldn't bear to watch her mate die.

A loud, piercing, warbling cry rang out.

Pinky shot her gaze at the sound and smiled her killer grin.

Lucy stood halfway down the staircase waving the spear in the air.

The Wolf Monsters stopped climbing. For a few moments they did nothing other than stare at the strange creature, then five split off from the group and rushed at the new prey while the three remaining beasts continued their climb.

Pinky leaped from the bushes and rushed across the room.

Lucy watched the five vicious beasts approach and noticed Pinky's rapid dash for the rock to help her mate. Lucy hoped she had bought them both enough time and they both survived. When the Wolf Monsters reached the bottom of the staircase, Lucy could wait no longer. She turned, ran up the oversized treads and rushed through the open door. A sprint along a short corridor brought her to another door she had already checked was operational before alerting the Wolf Monsters to her presence. As the door opened, the first of the Wolf Monsters skidded into the room. Its claws scratched on the metal floor as they sought traction on its smooth surface.

A second beast slammed into it, knocking them both to the floor. As two more entered, Lucy nipped through the opening and closed the door.

Though she thought it unlikely the Wolf Monsters could open the door, Lucy didn't want to linger and be proved wrong. She moved through the short corridor and opened the door at the far end. Her face dropped when she stepped onto a balcony entwined with alien ivy and gazed at the jungle-choked room. The tall foliage was too dense for her to see the far side of the room or how far away it was. Aware she had to keep moving, Lucy climbed down the stairs overgrown with creeping fauna and entered the jungle.

Pinky arrived at the rock wall and scurried up the side towards the nearest beast. She grabbed its leg and yanked it down hard. The Wolf Monster slipped and lashed out at the creature responsible. Pinky easily dodged the claw and jumped onto its back. She grabbed its ears and yanked its head back and to the side. Her head shot forward. Her teeth latched onto its neck and ripped a large gash in its throat. She leaped off as her victim fell and climbed up the cliff. The first beast had already reached the top. She scrambled onto an outcrop of rock and leaped at the second beast. She slammed into its side, freeing its grip on the rock, and raked claws down its belly as she dodged away and watched the wounded Wolf Monster tumble down the cliff.

Pinky climbed over the ledge and looked at her mate facing down the Wolf Monster. It smiled at her and nodded.

They both attacked at the same time. The Wolf Monster screeched as it lashed out at the fast moving creatures, but they ducked and dodged its claws as they made contact with their own. It fell to the ground panting heavily. Blood poured from its many wounds.

Howls rang out as the pack announced their return.

Pinky and her mate left the wounded creature as a distraction for its comrades and leaped over the cliff. They slid to the bottom and rushed across the ground as the pack arrived.

The Wolf Monsters instinctively gave chase, but skidded to a halt, raised their vicious snouts, sniffed and turned their heads back towards the cliff and the strong scent of blood. After a brief glance at the two fleeing creatures they headed back to the cliff to begin feasting on the food they didn't have to chase.

CHAPTER 17

Fields of Fear

THE WARM HUMID room the Russian salvage team had entered was lit by rows of light cells hanging from the ceiling. It stretched into the distance and was filled with raised growing beds one-hundred-feet wide and what seemed three times that long. Each contained a single variety of crop that included fruit trees, vegetables and grain crops similar to wheat or barley. Untended, the crops had run wild and a carpet of rotten fruit and vegetation covered the floor between the crop trays and filled the air with the stench of cloying decay. Lines of one-inch wide black pipes, which seemed to be part of an irrigation system, were suspended above each crop area and led to large, tall tanks positioned at intervals around the room.

Sergei Antonoff walked over to a fruit-laden tree and plucked one of its purple fruits, similar in size and shape to an avocado. He sniffed it. "It smells sweet, a cross between a grape and a pear."

"I wouldn't risk tasting it," said Brusilov.

Sergei had no intention of doing so. He dropped the fruit and when he gazed down the long path, he thought he glimpsed movement. "Captain, I think crops aren't the only thing in here."

Brusilov followed Sergei's gaze. Though he saw nothing, he trusted the man's judgment. "Okay, let's leave. There's nothing in this room we want."

As if it had patiently waited for those very words to be spoken, the door rasped closed just as ominously as it had opened. Weapons were brought to bear on the closed door but no one was nearby to have operated it.

"Probably on a timer to protect the warm, moist atmosphere," Viktor Rozovsky suggested, feeling a bead of sweat run down his neck.

A distant shriek rang out.

Weapons swiveled towards the sound.

Nothing moved except for their rapidly beating hearts and the blood pumping through their veins.

"Let's go," ordered Brusilov.

Their weapons roamed the room for danger as they backed towards the exit.

Petya Babinski reached the door first and searched for the door control. He found it smashed on the floor. "Captain, we have a problem."

Brusilov glanced at the broken control highlighted in the beam from Babinski's flashlight and received an uneasy feeling they'd walked into a trap. He watched as Rozovsky and Vadik tried to force the door open. When it was obvious they wouldn't succeed, he glanced around the huge room. "There has to be another exit in here somewhere and we need to find it before whatever's in here finds us." He led his men down the nearest path.

Another screech closer than before, came from ahead and to their right.

Vadik aimed his weapon at the point where he thought the sound had originated from. "Whatever it is, it's in that alien wheat field."

Brusilov thought it wise they move before it attacked. "Pick up the pace."

All were glad to do so and they hurried along the path. Each footstep squelched into the thick carpet of rotted vegetation. The rustle of crops on their right indicated something homing in on them. All were startled by the sprinkler system when it sputtered out jets of water that filled the room with fine rain and cut their limited vision even more. Without making a sound, something leaped from the crop field on their left. It had been waiting for them.

Horror spread across Yegor Kristoff's features when he turned and stared at the ten-foot-long creature. Patches of scraggy fur and scaly, snakelike skin covered its muscular brown body. He stumbled into Babinski when one of the monster's three-clawed front limbs lashed out, ripping three deep gashes across his chest that continued up his neck and across his face. Blood gushed from the wound as the creature sailed overhead. Its long tail, ridged with short, sharp spikes, ended in a jaw the size of a large melon and crammed with sharp teeth. It gripped Yegor's face and flipped him into the air, sending the dying man soaring over the path. The creature disappeared into the opposite crop field and then reappeared briefly to snatch Yegor's screaming body from the air. The grisly sounds of tearing flesh quickly followed, ending the Russian's harrowing screams.

Rozovsky sprayed bullets after the monster crashing through the field away from them.

Sergei gripped his shoulder. "Stop, you'll hit Yegor."

Rozovsky sprayed one more burst before stopping. He looked at Sergei. "What's it matter? He's already dead."

"Quiet everyone," ordered Brusilov. He was worried that the creatures had shown intelligence and there were at least two of them—the one that had lain in wait and attacked and the other that had distracted their attention.

Though the rain made it hard to hear anything more than a short distance away, they all heard the cacophony of excited squeals that rippled across the room. There were more than two monsters and they had smelt blood—human blood.

Expecting an attack at any moment, Brusilov scanned the room. His eyes halted on the nearest water tower. It was their only chance. The higher vantage point would give them a good view of the room, the approaching monsters and an ideal defensive position. "Head for the water tower."

They sprinted for the tower and while the Captain and Vadik kept guard, the others climbed the ladder. Its widely spaced rungs were evidence it had been designed for someone with longer legs than humans. Once the others reached the top, they covered Brusilov and Vadik's climb.

The height of the tower had brought them above the rain, but the fine mist it created still impaired their view of anything moving through it. The men spread out around the edge of the tank and scanned the room below.

Brusilov switched off his weapon-light and advised his men to do the same to conserve the batteries; they could be stuck here for some time.

Babinski pointed at something moving through one of the crop sections, leaving behind a trail of flattened growth. "Something's coming from over there."

"Two more coming from this side," called out Vadik.

"I see four coming in fast over here," added Sasha Petroff.

The Captain joined Petroff in watching the four trails of flattened growth move across the width of a field two crop sections away. The tall crops hid the creatures until they jumped across the path. Four vicious, fanged faces snarled up at them.

The Captain gazed around as more creatures joined in the hunt. He counted nine. "Fire when you have a target, but don't waste ammo. I've a feeling we're gonna need more than we have."

Brusilov lay flat on the tank and sighted along his weapon, following the leading edge of a flattened trail snaking through a field. When the creature appeared and leaped across the path, he adjusted aim slightly and fired a short burst. The creature screeched, crashed to the ground, tumbled head over heels and lay still.

More shots rang out. Two more creatures died. The remaining creatures turned and retreated. While Brusilov watched them retreat, he wondered why they had halted their attack so quickly. Did their weapons drive them back, or were they testing their defenses? He glanced around at his men.

Vadik approached. "Now what do we do, Captain? We're stuck up here and I can't see those things going too far when a cornered meal's on offer."

"I've no idea, Vadik. This is as new to me as it is to you. We now know they can be killed and they also now know we have the means to do so. We'll stay here for a while to see what they do before I make a decision."

"Now they've seen we aren't the easy prey they no doubt assumed we were, maybe they'll leave us alone and give us chance to leave?" said Babinski, hopefully.

Brusilov climbed to his feet and stared down at the surrounding crops, but saw no sign of the monsters he knew were down there, watching and waiting. "I think them leaving us alone is wishful thinking. They are up to something."

The rain stopped to be replaced by occasional drips of water from the irrigation pipes.

Brusilov suddenly crouched and placed a hand on the metal tank. He glanced at Rozovsky. "Check the ladder."

Rozovsky moved to the ladder and peered down its length. Half a body length away a monster growled at him. Its tail head lashed out, gripped his shoulder and flung him over the edge. The creature bounded up the last few rungs and onto the tank. Startled by its sudden appearance, Sergei froze. The captain barged the shocked man aside as the monster lashed a claw at Sergei's face. Brusilov fired. Bullets struck the monster's chest. It collapsed to the ground. Babinski kicked it in the head, sending it rolling off the tower.

Rozovsky, though shaken by the fall, had been saved from injury by the cushioning effect of the thick carpet of decayed mulch covering the floor. When he gazed up and saw the monster plummeting straight for him, he rolled out of the way. The monster crashed to the ground beside him. Blood oozed from the bullet holes in its chest. Though it was undeniably dead, the message had not yet been received by the tail head. It snapped its jaws and lunged for Rozovsky. Having dropped his weapon during the fall, Rozovsky snatched the knife from its sheaf on his thigh and stabbed at the head. The blade entered just behind its snapping jaw and after a few seconds it fell still and drooped.

"Are you okay, Rozovsky?" called out Sergei.

Rozovsky gazed up the tower to see his comrades staring down at him.

"I was until someone dropped a bloody monster on me." He used a hand to push the head from the blade and threw it aside.

Babinski grinned. "That was me."

Rozovsky turned his head and stared at the monster's face only two feet away. No flesh or hair covered its head from its ears to the tip of its long snout. It gave it a skeletal appearance and revealed the full wickedness of its sharp, scythe-like fangs.

Brusilov noticed two creatures heading for Rozovsky. "If you're finished playing with your new friend, I suggest you climb back up here before its comrades join the party."

Rozovsky took the hint. He climbed to his feet, grabbed his rifle and rushed up the ladder. He was halfway up when gunshots echoed through the vast room. A screech indicated one monster had been hit. The other was not so easy to kill. It didn't move in a straight line, but constantly dodged and changed direction, making it hard to hit. They were learning. It leaped out of the crop below the water tank and onto the ladder.

Rozovsky fumbled with the weapon he'd slung over his shoulder for the climb.

Brusilov dropped his rifle, grabbed his pistol and shot out an arm behind him. "Someone hold me."

When someone grabbed his wrist, Brusilov leaned out over the edge, took aim and fired four shots at the monster's head and two in the tail head. It fell to the ground and lay still. Brusilov glanced at Rozovsky and nodded.

Rozovsky returned the nod. "Thanks, Captain."

When Brusilov was pulled upright, he reloaded and holstered the weapon and reclaimed his rifle.

A creature, slightly paler and larger than the others, stood in the shadows watching the strange new arrivals trapped in its domain. Though they were proving difficult to kill, it wasn't beaten yet. It had a plan. It tilted its head and looked at the rows of yellow lights hanging from the ceiling. It wouldn't be long now. It turned to face the hoard of creatures waiting for instructions and barked a command. The creatures glanced towards the prey atop the water tower and then rushed off.

The men on the tower stared in the direction the bark had come from. They glimpsed the bulk of a larger, paler creature before it slunk into the shadows.

Wondering what the creatures were up to now, Brusilov eyes searched the room for a clue and noticed the farthest row of lights go out and then the next. One by one the rows went dark. Pitch-blackness sped towards them.

Sensing something bad was about to happen, the Russians switched on their flashlights and waited.

"You know the drill, comrades," Brusilov said. "Spread out and keep your eyes and lights trained below. The only way they can get to us is by climbing the tower. If we stay alert we'll survive. Pick off any that venture too close and hopefully we can reduce their numbers enough to risk climbing down and search for an exit."

The men spaced themselves around the edge of the tower and roamed their lights over the area below. When thirty minutes had passed and the creatures still hadn't shown themselves, Brusilov became concerned. He didn't like the inactivity. He preferred they attack so one way or another they could bring an end to this stalemate. His eyes searched the ground as he walked the tower's circumference, but nothing moved below. He cocked an ear when he thought he heard something. There it was again. It was faint, but continuous—the sound of something sliding, slithering. He stared into the patch of darkness he thought it originated from and raised the light fixed to his weapon. Caught in his beam nine feet away was the open jaw of one of the creatures hanging upside down from a ceiling beam. He shifted the light left and right, revealing rows of the monsters, one behind the other.

"They're on the ceiling!" he shouted.

Bullets sprayed from his rifle. A creature screeched and fell to the floor. A second soon followed. The others raised their lights, glimpsed the creatures moving along the roof girders all around them and fired.

One leapt and twisted in midair with its claws aimed at Babinski. Babinski fired as he dodged back and smashed the rifle butt into its head when it flew past. The creature slammed into the tank and rolled.

Rozovsky jumped over it to prevent the tumbling monster from knocking him over the edge and glared at Babinski. "Stop throwing monsters at me."

Babinski shrugged and grinned as he shot another creature. "I assure you, Rozovsky, it's not intentional."

As the men dispatched more of the horrors, Brusilov went through their options. They would soon run out of ammo if they remained here and if the creatures were on the ceiling, perhaps—if they were really lucky—there wouldn't be any below or reduced to a number they might be able to handle. He glanced at the men firing beside him. "Sergei, Petroff, climb down and take position at the bottom of the ladder. It's time we found that exit."

The men shot two more creatures as they moved for the ladder. Petroff slid down first, Sergei quickly followed. Bullets continued to find their targets from the remaining men on top. The creatures that had witnessed the deaths of those in front now moved more cautiously or had stopped.

Brusilov placed a hand on Vadik's shoulder. "I'm going down next. The rest of you follow in quick order."

The men nodded and followed the captain down the ladder. When Rozovsky was the only one on the tower, he sprayed bullets in all directions at the creatures until his foot touched the top rung. He quickly shouldered his weapon, gripped the side rails and slid to the bottom.

Brusilov explained his escape plan. "We head to the far side of the room and hope we find a usable exit."

"And if we don't, what then, Captain?" asked Babinski.

"I'll let you know if and when that happens. Let's go." Brusilov sprinted into the darkness with his weapon raised and moving from side to side. His men followed close behind in staggered formation.

Their feet squelched and slipped in the rain-moistened compost covering the floor. They had crossed over half the room before a creature attacked. It leaped out of the crop at Sergei, who was at the back. He sensed the creature's presence, turned to the side and fired without breaking stride. The dead creature dropped to the ground. Two more rushed from a side turning in front and were mowed down before their claws found flesh. The leading men jumped over their bodies and dodged the tail head that lunged for them. A single shot from Vadik's weapon rang out and the snapping head exploded in a spray of blood and teeth.

Brusilov's light fell on the far wall and searched for a door. Finding one identical to the one they had entered and hoping this one would open, he led the team straight for it. Five more monsters attacked and died before they reached it. Brusilov groaned on spying the smashed control panel. There would be no escape this way. His flashlight and eyes searched the length of the wall until they halted on a dark opening a short distance away. He led the men over and when he paused outside, they formed a defensive shield around him while he checked the room. Brusilov peered inside and swept the light around the chamber before entering. The floor was covered in a thick layer of alien crops collected from the growing beds. Circular impressions dotted across it, hinted it might be where some of the creatures slept. Though his senses screamed at him to turn around and go back, he and his men needed to find a way out of this hellhole.

"Rozovsky, you're with me. The rest of you wait here."

Brusilov and Rozovsky crossed the stench-filled room and stepped through the opening in the back wall where a ramp led down to a lower level. On hearing movement, the two men stopped halfway down, crouched and peered through the railings into the lower area. Their lights revealed the room was occupied. Nests formed from gathered crops were occupied by female creatures and their young. All stared at the two intruders, their eyes bright beacons in the reflected light. Some of the females' bloated bellies indicated they were pregnant. One creature that seemed to be newborn, suckled at its mother's breast. It was a birthing chamber. Four of the larger young creatures stepped nearer and growled and snarled up at the intruders. Brusilov indicated for Rozovsky to retreat and they slowly backed up the ramp and returned to the exit.

"No exit that way," Brusilov informed the others as he glanced around the room. "Have any more attacked?"

Vadik shook his head. "Not yet. We've glimpsed them moving about in the shadows, but for the moment they're keeping their distance."

A worried frown creased Sergei's brow. "Maybe they're waiting for the ones from the ceiling to join them so they can attack in a large group."

Babinski glanced around the room at fleeting shadows too quick to target. "If they do, we won't stand a chance out in the open like this."

"How's the ammo situation?" Brusilov asked.

"Not good," Petroff replied. "We did a rough calc why you were away—about two mags each plus what we have loaded."

Brusilov searched the walls for another exit. The monsters seemed too intelligent to trap themselves here; they must have a way in and out of the room. He stepped back from the wall, roamed his light along the higher reaches and noticed a high walkway. A dark opening at one end indicated it led somewhere. The thick metal columns running up the wall to support the ceiling beams would provide the means to reach it.

Vadik had seen the object of Brusilov's gaze. "We go up, Captain?"

Brusilov nodded. "There's an exit up there. Though I have no idea where or what it leads to, it's better than waiting here for the attack that's sure to come."

"Amen to that, sir," said Sergei.

The men spread out, picked a column to climb and began their ascent. When they neared the top, a group of monsters surged forward. Though they snarled and screeched, they made no attempt to climb up after them, as they had proved they could easily do from their ceiling maneuvers. When the men had climbed another few feet, the reason why they remained below became apparent. Followed by some of its pack, the large, paler-skinned leader stepped onto the metal walkway and peered down at them. It swiped its tongue over its hungry teeth and snarled.

The men couldn't go up and they couldn't go down.

The lead creature raised its head and barked three times.

Creatures poured through the doorway and along the walkway and the creatures below started climbing.

Weapon fire echoed through the room as the men picked off the monsters climbing towards them from both directions. Fresh cartridges were quickly exchanged for empty as their bullets rapidly dwindled. One by one the click of a firing pin striking an empty breach moved through the men. Those who had pistols, slung their rifle over their shoulders and resumed shooting; those who didn't, brought their knives into action, slicing and stabbing at any monsters that ventured close enough.

Their chances of survival had dwindled drastically.

Brusilov dodged the creature that leapt at him, almost falling to the ground in the process. While swinging from one hand and firing two shots into the creature's head, he noticed lights sweeping the dark room. He glanced at the lights at the far end of the room by the entrance. It had to be the engineering team. He shouted out a warning. "Don't let the door close. It can't be opened from the inside." After regaining his footing on the column, he glanced across the room. "If that's you, Chief, we could do with some help here. There are monsters in the room and we're almost out of ammo."

The lights held by the engineering team focused on the Captain's voice at the far end of the room and highlighted the monstrous creatures attacking their comrades.

Recovering from his shock at seeing the strange alien monsters, Nikolay turned to his men. "Alexei and Mikhail, stay in the corridor and make sure the door remains open. Yelchin, you are the best shot. Take position here and pick off as many monsters as you can. The rest of you come with me."

The men followed his hurried dash through the room. Yelchin took up position by the end of a crop bed, knelt on one knee and looked through the Ak-12's sight. He focused on a creature above Vadik and fired. Blood spurted from the creature's head when it fell. He moved to the next creature and fired. It joined its dead comrades on the floor. He focused on the next.

Brusilov heard the single shots and saw the results. He knew it had to be Yelchin picking off the creatures. The man's talent with a rifle was wasted in the engineers. When he glanced back across the room and saw the engineers were barely halfway, he observed some of the creatures splitting off from the pack below and bounding swiftly through the crop fields towards the new arrivals. His warning echoed through the room. "Chief, you have three creatures attacking from your right and four from your left. They'll be with you in three, two..."

Nikolay halted his team on hearing the Captain's warning. They split into two and focused their weapons on the rustle of crops pinpointing the approaching threats. When the monsters were almost upon them, bullets tore into the fields, cutting crop stems and punching through monsters flesh. One leaped out with savage claws reaching for the men. Bullets riddled its monstrous form. The men dodged its falling carcass and shot the tail head that lunged at them with gaping jaws. After a few more shots rang out to kill the remaining two, Nikolay urged them forward again.

Rozovsky shoved the barrel of his shotgun into the mouth of the monster that lunged at him from above and pulled the trigger; the beast's head exploded, adding its blood and gore to that already covering his face and clothes. The weapon, held in one hand while the other gripped the wall beam for support, was pulled from his grasp when the creature crashed into his shoulder. Man and monster tumbled to the ground. While they fell, the tail head appeared and headed for his face with jaws spread wide. Just before it struck, it exploded in a spray of blood. The sound of a single shot chased the carnage. Rozovsky made a mental note to thank Yelchin if he lived through this. He landed on the pile of creature corpses littering the floor and slid down their blood-slick bodies. Creatures shrieked too close to make Rozovsky believe he would survive. He scrambled about for his lost shotgun, but it was nowhere to be seen.

Petroff's pistol clicked on empty. When he holstered it and pulled out his knife, he noticed a creature below climbing the pile of corpses towards Rozovsky. He jumped from his high perch.

Rozovsky tried to free his knife, but hemmed between two dead creatures, he was having trouble reaching it. He saw the tail head and then its owner's vicious face appear over the top of the corpse pile. Slowly it crept closer. Its jaws parted in a shriek the foulest demon would have been proud to call its own. The tail head attacked first. Rozovsky shot out a hand and grabbed it behind the jaws. It squirmed to be free. The creature attacked with claws and teeth prepared to rip and bite. Something landed on the creature's head, slamming its jaws shut so forcefully its teeth cracked and splintered. A hand grabbed the creature's head and yanked it back. A knife severed it throat. Blood gushed as the creature died.

Rozovsky stared at Petroff's grinning face and held out the writhing tail-head. Petroff obliged with a swipe of his knife that parted the head from the tail.

Rozovsky slung it away and nodded at Petroff. "Thanks."

Petroff smiled. "You're welc..."

A creature that had leapt from the wall above slammed into Petroff and gripped the man's head with its claws. Petroff screamed as they rolled down the corpse pile. Creatures shrieked. Flesh and clothes ripped. Petroff fell silent.

Rozovsky scrambled to his feet and, horrified by what he saw, stared at the five creatures ripping Petroff apart.

Shots rang out. Bullets ripped holes in the feasting monsters.

Rozovsky rushed over to Petroff as the Chief and his men arrived and started picking off the attacking creatures.

Rozovsky stared at his friend's body ripped open in a hundred places. Without turning his head, Rozovsky grabbed the tail-head that shot towards him and used both hands to rip the jaws from the tail. He threw both parts away.

The pale alpha male monster had remained on the high walkway observing the battle and had seen its pack mown down by the fresh onslaught. The intruders' weapons were no match for their teeth and claws; they couldn't get close enough to use them. A new plan was needed. When it barked a series of commands the creatures ceased their attack and retreated into the shadows.

After the creatures had moved away the men climbed down.

"Thanks, Nikolay," said Brusilov. You and your men arrived just in the nick of time."

The Chief smiled. "Just like in American movies."

"Yeah, just like that, but let's not push our luck. We'd best get out of here before they regroup." Brusilov noticed Rozovsky by Petroff's gruesome remains; this wasn't the time to mourn. The creatures could stage a fresh assault at any time. "Rozovsky, it's time to leave."

Well aware of the danger and the need to get out of the room, Rozovsky gave Petroff a respectful nod and rejoined the men.

Wary of a fresh attack, they rushed across the room alert for danger and reached the exit without encountering any. Mikhail pulled the salvage cart out of the opening and Alexei closed the door when the last man stepped through.

"Bloody hell!" said Babinski, panting. "That was a rush."

The men rested for a moment to catch their breath.

Brusilov glanced along the corridor. "One thing's for certain, we're not going any farther into the ship until we fetch more firepower."

"Amen to that," said Sergei.

All heads spun towards the screeching that blasted along the corridor. A mass of creatures from the crop room that had somehow cut off their retreat rushed at them.

The Chief's men fired at the tidal wave of horror.

Blood and flesh sprayed the walls from the dead and wounded monsters that tumbled and tripped those behind, packed as tightly as they were in the corridor.

Aware that with the limited ammo they had between them they couldn't kill them all, Brusilov took the only option open to them. "Run!" he ordered.

The men rushed along the corridor and headed deeper into the spaceship.

The monsters chased them.

CHAPTER 18

Please Don't Let Me Die...

LUCY WAS SCARED. Frightened that at any moment something would leap out from the dense foliage. Her imagination, fueled by flashes of her nightmarish journey through Hell's Garden, perceived every rustle of leaves or sway of leafy branch as being put in motion by a monster stalking her. Her eyes darted anxiously in all directions while her head swiveled constantly, shooting fearful glances behind and above, but she saw nothing physical, only shadows—ghosts of implied threats that accompanied her journey through the jungle undergrowth. She took a deep breath and forced her nerves to regain a semblance of calm before panic overtook her and made her to do something rash. Her hands gripped the makeshift weapon tighter as she carried on.

On reaching the edge of the jungle, she found her way blocked by a metal wall. A search along its length revealed a staircase that led up to an open door choked with undergrowth that had sought new areas to expand its creeping tendrils. She forced her way through and stepped away from the encroaching plants. Once she was past the layer of dead and rotted vegetation underfoot, she stepped onto a cold metal floor. It brought her comfort that she had at last reached a normal part of the spaceship—if anything could be described as normal on this bizarre vessel. Though a few small lights blinked on some surfaces of the strange machines and objects dotted around the room, there was no ambient light to reveal what might be lurking in its many dark recesses.

Lucy glanced at the flashlight beam that no longer seemed as bright and wondered how much longer the battery would last. Chills ran through her at the thought of wandering blind through the monster-infested darkness. Her head turned as she listened for telltale signs of creatures that might be in the room. Though she heard no growls, sinister breathing or scrape of claws, only the groans of the ship and the protesting creaks of its stressed metal, she sensed she was not alone. When the light she swept around the room failed to pick out the object of her concern, she steeled herself for the journey and headed across the room in search of an exit.

Her feet barely made a sound as burglar-like she crept around the pieces of machinery that lay dormant, but ready to spring to life if their function, whatever that might be, were required. Cables, which hung like the limbs of an alien creature waiting to grab her if she ventured near, were offered the impression of life when the flashlight beam moved over them. There were so many tubes, pipes, cables and organically shaped pieces of machinery, Lucy worried that she might fail to recognize a monster if it remained still and silent. Her journey past them was nerve-wracking as she studied everything for the slightest movement or sign of life.

She was so intent on looking ahead that she failed to see the cable snaking across the floor. She tripped and stumbled into a mass of black tentacles that entwined her in their cold embrace. Lucy screamed. The flashlight spilled from her hand and clattered to the floor. When the beam swept across the tentacles she fought to be free from, she saw what they really were—inanimate cables stretching from the floor to the ceiling. A nervous sigh escaped her lips as she began to untangle herself, but froze. Shrieks erupted from various parts of the room as Lucy's fears came true; there were monsters in the room and they were on the move.

Lucy pressed her body deeper amongst the cables and tried to bring the spear up to defend herself if necessary, but it was caught in the cables. She was about to free it when something scraped on the floor nearby. She stared along the path that led between the machines where shadows and shapes converged. Something slightly lighter than the surrounding darkness stepped into view and turned its head to peer at the flashlight pointing off to the side. With sharp claws and teeth brandished for the kill, it approached the light cautiously. Lucy almost gasped in terror at the clawed foot that stepped into the beam of light. Her legs began to shake and thrummed on the cables. The monster's head darted at the sound and stepped nearer. Though her terror remained, Lucy somehow forced her legs to be still. The monster halted close enough for her to reach out and touch. It reeked of promised death and ancient kills. Its head swayed from side to side as it attempted to pinpoint the area the sound had come from.

Another monster that stalked the cause of the scream crawled along the top of the machines and paused to stare at the light and another of its kind below.

Lucy's monster stretched its head at the new arrival and snarled viciously. The two stared at each other for a moment before the new arrival took heed of the warning, lowered its subservient head and retreated.

A whimper escaped Lucy's lips when the vicious face swung back and looked straight at her. She turned her head away when it poked its vicious snout between the cables and sniffed her face. Lucy moved her fear-filled eyes to stare at the monster that emanated the scent of malevolence and decay. Its lips curled into a savage grin that exposed rows of sharp teeth stained with the blood of its past victims.

"Please don't let me die. Please don't let me die. Please don't let me die," Lucy repeated, softly. Her breathing ragged with terror.

The monster snarled as its clawed hands reached out and parted the cables.

On the verge of panic, Lucy maneuvered the weapon around the cables. When it sprung free she gripped it with both hands and shoved it up into the creature's neck. Blood—black, warm and thick—splashed her. The monster shrieked, filling Lucy's mouth with its foul, predatory breath. Fighting the response to gag, she dodged the claw that swiped at her, yanked out the spear and repeatedly thrust it into its flesh. The monster stumbled back screeching in pain. Viscous blood oozed from its wounds. Multiple shrieks again filled the room when other hungry monsters detected the scent of blood in the air and came to claim their share.

Lucy emerged from her protective cover, grabbed the flashlight, dodged around the wounded monster and ran. As she careened around a corner she almost crashed into another of the monsters following the blood trail. She dived for the floor, rolled past and jumped to her feet. When the surprised monster turned, she thrust the sword into its side. It squealed in pain. Lucy ran.

A closed door up ahead appeared in the flashlight's erratically dancing beam as she sprinted towards it. Lucy prayed it would open. She slapped the door control and let out a sigh of relief when it moved. She looked down at her feet when cold water surged around them and spun when shrieks rang out too close for comfort. Two monsters stepped onto the path leading to the door and stared at her. One moved its head, sniffed the air and turned away to face the monster she had stabbed in the side. The wounded creature that was now prey, backed away, but it was too slow to avoid the claw that slashed open its chest. Its attacker moved in for the kill and ripped out its throat.

The other monster glanced behind at the carnage and the enticing scent of fresh blood, but looked back at Lucy when she backed through the doorway. It growled menacingly as it rushed forward. Lucy nipped through the opening and pressed the close button. She aimed her weapon at the approaching monster and prepared to fend it off, but the door slid shut before it reached her. Lucy panted heavily as she caught her breath. The sound of trickling water turned her around and the flashlight highlighted the new hell she had stumbled into. Her scream echoed through the room.

CHAPTER 19

The Iceberg

JANE AND JACK had arrived in Antarctica the day before and had spent the night on the American container ship. The following morning, after they had been briefed and studied satellite images of the iceberg, the crack along its top and the entombed spaceship, it was time for a closer look at the icy behemoth.

John Devonport, their assigned pilot, and Lieutenant Christopher Northwood, the British soldier who would babysit them, greeted Jane and Jack when they arrived at the waiting helicopter and introduced themselves.

"Miss Harper, where do you want go first?" asked Devonport.

"I need to take a look at the edges of the iceberg so I can judge its condition."

Devonport indicated the open rear passenger door of the helicopter. "Climb aboard, strap yourselves in, put on the headsets and we'll be off."

"I'd prefer to sit up front for the better view," said Jane.

The pilot nodded. "Okay, I'm sure Lieutenant Northwood wouldn't mind sitting in the back."

Northwood nodded his consent.

Once they were all aboard, the pilot lifted the helicopter from the deck and headed for the drifting iceberg.

As the helicopter approached the iceberg, Jane and Jack stared down at the men busy on the ice ledge around the tunnel where a helicopter had just dropped off a forklift which headed for the tunnel they had flown through in Haax's scout ship. It seemed to have happened ages ago instead of the few days that had passed.

Jack spoke into the mic of his headset they all wore. "I don't envy those inside."

Jane was in total agreement. "I wouldn't set aboard that spaceship again if they offered me ten million."

The ice cliff that formed this side of the iceberg filled the screen and slid by when the pilot turned and flew alongside. Jane scrutinized the ice for cracks or telltale signs of deterioration. The iceberg's immense size worked against its stability and the bobbing action of the waves would place stress on any fractures or weaker points; these were what Jane searched for. The gigantic spaceship at its heart was an unknown variable and it was difficult to predict what adverse effect it would have on the iceberg's stability.

After a few minutes, Jane pointed out of the window. "Who's that?"

Devonport's gaze followed Jane's outstretched arm. "The Russians."

Jack looked at the men working on a small ledge of ice and a flat ship by a neat hole in the side of the ice wall. "It seems the Russians are carrying out a salvage operation of their own."

"Rather them than me," said Jane. "They are welcome to what they can get. The alien technology should be shared with everyone, not just those lucky to be first on the scene."

Devonport's eyebrows rose. "I wouldn't let Admiral Thomson hear you say that. If it was up to him he would plant an American flag on the ice and blow anyone other than Americans who got too close out of the water. He can barely stand us British being involved, so you can understand his feelings towards the Russians."

"I'm glad they are here," Lucy said, defiantly.

Devonport smiled.

It took them two hours to circle the huge iceberg and arrive back at the ice tunnel. When Jane had noticed anything that caused her concern, the pilot had moved nearer so she could get a closer look. They had been lucky and witnessed a couple of incidents of ice calving from the ice walls. Though none had been of a size to affect its stability, yet, it was a sign the iceberg was deteriorating and the approaching storm they had been warned about would speed up the process when it arrived.

Jane and Jack looked down again at the activity around the ice tunnel as a large helicopter lowered a shipping container beside one already in position on the ice ledge.

"What are the containers for?" Jack asked.

"The aliens' storage pods," replied Northwood, glancing out the window.

"Where to now, Miss Harper?" enquired Devonport.

Jane turned to the pilot. "I want to check out that crack in the ice that has the Admiral and the others so worried."

"Okay, on our way." The pilot took a wide berth around the entrance so it didn't interfere with the larger helicopters and flew over the top of the iceberg.

While they flew the length of the crack, Jane studied the satellite scan of the iceberg on the tablet she had borrowed and overlaid it onto the spaceship image. It was as she suspected—the crack stretched out from the front edge of the spaceship. The conflicting movement of ice and metal must have caused the fracture. Jane glanced at the pilot. "Can you set us down on the ice so I can take a closer look?"

Devonport nodded and turned the helicopter to search for a suitable landing zone. He found a level area about one hundred and fifty feet from the crack and set the helicopter gently down on the ice.

Jack, Jane and Lieutenant Northwood climbed out onto the wind sculptured surface and headed across the ice in places frozen into waves of glass-like hardness.

They halted at the edge of the two-yard-wide crack and stared into the void that was much deeper than Jane had expected. Jack shone his flashlight into its dark depths, but the beam failed to pick out the bottom.

Jane glanced each way along the crevice that almost stretched from one side of the iceberg to the other. "This isn't good. I was hoping it was only a surface crack, but it's too deep for that. The iceberg's definitely breaking apart."

"Any idea how long before that happens?" Jack asked, pulling the hood of his jacket over his head to keep out the chill.

Jane shrugged. "It could be a few days, a month or happen in the next five minutes. Predicting what the ice will do is like trying to predict next week's lottery numbers. However, I think it will happen sooner rather than later now I've seen how deep it is."

"So the iceberg breaks in two pieces—it's so big I can't see that matters an awful lot," said Northwood. "I mean, look at the size of this thing. I've been on islands that were smaller."

Jane looked at Northwood. "The problem is, Lieutenant, over two thirds of an iceberg is under water. When the ice below melts or breaks away, or large sections calve off from one side, it destabilizes its mass. If it becomes heavier on one side or becomes top-heavy it could roll on its side or flip completely over. The smaller the iceberg, the more likely this will happen. We also have an added unknown variable, the spaceship. It must weigh thousands or millions of tons, much heavier than the volume of ice it replaces."

The soldier realized the danger. "And because it's situated nearer to one side of the ice mass, its weight will increase the chances of the iceberg flipping over."

"Exactly!" When Jane gazed along the crack and noticed something on the far side, she moved along to where a zigzag in the ice reduced the width of the opening and jumped across.

Jack shook his head in dismay as he eyed the edges of the crevasse that might be unstable and he promptly followed her across. He wished she wouldn't take so many risks.

Jane dropped to one knee and examined something on the ice.

Jack halted beside her. "What is it?"

Jane's eyes roamed the ice before pointing at something on the ground. "What do you think these marks are?"

Jack knelt and examined the lines of scrape-marks Jane's finger pointed at. He saw nothing to distinguish them from the thousands of marks, grooves and scratches covering the weathered surface. "More to the point, what do you think they are?"

Jane glanced around as she stood. "I'm not sure, but something's not right. Most of the marks are in straight lines, scoured by pellets of ice blown by the wind, but the way these tracks curve from side to side isn't natural."

Jack cast his gaze over the ice and followed the tracks that curved in an erratic winding path. If he didn't know better, he would say they were animal tracks, but there weren't any animals in Antarctica that could have made them.

Jane suddenly had a sickening thought and grabbed Jack's arm. "What if we're not the only ones on the iceberg?"

Jack knew exactly what she meant. "That's impossible, isn't it?"

Their eyes followed the tracks that led to or from the crack out onto the ice.

Noticing their anxiousness, Northwood jumped across the crevice and approached. "What's the problem?"

"We're not sure," Jack replied. He glanced at the soldier's assault rifle. "Is that thing loaded?"

"It wouldn't be much use if it wasn't."

Jack took that as an affirmative. He followed the tracks over to the fissure twenty-five feet away, shone the flashlight into the void and moved the beam along the crack. Something glinted. He froze and stared at the two reflected points of light when they moved. Something rose into the circle of light. It was the head of a Hunter climbing up the ice wall. Jack moved the beam and counted six more.

Shocked by the sight, Jack was unable to move for a few moments until his brain had processed the terror. He stumbled back and turned to Jane. "Hunters!"

Screeches erupted from the dark crevice.

A fearful chill shivered through Jane's body.

The soldier raised his rifle, aimed it nervously at the crack in the ice and fired at the first two to appear. Their dead carcasses toppled back into the crevasse.

Jack grabbed Jane's hand and shouted, "Run! We have to get back to the helicopter."

They sprinted across the ice and jumped across the crack.

Northwood quickly followed.

The Hunters emerged from the crevasse and rushed across the ice in pursuit.

Northwood turned and fired a short burst at them. Blood sprayed from the side of one. It took a few more bounding strides before it tripped and rolled across the ice. Unable to fight their instinct to feed, two Hunters leaped on the corpse and ripped off chunks of warm flesh. Northwood aimed at the two feeding Hunters, easier targets now they were stationary, and fired a short burst at each. Both collapsed across the corpse they had been devouring. Wary of the loud weapon that turned in their direction the remaining two Hunters drifted away and ran in a wide arc towards the helicopter. They were trying to cut off the humans' retreat.

The pilot, who had stepped out of the helicopter for a smoke, was busy observing the dark skies on the horizon growing speedily closer, and fretted that it would soon be upon them. When gunshots rang out, he at first credited them to distant thunder, but the second burst turned him around. He stared in the direction his passengers had headed to see if they were on their way back and glimpsed two dark shapes amongst the airborne ice and snow sweeping across the iceberg and three smaller shapes rushing towards him. He thought he detected shouts carried on the wind and peered at the three hazy shapes that had to be Jane, Jack and the lieutenant. The flashes of gunfire from one of them confirmed it, but who were the other two? As far as he was aware they were the only ones on the ice. He gazed at the two shapes in an attempt to bring form to their indistinct outlines. *Was it the Russians?*

When the two shapes came nearer he saw exactly what they were—monsters—and they would reach him before his passengers did. He climbed back though the rear door he had left open, threw himself in the pilot's seat, and revved the idling engine while fastening the seat harness.

The Hunters fought their fear of the loud machine that had previously caused them to seek refuge in the ice crack, and focused on the food inside. When it began to rise into the air the lead Hunter jumped. It landed in the doorway and gripped the frame to stop from toppling out when the helicopter tilted.

The pilot fought the controls when the sudden extra weight tipped the machine off balance. He glanced back and physically trembled at the horrific monster that turned its evil head and snarled at him. Two gunshots rang out. The Hunter jerked and screeched when it toppled back through the doorway. The pilot, momentarily shocked, recovered when he turned back and realized the helicopter was heading for the ice. He quickly compensated, skimming a few inches across the surface before lifting the machine into the air. Shaking from the adrenaline rush, he glanced down at the ice. The lieutenant had his rifle raised and beside him Jack pointed and shouted, his words drowned out by the loud engine. *No doubt they were pissed because he had*

abandoned them, but he would have been dead if he hadn't.
He would pick them up, but not until he knew where the
other monstrosity was. His searching eyes swept the ice as he
spun the helicopter, but he saw no sign of the second
monster.

Something breathed behind him and sent a blast of
warm putrid air over his neck. Fearing what he already knew
was there, he slowly turned his head. The Hunter's snarl
seemed like a grin to the pilot. Its head darted forward and
blood splashed the cockpit controls and canopy.

After Northwood had shot the Hunter clinging to the
helicopter, Jane and Jack had watched the helicopter
plummet. When it had swerved perilously close to the ice,
they had thought it would crash, but at the last second it had
lifted into the air. It had been enough time for the remaining
Hunter to climb aboard. The pilot was unaware he had
gained an extra passenger and though Jack had screamed a
warning, his voice couldn't compete with the helicopter's
deafening engine and went unheeded. Northwood was unable
to get a clear shot at the Hunter as the helicopter had turned,
putting it on the far side. They were helpless to do anything
as the monster climbed inside. A few moments later the
helicopter danced erratically and then headed straight for
them.

Jane, Jack and Northwood ran out of its path.

The helicopter crashed and screeched along the ice
until it struck a lump and rolled over. The rotors sheared off

and flew through the air like missiles. The tail snapped free and was dragged across the ice by its spinning rotor. It cut a circular path in front of the three runners before running out of momentum.

Jack glanced behind at the sound of buckling metal and saw the body of the helicopter tumbling towards them. "Head right," he shouted.

The three runners veered right. The rolling carcass of the helicopter missed them by inches. They halted and watched the helicopter come to a hesitant halt.

Jack rested his hands on his knees and panted heavily.

Jane, also panting heavily, lay on the ice to rest.

Northwood, the fittest of them all, breathed heavily but remained standing. "I'm going to check on the pilot." He headed for the mangled wreck.

Jane sat up and looked at Jack. "No one could have survived that crash, could they?"

Jack shrugged. "It's unlikely, but I've seen cars mangled almost beyond recognition and the drivers walked away with only a few scratches and bruises."

Jane looked at the helicopter. "But if the pilot could survive, so could the Hunter."

Jack gazed over at the wreck for signs of movement. Though he doubted there would be any survivors, there was always a slim chance. "Hey, Lieutenant, remember the monster," Jack called out.

Northwood turned his head. "It's not something I'm ever going to forget."

Jack helped Jane to her feet and she glanced around at the desolate surroundings. "Now what do we do? We're stuck on the ice with the damn monsters *again.*"

Jack smiled. "Maybe only those few Hunters got out, but if the helicopter's radio isn't damaged, we can call for help."

Jane held his arm as they walked towards the crash. "That's one of the things I like about you, Jack, you are forever the optimist."

Jack smiled. "I'd be happy to hear the whole list if you..."

A crunching of metal cut short Jack's reply.

The helicopter rocked as something moved about inside.

Northwood aimed his weapon at the wreckage while cautiously moving around to the cracked canopy.

"Maybe the pilot did survive," said Jane, hopefully. "He was strapped in—the monster wasn't."

Northwood stared at the front of the helicopter. Blood, human or alien, covered much of the cracked transparent canopy and blocked his view of the interior. When he stepped nearer he glimpsed something moving within. It was nothing more than a shadow and revealed no details to whom or what it was. He stepped closer. There was a clear patch on the left side that would allow him to peer inside.

Jack and Jane halted a short distance away and apprehensively watched the soldier. Both sensed something was going to happen.

"This is a bad idea," whispered Jack, reluctant to distract Northwood with a warning now he was so close to the crashed vehicle.

The cockpit windscreen erupted in a spray of transparent shards when something crashed through it and landed on the ice between Jane, Jack and Northwood. It was Devonport's head.

The Hunter leaped from the helicopter wreckage, skidded towards Northwood and slashed at him with a claw, knocking the weapon from his grasp. Northwood tripped to the ground and stared at the horror that attacked him. Its head and skin was covered in cuts and one eye a mangled mess. The Hunter slashed savagely at Northwood's face, neck and chest with raking claws, dishing out a death that was mercifully swift if not pain free.

Jack thrust the flashlight into Jane's hands and snatched Northwood's rifle from the ice, aimed it at the Hunter and pulled the trigger. Nothing happened. He gave it a quick examination, but unfamiliar with the weapon, he failed to see the problem.

Though little snow fell day to day in Antarctica, thousands of years of the accumulated stuff was picked up by the increasing gusts and formed a curtain that hid the gruesome sight of the Hunter feeding upon the soldier.

Ben Hammott

Jane grabbed Jack's arm and pulled him away. "We can't help him now and we need to go before it comes for us."

They headed off across the ice, jumped across the crack and ran.

Jane glanced at her companion as he slung the rifle over his shoulder. "What's the plan, Jack?" She was confident he would have one.

"If we head for the back of the iceberg where the Americans are working at the tunnel, we should be able to attract someone's attention to come rescue us."

"Then we fly back to New Zealand and never come back."

Jack looked her skeptically. "Whatever you're offered?"

Jane nodded. "Nothing's worth the risk of facing these alien monsters again. Greed brought me back, but it won't a second time."

Jack glanced behind for any sign the Hunter was in pursuit, but the weather had quickly grown worst, impeding his vision after a few yards. He looked ahead. They had a long way to go before they could hope to be rescued, but the worsening weather, for once, might actually help them. If they couldn't see, neither could the Hunter. He glanced at Jane running beside him. Though they had only recently met, he already knew he wanted to spend the rest of his life with her. He was almost certain she felt the same towards him. In a few months, if he could wait that long, he would ask her to marry him.

As if sensing his eyes upon her, Jane turned her head to look at Jack. She wondered the reason for the thoughtful expression he wore, which quickly changed to a smile.

Jane screamed when she fell.

When Jane disappeared, Jack skidded to a halt.

A piercing shriek answered the scream. The Hunter *was* on their trail and now it knew roughly where they were.

Jack gazed in horror at the hole in the ice that had swallowed Jane. The claw marks covering the sides of the sloping shaft identified who had dug it—the Hunters. This was how they escaped from the spaceship. He fell to his knees and peered into its dark depths. "Jane!" he shouted.

Jane's surprised scream uttered when she fell, turned to a painful groan when her back jarred against the ice. The roof of the ice tunnel speeding by filled her vision. She dug her heels into the ice, marginally slowing her rapid descent and regretted the lack of an ice axe that might have halted her slide. The flashlight she aimed past her legs revealed nothing helpful; the tunnel seemed to go on forever. After a few moments and a long uncomfortable ride, thankfully cushioned by the padding of her extreme weather clothing, the beam picked out the tunnel's end twenty feet away and the nothingness beyond. Something glinted in the light—a piece of metal protruded past the entrance. When she reached the end of the tunnel her hands grabbed at the object and gripped it tightly, swinging her out over a dark void. The flashlight swaying from her wrist highlighted the tree canopy below.

The thing Jane hung from, and that had prevented her from plummeting to the ground, bent slightly with a metallic groan. Though reluctant to do so, Jane released her hold with one hand, grabbed the flashlight hanging from her wrist and shone it above her. She immediately recognized what the light picked out—the transparent roof of Hell's Garden. She hooked a thumb under the plastic handle of the flashlight, re-established her hold on the metal bar, and moved along it until she could grab one of the metal window sections that seemed more firmly attached. She swung her legs up, hooked them over the frame and was thankful for the pressure released from her arms.

"Jane!"

Jane tilted her head back and gazed up the tunnel on hearing Jack's worried voice. "I'm okay. A little battered, but nothing broken," she shouted back. "You need to find a rope so I can climb out."

Though Jack was relieved Jane had survived the fall and wasn't injured, there was still the problem of rescuing her. *Where the hell am I going to find a rope?* Jack fretted. The helicopter was his only hope. If not, he didn't know what he would do.

"There might be a rope in the crashed helicopter." Jack rushed off to find out.

Jane glanced below. She couldn't believe she was aboard the spaceship and in Hell's Garden again. Her ears strained to hear any sounds of creatures that might be moving through the undergrowth. Apart from a slight rustle of vegetation caused by the chill draft funneled down the tunnel, all was still. The lack of movement inspired no confidence in her that there weren't any monsters below.

"Be as quick as you can," she shouted up the tunnel.

The Hunter headed towards the voices. When it arrived at the hole and saw no sign of the humans, it glanced around. It was about to chase after the dark form moving swiftly away before the swirling snow concealed its presence when a voice drifted from the hole.

"Be as quick as you can."

The Hunter's lips formed into a cruel snarl when it climbed into the hole and dug its claws into the ice to prevent it sliding down the chute.

Wary of the one-eyed Hunter prowling the iceberg, Jack constantly scanned his surroundings for any sign of it, but the snow and ice borne by the increasing wind hampered his vision. The Hunter would probably be upon him before he realized it was there. While he ran he checked the weapon in the hope he would discover why it didn't work. He pressed, prodded and slapped various parts of the rifle until something clicked into place. Hoping he had fixed whatever had caused it to fail before, he held it ready to fire.

When he arrived back at the crack in the ice, he followed it until he arrived at a place where the edges were close enough for him to leap across. No sooner had his feet touched the ice when the iceberg trembled. Though it only lasted a few seconds, Jack knew it didn't bode well for the iceberg's stability. A short distance later he spied the dark shape of the mangled helicopter. He approached cautiously with the weapon raised to fire, but when he had circumnavigated the wreck without spying any sign of the Hunter, he moved closer.

Avoiding more than a brief look at Northwood's gruesome remains surrounded by bloodstained snow, Jack peered through the broken windscreen into the cockpit. The pilot's headless corpse, still strapped upright in the seat, showed signs of having being feasted upon. Jack averted his gaze and examined the space behind the pilot seats. The Hunter wasn't inside. The helicopter was so crushed, Jack didn't waste time trying to open the other door now facing the heavens; it would most likely be jammed shut, he entered through the broken canopy. Metal groaned when his weight rocked the helicopter. A tapping, like that of a ticking clock's pendulum, turned Jack towards the sound. He snatched up the radio mic swinging from the console and pressed the talk button.

Even though the lack of static indicated it probably wasn't working, Jack nevertheless, tried. "This is Jack speaking from the iceberg. Can anyone hear me? Over."

Jack released his finger from the talk button. There was no reply. He tried twice more before giving up.

A search of the seating area and storage cupboards in the back produced a coil of rope, a flare gun, a first-aid kit and a rucksack to store them in. He added the bottle of water he glimpsed under a seat before returning outside. The flare he fired into the sky was their only chance of help if someone on the ship noticed it; however, the worsening weather made it unlikely. Jack turned to leave. A man's voice brought him to a halt after only a few steps.

"Lieutenant Northwood, this is Starlight Control. Report your situation. We have lost all contact with your helicopter."

Jack turned. The voice had come from Northwood's bloody corpse. Realizing he must have a radio, Jack rushed over and grimaced at the horrific sight of the man's ripped-open chest. Though Jack had no medical experience, it was obvious by the broken ribs and empty cavity that the Hunter had feasted on the man's internal organs.

"Lieutenant Northwood, I repeat. Report your situation."

Jack knelt beside the body and searched through the man's pockets. He found the radio and ignoring the blood that covered it, pressed the talk button. "This is Jack, can you hear me? Over."

"Jack, where is Lieutenant Northwood?"

"He's dead and so is the pilot. The helicopter crashed..."

Back in the control room aboard the container ship, Admiral Thomson snatched the radio from Norton. "Crashed! How? Was it the Russians?" It sounded like he half-hoped it was.

"No. A Hunter monster boarded the helicopter when it took off and killed the pilot," was Jack's crackled reply.

Thomson glanced at Norton in disbelief. "The aliens are on the iceberg?"

"Yes. They dug a tunnel through the ice to escape from the spaceship. Jane has fallen into their tunnel. I have some rope and will try to rescue her, but I could do with some help. The hole is about two-hundred yards from the crash site, direction northeast." Jack stared at the radio.

There was a slight delay before Thomson spoke again. "Help is on its way, Jack. Over."

"One other thing, Admiral, the crack in the ice is serious so you might need to think about getting everyone off the spaceship as it could break apart at any moment and might cause the iceberg to roll over."

"Okay, Jack, thanks for the heads up. Help will be with you shortly."

Jack slipped the radio into his pocket and gazed around the wreckage. He needed an anchor for the rope. He picked up a piece of metal that should do the job and hurried off to rescue Jane.

Norton took the radio from Thomson. "Shall I notify the team on the ice to start the evacuation, Admiral?"

"What for? The iceberg is still stable. No, they stay there until I'm certain we've salvaged as much of the alien technology as possible."

"Yes Admiral." Norton placed the radio back on the console.

Jane glanced over at the small pieces of ice rolling from the end of the tunnel a few moments after Jack had gone to fetch a rope. The scraping sounds indicated someone was climbing down. She wondered where Jack had found a rope so quickly.

"Jack, there's no need to come down. Throw down a rope end and I'll climb out."

When Jack failed to reply, anxiety washed over her. She moved position slightly and aimed the flashlight up the tunnel.

"Jack, is that you?"

The Hunter entered the beam and snarled at her.

Though panic threatened to overwhelm her, Jane forced it to keep its distance and directed the light over the ceiling. The large domed roof was her only hope. The buckled frame wobbled precariously as she climbed over to the lump of ice protruding through the dome. If she could get behind it and hide, the Hunter might think she had fallen and go look for her. She stretched her right arm around the ice and grabbed a twisted part of the frame that stuck out. She picked out her next handhold, let the torch dangle from her wrist, unlatched her legs so she hung and released her left hand. When she swung, her left hand reached for the handhold she visualized in the darkness and her fingers wrapped around it. The sound of the Hunter's movements, louder now, indicated it would soon reach the end of the shaft. Hand over hand, Jane moved behind the ice and swung her legs over the frame. With her right arm hooked over the metal, she switched off the flashlight and waited.

The Hunter paused at the end of the ice tunnel and stared in the direction the human had gone. When it didn't see her, it looked down and explored the foliage with its eyes for signs the human had fallen. When it detected none, it stared at the ice that jutted through the ceiling, but focused on the metal that moved slightly. Its lips curled into an evil smile and as it climbed onto the frame a lump of ice at the edge of the opening broke free and dropped below.

An almost silent sigh of relief escaped Jane's lips on hearing something crash though the foliage. Her ploy had worked; the Hunter had gone. Now all she had to do was wait for Jack to return and rescue her, as she was confident he would.

When the frame Jane clung to swayed, she knew there could be only one cause. She switched on the flashlight, poked her head around the ice and lit up the menace. The Hunter, a creature of claws, fangs and unending malice, hung upside-down from the frame and climbed towards her.

Jane had nowhere to go.

When Jack arrived at the hole without catching a glimpse of the Hunter, its absence brought him some comfort. Perhaps the worsening weather conditions had driven it to seek shelter, or the best scenario, it had fallen off the iceberg into the freezing ocean.

As Jack hammered the two-foot long piece of metal into the ice with the butt of the rifle, the iceberg trembled again. He paused and glanced around until the ice grew still. He ignored the bad omen; he wasn't leaving without Jane. Once he was satisfied the anchor was secure, he attached the rope and crossed to the hole. He gazed down the shaft and called out, "Jane! The rope's coming down."

The coil of rope unfurled as it slid down the steep chute.

Concerned that Jane hadn't answered, he called out again, "Jane, are you okay? Can you see the rope?"

His brow remained creased when he again received no reply. Something was wrong. He snatched up the rope and backed down the tunnel.

Jack glanced up at the entrance now far above, an eye gazing out at the dark clouds skidding across the sky through gaps in the windborne snow and ice. The storm had arrived. He switched on the light attached to the weapon slung across his back and continued his descent.

The Hunter ignored the voice from the tunnel and continued its hunt for the much closer prey.

Jane also ignored Jack's voice, but for a different reason. If she told him she was in danger, she knew that—damn hero that he was—would make him rush down without thinking in an attempt to try and save her. If he fell to the ground they'd likely both end up dead. She climbed across the frame away from the ice until the frosted transparent panels still attached to the frame halted her. She aimed the flashlight behind her. The Hunter's arm that groped around the ice and grabbed at the frame was followed by its vicious, evil head.

The frame that shook and swayed with its movements made the Hunter's progress slow and cautious, but it had no need to hurry; its prey couldn't go anywhere.

Adamant she wasn't going to give up without a fight, Jane turned away from the approaching threat and kicked at a cracked window. If she could break it she could move a little farther and prolong the onslaught of pain and her death and perhaps buy her enough time until Jack arrived. If he still had the weapon and had managed to get it working, he could shoot the Hunter and they could climb out. Each forceful kick shook the frame violently. The loud crack that rang out was a harbinger of danger. The frame dropped with a screech of tortured metal. Jane clung on tightly, the monster likewise. Glass cracked and splintered, showering the jungle below with sharp, transparent shards. One edge of the frame, its only remaining support, bent but refused to snap, pivoting its unwelcome passengers through the air.

Worried she would be cast to the ground, Jane gripped the metal tighter with her legs and hands. The squeal of metal faded as the swinging frame settled to a gentle sway. Upside down now, she looked up the length of her body at the Hunter moving nearer. Jane righted herself and glanced below. The ground was still too far away to risk jumping, but a thick tree limb, though not directly below her, was much nearer. She climbed to the edge of the frame and maneuvered around to its other side. The sway of her body swung the frame back and forth and metal squealed with each swing.

The Hunter paused when the human moved. Though it had noticed none of the deadly weapons that killed from afar on this human, their layers of strange, thick, blood-less skin, contained places where things could be hidden. When the human didn't produce such a weapon and started swinging the frame, the Hunter decided it was time to end the hunt.

Jane glanced at the thick bough below. Each complete swing brought her a little nearer. One more and she would be right above it. Dropping into the tree to escape the Hunter was as far as her plan went. She would work out the next part if she survived the fall uninjured. As the frame swung out above the branch, Jane prepared to jump.

Metal snapped with barely a whimper. The frame dropped, taking Jane and the Hunter along for the ride. The edge of the frame struck a branch, almost dislodging its terrified passengers, and tipped ninety-degrees until it crashed into the branches of the tree opposite, forming a bridge between the two. When Jane's tired grip failed her, she hung upside-down from legs hooked over the frame.

The Hunter slammed into the frame when it came to a jarring halt and looked through the metal bars at the human hanging below.

Terror gripped Jane as she gazed at the one-eyed monster running its foul tongue over wicked teeth eager to taste her flesh. She contemplated letting go. Breaking her neck on impact with the ground had to be a quicker and hopefully a far less painful death than ripped apart by foul thing creeping towards her, but she couldn't bring herself to do it. She glanced up at the ice tunnel opening. Now would be the perfect moment for Jack to heroically appear and save her. The dark tunnel mouth remained empty of her saviour.

When Jack reached the end of the rope, he realized he had a serious problem; it was too short. He wound the end around his wrist, fumbled the weapon into his hands and pointed the light down the dark passage. He thought he could make out the end about fifty feet away, but there was no sign of Jane.

He tried to make out what lay past the tunnel's end, but it was too far away. If he released his grip on the rope and slid down into the unknown there was a good chance he would be killed and Jane would be left down here alone. He gazed back up the passage and contemplated the merits of climbing back up. Maybe help had arrived or soon would. If they had, they would surely have another rope. It was the safest course of action. Just in case Jane could hear him but for some reason couldn't reply, Jack voiced his plan.

"Jane, the rope is too short. I'm going back up to get another." Jack began to climb up the tunnel. He hadn't gone very far when a voice echoed down to him.

"Jack, Are you down there?"

*****

The three British soldiers in the helicopter hovered over the wreck of the downed helicopter and gazed at Northwood's gruesome corpse and Devonport's decapitated head.

Sergeant Fredrick Hopkins tore his gaze away and looked at the pilot. "Head northwest, we need to find the others."

The pilot headed across the iceberg and the dark opening in the ice appeared a few moments later. Buffeted by the increasing wind, the helicopter landed a short distance away.

"You'll have to be quick," stated the pilot, as the men prepared to exit. "If this wind gets any stronger I won't be able to land on the ship."

Hopkins glanced at the dark clouds. "I assure you, this is not a sightseeing tour. It will take as long as it takes."

The pilot shrugged. "I'm just saying."

Hopkins followed Private Arkwright out onto the ice and across to the hole. Their gazes took in the rope tied to the pole and its trail into the hole.

Arkwright shouted to be heard over the roar of the wind and the ice pellets splattering his Gore-Tex clothing. "Jack must have already gone down."

Hopkins dropped to his knees besides the opening and poked his head inside. "Jack. Are you down there?"

Jack had rarely been so pleased to hear a man's voice. "Yes, I'm here."

"We don't have much time. What do you need?"

"A longer rope, this one's about fifty feet too short."

"I'm on it," said Arkwright, and rushed back to the helicopter.

"Is Miss Harper with you?" Hopkins asked.

"No, she fell all the way down. She was answering a while ago, but isn't anymore, so she might be injured."

"When we have a second rope secured, I'll come down to help." Hopkins glanced over at the helicopter and saw Arkwright heading back with a rope and an ice anchor.

The ice rumbled and shook violently.

"What the..." Hopkins threw himself away from the hole when the edges started cracking away.

*****

Because the Hunter was so close, Jane hadn't answered Jack as she was worried her voice might cause it to abandon its cautious approach and attack. Help had arrived, so if she could survive for a little longer she might live through this. She held on tightly when the ship trembled, causing metal to screech in protest and distant booms to thunder through the ship like a drumroll announcing her impending death. The frame vibrated violently, sending the Hunter that had climbed to its feet to its belly again and causing Jane to wrap her limbs tighter around the frame.

Both human and alien waited for the ship to settle before making their next move.

When Jane looked around for something that might save her from the monster, she noticed something directly above the Hunter. The large lump of ice protruding through the ship's hull shuddered and a crack formed around its base. As the vibrations faded, the ice lump fell.

Aware the ice would probably send the frame crashing to the ground, Jane climbed through and as the Hunted leaped at her she jumped for the branch a foot above her outstretched arms.

The leap saved the monster's life. Lumps of ice shot out in all directions when the ice exploded on contact with the frame that folded from the force and shot to the ground.

Lucy grabbed the branch and turned her head.

The Hunter flew towards her, its extended claws ready to receive her flesh. She tried to pull herself from its reach, but she lacked the strength. The Hunter's claws caressed Jane's jacket when it was swept aside by the large piece of ice smashing into its back. A smaller lump struck

Jane's chest, dislodging her precarious grip upon the branch and slamming her into the thick tree trunk. She fell and yelped in pain when her ankle struck something hard. She collapsed and smashed her head on the branch she had landed on. Draped over the limb, through hazy vision, she watched the Hunter fall until the undergrowth hid it from her view. A shrill chattering turned her throbbing head. An Alien Squirrel appeared around the trunk of a nearby tree and bared its small sharp fangs at her. Jane would have sighed in despair if she'd had the energy. She pulled her tired body onto the branch and backed away.

The Alien Squirrel observed the still creature for a few moments before deciding it was no threat. It glanced around worriedly on hearing others of its kind approaching to investigate the disturbance. Eager to be first to feed, it moved cautiously nearer the unexpected meal.

The Hunter's frantic grabs at branches it crashed painfully into during its fall, failed to provide a firm enough hold to stop them slipping from its grasp. They did however, slow its plunge, enabling the bush it landed on to cushion its abrupt halt with the ground. Dazed by the experience, the Hunter remained on the ground and gazed up into the trees with its single good eye. When a buzzing distracted its search for the human aloft, it turned its battered head at the sound. Alien wasps exited their huge nest a few feet away. Though it was a giant in comparison to the small insect, the Hunter was aware of the danger their numbers presented. The

Hunter slowly climbed to its feet and skulked into the undergrowth before it was noticed.

*****

The loud crack that accompanied the shaking ice signaled the tunnel's collapse.

Jack stared at the large chunks of ice sliding down towards him. "You have got to be kidding me."

With no way to avoid the oncoming avalanche, Jack let go of the rope and prayed for a soft landing. When he shot from the opening and dropped, he glimpsed foliage below a split second before he was amongst it. His hands grabbed at the thin branches he crashed through and he groaned when a larger branch halted his plummet. He bounced before coming still and stared at the ice pouring from the tunnel mouth. When his brain informed him it would be a good idea to move out of its path, Jack groaned from aches and bruises as he rolled onto his knees and crawled along the thick limb.

The ice slammed into the branch behind him, swaying and bouncing it forcefully. Jack slipped to the side. He grabbed hold of the branch to halt his fall and held on. He glanced down at the thick branch beneath his feet and dropped onto it. He swayed unsteadily before regaining his balance.

A scream alerted him to Jane's position. He snatched the weapon slung over his shoulder and aimed the light in the direction the scream had come from, but the trunk of the tree opposite blocked his view. He moved to the end of the branch and crossed to the other tree. When he moved around the trunk he saw Jane one tree away and the small but vicious Alien Squirrel creeping towards her. Jack put the weapon to his shoulder and aimed at the creature. A single shot echoed through the jungle. The creature lurched backward in a spray of blood. Jack moved through the trees and knelt by Jane.

Jane smiled at her saviour. "You took your time."

Jack grinned. "I was waiting for the most opportune moment to make my heroic entrance." He ran his eyes over her body, noticing a few rips in her clothes. "Are you hurt?"

"A few more scrapes and bruises to add to my extensive collection, but nothing serious."

Jack peered through the foliage at the sounds of things moving through the trees. The glimpse of another Alien Squirrel prompted him into action. "We need to move."

Jack helped Jane to her feet and led her along the branch and onto the next tree.

Jane glanced below. "Where are we going? That one-eyed Hunter is down there. It came down the ice tunnel after me."

Jack glanced behind. A group of Alien Squirrels jumped from branch to branch. "We may not have much choice if we run out of trees. The tunnel collapsed."

Jack fired off a couple of shots, killing one creature. It made the others cautious, but didn't halt them.

By the time they had crossed from tree to tree and reached the end of the room, the vicious squirrels had increased in number and were converging around them.

Jack pulled aside a branch and gazed at the rock wall and the waterfall pouring from an opening at the top that looked big enough for them to take refuge in. He pointed it out to Jane. "If we can reach it the creatures will only be able to attack from one direction and will give us a better chance of defending ourselves. Maybe when I've killed a few, the others will give up and leave us alone."

Jane admired Jack's optimism as she stared at the dark opening. Though she wasn't keen to be trapped in a space with only one exit, the squirrels had the advantage in the open. She studied the cliff the branch led to. It was rough with plenty of hand and foot holds. It would be an easy climb. "Let's go."

The branch sagged with their weight as they moved to the tip and stepped onto the rock. A short climb brought them to the cave. Jane entered first, stepping into the cold water pouring over the lip. She pictured the creatures in the pool below looking up at her, urging her to slip and fall into their world. Jane disappointed them when she moved to the back of the six-foot deep passage where a pipe fed water into the cave. Jack followed her inside and aimed the weapon at the opening.

The creatures weren't about to be kept from their food so easily. They had numbers on their side. Attacking en mass had worked before on larger creatures when hunger necessitated the riskier attack method. They climbed the rock and swarmed into the hole.

The weapon in Jack's hand sprayed bullets at an alarming rate at the creatures highlighted in the weapon-light and muzzle flashes. They shrieked and squealed when bullets tore into them. Their small bodies, shot back by the force, slammed into those behind and knocked them out of the cave. Some splashed into the pool below and were quickly dragged into its dismal depth by the amphibious predators happy to receive them.

Jane clamped hands over her ears in an attempt to block the deafening gunfire that exploded through the small cave and shrunk back in fear of the creatures pouring into the entrance. The bullets that currently saved them from being devoured wouldn't last long at the rate they were being used. Jack seemed to reach the same conclusion, as he changed to firing short, controlled bursts.

Jane glanced around for something she could use as a weapon; perhaps there was a loose rock or a piece of metal she could pry loose. Spying nothing on the ground, she examined the walls and then the ceiling. Her gaze paused on something set in the rock—a rusty hatch. Her hands reached for it and pushed. It didn't budge. She put her shoulder to it and shoved. It moved slightly. She pushed harder. The hatch opened with a loud protesting screech and tipped back on its hinge.

She tapped Jack on the shoulder and when he glanced behind, pointed at the opening. He nodded and when Jane had climbed through he backed towards the hole while still firing. The last bullet shot from the barrel. Jack dropped the weapon, grabbed the flare gun from his pocket and fired the last flare at the vicious squirrels. As the bright light exploded and the creatures sizzled and screeched, Jack dropped the pistol and pulled himself through the opening. As soon as his feet were clear, Jane slammed the hatch shut.

CHAPTER 20

Jaws

LUCY BACKED AWAY from the monster's staring eyes, stumbled, and crashed into the door she had just come through, causing the monster on the door's far side to screech and bang upon it. The amphibious creature only eight-feet away from Lucy, blinked all six of its eyes, three set in a row down either side of its monstrous head. All that separated them was the thickness of the twenty-five-foot high transparent wall that formed the circular aquarium that almost filled the room. The four, short, three-clawed arms that surrounded the monster's mouth, scratched at the transparent barrier as if trying to penetrate it to grab the prey it eyed hungrily.

Lucy altered her gaze when she noticed movement. Something, parasitic in form and about a foot long, moved atop the creature. Its head was surrounded by triangular growths of varying size; some had small spikes on their tips. It had no obvious sign of eyes, but when it halted its nibbling on the creature's skin, looked straight at her and spread its mouth, Lucy had no doubts it had detected her presence.

More of the parasites fed on whatever it was they found so appetizing on the amphibious monster's large body.

When the Leviathan tapped its snout against the side of the tank, Lucy's eyes darted to the water trickling from the crack in the aquarium wall a few feet away as the increased pressure forced the fracture to spread with a splintering sound.

As if curious as to what had emitted the sound, the amphibious monster backed off and stared at the crack for a few moments, as if calculating the discovery for the first time. When it turned away, Lucy stared at its long, sleek body, which shimmered blue, red and green in the beam of her flashlight when it swam by. Some of the large parasites dotted over it body, turned their heads in her direction and opened and closed their beaked jaws menacingly. Two spiked-fins were attached to the Leviathan's back. Ribs of bone ran the length of its forked tail and protruded past its skin to form thin, sharp spikes. Lucy thought it to be about twice the size of a great white shark. After a few flicks of its tail, it vanished into the gloomy, green water.

The skeleton of a creature that seemed to match the species that had just swum away, though slightly smaller, rested on the bottom of the tank, its bones being picked clean by small, strange alien scavengers. Lucy thought she noticed another skeleton farther away, its ghostly form almost concealed by the green tainted water.

Lucy recovered from her latest fright. She had to keep moving. The monsters in the machine room she had just escaped from might be able to open the door. She was about to turn away when movement in the tank distracted her, a hazy dark shape grew larger. The Leviathan was coming back. More worriedly, it was speeding straight for the tank wall. Lucy's gaze shot to the water dribbling from the crack and guessed its intention. She rushed around the edge of the huge aquarium.

A loud boom rang out behind her.

The aquarium wall shook.

The tank splintered.

The loud crash echoing around the room was followed by the roar of escaping water.

Lucy shot a glance behind. Water gushed from the broken tank so furiously a tidal wave formed and sped along the gap between wall and tank. The large creature carried through the hole by the escaping surge, collided with the wall before the torrent of escaping water grabbed it and carried it towards Lucy. Too fast to outrun, the wall of rapidly rising water gained on her. Its front edge scooped her up and sped her forward. She kept a tight hold on the weapon and flashlight as she tumbled in the turbulent water, catching glimpses of the Leviathan growing steadily closer on each roll. She turned her head at the pipes running along the wall and checked the flashlight strap was still hooked around her wrist; she would rather lose the weapon than the light, but she'd keep both if she could. She let the light dangle, reached out for one of the pipes and used them to steer herself towards the surface while the flood carried her around the circular room. She gasped in deep breaths when her head surfaced and looked at the pipes that continued almost to the ceiling. She grabbed at a bracket fixing the pipes to the wall. Her hand slipped from the first, but gripped the second. The current swung her body on its anchor point lengthwise along the wall and she slipped between two pipes, half in and half out of the water. The Leviathan broke surface thirty feet away and looked at its prey. With a flick of its tail it headed for her. Its mouth opened to reveal the sharp triangular teeth that lined its upper and lower jaw. The frightening vision reminded Lucy of the movie, *Jaws*, though this was far more terrifying.

A parasite clinging to the monster's head, released its hold on its host. The current propelled its light body through the water it grabbed at with its stubby, eight-clawed limbs to steer it towards her. Lucy jabbed the spear at it. The tip entered its mouth, smashing through its teeth. When she shook the revolting parasite free, creamy blood spewed into the water.

The Leviathan approached rapidly with its clawed mouth-hands reaching out for her, their task to guide her flesh between its terrifying jaws. Lucy pressed her body deeper between the pipes as one clawed hand screeched along a pipe. Lucy prodded it savagely with the spear. The arm retracted. Aware its head was too large to reach its prey, the Leviathan's eyes glared at her when the current sped it past and Lucy watched the scaled-body of the beast glide by. Its tail flicked and smashed against the pipes. The wash from the force loosened her hold and the current grabbed her in its grasp again.

Lucy turned herself around so she faced forward. The monster tried to turn to reach its prey, but it was too large for the limited space and the parasites weren't strong enough to fight against the surging current. When the Leviathan sped away, Lucy guessed its plan was to swim in a circuit and come up behind her. She struggled to the surface, gulped in air and grabbed hold of a smaller pipe to halt her drift. Her searching gaze fell upon the grill of a ceiling vent. She climbed the pipes free of the water and grasped the vent with her fingers and pulled. It refused to budge. She laid the weapon on top of a pipe free of the water, wrapped a leg around another and gripped the vent with both hands. The Leviathan rose above the ever-rising water fifty feet away. Horror spread across Lucy's face as she again stared into the wide open jaws that promised pain and death, and at the evil, grabbing-claws impatient to grasp her flesh. She frantically yanked at the vent. It came free as the monster leaped. Lucy screamed when she lost her balance and splashed into the water. The Leviathan spurted forward. Lucy slammed the metal grill at the vicious mouth, jamming it between its jaws. She let go and spun her body around. Aided by the current she swam away as fast as she could.

Two parasites launched themselves from the back of their host and let the current rush them toward their prey.

The Leviathan shook its head as its mouth-claws grabbed at the vent in attempts to free it. The monster clenched its powerful jaws. The metal edges bit into its skin before it folded. When the mouth-hands pulled the grill free and threw it clear, the Leviathan's tail swished and sped it through the water.

Carried by the surging current still draining from the massive aquarium and her adrenaline fueled thrashing, Lucy sped around the circular tank. Worried she'd miss the open vent, her only chance to escape the monster fish and its evil passengers, Lucy gulped down a few breaths of air and dived below the surface. The featureless circular tank had only one landmark she could rely on, the hole smashed in its side. She glimpsed it up ahead. Not far to go now. She glanced behind. Two small, pale shapes loomed up on her. One snapped at her toes. Regretting she didn't have the spear, Lucy jerked her foot from its reach. The other parasite had used the distraction to launch its attack and headed for Lucy's thigh. Lucy screamed and swallowed water when the parasite's eight sets of claws latched onto her skin. When its head moved to bite her, Lucy grabbed it and pulled it free, ripping her skin in the process. It had the revolting consistency of a maggot. She slammed it against the side of the tank and released it. She wasn't sure if it was dead or stunned, but for the moment it was no longer a threat. Its companion though, was. She kicked out at it, landing it a blow. It shot to the side and disappeared between the pipes on the wall. Though she had slowed it down, she spied the parasite swimming along the gap between two pipes.

Lucy needed air. She swam for the surface and looked ahead. The vent opening was approaching fast. She would only get one chance. Her hands grabbed at a pipe bracket and gripped it tighter when she jerked to a halt. The parasite; upside-down with its feet pushing on a pipe to propel it forward faster, would soon reach her. A larger shape entered her vision. The Leviathan had arrived. Lucy scrambled up the pipes, snatched up her weapon and slid it between the pipes at the parasite. A cloud of pus-coloured blood seeped out, an indication her aim had been true. When she threw the spear into the vent, movement glimpsed from the corner of her eye spun her head around. The Leviathan rose above the surface twenty feet away with its jaws parted in anticipation of a meal. Lucy climbed through the opening and pulled her feet clear just before the Leviathan's head slammed into the ceiling. Lucy stumbled from the force that buckled the vent floor and sent her crashing into the side wall.

The Leviathan, reluctant to let its prey escape, fought the lessening force of the water pushing against it and held its position beneath the opening. It pressed its snout against the hole and forced it inside. Metal screeched, buckled and tore. A clawed hand snaked past the tip of the monsters head and groped around for her. When it brushed against her leg, the claw snatched at it. Lucy yanked her foot away, but it was faster. It grasped her ankle and squeezed painfully. Sensing its prey had been caught; the Leviathan backed out of the hole and pulled Lucy towards the opening. Fighting back the panic that again threatened to overwhelm her, Lucy kicked at the claw, but it held on tight. Remembering the weapon, she snatched it up and stabbed at the monster fish. The blade slid harmlessly on the hard scales covering its head as efficient as medieval armor. Lucy changed tactic when her foot entered the opening. She stabbed and sliced at the hand around her ankle. When dark blood oozed from the wounds, the grip lessened. She kicked the claw free, pulled her leg back inside the vent and scrambled away from the opening. Except for the sound of rushing water, silence prevailed.

After a few moments staring at the opening, Lucy relaxed and checked her ankle for damage. It was an angry red and throbbed painfully, but no serious damage had been inflicted. Though blood oozed from the eight small wounds on her thigh, it also wasn't serious, unless the parasite carried smaller parasites. Lucy shivered, suppressed the thought of micro-monsters crawling through her body, and aimed the flashlight into the dark, cramped passage she had sought refuge in and started crawling.

A loud boom rang out. Metal screeched. Lucy screamed when she shot into the air and collided with the top of the vent before falling onto the buckled floor. It was evidence the vicious amphibian hadn't given up on its chance of a meal. As Lucy slithered over the raised dented section, the floor in front buckled as another loud boom assaulted her ears. Fearful of giving away her position again, Lucy held back the surprised yelp that threatened to escape her lips and eyed the narrowed gap left by the dented floor. There was just enough clearance for her to slither over the raised section of warped metal. She crawled as quickly and silently as she could along the passage. Only when she had traveled past the walls of the aquarium room would she be safe from the monster. A third boom shot her legs into the air. This time the Leviathan continued to apply pressure, forcing it higher. The floor of the vent pressed against her legs. She pulled one leg free, but the other was trapped, metal cut into her skin when her leg was squeezed against the top of the vent. A trickle of blood oozed out and ran down the sloping floor.

In the aquarium room below, the water continued to rise and lapped at the edges of the vent opening before pouring inside. The ever-rising water level carried it over the first buckled area and flowed onward.

When the cold water tickled her toes, Lucy stopped struggling to free her leg. She peered through the gap that trapped her foot at the steadily rising water and then saw something more immediately life threatening than the possibility of drowning; six parasite creatures entered into the vent. She twisted her foot and pulled. Her ankle-bones scraped on the metal. The parasites surged towards her with chomping jaws.

The parasites hideous cream bodies and sightless heads were even more frightening in the confines of the vent. Unexpectedly, the pressure on her foot released with a squeal of metal; an indication the Leviathan had moved. Lucy pulled her foot free as one of the parasites lunged at her toes and scrambled away along the vent.

Lucy halted at an intersection and quickly considered her options; left, right or continue straight ahead. The water ebbed beneath her. The parasites wouldn't be far behind. Confident the right-hand turning would remove her from danger the quickest, she turned right and sped along the passage. The Leviathan struck again. The boom and screech of metal drifted through the vent from behind. She had passed the edge of the room and was out of the Leviathan's reach. That just left the parasites to deal with. She glanced back. Though the water was only a few inches deep, the parasites continued their pursuit, an indication they were just at home in or out of the water.

Thirty-feet farther, she stopped beneath a hole in the top of the vent and shone the flashlight up its length. Another side-turning about twenty feet above her might be her chance to escape the fast approaching parasites. She doubted, even with their eight clawed limbs, they would be able to climb the smooth metal sides. Lucy climbed upright, pressed her hands and feet against the vertical chute, and hoisted her body up. It was awkward with the spear in one hand and the flashlight dangling from her wrist, but she was reluctant to lose either if it was possible. She had climbed about halfway when the parasites appeared below. Their sightless, evil heads tilted up and watched her. One tried to climb the wall, but failed to get a purchase on the smooth metal. It brought Lucy a little comfort. All she had to do now was climb a few more feet without falling and she'd be safe. Well, as safe as she could be aboard the alien monster-infested vessel that constantly threw surprises at her. She didn't think it would be long before she was fleeing from another vicious, nightmarish monstrosity keen to taste her flesh.

Lucy pulled her tired body into the horizontal vent and collapsed on the floor to catch her breath. Panting heavily, she wondered when and how this nightmare she desperately wanted to escape from would end. She aimed the flashlight along the dark vent. Whatever the outcome, it would be found in that direction. When she felt rested, she continued her journey.

CHAPTER 21

Power

THE MEN AT the rear of the fleeing group continued firing short bursts at the monsters chasing them. Brusilov glanced back at the vicious creatures that filled the width of the corridor, an avalanche of monstrosity that would soon wash over them. Their horrific screeches and howls increased the men's already high anxiety. Even the bravest among them feared what was coming.

The men rushed around a corner to find their escape blocked. The floor of the corridor above had collapsed. Brusilov shone his flashlight at the dark void in the ceiling above the pile of twisted metal. It was large enough for the men to fit through, but too small for the monsters to follow. It was their only chance. Shots rang out behind him as the chief's men picked off more of the monsters, but it was a battle they couldn't win.

"Climb up through the hole," shouted Brusilov.

The barricade shifted and groaned when they climbed the precarious pile of scrap and squeezed through the small gap. As the last man scrambled up, the barricade shifted and dropped a few feet. Babinski slipped and rolled to the floor as the monsters surged ever nearer.

"Babinski," called out Nikolay. "Jump and I'll grab you."

Babinski glanced at the approaching monsters and jumped to his feet. He ran at the collapsed metal pile, leaped onto a beam amongst the wreckage and jumped for the chief's arms stretching from the opening. They clasped each other's wrists and helped by Obolensky, the two men pulled Babinski through the opening. The two lead monsters dived at the man's dangling legs. Their claws grabbed air as the prey was yanked from their grasp. The barricade collapsed and tangled them amongst its twisted forms when they landed on it.

The damaged section of floor the men were on groaned and shuddered as it began to tilt. The men rushed away as it fell and gazed back when they reached solid ground. The sloping floor was an ideal ramp for the monsters below to climb. A few shots were fired in an attempt to deter them from following, but it failed and the men fled when the monsters rushed up the slope.

The chief glanced at the creaking ceiling as they rushed through the corridor and thought it could collapse at any moment. "The ship seems to be falling apart."

Brusilov agreed. "It's ancient." It felt strange giving the ship such a label with its advanced nature when compared to human technology. "It's lain dormant for thousands of years and now it's on the move the stress is ripping it apart."

The sounds of stressed metal that had quickly increased in volume and frequency enforced Brusilov's reasoning and accompanied their hurried dash away from the monsters in pursuit. They rounded a corner and noticed water trickling from a ceiling vent. The chief placed a hand in the stream as they passed and put it to his nose. "It's not ice melt—it smells briny. I wonder where it's leaking from."

"Does it really matter?" said Brusilov. "We can't stop it, but let's hope the sea isn't leaking in somewhere or the monsters might not be our only problem."

A loud crash echoed along the corridor when something struck the ceiling behind them from above. The men still around the corner who had their gazes and weapons aimed back along the corridor as they fired occasional shots at the approaching monsters, saw the ceiling buckle before it fell and the wall of water that gushed through the gap. The wave picked up the lead monsters and sped towards them.

Bullets were useless now.

The men turned and ran.

The water flowed after them.

Alexei and Kolya, the two engineers at the back, shot glances behind at the tidal wave only a few yards away. A large dark shape, hazy and indistinct, surged forward and attacked the monsters desperately trying to escape the water before they drowned, swallowing them whole.

Alexei glanced at Kolya. "Did you see that?"

Kolya nodded. Though he had witnessed it, he wished he hadn't. There was something in the water.

The dark shape swam forward to the front of the wave and observed the fleeing men with its six eyes for a moment before opening its massive jaws, as if proud to display the wicked teeth within to its intended victims. Something leaped from the water and latched onto Kolya's back.

Kolya screamed and stumbled.

Alexei grabbed his arm to prevent him from falling. "Don't stop, I'll get it off."

Alexei grabbed the alien parasite and yanked it free, ripping Kolya's skin in the process. The parasite turned its head at Alexei as its jaws chomped on a chunk of Kolya's flesh. Alexei threw it against the wall.

Brusilov's light picked out an open door ahead. As soon as he was through he searched for the door control. With a hand hovered over the button, he stared back through the opening his men rushed through and caught his first glimpse of the water rushing towards them through the corridor and the horror it brought with it.

Alexei and Kolya saw the doorway ahead. Not far now and they would be safe. The Leviathan surged forward and shot out of the water. It slid along the floor and plucked Kolya up in its mouth. Kolya screamed when the monster fish clamped its jaws around him.

Blood sprayed Alexei's shocked face. Blinded by the blood filling his eyes, Alexei stumbled and crashed into the wall as the water caught up and flowed over the giant amphibian.

The men in the doorway had watched in horror as another comrade died a gruesome death. When Alexei stumbled into the wall, Brusilov knew there was no saving him now and closed the door.

As Alexei regained his balance, he cleared his vision with his hands. He saw the door close and the guilty look on the faces of the men staring at him through the ever-narrowing gap. To save themselves he had been sacrificed. There was no escape for him now. The wave gripped him in its cold grasp, carried him along the corridor and smashed him against the door. As soon as the pressure subsided, he turned. Teeth filled his vision. Bubbles poured from his mouth when he screamed. Pain flooded his senses when the monster's mouth-claws grabbed hold and fed him into the Leviathan's maw. His blood clouded the water before his dimming eyes.

The men stared at their captain when he turned his gaze away from the door. All knew why he had done it and all knew it was a decision that would weigh heavily on his shoulders.

Brusilov glanced around at the men. Brave as he knew them to be, none were prepared for the horrors they had recently encountered. He now knew the Englishman, Richard Whorley, had not exaggerated his retelling of his own encounters with the alien monsters; if anything, he had underplayed their ferocity.

The door holding back the tons of water creaked from the pressure.

The captain glanced down the dark corridor a couple of the men shone their lights along. "Rozovsky, Vadik, lead the way," he ordered.

As the men set off along the corridor, Brusilov glanced back at the door.

Nikolay laid a hand on Brusilov's shoulder. "To save us you had no choice, my friend. Alexei would have known this and understood."

Brusilov looked at his comrade. "That doesn't make it rest any easier." He headed along the corridor and Nikolay followed.

"Are my ears ringing or can anyone else hear that humming?" asked Vadik a few moments later, slapping his ears to try and clear them of the sound.

"It's not your ears, you idiot," Rozovsky pointed his rifle at the door at the end of the corridor. "It's coming from behind there."

The captain and the chief moved to the front.

Nikolay cocked an ear to the sound. "It sounds like machinery."

Brusilov stared at the distant door. "We have nowhere else to go, so I guess we're about to find out."

The humming grew louder as they headed for the door.

Brusilov looked back at his men. "When the door opens, be prepared for anything."

Weapons were aimed at the door and when it slid open a green glow seeped out, bathing the men in eerie light.

Brusilov peered through the opening and gazed around the room before stepping through onto a walkway that crossed to a door on the far side. The men followed close behind. The green light emanated from a series of clustered, six-foot diameter transparent pipes that ran the length of the long round tunnel. Contained within the pipes was a liquid that glowed green and crackled softly. Smaller transparent cables snaked out from the larger pipes and connected to black tubes or cables that disappeared into the curved walls and ceiling. A walkway raised a foot above the pipes and cables that covered the floor led off down the center.

Brusilov glanced at his chief engineer, who roamed his eyes over the tunnel. "What do you make of it, Nikolay?"

Nikolay was fascinated by the discovery. "It could be the main power and utility conduit that feeds the ship with whatever it needs to keep running." He pointed along the tunnel towards the main source of the humming. "I assume there's some sort of distribution plant that way."

He turned to the captain. "It could be worth checking out. As well as weapons, its technology we're after and we might find some there."

Brusilov nodded. "It's a good an option as any."

The men, alert for danger, walked along the tunnel and entered the large room at its end. Tubes and cables of varying thicknesses snaked out from a large device that hummed steadily. Pieces of complex machinery, fittings, dials and small red lights covered the large machine. One of the wide tubes connected to it had pulled away from its housing on the machine, revealing thousands of smaller cables crammed inside.

Nikolay gazed at the machine that towered from a lower level to almost reach the seventy-foot high ceiling. "It seems to be a transformer, or the alien equivalent, to distribute power throughout the ship."

The captain walked up to the rail of the balcony that ran the entire circumference of the room and peered over the edge. Strange pieces of smaller machinery covered the floor twelve feet below. All had cables attached that disappeared into ducts, the walls, under the floor or into the ceiling and some connected to other pieces of machinery. Though no doubt technologically advanced, he saw nothing easily transportable. "Let's keep moving."

He led the men along the pathway that hugged the edges of the room. They hadn't gone far when Nikolay paused before an area set back from the path and stared at the banks of switches, levers and dials dotted with small green, red and yellow lights that adorned the console at the far edge. He glanced at the captain.

"I think this might be the power control center."

When his gaze fell upon something on the wall to the left of the long console, he moved over for a closer look. Etched into the metal wall were detailed floor plans of every level and room in the spaceship labeled with strange symbols. He glanced over at the men training their rifles around the room.

"Mikhail, come take a look at this."

Mikhail, an electrical engineer, walked over to the console and ran his eyes over the hundreds of controls and the small diagrams beside each.

Nikolay pointed at the spaceship floor plan on the wall. "Because those symbols match those labeling each of the console controls, I'm thinking they manage the power to each floor and each room on that level?"

Mikhail glanced between the console and the ship's floor plan diagrams and nodded. "It's logical the alien crew would need some way of manually controlling and distributing power around the ship." He pointed at the larger symbol beside a lever on one of the many raised sections that covered the long console, separating them from each other. "I assume the levers cut the power to the marked level, and the switches in the same section control the power to each room on that level."

Brusilov was eager to move on. "I'm sure it's all very interesting, but if it doesn't help us find what we're searching for, it's of no use. We can't risk remaining in one place for too long."

"It may not help us find the armory, Captain," said Nikolay, "But it could delay our competition, the British and Americans."

He had caught the captain's attention. "How?"

"If we can kill the power to the levels they are on, it could slow them down and buy us some time." Nikolay glanced at Mikhail. "Can you work out the power controls for the upper three or four levels?"

After Mikhail had scanned the controls and the floor plans again, he nodded. "I think so. All we have to do is match up the symbols and flick the switch."

Brusilov liked the idea and smiled. They needed every advantage they could get. "Do it." He turned to the rest of the men. "While he's doing that, the rest of you set up a defensive position in case of attack."

Mikhail moved across the control panel while shooting glances at the deck plans on the wall before he stopped and glanced at Nikolay. "I think I've found the controls for the top levels. Shall I kill the power?"

Nikolay nodded.

Mikhail pushed one of the power levers from down to its up position. The lights on the raised panel beside it turned from green to red, an indication something had changed. He did the same with the next three upper level levers he had picked out and stepped away from the console.

"All done," stated Mikhail. "The Americans should now be stumbling around in the dark."

"I'm sure even the Americans aren't stupid enough not to bring some kind of light with them," said Brusilov, "but the darkness should slow them down and perhaps any closed doors they come to won't be opened so easily. Now let's move. We have a lot to do and little time to do it."

CHAPTER 22

Map Room

RICHARD POINTED AT the open door a short distance along the corridor and, with some relief, stated, "That's the room you're looking for."

Colbert called the SEALs to a halt and scrutinized the opening ahead. It had taken them longer to reach than he had expected. Their damn fool of a guide had led them in the wrong direction twice before realizing his mistake. He looked at Richard. "Are you certain this time?"

Richard nodded vaguely. "I think so. It's not my fault all the corridors and doors look the same in this part of the ship."

Colbert picked out two men. "Sullivan, Cleveland, check it out."

The two men moved to the doorway and peered inside before entering. Their eyes and weapons swept the room as they walked to the balcony and peered into the lower level. They assumed the strange table below was the one they searched for. Ignoring it for the moment, they descended the ramp and searched the room.

"All clear," called out Cleveland.

The others entered and joined them on the circular platform with the map table at its center.

Richard pointed at the control panel Jane had used to operate the map table. The screen was lit, indicating it still had power. "That's what we used to operate the 3D blueprint of the ship."

Ramirez, the team's computer wizard, moved to the controls and studied the screen. He shifted through a few menus and selected the option to show the complete spaceship. Fingers of the gel-like substance rose into the air, stretched horizontally and morphed into a detailed model of the ship's interior.

Though the men had been told about the map table, they were still stunned by the amazing technology. Even Richard, who had only seen part of the ship before, was shocked by the ship's immense size and the amount of floor levels and rooms it contained, some of which were far larger than those he and the team had encountered previously.

Back in the control room, Admiral Thomson, a few others and NASA scientists and technicians, stared in awe at the large screen filled with the different viewpoints from the SEALs head cams of the 3D model.

The SEALs stared at the model for a few moments, but there was too much detail crammed in such a small area for them to get a clear idea of the purpose or layout of the hundreds of rooms laid out before them.

Colbert looked at Ramirez. "Can you zoom in or something so we're not looking at such a large area?"

"He can," stated Richard. "When we operated the map before it didn't show the whole ship, only the sections we needed to escape through. I think the computer set it up for us."

After a few moments Ramirez found the menu he wanted and the map changed to represent a smaller area of the ship centered on their position.

Richard pointed out the areas the scientists and he had explored. "There was no armory in these parts, not that we went into every room."

Ramirez scrolled the map to nearby unexplored areas and levels.

While the men examined the constantly changing map, Richard stepped away from the group. He didn't like staying in one place for too long. "It's time I was leaving. I've filled my part of the bargain."

Colbert was about to reply when Ramirez interrupted.

"Sir, I think I've found what we're looking for."

Colbert redirected his gaze at Ramirez. "The armory?"

"Not exactly. A list of the spaceship's rooms. Though there seems to be no direct translation for everything, thank God most are in English." Ramirez scrolled down the list.

Colbert moved to get a better view of the screen. "Does it tell us where the weapons are located?"

"I'm looking, sir. It's a damn long list." Ramirez stopped scrolling and pointed at one word. "There you are, sir, the weapon store."

When Ramirez selected the room, the map changed, scrolling and zooming out until it settled into stillness again. The weapon store was longer than it was wide with a door at each end and contained racks filled with weapons of different types and sizes.

Richard moved in for a closer look and pointed at a rack on the wall filled with weapons he recognized. "Those look the same as the light-beam rifle Haax had."

"There are a lot more weapons than I visualized," said Colbert. He moved his mouth towards his mic. "Control, I assume you are seeing this. There's no way we can collect them all."

In the control room, Admiral Thomson stared excitedly at the store of alien weapons. Colbert was right. It would take more men and a lot more time than they had to salvage them all. The feed was also being watched by the President, so he would need to confer with him before making a decision. He pressed a button to speak to Colbert. "Make your way to the armory. By the time you arrive I'll have new instructions for you, but if we lose comms grab what merchandise you can and instigate operation Phoenix."

"Yes, sir, orders acknowledged." Colbert glanced at Ramirez. "We need a route planned from here to the weapon store."

Ramirez was scrolling through different options. "I'm already on it." He found what was required and chose the destination they wanted to travel to.

The map reformed and depicted a route to the armory, but as the men examined the route, the lights flickered. The map collapsed and reformed.

Colbert glanced at Ramirez. "Did you do something?"

The man held his hands away from the controls and shook his head.

The map collapsed and the lights went dark. The men switched on their flashlights and swept them around the room.

"Maybe the ship's losing power," Ramirez suggested.

"From here on in it's all in the dark," said Stedman, a little too cheerily for Richard's liking. He was glad he wasn't going with them.

"Has anyone got a spare flashlight?" asked Richard.

"No Richard, they haven't," replied Colbert.

"Just smile and let those shiny white teeth of yours light up the way," said Crowe.

A couple of the men sniggered.

Richard sighed. "I want to leave. I did what was asked of me and you don't need me tagging along and getting in your way."

Colbert couldn't get rid of the man quick enough and glanced at his escorts. "You can take him back now. The rest of you, follow me."

After the SEALs had gone, Talbot, Jenkins, and Richard moved up the ramp, out through the door and headed along the corridor towards the back of the ship and the hangar. None of them envied the SEAL team heading in the opposite direction.

CHAPTER 23

Smoke and EV1L

LUCY STOPPED WITH the flashlight and her gaze aimed at the turning in the vent ahead. Movement she thought she had heard from around the corner had caused her imagination to picture some horror waiting in the darkness for her. She strained her senses to the limit in an attempt to pick out anything above the continuous creaks and groans of the large vessel that might signal danger was nearby. Though she thought she detected something breathing, she wasn't sure if her imagination was to blame.

Lucy took a few deep breaths to calm her anxiousness and aimed the light behind. Perhaps it would be safer to go back and seek out different route. After a few moments thought she decided to continue forward; there were nightmare creatures in any direction she took. With the spear ready to counter any attack, Lucy cautiously edged nearer the turning.

One of her worst fears—the list far longer now since her time aboard the spaceship—confronted her; the flashlight's beam faded to a dim yellow glow. When a few slaps on the casing failed to revive the light, Lucy stared at the pale glow dimming before her eyes until the dark engulfed her in its lightless embrace. She stifled the sob that threatened panic in its wake and moved forward before she became rooted in terror. Her heart rate increased as fear screamed for her to turn back. She pressed her body against the cold side of the vent when she judged she was almost at the corner and slid closer, expecting some foul monster to appear at any moment. When her fingers felt the edge of the passage, she prodded the spear around the corner. When it failed to pierce flesh or invoke a reaction from anything that might be lying in wait for her, she leaned forward and peered around the corner into the never-ending darkness and cocked an ear. Her heartbeat, amplified in the pitch-black that shrouded her, was all she heard. Forcing her body to keep moving, she scrambled around the corner and continued along the passage.

She hadn't travelled more than a few yards when an ominous slithering froze her. Something was in here with her and moving closer. Though the vent's acoustics made it difficult to determine from which direction it came, Lucy thought it sounded slightly louder behind her. Because she doubted the parasites could have climbed the vertical vent, it had to be another monster that stalked her. She spurted away from the sound, haste now more important than caution.

A surprised scream flew from her throat when her hand fell into nothingness and ended with a pained groan when her shoulder slammed into the floor. She quickly recovered and ignored her aching shoulder whilst she searched the darkness with her hands and discovered a crossroads of passages. One of which dropped to a lower level. It was this she had stumbled into. The slithering grew louder and now came from more than one direction. Slowing her rapid fear-induced breathing, Lucy glanced at something she noticed in one of the passages—a faint glow of light. It gave her hope. She rushed towards it and the slithering coming from the same direction. She was almost at the light when something entered its glow and stopped, as if proudly presenting its vile form to its prey. Arms or tentacles with net-like webbing stretched between them, reached out from its body to grip the vent walls and propel it along. The mouth, a circular orifice ringed with needle-sharp teeth, was surrounded by a ring of black, golf-ball eyes that stared at Lucy.

Lucy shot a glance behind. Though she saw nothing, she heard the slithering approach. She slipped the useless flashlight she had been reluctant to part with before, from her wrist and threw it back along the vent. Something screeched before the flashlight clattered loudly to the floor, evidence something had been struck. Hoping she had held it at bay temporarily, Lucy sped along the vent towards the light and the monster in her way that now rushed towards her. When it was within reach, Lucy held the spear at arm's length and jabbed it at the creature's flesh, aiming for its eyes, but missed and instead stabbed it between two of them.

It screeched and lashed out a tentacle that grabbed her leg. Pulled off balance, she fell onto her back. Lucy sat up and thrust the weapon at the creature reeling her in. Conscious of the second creature coming up behind her, she stabbed frantically at this one's flesh in the hope of hitting a vital organ. Lucy yanked the spear up when it entered flesh and tore a long gash in the monster's skin. The monster's piercing screech was deafening in the vent's confines. It pulled away and writhed, its tentacles thumping the metal sides loudly. Lucy shot her shoulders to the floor and thrust the spear over her head. The screech that followed indicated her target had been hit. She repeatedly stabbed at the creature she couldn't see until it moved out of the weapon's reach. Lucy rolled onto her stomach. The wounded creature's eyes reflecting the dim light behind her was all she could see of the Lovecraftian monstrosity that seemed wary to approach too close again. A glance behind revealed the withering creature collapse to the floor and lay still. Keeping one eye on the wounded monster, Lucy backed towards the light. She almost slipped on the warm blood that had pooled around the dead creature when she climbed over its hideous corpse that squelched beneath her. When she reached the light she glanced at the weak glow highlighting the slats of the grill from below. It was a way out of the rathole she was trapped in.

As she kicked out the grill and watched it drop to the floor below, the wounded monster used the distraction to try a second attack. With surprising speed it shot along the vent.

Lucy raised the spear at the sound. The monster's speed impaled it on the tip and knocked Lucy to the ground. She jerked the weapon from side to side, smacking the monster hard against the walls as its tentacles grabbed at her. She pushed it away and forced it through the opening. Its tentacles unwrapped from her arms with a moist slithering as it fell. The spear, pulled from her tired grasp by the monster's weight, journeyed with the Lovecraftian horror to the floor of the room below. The slap of flesh on the hard ground echoed through the room.

Lucy poked her head through the hole. The monster, though wounded, still lived and left a trail of green blood when it slithered away and sought refuge in the shadows. Her gaze around the gloom-ridden room revealed metal bars sectioned off a large alcove at one end and at the opposite end faint blue light shone through an open door from the corridor outside. The drop to the floor fifteen feet away would be a one way trip, but whatever lay below had to be preferable to remaining in the vent lacking an escape route if she was attacked by more of the monsters. She would stand no chance without the weapon she would have to retrieve. She hung from the opening and dropped softly to the floor of the room dimly lit by a single ceiling light.

Wondering if the barred area contained anything she could makc usc of—alien weaponry would be a godsend—Lucy took a wide berth around the tentacle monster's position, given away by its ragged breathing, and approached the bars, but stopped a short distance away when she noticed something strange. Though the bars appeared to be metal that had a dull copper sheen, they intermittently shivered a rich, rusty orange. Believing it best she refrain from touching them, Lucy peered through the bars. A faint whirring came from inside a transparent container barely visible in the middle of the barred room. After she had moved around the edge of the bars she got a better look at what was contained within the glass prison. A fan at the top of the container swirled thick grey smoke around its inner sides. A four-inch tube connected to the side of the container led to a machine fixed to the wall with a smaller eighteen-high by twelve-inch-wide transparent container that had the appearance of a vacuum cleaner. Wondering what it was, Lucy stared at the trapped smoke. Though she thought she glimpsed eyes and a screaming mouth form briefly amidst the dirty grey fog before it was ripped apart by the turbulent wind, she assigned this to her present anxiety and nothing more than identifying shapes in natural cloud formations. When she turned away she noticed a door in the bars and a tiny green blinking light on the lock that secured it closed. An indication it might be a prison cell. *But for what?*

She glanced back at the swirling mist that had to be the reason for the excessive means of imprisonment. Whatever it was, if the spaceship's crew thought it was dangerous enough to keep confined, she was glad it hadn't gotten free. Lucy studied the sign fixed to the barred door. Though in alien text, Lucy's mind tried to make sense of the strange symbols and formed images of an E, a V, a 1 and an L.

"Evil," Lucy spoke aloud, shivering at the coincidence between the strange alien letters and the English word and hoped it wasn't a forewarning of something worse to come.

Her gaze surveyed the rest of the room, but saw no more than she had seen from above. It was time to retrieve her weapon. With extreme caution, she approached the dark area that concealed the wounded creature, hoping to yank the spear out of its body and be gone. As she drew near she noticed it looked at her, its many eyes reflecting the room's dim light. It moved. Something shot out of the darkness. Lucy glanced at the spear that slid loudly across the floor. It was a distraction. The monster sprung at her with its tentacles spread wide like a gruesome, living net to entrap its prey.

Lucy reacted quickly. She dropped to the floor and rolled beneath the creature. It flew over her and landed on the cell bars. Though the bars reacted with an increased brighter color shift where the monster's flesh touched, the Tentacle Monster showed no indication it was affected by the change. Its vicious mouth and evil eyes melted through its body to face her. Momentarily stunned by the creature's macabre and unexpected peculiarity, Lucy missed the chance to flee across the room and grab the spear before the room plunged into darkness.

The whirring drone of the fan slowed.

The green light on the cell's lock turned red.

The click of the electronic mechanism was loud in the silence that had prevailed. Even the constant creaks and groans of the spaceship had ceased. It was as if the vessel held its breath. Lucy stared at the red light that flashed intermittently on the cell door.

A series of hisses emanated from the darkness within the cell.

Something groaned.

Whatever had been imprisoned inside the cage had awoken and was free.

Cloaked by the darkness, the Tentacle Monster attacked. Knocked off balance, Lucy fell to the floor. As the Tentacle Monster's cold limbs wrapped around her body, Lucy lashed out with a fist. The monster screeched when the punch popped one of its eyes. She gripped the monster's slimy head, her thumbs slipping in the gaps between its teeth, and kept its head at arm's length. She rolled over when its tentacles slithered tighter around her arms, legs and body, clambered to her feet and rushed at the wall. The monster slammed against the bars of the cell. Caught off guard by the unexpected halt in the darkness, the momentum shot Lucy forward, stopping with her head only inches away from the monster's snapping mouth. She jerked away, but it was a stalemate. The monster wasn't going to release its grip on her and Lucy couldn't or she would be killed.

When Lucy sensed movement in the cell, she leaned her head to the side so she could see around the monster and peered into the darkness. Suddenly the Tentacle Monster screeched as it was yanked backwards, dragging Lucy with it. Her head slammed into the bars, the blow cushioned by the Tentacle Monster's thin body being pulled through a gap between the metal bars. She moved away when the tentacles released their hold upon her. Silence filled the void left by the ceasing of the Tentacle Monster's screams.

As Lucy dashed across the room to retrieve the spear, she noticed a square of red light that hadn't been there before. She rushed over to investigate. It was a cupboard and through the transparent door she saw objects bathed in the red glow that by their shape could only be weapons. She pulled the door open, snatched up the two weapons and fled through the exit.

The squeal of the cell door's protesting hinges drifted along the dark corridor behind her.

EV1L stared at the open lock of the door trapping it in its cell. Though touching the bars would cause it pain, it was its only escape. It had been imprisoned for long enough. A smoke-formed hand reached out from its hazy mass. Oily darkness poured down the limb to solidify the hand when it gripped a bar and pushed open the door. The metal around its touch grew bright and seeped along its hand. A mouth formed amidst the smoke and let out a pained scream that only ended when its hand released its hold on the metal. Drained of the energy it had gained from the recent meal it had hungrily consumed, EV1L's mass had shrunk and turned the wispy grey of early morning mist.

The strange two-legged creature that had escaped would have provided it with a little extra of the sustenance its mind and body desperately craved. As EV1L slowly exited its cell and floated across the room, wisps of its form drifted free and dissipated into nothingness. EV1L was dying. To survive it needed to find further sustenance quickly.

CHAPTER 24

A Sudden Change of Direction

SO FAR RICHARD and his two escorts' journey towards the exit had gone without a hitch. No monsters had made an appearance and they had taken no wrong turns.

Richard was aware if their good luck continued they would soon reach the cargo bay and once through the hangar he was out of the damn spacecraft, free and safe. He wasn't sure what would happen next. Transporting him back to civilization wouldn't be a priority of the Americans or the British. He'd probably be confined aboard the American ship until the salvage operation had been completed before any transport could be arranged. Anything was better than being aboard this death ship. Once he'd left this godforsaken frozen world, he would never return.

Richard paused at the top of the staircase and glanced at the two Clickers the SEALs had killed earlier highlighted by Jenkins flashlight.

Talbot glanced around worriedly, his weapon light searching the darkness. "Why have you stopped?"

Richard pointed at the corpses. "Relax. The Clickers haven't been eaten. It's a good sign the area's free of monsters."

Richard's observation brought the soldiers a little comfort. They too would be glad to reach the exit. Though they wouldn't be allowed to leave, duties around the hangar were far preferable to roaming through the ship where death could strike at any moment.

Talbot took the lead down the staircase and along the corridor at its base. He stopped after a few feet and stared ahead as his eyes and flashlight searched the darkness.

It was Richard's turn to worry. He frowned. "What is it?"

Talbot shook his head. "I'm not sure. I thought I heard something."

"Maybe it was just the ship creaking," suggested Jenkins, hopefully, who had turned to point his weapon back along the corridor.

"Maybe, but shouldn't one of you go and check?" Richard suggested. "Your orders are to protect me." He was so close to the exit now he didn't want to take any risks.

Talbot scowled at Richard. "If you think your death would cause anyone concern, think again. All our lives are expendable when compared to the salvaging of alien technology."

Richard was under no illusions the man's words weren't the truth. "That's as maybe, but if my life's at risk, so is yours. I'm only trying to keep you alive."

"That will be a cold day in hell when I put my life in your hands, however..." Talbot looked at Jenkins. "Keep me covered while I go check."

Jenkins nodded and pushed Richard to the side so he had a clear view of the corridor. They watched Talbot cautiously approach the intersection and after a brief pause he disappeared around the corner.

Neither Jenkins nor Richard noticed the floor hatch lift slightly behind them or the tentacle that slithered out and searched for the disturbance it had heard above its domain. It moved between Richard's feet without detecting his presence, but when its probing tip touched Jenkins' boot, it seemed to sniff the strange object. Satisfied it was something that could be consumed, it rose into the air and coiled back like a snake about to strike before shooting forward. It wrapped around Jenkins's ankles, clamped his legs together and pulled. Jenkins toppled to the floor when his feet were yanked out from under him. Richard was knocked off balance when Jenkins crashed into him and collided hard against the wall before dropping to the floor.

Jenkins screamed as he was dragged backward. His hands scrabbled about for something to stop him. The only thing within reach was Richard's leg, and he grabbed it.

Richard recovered from his shock and glanced at the hatch cover that slammed loudly against the floor, the tentacle attached to Jenkins' ankle snaking from the opening, and Jenkins's terrified expression.

"Help me," pleaded Jenkins.

The man's desperate plea fell on deaf ears; there was only one person Richard planned on helping, and it wasn't Jenkins.

"Let go of me!" yelled Richard savagely. Ignoring the man's screams, he kicked at Jenkins' hand with his other foot. When he was free, he crab-walked out of the man's reach as Jenkins grabbed for his foot again.

Running footsteps approached from behind Richard as Jenkins was pulled through the opening so forcefully the back of his head slammed against the edge. Talbot ran past Richard and threw himself to the floor. He thrust his arms into the hole to help his friend, but Jenkins was already out of reach. Highlighted by the rifle falling with him, Talbot watched Jenkins disappear into the darkness until he was lost from his sight.

Talbot turned and glared at Richard accusingly. "What the fuck just happened."

"Hey, it wasn't my fault. Something grabbed him and pulled him into the hole. I told you weapons wouldn't protect you from everything in this ship."

"And I bet you're so pleased you've been proven right," Talbot replied angrily.

Richard shook his head. "Not at all! We now only have one weapon. The good news is that we don't have far to go now, so I suggest we move before that thing returns."

Talbot turned away before he struck the man, and shone his light into the hole. "Jenkins!" he shouted.

Richard climbed to his feet. "You're wasting your time. The man's already food for whatever monstrosity lives down there."

The stare Talbot aimed at Richard was fierce and angry. "Go if you want, but it's my time to waste and I'm not leaving until I know for certain if Jenkins' alive or dead."

Richard, oblivious or unconcerned by the man's temperament, continued to rile him. "Stick your ear in the hole and you'll probably hear his bones crunching." Richard's eyes flicked to something behind Talbot. "Shit, we need to leave, now!"

Talbot spun and dodged back to avoid the tentacle zooming towards him. He aimed his weapon and fired a short burst, cutting the tentacle to shreds. A screech drifted up the shaft and something thumping on the metal sides quickly followed.

Richard backed away. "Well done, now you've really pissed it off."

"And you think that makes it any less friendly than it was before?"

Richard shrugged. "It can't have helped."

Talbot cautiously approached the opening and peered inside. A mass of tentacles surged up the shaft. He fired into the hole. Tentacles peppered with bullet holes shot from the opening and grabbed him. They twisted around his legs and waist and pulled him off his feet. Talbot tried to aim his weapon at them, but his shoulders slammed into the floor when he was jerked towards the hole.

Richard's first instinct was to flee. His second was there might be monsters between him and the exit. Unarmed and without a light he might not make it very far. He sprinted for Talbot and grabbed the rifle.

Talbot kept a tight grip on the weapon and glared at Richard. "Let go of the damn rifle and grab my arms."

"I can't kill monsters with your arms. Let me have the rifle and I'll save you."

"Like fuck you will." As Talbot slipped into the hole, he grabbed Richard's leg, tripping him to the floor.

Richard kicked at Talbot's head in an attempt to release the desperate man's grip, but it was too late. Both men were pulled into the shaft and both screamed as they fell.

*****

With the route to the weapon store memorized as much as they could in the brief time they had managed to study the map before it went dark, the SEAL team moved through the ship towards their goal. The threat of constant attack by the spaceship's vicious inhabitants hampered their progress as every open side door, turning and intersection had to be checked before they could progress past it.

Their latest holdup was a staircase leading down to a half-landing before turning back on itself. They briefly paused at the top to look below and alert for monsters they slowly descended with their eyes searching below for anything that might be waiting to surprise them.

When Sullivan reached the bottom with the others close behind, he turned his light each way along the corridor and called out, "It's clear for as far as I can see."

Colbert pulled the image of the map into his thoughts and pictured the staircase they had just climbed down. "Head right."

Sullivan and Cleveland led them along the corridor.

Another boom like the sound of a distant explosion vibrated through the ship, a reminder from the iceberg that they were at its mercy. Creaks, groans and the distant sounds of collapsing metal followed in the wake of the disturbance.

Sullivan nudged Cleveland with his elbow. "I know this mission has turned out to be the shittiest one yet, but if we ever get out of here we're going to have a great story to tell our kids."

Cleveland humphed. "It's alright for you, you're white. I've seen the movies. The token black man never survives."

Sullivan laughed. "Yeah, you're right. Maybe I shouldn't stand so close, collateral damage and all that."

"Quiet you two and concentrate on the mission," Colbert ordered. He knew it was only nervous banter, a way to push aside their anxiety, but he needed his men to stay focused.

"Sir, I think we have a problem," said Cleveland.

"You ain't farted again have you Cleve?" asked Crowe.

"You'll wish that was the problem," replied Cleveland, stepping aside so those behind could see the mass of wreckage blocking the corridor.

It looked like a couple of floors had collapsed. The floor they stood on sagged on one side towards the buckled wall and creaked unnervingly when they approached the blockage. Pieces of unrecognizable machinery lay entangled in the twisted lengths of metal and floor plates.

"I guess we go back and search for a workaround," said Stedman.

Colbert stepped nearer the barrier and examined the wall for a few moments before he knelt and aimed his light through the small gap caused by the buckled wall panel. The beam penetrated a space that might be a room. He slung his weapon over his shoulder. "Sullivan, give me a hand. I want to see if we can enlarge this hole."

The two men gripped the loose edge and forced it back with a protesting groan until the gap was big enough to crawl through. Colbert crouched and again shone his light into the room. "Hold here until I've checked it out."

After crawling through, Colbert swept his light around the room. He searched low, high and everything in-between. Only when he was satisfied it was free of any monstrous threat, did he start taking in the room's details. The beds situated at each end of the room were surrounded by strange mechanical arms. Cables hung from the circular pieces of equipment against the wall that looked like it might be some type of scanner that could move the length of the bed. Broken monitors and pieces of medical equipment were strewn across the bloodstained floor. The floor-to-ceiling transparent walls once forming what might have been a quarantine compartment lay in pieces on the floor. Even in its current state, it was obvious this room had once been a sterile environment and probably an operating theater, or some kind of medical facility. Screens as dead as the ancient corpse in the corner—patient or medical personnel was impossible to tell from the disarrayed skeleton—were placed around the room.

"You okay in there, sir?"

Colbert turned to see Crowe's head poking through the gap in the wall. "It's clear. Tell the others to come in."

As Crowe disappeared to inform the others, Colbert crossed to the double doors, each set with a window in the top half, and peered out into a corridor vastly different from the others they had journeyed through. Apart from being wider, everything was white—the floor, ceiling, doors and every pipe, cable or fitting fixed to it. Colbert briefly focused on the identical set of doors opposite before glancing at the exits at each end of the short corridor that led left and right. All were closed. He moved to the door control and pressed the button. He wasn't surprised it didn't open; the whole level seemed to lack any power. He turned on hearing the others enter. "We need something to jimmy the door open."

The men glanced around the room for something suitable.

Cleveland picked up a tool with one flat end and the other shaped like pincers. He held it up as he crossed to Colbert. "This should do it."

Colbert glanced at the tool. At about eighteen inches long, it wouldn't offer much leverage. "Give it a try. Ramirez, Stedman, get ready to pull the doors open."

Cleveland forced the flat end between the doors and was surprised by how easily they parted when he pushed the lever to one side. Ramirez and Stedman pulled them apart wide enough for them to fit through.

Colbert stepped into the sterile, white corridor and looked at the door that led back to the corridor with the blockage. It was obvious from the bulge in one side of the door, the frame and the wall that it wouldn't open. The door at the opposite end of the corridor would take them away from the corridor and their route to the armory. That left the door directly opposite the medical room. He stepped back, glanced at Cleveland and nodded at the door.

The men set to work and it was soon opened, setting free a fetid whiff of decay and acrid-scented air that wafted over them. The vision that greeted them was equally unpleasant. Though the bloodstained beds that lined each side of the room and the skeletal remains of long dead patients that occupied some of them were a concern, it wasn't these that caused them the most alarm. This honor fell to the large, brown cocoons hanging from the ceiling throughout the room.

Not one of the men believed it would be a good idea to go anywhere near them.

"Close the door," Colbert whispered.

The men were glad to do so and slid them together.

Colbert nodded at the door along the corridor. "Let's try that one, but only open it a crack until we find out what's on the other side."

As soon as the door was open a few inches, Sullivan aimed his light through the slit. At first he saw nothing, but as his eyes adjusted he glimpsed something—two small points of lights.

"What do you see?" asked Ramirez, placing his eye to the gap when Sullivan moved.

"A couple of lights, so maybe the power's on."

A rhythmic thumping emanated through the door gap.

Ramirez saw the lights now bobbed up and down and were growing bigger and then the monstrous head rush into the light.

Sullivan looked at the floor when it started vibrating.

Ramirez stepped back. "I suggest we move as that direction is definitely not an option."

Cleveland peered through the gap. "What did you see?"

"What do you think I saw, a bunch of pixies sitting on toadstools singing a merry song? It's another damned monster, and it's coming this way."

"Do you see it, Cleve?" asked Colbert.

Cleveland stepped back from the door. "It kinda hard to miss, it's a bloody big 'un."

Thumping footsteps approached the door.

"Everyone back," ordered Colbert.

The men retreated from the door but kept their eyes and weapons aimed at it.

A loud crash rang out when the monster struck. The force was enough to buckle the door slightly and send vibrations rippling along the floor, walls and ceiling.

As if in competition to the noise, another crash came from the medical room.

Colbert glanced behind. "Ramirez, Sullivan, check it out."

The two men rushed back along the corridor.

The remaining men gazed at the damaged door.

A loud snort that sent a jet of misty breath through the breach was followed by a scraping sound and then a large eye peered out at them, glowing brightly in the reflected flashlights aimed at it. A thick black tongue snaked through the gap and waggled at them, as if it tasting their scent, before being pulled back inside its owner's mouth. The eye disappeared from the gap and heavy footsteps moved away from the door.

Cleveland let out a relieved sigh. "Thank God it's gone."

"What do we do now, sir?" asked Crowe.

Colbert glanced behind at the approaching footsteps. The concerned expressions worn by Ramirez and Sullivan did not bode well. "My first reaction was to head back the way we came, but something tells me that not's going to be possible."

"The wreckage in the corridor shifted and blocked the opening. There's no way we can go back through," Sullivan reported.

Thundering footsteps that grew louder with every thump pounded the floor.

All faces swiveled to the door.

The beast's pounding footsteps didn't slow when they grew nearer. As if a silent command had been given, the men took a few steps back. The sound wave from the powerful crash sped along the corridor and thumped against the men. Metal screeched like it was screaming in agony when the two halves of the door bowed worryingly. The beast responsible pressed its face in the gap and growled at them before it turned away and loped back along the corridor.

"One more hit and it'll be through," stated Cleveland, his voice a little higher than normal.

Colbert looked at the only exit left to them. "Open it," he ordered.

Cleveland rushed to the door as the thumping footsteps started up again. As soon as he had made a gap wide enough, Ramirez and Sullivan forced their fingers in and pulled the two doors open. Ignoring the pungent stench that assailed them again, the men filed in.

When the beast struck the door a third time, one of the doors blasted free and sped along the corridor. Colbert pulled Ramirez to his knees a moment before the door skimmed over their heads.

Ramirez shot a worried glance at the approaching beast as he rushed through the opening and Sullivan and Cleveland pushed the doors closed after Colbert had stepped through.

The beast that was the size of an adult rhinoceros, just as powerful and twice as vicious, stared at the closed doors when it skidded by. It turned sharply, letting its back legs slide around into the wall, which shook with the force of its collision. It moved back to the door, nudged it with its powerful armored head and snorted angrily.

The men on the other side watched the double doors bow slightly when the beast pressed on it. Though it didn't have the long run up like before, none of them doubted the beast's capability to force its way inside.

Sullivan nudged Colbert and when the man turned, pointed his light at the nearest cocoon. Things moved inside. The forms of imagined horrors pressing against the interior walls of the leathery sack pulsated, as if something within breathed.

Colbert turned to his men and put a finger to his lips. If they didn't disturb whatever nightmare dwelled within the hanging pods, they might make it through the room to the exit he hoped lay on its far side. He nodded for Sullivan to lead the way.

The foul substance covering the floor squelched beneath their boots and set free a fresh wave of eye-watering stench with every step. That and their shallow breaths were the only sounds they made as they moved through the maze of narrow alleys that twisted between and around the grotesque, horror-filled piñatas.

The beast turned away from the entrance and forced its bulk between the partly open doors leading to the medical room. They screeched in protest as they juddered along the beast's rough skin and curled back from their runners and crashed to the floor. Looking neither left nor right, the powerful beast strolled lazily across the room and turned when it reached the far end. It lowered its head, snorted like a bull facing down a matador, and charged.

*****

Praying for a soft landing, Richard sped down the chute. He dropped into nothingness and gasped when something cold engulfed him. Foul, rancid sludge, thick as lumpy yogurt, slivered into his mouth until he clamped his lips shut. He clawed his way to the surface and dragged air into his lungs only slightly less foul than the putrid ooze he had fallen into.

Fearing the tentacles might be searching for him, Richard glanced around the foul chamber. A soft, blue glow highlighted the surroundings he took in at a glance. He was in a pool set in the middle of a long, vaulted room. Though there seemed to be some kind of machinery dotted about the floor and along the walls, all were covered in a thick carpet of mould with strands of growth tipped with tiny claws that constantly undulated. Thick metal columns, entwined with blue glowing vines festooned with red, barbed thorns, rose from the pool to reach the ceiling. The same vicious vines also trailed down parts of the walls.

A disgusting sucking and slurping put Richard's danger radar on full alert. He cautiously turned by paddling in a circle to reluctantly discover its cause. Before he even laid eyes on what made the sound, he knew it wouldn't be good. The shiver of revulsion that ran through him on seeing it was strong enough to send ripples across the thick sludge. Richard froze, lest he be detected by the grotesque slug-like creature that slithered down a short flight of steps and along a path away from the pool. The monstrosity emitted a sickly green glow that highlighted its grotesque pale form. It was difficult to work out if the mass of tentacles that surrounded the Lovecraftian horror were part of it or loyal worm-like followers. The pustules that adorned the creature's glowing skin constantly pulsated and with each throb a dribble of white, pus-thick liquid oozed from their tips. Richard couldn't imagine that a more grotesque or eye-offending monster existed on any other planet in all the universes that might exist. Staring at it had the effect of looking through night-vision goggles at a gigantic deformed glowworm with terrible acne. As Richard saw no sign of Talbot, he assumed the man had already been consumed by the Slug Monster.

Though Talbot was still alive, he was certain his death wasn't very far away and he would suffer the same horrific fate as Jenkins. He had witnessed his friend being fed into the monster's mouth and chewed by the thing's sharp teeth when he was dragged out of the vent. Because the tentacles wrapped around him squeezed tighter when he struggled to free himself from the monster's grip, he had stopped, hoping they would loosen if he remained still and acted dead. So constricted was his chest, it was difficult drawing each breath. As the thing moved and entered a tunnel, he was raised higher, allowing him to peer over the grotesque creature. His eyes searched for Richard, worryingly his only chance of rescue, and when he saw the man he locked eyes with him. He was well aware Richard wouldn't risk his life rescuing anyone, especially someone responsible for dragging him into such a foul place; however, the weapon, and just as important the light attached to it, would be something he would need to stand any chance of escape. If Richard came after them, he might be rescued in the process. Unable to scream or speak due to the tentacle that had smothered his mouth to silence his terrified screams, Talbot nodded his head as much as the living restraints would allow and darted his eyes at something pinned to his side by the tentacles wrapped around his body.

Just before the monstrosity Richard watched in loathing disappeared into a side turning, Talbot appeared above the foul creature. When the man's fear-filled eyes locked with Richard's and he indicated something at his side, Richard's eyes flicked to the object the man desperately wanted him to see—the rifle and flashlight.

Richard moved to the edge of the foul pool of porridge and dragged his gunk-covered body onto a level floor covered with a thin layer of the foul slush that filled the pool. Most likely the runoff from the pus he had noticed seeping from the Slug Monster's repugnant body. He nearly gagged on remembering he had swallowed some. Fighting the nausea that might turn out to be a losing battle as he swallowed the bile that rose in his throat, Richard climbed to his feet and looked at the foul substance covering his hands. A few tiny worms, sensing something breathing, wavered in the air towards his mouth. Richard shivered involuntarily and quickly scraped them off on the edge of one of the steps that led up to the slightly higher level recently occupied by the Slug Monster. He slipped off his jacket, heavy with the sludge that covered it and filled every pocket, and dropped it to the ground. He shook his re-soiled hands as clean as he could and removed as much of the gunk as was possible from his face and hair and looked both ways along the room. To his left, a wall blocked the way. Vine-entangled pipes or cables that ran along one side of the room turned up the wall and disappeared into the ceiling. There wasn't even a hint of a door or an exit. The only direction left open to him was past the turning the foul creature had disappeared along.

Richard approached the side turning and stared at the faint, green glow highlighting the wall from around the corner—an indication the monster hadn't strayed far. Worried he wouldn't survive long without a light and some sort of weapon, Richard sighed and entered the tunnel.

After a few cautious steps, Richard stopped and stared at the boot protruding from a mound of mustard-brown feces. A similar line of disgusting dollops stretched out in a row following the Slug Monster's route, evidence it passed its waste on the move. A closer inspection revealed the foot was still inside and slowly being devoured by the small worms he had encountered a few moments ago. As Talbot was alive a moment ago, Richard guessed the military boot had to belong to Jenkins. Hoping to find the dead man's weapon amongst the scraps of ejected clothing within the shit trail, Richard used a foot to hesitantly probe the disgusting mess and fought back the vomit that threatened to spew forth again, this time from the eye-watering stench his reluctant search threw up. When he failed to find the weapon, Richard suspected it probably fell into the pus pool when the man was dragged down the chute and was now lost forever.

Richard moved deeper into the passage, stopped at the corner and peered around the edge into the chamber the Slug Monster had made its home. From its position, he now knew the slug and the tentacles were joined. It hung upside down from tentacles latched onto the ceiling like a grotesque chandelier fashioned from a design straight out of Lovecraft's weird imagination. The head of the thing didn't vary much from the rest of its body, except for short tentacles that grew from around its mouth and eyes—thankfully, presently closed—and waved in the air in some macabre dance routine, twisting around and caressing each other. A ripple of flabby skin travelled the length of the monster's bulky body with each breath it took and each exhale produced a wheezing, rumbling snort. The thing was asleep. The smell the creature reeked of reminded Richard of the one and only time he had gone fishing. His friend, who had convinced him what a great sport it was, had opened a container filled with wriggling maggots and shoved it under his nose. The foul stench that had invaded his nostrils then was a similar smell, albeit the stench that invaded them now was much stronger.

Richard's eyes searched for Talbot—well, for the weapon mainly, but as the two were connected last time he saw them, he thought if he found one the other wouldn't be far away, and Talbot would be easier to spot. However, there was no sign of either. Thinking the man might have been devoured as a pre-nap snack, Richard searched the ground around the monster for any evidence the man had been eaten or the weapon that may have slipped from his grasp. He again found no sign of either, and careful to time his movements to coincide with the Slug Monster's snores to cover the sound, he took a few cautious steps nearer Sleeping Ugly and noticed Talbot's boots poking out past the monster's far side. A few more snore-timed steps brought the soldier into view. Talbot lay on the ground held in place by tentacles that entwined his body. With his eyes watching the hanging monstrosity in case it awoke, Richard moved closer and knelt beside Talbot. The man actually looked relieved to see him. It wasn't an emotion Richard experienced very often, if ever. Richard gripped the butt of the rifle and pulled, but stopped when the tentacles squeezed the weapon and their victim tighter.

Talbot shook his head desperately as he struggled to draw another breath through his partially smothered nose and flicked his eyes at his feet. Deciphering the signal, Richard examined the man's boots and noticed the knife strapped around one ankle. Though a tentacle was wrapped around the sheath, the handle was free. A gentle tug saw it transferred to his hand. Richard showed it to Talbot to let him know he had it, and then examined the three tentacles holding the weapon in place. He assumed, as soon as the blade started cutting, the monster would awake to find out the cause of the pain and viciously retaliate when it saw the human holding a knife stained with its blood. He would have to be super quick if he was going to cut through all three, grab the weapon and kill the monster before he became its next victim.

As Richard held the knife above the first tentacle, he wondered how tough they were and if the knife would be able to cut through them. As soon as he made the first cut he would be committed; there would be no second chance. Two of the worm-like tentacles were about two inches across and one about four. Sweat poured from his brow. His hands shook and fear of failure and his resulting painful death almost stopped him. The thought of wandering through the ship unarmed and in darkness persuaded him he had to take the risk. The knife moved closer until it was almost touching the thing's flesh before Richard jerked it away. He looked at Talbot, who stared at him pleadingly to do it. Certain the monster would be upon him before he had cut through the first ghastly limb, Richard stood and backed away. Self-preservation forced him to alter his plan. A few steps positioned him in front of the monster's grotesque rippling body. Hardly believing what he was about to do and before fear changed his mind, he raised the knife clutched in both hands, plunged it into the monster's flesh and dragged it quickly down its vile body.

The monster screeched and its eyes sprung open and looked at Richard as soon as the blade had pierced its flesh. When tentacles darted out to seize the attacker, they released their hold on the ceiling. When the monster flopped to the floor, its innards burst from the rip in its body with a loud, squishy, slurp wrapped in the foulest of stenches.

Blood, gore and all manner of foul excrement sprayed Richard as he dodged away and slashed at the tentacles groping for him. When he was tripped to the ground by the mass of slithering, slippery innards beneath his feet, tentacles grabbed his legs and hoisted him into the air.

The Slug Monster, that seemed unaffected by the loss of some of its internal organs, climbed upright, turned its many eyes upon its attacker and bared rows of sharp, chomping teeth. The tentacles around its mouth danced frantically as they stretched towards the prey.

Though more terrified than he had ever been before, Richard stared at the vicious mouth the tentacles planned to feed him into and bent his body to bring the knife in range of the nearest tentacle gripping him. He slashed out, but only managed to scratch it. Another tentacle snatched the knife from his hand and threw it across the room. Dangled above the gaping mouth eager to receive its attacker, Richard was horror-stricken by the Slug-Monster's obvious intention. He placed a hand either side its jaw and grabbed hold of two small tentacles, which protested vigorously and tried to shake his grip free. Other smaller tentacles wrapped around his wrists and pulled. The ones he refused to let go of snapped. Thick, white, goo oozed from the stumps he dropped into the monster's gaping maw.

As he swayed back and forth over the teeth-lined cavernous mouth, Richard realized there was no escape for him now. This would be how his life would end. His body would be chewed into bite-size chunks by a monster maggot from another world. Who could have predicted such a thing? Soon he would be nothing more than a brown stain on the sludge-covered floor. He closed his eyes and hoped the monster would bite through his neck to give him a quick death. He sobbed in terror as he was lowered towards the waiting teeth and felt the warm, waft of the monster's foul breath wash over his face.

Gunfire echoed around the chamber.

The monster's painful shrieks quickly followed.

Richard opened his eyes when he was thrown across the room by the tentacles that had discarded him to fight off the latest threat. Richard struck the wall hard and fell to the floor. Slightly dazed, he watched blurred flashes light up the foul room.

Talbot cursed Richard when he left him at the mercy of the monster. He should have known better than put his hope in the cowardly man. His accusing eyes followed Richard until the sleeping monster's ugly form hid him from view. A tearing noise that followed Richard's cowardly flight was in turn followed by an unholy screech, a gruesome slurp and a wave of stench that surprised him almost as much as the monster crashing to the ground. When the tentacles that imprisoned him as secularly as any caged cell uncurled from his body and left him free, he rolled away and climbed to his feet. Fearing the monster would realize its mistake and the tentacles would return at any moment, he aimed the rifle at the monster's grotesque form and sprayed it with bullets. The monster writhed in pain and its piercing shrieks were almost as deafening as the gunfire. Talbot rushed past the Slug

Monster and almost slipped on the slimy mess of offal that had slipped from the long gash in its stomach. Richard had to be responsible. He glanced at the man he now thought he might have misjudged sprawled on the ground. "Richard, it's time to leave."

Richard glanced at the monster riddled with holes oozing thick pus when it toppled to the floor with its tentacles waving frantically in all directions. He snatched up the knife he noticed beside him, climbed to his feet and in a staggering dazed run, followed Talbot back through the passage.

*****

The soldiers moved quietly through the room, which they assumed by the rows of beds lining its walls, to be a hospital ward. Some of the contorted skeletal remains of the patients' corpses remained on the dark-stained beds where they had come to be healed, but instead, by the evidence of missing body parts and gnawed bones, had suffered a horrifying and brutal demise. Remains of other unfortunate victims who had attempted, but ultimately failed, to flee from whatever horror had confronted them lay in pieces strewn about the floor. The gruesome remains both horrified and fascinated the men who cast anxious gazes at the bones of the crew who had once piloted the huge spaceship through space. It was a sobering thought to them all that advanced technology was no match against nature's primal instinct to slay and feed, whatever planet it originated from.

Startled by the loud boom and the crunching of metal that thundered through the room, some of the men instinctively glanced back at the sound, but found the door the beast had just struck blocked by rows of monstrous cocoons.

Colbert and Sullivan turned their gaze upon the cocoons surrounding them when the movements of whatever was inside increased. They were waking up. Bulges appeared over their surfaces like fast-forming boils about to erupt. Sullivan wasn't eager to be around when they did and pressed on. Equally eager to put as much distance as possible between them and whatever horror emerged from the now swaying sacks, the rest of the SEALs quickly followed. Haste had replaced their previous priority of silence.

Metal skidding across the floor followed the loud crash and rending of metal as the beast announced its arrival and charged through the room in search of its prey. The cocoons it barged aside, slammed into others. Casings split and dark-brown shiny things the size and shape of a soccer ball poured out. Some bounced slightly, others drifted in circles before coming to a stop, while others rolled across the floor.

Confused by the mass of cocoons blocking its view, the beast slowed and nudged another of the obstructions aside. Unaware of the object that rolled beneath its belly, it kicked it when it moved forward.

Hearing something approach, Brody glanced behind and stared at the strange ball rolling towards him. Though he had no idea what it was, he assumed it wasn't anything he wanted anywhere near him. When he lashed out a foot to kick it away, the ball changed.

As a head uncurled from the round mass, strands of sinewy hair sprung out from around the top. Dark eyes, more like shapeless holes, appeared. A crack on the lower part of the skull-shaped head separated and dropped to form a jaw displaying shiny, black teeth splayed at various angles. Committed to the maneuver, Brody was powerless to pull his foot away from the frightening monster that had formed in a split second. Two slender arms sporting four-fingered, clawless hands, unfurled from its body as it sprung over Brody's foot, scampered up his body, grabbed his face and pressed two fingers into his eyes. Brody screamed and pawed at the beast gnawing his cheek.

The beast snapped at the fingers, biting off three at the knuckles.

Brody screamed louder and staggered back into a cocoon.

Ramirez spun towards the scream and, for a moment, stared at the grotesque creature perched on Brody's chest. When the creature looked back at him, its hair splayed out like a bizarre crown as it dropped its blood-dripping jaw and let out a scream so high-pitched it hurt Ramirez's ears.

A single shot rang out.

The hole punched through the creature's head, ran with thick blood so dark it was almost black, like crude oil.

Ramirez knocked the dead creature to the floor and examined Brody. Blood poured from the man's eyes, cheek and hand. He was in bad shape, but still alive. "Okay, buddy, it's gone."

"I can't see," screamed Brody. He wiped at his eyes with fingers oozing blood from severed digits.

More of the creatures poured from the top of the cocoon behind Brody and headed for the scent of blood. Ramirez dodged back when they swarmed over Brody, biting and pulling free lumps of flesh.

Colbert arrived, saw the carnage taking place, aimed his gun at Brody's head and fired. The bullet brought a merciful end to the man's agony. He grabbed Ramirez's shoulder and turned him away from the horrific sight.

"We have to go before more come—we've found an exit."

The beast appeared and rushed towards them. It snorted loudly, its eyes wide and full of terror. Colbert and Ramirez dodged aside and watched it bolt past. Creatures feeding on its flesh clung to its sides and back. More of the creatures were in pursuit, chasing the beast for a share of the feast. One leaped at Ramirez. His rifled barked, killing it in midair. Colbert joined him in spraying the oncoming hoard as they moved back and as soon as they saw a space, they turned and fled.

Creatures poured from every evil sack. There were hundreds of them. Gunshots echoed through the room from different positions, a sign the others were having their own problems. Colbert prayed they had managed to get the door open.

Colbert and Ramirez veered to the side and sought sanctuary on the nearest bed when a group of creatures blocked their path. A commotion raised their heads.

In its attempt to be free of the creatures eating it alive, the beast slammed into the wall, crushing those on that side. It bounded forward, knocking beds aside with its massive head and shoving others in front like a bulldozer pushing soil. Beds, mixed with the crew's ancient skeletons, tumbled over each other in a mass of metal and bones. A cocoon ripped from the ceiling joined the oncoming wreckage, adding the screams of the foul creatures trapped inside to the screeching clash of wreckage.

Colbert glanced at the floor crawling with creatures and realized they had nowhere to go. He shot the creature that crawled from the top of the cocoon nearest the bed, shouldered his rifle and shouted loud enough to be heard above the speedily approaching ruckus, "Ramirez, follow me."

Ramirez turned as Colbert leaped onto the cocoon. His weight swung it away from the bed. When it was within reach, he climbed onto the next one. Ramirez kicked away the creature that jumped on the bed before it could attack and leaped as the mangled pile of beds, skeletons and creatures tore the one he stood on away. Trying to ignore the things moving about inside, he moved around the grotesque sack, and climbed onto the next one when it swung into reach. He grabbed his pistol and shot the creature that poked its head out the top and glanced at Colbert, two cocoons away when he dropped to the floor. He glanced down. The creatures ignored them and swarmed after the beast like rats drawn to the Pied Piper. Ramirez dropped to the floor and rushed after Colbert towards the exit.

Cleveland pointed. "Here they come."

"Where's Brody," asked Sullivan, gazing behind them.

No one answered. They knew the commander wouldn't have abandoned Brody if he still lived. Stedman and Sullivan slid the doors closed when Colbert and Ramirez were safely through.

"Brody?" questioned Sullivan.

Colbert shook his head sadly and glanced at the door at the end of the short corridor. It looked intact and would take them back onto the route to the armory. He didn't think mentioning he ended the man's suffering with a bullet would boost their morale, so he skipped past it and forced the men to concentrate back on the mission. He glanced at the tool in Cleveland's hand, pleased the man had kept hold of it. "Let's get that door open and find out if the corridor's clear."

When the door had been forced open, Cleveland stepped through. The barricade of debris ended a few feet away. "It's clear."

Keen to keep the men moving and their thoughts, for now, off the brother they had lost, Colbert urged them onwards.

*****

As Talbot and Richard sprinted through room away from the foul pool, Talbot slowed to let Richard catch up. "I suppose I should thank you for saving my life."

"Yes, you should, but give me your rifle and I'll consider the debt repaid."

Talbot smiled. "Not going to happen. I know it's the only reason you rescued me."

When a loud, piercing shriek echoed through the room, they turned. The Slug Monster emerged from the tunnel and turned its gaze upon the fleeing men. Its tentacles reached for the ceiling, pulled its bulk from the ground and as fluidly as any chimpanzee swinging from branch to branch, swung through the room towards them at an amazing speed for its bulk.

Richard sighed. "What is it with these aliens? They never give up."

"Probably the scarceness of food has something to do with it, but what surprises me more is how is that thing is still alive. You gutted it and I shot it."

The two men fled the pursuing monster that quickly gained on them. Its excited shrieks growing ever nearer filled the men with dread.

Talbot's weapon-light fell on a door a short distance ahead. It was neither open nor closed. A small gap in its center provided their only means of escape. They rushed for it. Richard glanced behind and wished he hadn't. The monster was barely twenty feet away. Globules of white pus dripped from its body wounds and its teeth chomped menacingly.

Talbot didn't slow when he approached the door, but dived and passed smoothly through the hole barely wider than his shoulders.

Richard looked on in dismay as Talbot's feet disappeared through the small opening. He was a terrible diver. Though he had practiced when he was a teenager, so he could impress the bikini-clad girls at his local swimming pool, he had failed miserably. Every dive had turned into a clumsy and extremely embarrassing belly flop; the chances of him diving through such a small hole without hitting the side was something he thought impossible. A tentacle appeared beside his face and seemed to look at him. With doubts he would make it, Richard dived for the hole. His arms and shoulders went through smoothly, but his knees struck the edge painfully, causing him to crash to the ground. Panting heavily, he remained where he fell to catch his breath.

When the monster smashed into the door, Talbot aimed the weapon at the bulbous skin that filled the hole briefly before moving away. Though its body was too large to fit through the small opening, its tentacles weren't. They snaked through the opening and whipped out erratically in all directions in an attempt to snare their prey. Talbot prodded Richard with a foot. "I suggest you move."

Richard rolled onto his back and glanced at the tentacles reaching ever nearer. He climbed to his feet, ducked beneath one and moved until he was out of their long reach.

"We're safe now," said Talbot.

Richard snorted as he examined his scraped knees. "Safe! Nowhere aboard this damn ship is safe."

Talbot roamed the light around until it settled on something fifty feet away. "What do you make of that?"

Hoping it wasn't another monster, Richard dragged his gaze away from the wavering tentacles to find out the reason for Talbot's question. Though large and unexpected, it wasn't anything alive. He gazed at the thing perched on a thick rail that ran along the center of the floor. "Well I'll be damned—it's a train."

Talbot nodded. "The crew must have used it to move through the ship. Which stands to reason, I suppose. The ship's so large it would take ages to walk back and forth."

Though two carriages had dislodged from the rail, one was still connected to the train. The other had broken free, slewed across the platform and smashed against the wall. Dim yellow lights lined the sides of the tunnel and led off into the distance.

While Richard headed for the train, Talbot climbed onto the wide platform beside it and looked down the side of the carriage that had struck the wall. He glimpsed two doors as buckled and dented as the wall. Even if they could move the twisted wreck, he doubted the doors would ever open again. He glanced along the platform dotted with seats, columns and walls adorned with alien posters and information signs, but saw no other exits. He glanced at Richard climbing onto the platform and walked over.

Richard placed his face against the window of the first upright carriage and peered inside. "I wonder if it still works."

"It wouldn't do us any good if it does." Talbot pointed the weapon behind him. "The way out is back there. We need to go up and head for the back of the ship."

Richard looked at the carriage leaning against the wall and the tip of the door tops it blocked. "Good luck with that. In my experience aboard this vessel, it's never that simple. If you see a handy exit, point it out and I'll gladly follow, but failing that, I'm going to search the train. There might be weapons aboard." Richard increased his pace.

"Or monsters," Talbot added and smirked when Richard's pace suddenly slowed.

Richard turned. "As you have the only weapon, it's best you lead."

"Not true, you have the knife."

Richard glanced at the knife in his hand. He couldn't imagine fighting any monster in such close proximity to be able to use it. He held it out to Talbot. "Swap it for the rifle and I'll go first."

Talbot strode past Richard. "I'm fine, thanks."

They passed two more carriages before they found an open door. Talbot shone the light inside at the obvious neglect and deterioration. Two rows of large, facing seats lined both sides of the compartment. Tuffs of spongy filling poked from the many rips in the orange padded seats, evidence that sharp-clawed creatures had been inside. When they were confident it was free of danger, they entered and cautiously made their way through the train.

To Talbot, though on a larger scale, the seats and the layout of the train seemed remarkably similar to trains he had travelled on and abnormally out of place in an alien vessel. "Richard, do you have any idea what the crew looked like?"

"I never saw one, but the other scientists found the well preserved corpse of an alien they thought might have been the Captain. Apparently it was humanoid, taller than humans and, surprisingly, not that scary compared to the other creatures they transported. I'm not sure how much you know, but when the aliens were forced to leave their planet they built an armada of these gigantic Ark ships to evacuate their world. They filled it with a variety of species and plants and set off through space to search for a new planet to inhabit. After the crew had evacuated this one it was damaged by meteoroids and crashed on Earth."

They moved through a small articulated corridor into a compartment identical to the previous.

"So this spaceship is the alien version of Noah's Ark."

Richard shrugged. "I suppose so, though Noah didn't fill his ship with bloodthirsty monsters."

The next compartment they entered was absent any seats. A pair of large doors in both side walls indicated the space big enough to fit an articulated lorry in was probably used for transporting cargo.

Three compartments later they arrived at one that gave them the most concern. Cages down the center of the room could only have one function—transporting live cargo. Monsters. Richard kept close to Talbot as they moved down one side, peering through the crisscrossed bars of each cage for any inhabitants. The first, second and third, though occupied, posed no danger; the creatures were a long time dead, nothing but yellowed skeletons. They paused at the fourth and stared at the gaping hole. Unable to get through the cage walls, whatever was once imprisoned here had burrowed through the floor.

Talbot looked at Richard. "Maybe entering the train wasn't such a bad idea after all."

Richard grinned and held out a hand. "Does it earn me the rifle as a reward?"

"It wasn't that good an idea." Talbot gazed ahead. "Let's keep moving."

As they entered the next compartment, another cargo hold, Talbot held up a fist to halt Richard.

"That I understand, but I don't speak army talk. Anything more complicated you'll have to verbalize."

Talbot turned, placed a finger to his lips and shushed.

That, Richard understood.

The two men tilted their heads up at the ceiling and their eyes followed the click-clacks that moved along the roof until it stopped directly above them.

Richard tapped Talbot on the shoulder and pointed through the window at the creature's shadow cast on the wall by the dim yellow lights stretching the length of the tunnel. It looked more like a spindly tree covered in thin, twiggy branches than any creature either of them could visualize.

Talbot pointed forward. Richard nodded and one careful step at a time they moved through the carriage. They stopped when the click-clacking started up again, moved to the edge of the roof and down the side of the carriage.

Talbot switched off the light when something appeared at a nearby window and looked inside. "Don't move," he whispered. "It might not see us and leave."

Richard huffed softly and whispered back, "Yeah, that's what's going to happen. It's probably got infrared vision or whatever ability it needs to see us in the dark."

The head turned and looked straight at them.

Richard refrained from telling Talbot '*I told you so.*'

Talbot raised the rifle, switched on the light and aimed it at the creature. Caught in the glare, the creature didn't move.

The twig-like growths they had first glimpsed from its shadow grew out from along its back and from a silver, almost metallic, head that reflected Talbot's light. Flat pieces of bone, the hue of ancient parchment, protruded in two lines along either side of its head and the top part of its torso.

Exterior bone ribs, tightly packed together, adorned its chest. Its legs, which seemed to surround the body, matched the style of the twig-like appendages on its head and back, though these were slightly thicker and doubled jointed with smaller growths brandishing sharp points spouting from its knee joints. The creature, at three feet long, wasn't very big, but what it lacked in body mass it made up for with menace that wasn't lost on the two anxious men.

When it opened its small jaw set on the tip of its long head and let out a series of deep-throated squeaks and clicks, Talbot fired twice. The bullets smashed through the window and tore through the creature's skull, sending it flying against the wall before it dropped to the ground.

Talbot relaxed. "One wasn't so bad."

Richard looked at Talbot and shook his head. "You really need to acclimatize to the way everything in this ship behaves." He pointed at the recently deceased creature. "That thing won't be alone. At this very moment hoards of them will be converging towards its call or your gunshots."

Talbot cocked an ear, but heard nothing to hint Richard's prediction was about to come true. "You're paranoid. Nothing's coming."

"You keep telling yourself that, but they are coming, trust me, they are coming."

"We'll see." Talbot continued along the train.

Richard glanced back along the train before following. He hoped he was wrong.

When they reached a door that prevented any further progress through the train, Talbot searched for the door control, but soon discovered there wasn't one. "Stick the knife blade in the join and lever it apart so I can get my fingers in."

Richard did as instructed and forced the knife to the side, parting the two door sections slightly. Talbot forced his fingers into the gap, placed a foot against the frame and pulled the door open a few inches. Richard gripped the opposite door and together they forced it open and stepped inside the train's control room. It was obvious by the absence of lights on the wraparound console that the train lacked power. The padded backrest and seat of the large single seat set in the middle of the surrounding console was in better condition than the carriage seating. Richard glanced around for a power switch and spied a small door on the wall labeled with red, alien text, and pulled it open. Inside was a red lever. He was about to shift its position when Talbot stopped him.

"Did you hear that?"

Richard joined Talbot in staring out through the large, age-stained windscreen that curved around the sloped nose of the train. Something in the distance moved in and out of the pools of yellow light.

Richard operated the lever. The train hummed as whatever powered it sprung to life. The console lights flashed on and a bright light filled the tunnel when the train's single headlight came on. Caught in its blinding glare were more creatures of the type Talbot had just killed.

Now Richard could see them more clearly, they reminded him of Insectoids. He couldn't remember if they were from a cartoon or a range of toys, but one species were mantis-like aliens—a metamorphosis of an arachnid and a praying mantis—it described these creatures perfectly, though these didn't move like insects. They raced along the tunnel as gracefully as thoroughbred racehorses.

Richard barged by Talbot and climbed into the driver's seat. "Now do you believe me?"

"Okay, but it's not what I'd call a hoard. There's only about twenty of them."

"How much ammo do you have left?"

Talbot shrugged. "Probably not enough."

Richard swept his eyes over the controls. Luckily there weren't that many and the dials and gauges he could ignore. He had to sit on the front edge of the seat to reach the lever he thought would move the train.

"You're seriously going to try and drive this thing?"

Richard nodded. "We can't outrun them, so unless you have a better plan?"

Talbot didn't. "Will it work with the derailed carriage attached to the back?"

"Let's find out, shall we?"

Richard pushed the lever forward. The humming increased, but the train didn't budge. He pushed it farther and stared at the approaching creatures, now only thirty feet away. The train began to vibrate. The humming grew in intensity. The Insectoids grew nearer. The train jerked forwards an inch.

The derailed carriage trembled and jerked slightly with a protesting groan of tortured metal and slowly screeched along the track.

"It's working!" stated Talbot, surprised the train was moving, albeit at a snail's pace.

Richard pushed the lever to its limit. The high pitch of the humming engine was an indication of the strain it was under from dragging the dead weight of the damaged carriage.

When the Insectoids reached the train, some leaped onto the front while the remainder flowed down either side of the track before jumping onto the train. All searched for a way inside.

Richard recoiled slightly when three Insectoids landed on the windscreen. Two scrambled onto the roof while one remained and stared at him. It bared its small teeth into a snarl before disappearing onto the roof. The click-clack of their feet on top of the train was unnerving.

"We're up shit creek, aren't we?"

Richard glanced at Talbot, who had his weapon aimed back along the carriage. "You might think so, but a few minutes ago we both faced something far worse and survived, so don't give up just yet."

Talbot shot a disbelieving glance at Richard. Even though they had both survived their encounter with the alien maggot monster, he found it hard to imagine a similar outcome would present itself in this death-imminent predicament with the odds so stacked against them. "I admire your optimism, Richard, but if it comes to it, I'll put a bullet in your brain to save you from the pain."

"Not if I stab you in the eye first you won't."

The two men grinned at each other.

"At first I took you for a cowardly, self-serving, conniving, sneaky bastard and a stab you in the back kinda guy, but actually, Richard, you're not such a bad sort after all."

"Thanks, I think," said Richard, "but I'm certain you'll change your mind when you get to know me better."

"Here they come." Talbot fired off two shots, killing one of the Insectoids that had found a way inside the train.

Richard glanced past Talbot at the creatures swarming through the carriages. They moved along the floor, the seats, the walls and ceiling to form a tunnel of teeth and death. They didn't have long now. He had to think of something.

Metal screeched against metal when the dragged carriage skimmed along the wall. The rear end struck a support pillar, careened across to the other side and slammed against the platform edge with enough force to crumple the side. Windows shattered, sending glass tinkling across the platform and spraying the seats long absent any waiting passengers. The carriage tipped slightly before it rolled back and bounced at an angle across the single track.

The movement tore the back of the carriage it was tethered to away with a loud screech of tearing metal and slid a few feet before coming to a halt.

Richard was thrown back into his seat when the train lurched forward like a greyhound out of the stall on seeing the mechanical rabbit race by. Talbot tumbled forward, smashing his head against the wall before spilling through the doorway.

Richard leaned forward to accelerate the train that had slowed after his hand had been snatched from the lever.

As the train speeded up again, Talbot jumped to his feet and fired off a couple of shots. Both were on target, taking out two more Insectoids. He fired off another two shots while he backed into the driver's cab. A wounded Insectoid crashed into another and they tumbled in a tangle of limbs. Bones cracked in the scuffle.

Talbot grabbed the doors and tried pulling them closed, but he couldn't do it alone. "Quick, Richard, give me a hand."

Richard glanced behind. "We have power now, just press the damn button."

Talbot punched the button and the door closed.

A few moments later the creatures scratched at the door.

"That should hold them," said Talbot confidently.

"I wouldn't relax just yet. We have another problem."

Talbot turned and peered through the windscreen. About one hundred meters away a large section of collapsed ceiling rested on the rail and formed a ramp that sloped to a higher level.

*****

The SEALs arrived at a circular room that seemed to be the main hub of the intersecting corridors that led off in all directions from around its circumference. Elevators, positioned on one wall, allowed quick access to the upper and lower levels. A spiral staircase set in the room's center provided a slower way to get there.

Light beams roamed the room as the men crossed to the center.

Stedman aimed his light over the rail and peered down the spiral staircase that twisted to the lower levels. It seemed to go on forever.

Cleveland joined him and let out a whistle. "Damn, that's a long way down."

"Stairway to Hell," said Stedman, ominously.

Sullivan crossed to the elevators and forced one set of doors apart. The light he shone into the deep shaft failed to reach the bottom. He directed the flashlight overhead and picked out the bottom of the elevator two floors above. Curious to discover how deep it was, he fished a flare from a pocket, struck it and dropped it into the shaft. It was a long time before it stopped falling. He went to move away when a faint clicking drifted up the shaft and halted him. He cocked an ear. He wasn't fooled by the silence. Though he thought it might have been the ship groaning, he suspected something else was responsible. Something was alive down there. Luckily it was so far below it shouldn't cause them a problem.

Colbert gazed around the space he had first glimpsed on the 3D map. It was proof they were heading in the right direction. The next step was to go down a few levels. He crossed to the top of the staircase and gazed down at the thousands of treads spiraling into the dark bowels of the ship.

"If I remember correctly, we go down three levels," said Crowe, joining Colbert at the top of the stairs.

Colbert nodded; his thoughts preoccupied with what horrors lay below waiting to surprise them. Though they were running low on ammo, it wasn't yet at a critical level. But they hadn't reached their goal yet, and they still had to make the return journey. Their chances of success were growing slimmer the farther they distanced themselves from the exit.

"You okay, Captain?" asked Cleveland, quietly.

Colbert turned to the man, smiled weakly and nodded. It was time to move. "We're going down."

When the men were ready, Colbert started down the staircase.

*****

Brusilov took the lead and led the men along the corridor that ran straight for about five hundred feet before opening onto another metal walkway that stretched along each end and one edge of the long room they had entered. Their lights roamed the room and revealed part of the walkway had collapsed, preventing them from reaching the staircase at the far end that led down to an exit. The walkway groaned and shifted slightly when they walked to the rail and peered at the pieces of strange machinery in the lower level. Some blinked small red, green and yellow lights and some hummed softly.

Flashlights searched the gloom below, but there were so many places of concealment it was impossible to tell if any horrors waited in the dark for them. Nikolay leaned over the edge far enough for him to see under the walkway. He had hoped to find metal supports they could climb down, but the path was supported by brackets of metal angled towards the wall.

"We should be able to climb down here," called out Babinski.

Brusilov and Nikolay crossed to the edge of the collapsed walkway and looked at the four-inch wide cables running down the wall Babinski pointed out near the broken platform.

Though Brusilov was reluctant to go down, he couldn't see any other choice as they needed to keep moving. He glanced around the room again. It was obvious from what they had seen so far in the lower levels that they were moving through the spaceship's industrial areas, the machinery that kept the huge spaceship running. If there was an armory it had to be on a higher level.

Babinski slid down first and fearing something might be down here, waiting, as soon as his feet touched the floor he aimed his rifle and light around the room. Sergei came down next and the rest of the men quickly followed. They cautiously moved between the machinery, heading for the door they had spotted from above on the far side. All expected an attack at any moment. Something had been killed in the corridor they had just passed through and it was a good bet whatever was responsible was down here somewhere. The ship's creaks, groans and the humming of the machines that started and stopped erratically with sinister whirrs and chugging clacks filled the room with an atmosphere of spookiness the men had rarely experienced. All felt relieved when they reached the far door safely.

Rozovsky was first to arrive at the open door. He peered around the frame and after shining his light into the next room, turned to those watching him with a frown creasing his brow and a shake of his head. "It's not good."

Rozovsky's concern increased the men's anxiety.

"From what we've experienced so far, how bad can it be?" said Nikolay, attempting to quell the men's fears. He stepped through the doorway and glanced around the room while the men crowded behind him.

"I guess it's as bad as it can be," stated Yelchin, who halted beside Nikolay and gazed at the thing above.

"And then some," added Vadik, as he joined them in gazing at the thing that hung from the strange formations covering the walls and ceiling.

Though mostly a skeleton, enough of its tattered and ripped skin remained to give a sense of its appearance when alive and evidence something had fed upon the carcass. Its large skull had four empty eye sockets, two either side of a raised strip of bone that ended above its jaw. The top of the skull spread out in a fan with three holes spaced out near the top. Its chest, partially covered in taut ripped skin that exposed its thick ribs, was triangular, tapering down to hips that stuck out at an angle. Attached to these were two long legs jointed in two places. Attached to its spread out arms and legs were strands of what seemed to be thick webs suspending it from the ceiling. Its posed posture gave the impression the monster's corpse was flying, swooping down to snatch them up in its claws.

"Whatever it is, I'm just glad it's dead," said Nikolay, tearing his eyes away from the frightening spectacle.

Mikhail scanned the room, his eyes darting nervously at the many dark areas where anything could be concealed. "Yeah, but whatever hung that thing up there might not be."

Brusilov pushed to the front and gazed past the macabre ceiling decoration. The room stretched up three levels and dropped down one. This could be their chance to leave the bowels of the ship and climb nearer to their goal. It wasn't only the Motherland that desperately needed to get their hands on the alien weapons; their ammo had reached such a critical level if they didn't find something to defend themselves with soon it was doubtful any of them would be leaving the monster-infested vessel.

Nikolay read the captains thoughts. "You think we can climb it?"

Brusilov walked over to the nearest growth and tapped one of the brown, bonelike skeletal ribs that covered the walls and creaked with every movement of the ship; though a hollow thud rang out, it was as hard as stone.

"It seems strong enough."

Brusilov gazed the length of the long room, its machinery and purpose smothered by the brown growth. Curved vertical formations linked the horizontal ribs together, adding to their strength and gave the impression of macabre curved ladders set on their sides. At intervals, bridges formed of the same substance connected the two sides. He made his decision and glanced at his men. "We climb."

As the men started the ascent, Brusilov shone his light into the deep hole. The bone-like constructions continued down, becoming thicker as they neared the bottom and formed cave-like entrances. Shrouded in darkness the light failed to fully banish, it was easy to imagine monstrous creatures roaming its depths. Hell would probably look more inviting.

For all their strangeness, the ribs were easy to climb. Though they creaked and sometimes moved slightly, they supported the men's weight. They were almost halfway up when they heard it.

Clack clack. Clack clack. Clack clack.

The sound brought the team to a halt and all turned their gazes below.

A couple of the men aimed their flashlights at the clacking and highlighted the creature responsible for creating the sound. Each landing of one of its six skeletal limbs clacked on the hard growth it climbed. It stopped, raised its head and looked at the humans that had strayed into its domain.

The men stared back at the creature. It wasn't very big, about two and a half feet in length. Its head was little more than a skull so tightly was the skin stretched over it, but, surprisingly, it didn't look frightening or vicious. It had two small eyes, a hint of a nose and a tiny mouth. Its six almost fleshless limbs were tipped with a flat knob of bone, conspicuously absent any claws, and its body was covered in a wiry mass of brown hair. Even though it had the appearance of a six-legged spider, it was the least frightening alien they had seen thus far.

Vadik sighted along his rifle at the spider creature. "Shall I kill it?"

Brusilov shook his head doubtfully. "No. It hasn't shown us any aggression. It might just be curious about us."

"Shooting it might also attract others of its kind if there are any," added Rozovsky. "I think we should ignore it and press on."

All agreed and they continued their climb.

Noticing movement from out the corner of his eye, Yelchin glanced to the right and froze. A spider creature too close for comfort stared at him. It cocked its small head to one side and then the other as it briefly examined Yelchin before edging a little nearer.

Yelchin moved to the side so he could climb around it. The creature jumped on the rib by his head and hissed.

"Errrh, comrades, I could do with some help here," whispered Yelchin, keeping a smile on his lips in the hope it would convey to the creature he meant it no harm.

The men stopped and looked at the reason for Yelchin's concern. The creature they saw was about half the size of the one below.

"It's only a young'un, slap it away," said Vadik.

Yelchin reached out a hand towards the creature. "It's okay I'm not going to hurt you. I just want to push you back a bit."

The creature jerked its head from side to side as it watched the hand moving closer. When the hand was almost touching it, it sniffed the tips of the fingers and then looked at Yelchin.

Yelchin stared at the creature, partly in fascination, but mostly in apprehension. When its pupils grew until they filled its eyes and an intensely bright tiny orange dot glowed in their centers, he sensed something bad was about to happen and withdrew his hand. The creature's head spun around. The large mouth that filled this side of the head opened, revealing rows of needle-sharp teeth. The creature darted forward. The mouth snapped shut on Yelchin's hand and drew back with two of his fingers in its mouth. Yelchin screamed as he recoiled. His foot slipped and the creature's head spun again. It looked at him curiously as he fell back, blood spraying from his wounded hand.

Vadik grabbed at Yelchin when he fell, but his grip slid from the man's jacket and they all watched Yelchin fall. His body crashed into the walls, breaking some of the growths on his way to the bottom.

The spider creature at the bottom walked over to the body when it landed, turned its head around and began ripping off chunks of flesh.

Babinski aimed his rifle at the small creature responsible for the man's death and fired. The small creature dodged the bullet and agilely leaped from rib to rib to avoid the trail of bullets that followed it.

"Hold your fire," shouted Brusilov. "It's too fast, you'll never hit it."

Babinski reluctantly released his finger from the trigger.

The spider creature below swallowed a piece of flesh and shrilled softly.

The clack-clacking started up again, but this time more than six bony feet were responsible. A hoard of the spider creatures emerged from the darkness at the bottom of the hole and raced up towards them.

"Move!" shouted Brusilov.

The men scrambled up the ribs.

They climbed onto the highest level and peered down at the swarm climbing ever closer. Some shrilled piercing cries, while others spun their heads and snapped their vicious jaws at the intruders.

Brusilov's gaze searched the room for an exit, but if there was one it was hidden behind the brown growths that covered the walls. He glanced down at the oncoming menace. Thirty seconds and they'd be upon them. Even fully armed they wouldn't stand a chance against so many. "Spread out and search for an exit," he ordered. "There has to be one here somewhere."

Aware they had precious little time, the men hurried around the edges of the room and peered behind the ribs of growth.

"Found one," called out Sergei.

The men rushed over.

Sergei tore the growth from around the door control and pressed the button.

The door groaned and vibrated but remained closed.

Their time ran out when the creatures poured out of the hole and rushed towards them.

*****

Talbot stared at the fast approaching obstruction that would surely derail the train and kill them both and, not for the first time since setting foot aboard the treacherous alien vessel, wished he had chosen a different profession.

Richard glanced at Talbot and noticed his worried expression. "Don't despair just yet. I have an idea. Shoot out the window." Richard stabbed the knife into the console to keep the lever in the full-speed position.

Talbot, surprised and enthused by Richard's relative calmness, raised the rifle. "Why?"

"We're climbing onto the roof, but hurry, we don't have much time."

Though not altogether agreeable to the mad plan, with the monsters blocking their only exit, Talbot could see no other option. He shot out the window.

Glass sprayed into the cab and wind whistled around them. Richard climbed across the console and stood so the top of his body protruded through the opening. He grabbed a lip formed on the roof edge and hauled himself up.

Talbot glanced at the rapidly approaching ramp as he scrambled onto the console, made the sign of the cross on his chest and climbed onto the roof. Richard was already running along the top. He set off in pursuit. The wind pressing against their backs gave an extra boost to their leaps across the gaps between carriages.

When Richard glanced behind, he saw the train had reached the ramp. The front shot up with a loud squeal as it slid up the floor. The second carriage quickly followed, as did those in line. Richard turned away and increased his sprint for the back. They might just make it. As he neared the end of the last carriage, he saw the large group of Insectoids chasing the train. There would be no escape for them this way.

Talbot caught up to him and looked at the oncoming monsters. "Now that's a hoard."

They turned when their carriage headed up the ramp.

The train sped up the incline so fast it shot off the top and crashed through a wall. Richard and Talbot dived to their stomachs to avoid the debris flying by above them and bouncing along the carriages. The train jerked and shuddered from side to side. Talbot gripped a ridge running the width of the roof to stop from sliding off. Richard wasn't so fortunate; he rolled onto his back and slid towards the edge. When he spied Talbot's feet waving in the air above his face, Richard grabbed his ankles and held on. The sound of metal being crushed and ripped apart was deafening. Talbot lifted his head. A large section of metal staircase headed straight for him. He ducked as it struck the roof a foot away and bounced over him. Richard watched the staircase shoot by and then glimpsed something high above—men standing and hanging on another higher section of staircase. It was the SEAL team. He recognized Colbert and couldn't resist flashing the shocked man a grin before he was carried from his sight as the carriage shot through the far wall of the stairwell.

*****

The SEALs had only descended one flight of stairs when the rumbling began and the staircase vibrated. Wondering what new life-threatening event was about to unfold, they stopped and peered down the stairwell. An almighty crash rippled up the walls. Metal screeched. The staircase shook so violently some of the men were thrown off their feet. Others tumbled down its treads when it collapsed. When Colbert and Cleveland were thrown over the side, their hands grabbed at the rail as the staircase stretched out like a coiled spring unwinding, bouncing the two men hanging on up and down when the stairs below them broke away.

Colbert watched it crash against the walls as it fell and far below what seemed to be a train speed by. He stared in disbelief at the person riding on its roof. It was Richard. The damn man smiled at him before being dragged out of his sight through the wall. *What was the fool playing at? I thought he wanted off this ship?*

"Was that Richard?"

Colbert looked over at Cleveland hanging a little way above him. "It was. The man's a damn curse."

When Colbert glanced below again he noticed movement. A group of strange creatures rushed over the wreckage and headed after the train. He smiled. It seemed Richard's luck had finally run out.

Lights swept over Colbert and Cleveland from above.

"Are you two okay?" called out Stedman.

"Just about," Cleveland replied.

"We're gonna climb up," called out Colbert, pulling himself up the rail, which swayed and bounced preciously with his movements.

When they reached the relative safety of the still intact part of the staircase where his men waited, Colbert shone his light at the exit they needed to reach two floors below. It was too far away to jump and they had no rope. They'd either have to find another way to reach the level or abandon the mission.

"We could use the lift shaft," Sullivan suggested. "There's a maintenance ladder running down the wall."

Colbert thought it was worth a look. "Show me."

*****

The floor of the room the train had smashed its way into collapsed when the crumpled nose of the front carriage struck. The force of the plummeting wreckage buckled the walls when it impacted with the lower floor and punched a hole through. The following carriages twisted and crumpled with screams of protest. Some flipped over other carriages, their links snapping like twigs under the strain; others crashed into the ones in front and buckled from the force.

When the carriage Richard and Talbot were still reluctant passengers on flew through the air towards the twisted crumpling wreckage disappearing into the lower levels, they glimpsed an approaching patch of floor that was still intact. They slid down the tipping carriage and jumped off. They hit the floor hard, rolled and crashed into the wall.

The carriage they had just disembarked from struck the damaged piece of floor they had sought refuge on and tumbled Richard and Talbot over the edge when it ripped free from its supports. They landed on the side of a lower carriage and burst through the window. The seats cushioned part of their fall and bounced them to the floor. They slid down the upended carriage towards the group of Insectoids gathered in a heap of entwined limbs at the bottom. Talbot reached out and grabbed a seat leg with one hand and Richard's flaying wrist with the other. When Richard had secured a hold on the seat leg opposite, Talbot released him.

Richard grinned at Talbot. "See, that wasn't so bad."

Calming down from the rush of adrenaline and the hellish ride, Talbot looked at Richard. "I'm not sure if you are brave, mad, or utterly stupid. We're no better off. We are back on the train with the monsters and this time there's no door separating us."

Richard shrugged. "I never said my plan was perfect, but we're still alive."

Talbot glanced at the mass of wriggling nightmares below as an Insectoid untangled itself from the heap of twisted bodies and pulled its limbs free. He doubted alive would be something either of them would be for very long if they remained in the train.

The Insectoid looked up and let out a clicking call before climbing the carriage. A second Insectoid, dragging two broken limbs, emerged from the group and headed up towards them.

Using the seats to haul themselves away from the oncoming monsters, Richard and Talbot climbed. By the time they had reached the top, three more Insectoids climbed after them. The two men gazed around at the mass of twisted metal and mangled carriages that formed a mountain of sharp edges they had to climb down. Progress would be slow. Talbot aimed the rifle at the nearest Insectoid and fired. The creature tumbled down the carriage, knocking two others back to the bottom. As he shifted his aim to his next target, the train lurched, forcing him to grab hold of something to stop himself from falling into the Insectoids' twig-like clutches Metal creaked and screeched as the pile of wreckage shifted before settling to the occasional clang of something falling and the groan of the ship adjusting to the new shift in weight it was forced to support.

Richard glanced up when a series of calls revealed the Insectoids below weren't the only ones they had to worry about. A group of them stood at the edge of the hole the train had punched through the wall and stared down at them. Richard stepped off the carriage and started climbing down. Talbot shouldered the rifle and followed.

*****

Colbert examined the ladder running down the wall and then directed his flashlight down the elevator shaft at the door they needed to reach three levels below. "It seems easy enough. Climb down, force open the door, and it's a short sprint to the armory. We grab as many of the alien weapons as we can and then get the hell out of here. Mission completed." He stepped back while some of the others had a look.

Though the men remained silent, Colbert knew by their expressions he wasn't fooling them any more than he was fooling himself. The shit was bound to hit the fan and they'd all receive a large face-full.

*****

Shots rang out, killing some of the monsters that swarmed towards the Russians, but all were aware no matter how many they killed they wouldn't survive the onslaught from so many.

A loud crash from above shook the room like thunder and halted the monsters.

The ribs of growth shook, dislodging pieces that landed on the floor and bounced down the sides of the hole. The ceiling groaned. The agitated alien arachnids jerked their heads back and forth as they screamed short shrills, as if they were communicating.

Rozovsky joined the others at sharing their gazes between the halted creatures and the ceiling. "What's happening?"

It was a question none of them could answer.

A series of deafening crashes, clangs and screeches of metal foreshadowed the collapse of the ceiling that buckled before it gave way. Something appeared and, for a brief moment, hung poised above them before it dropped.

To avoid being crushed by the falling juggernaut and its accompanying wreckage, the creatures dived back into the hole and raced down the strange rib growths.

The train nose-dived after them.

Pieces of wreckage rained down around the men who pressed themselves tighter against the walls and watched the carriage dragged behind follow the front part of the train into the hole. The next carriage clipped the edge of the floor hole and tipped to the side, coming to a rest against the edge of the gaping hole it had forced through the ceiling. After a few minutes the falling debris ended. The carriage, the floor and the ceiling groaned as all settled.

The shocked Russians looked at each other.

Vadik grinned at his comrades. "I've been surprised by many things almost impossible to believe since setting foot aboard this alien ship, but I have to say, a train coming through the ceiling to save us, fuck me, I didn't expect that."

Momentarily forgetting the constant death and danger that stalked them, the others smiled at their good fortune.

Babinski took a step nearer the battered carriage. "I wonder where it came from."

Vadik stuck his head through one of the broken windows and gazed up the carriage. It was bent, buckled and full of sharp edges. It would be a brutal climb, but doable. He pulled his head out. "To use an American expression, let's not look a gift horse in the mouth, it saved us and has also provided us with an exit."

"Not more climbing," groaned Sergei.

Vadik gazed back into the carriage when something scraped the side. A head rose into view and before he could back away or defend himself, the Insectoid jumped through the window and knocked him to the ground. A blur of twisted twig-like limbs adorned with thorny tips, frantically slashed and stabbed at his body and face. Vadik's pain-wracked screams and convulsions ended when a spike entered his ear and pierced his brain.

The attack had happened so quickly, his shocked comrades barely had time to react before the monster turned on them. It leaped at Babinski. The Insectoid exploded in a spray of bullets. When it fell to the ground Rozovsky continued firing. Blood erupted from the wounds and limbs were sliced from its body. When the weapon ran out of ammo Rozovsky struck the monster repeatedly with the rifle butt, crushing its head to pulp.

Nikolay placed a hand on the man's shoulder. "That's enough Rozovsky, it's dead."

Rozovsky removed the flashlight from the rifle and let the gore-stained weapon clatter to the floor.

With weapons raised and senses on high alert, Mikhail, Sergei and Brusilov approached the carriage and peered inside.

Mikhail climbed through a window and glanced at the tangled heap of dead Insectoids and then up the wrecked carriage. "That seems to have been the only live one."

Brusilov glanced over at Babinski knelt besides Vadik's body. "You okay, Babinski?"

Babinski climbed to his feet. "I won't be until we leave this damned place."

"Well, hold it together and hopefully we soon will be." Brusilov cast a sad gaze at his dead comrade before he crossed to the train and peered inside as he worked out their next move. He glanced briefly at the dead Insectoids before gazing up the length of the carriage. At the top he spied another carriage they might be able to pass through, but beyond that wreckage blocked his sight. Another comrade dead and they were still nowhere near to finishing the mission. How many more would die before they left what was fast becoming their tomb. He briefly considered abandoning the hunt for alien weapons, but if he did, he argued, the men's deaths would have been in vain. At least if their mission was successful their lives would have had some purpose, and they still had to find a way back to the exit because they couldn't return the way they had come.

"What do you think, Captain, do we go up?"

Brusilov glanced at Sergei. "We do. Everyone in..." An ominous rasp of metal cut short his order.

They all turned towards the sound and peered at the door that opened.

"Looks like we won't have to climb after all," said Sergei, happily.

Nikolay and Mikhail moved to the doorway and peered through into the corridor. Though dark and unwelcoming, it was for as far as they could see, free from any blockage or monsters.

Nikolay looked back at the Captain. "It seems clear."

"Then we'll take it." Brusilov headed for the door and led his men along the corridor.

*****

As Richard neared the bottom of the treacherous pile of scrap, he paused on sighting an orange glow filtering into the darkness below. Though unsure of its cause, it gave him something to head for. Light was welcoming in this world of dark shadows and the monsters that dwelled among them. He shot a glance at Talbot a few feet away and then shifted his gaze to the Insectoids moving across the mishmash of jumbled metal forms as agile as any mountain goat; they would soon be upon them. When the wreckage shifted again and sent loose sections of metal and pieces of ripped off train sliding down the pile, the two men kept climbing.

A thick metal beam, previously hanging by a thread of sheared and twisted metal, fell from the upper room. It smashed into the carriage balanced precariously against the wall and sent it sliding into the hole. It crumpled loudly when it collided with the carriage lying at an angle on top of the wreckage mountain and screeched down its length before smashing into the carriage Richard and Talbot had recently vacated. It slid to the side and rolled down towards the two men. Unable to tolerate the additional strain, the floor supporting the massive weight of the train wreck and collapsed levels succumbed to the pressure and dropped away.

Though the terrible screams of tormented, shifting metal alerted them to the fresh danger, it was impossible for the two men climbing down the collapsing wreckage to move any faster. Every foot and handhold had to be carefully picked to avoid the many razor-sharp edges and unstable supports. They both clung to a thick metal beam as they rode the wave of shifting debris.

"Look out!" shouted Talbot.

Richard spun his head at the warning and saw the carriage rolling towards them. The creatures in its path jumped onto it and over to the far side to avoid being crushed, an acrobatic feat Richard and Talbot were incapable of doing.

His face a mask of alarm, Talbot raised his weapon and glanced at Richard. "The windows!"

Richard stared at the tumbling train anxiously. Its windows already covered in cracks, exploded when Talbot sprayed them with bullets.

Talbot climbed to his feet and glanced at Richard. "Get ready."

Though Richard doubted he would ever be ready for what was coming, he stood on shaking legs and watched the tumbling train bounce and slide nearer.

"Now!" Talbot ran up the metal beam and dived through a window.

Mumbling a prayer to a god he believed had stopped listening to his pleas long ago, Richard copied Talbot and dived into the train.

They slid across the floor and grabbed at a seat leg when the carriage rolled over. The men hung from the seat supports and then slammed into the side as the carriage continued tumbling until it came to an abrupt halt when it collided with the wall below. The force tore Richard's hands from the metal leg and shot him through the window he had entered a few moments before. His shoulder struck the wall and he slid to the ground. As the carriage rocked, Talbot released his hold and slid to the side. Click-clacks on the carriage reminded him of the pursuing creatures. He glanced up when they moved across the cracked windows above him that splintered with their weight, increasing the length of the many cracks. Talbot climbed out as an Insectoid fell through. Glass tinkled to the ground around the Insectoid as it moved after its prey.

Talbot grabbed Richard's arm, yanked him to his feet and dragged him through the triangle gap left by the train leaning against the wall. More creatures entered the carriage while others ran along the roof. One leaped at the two men. Talbot poked the rifle at it and pulled the trigger. The creature's head exploded, showering him with blood. The dead creature slammed into Richard's back, sending him screaming to the ground.

A swift kick from Talbot's boot sent the Insectoid's corpse flying. "Get up, there's more coming." Looking past Richard, he spied the orange light seeping through grimy glass. If there were windows, there might be a door.

As they fled, another section of floor gave way. The carriage tilted away from the wall and dropped into the hole with a loud crash. Some of the creatures still onboard jumped off; others not quick enough rode it down. Richard shoulder-barged the one that landed beside him and rose up on its rear spindly legs, knocking it into the hole and almost followed it down before he regained his balance. Another Insectoid a foot away snarled at him. Richard stamped on one of its legs, snapping it with a loud, satisfying crack. The creature screeched in pain. Richard followed through with a kick to its head. As the creature toppled back, Richard dodged past and ran.

Talbot shot two more Insectoids, killing one and wounding the other. When he leaped over the wounded creature writhing on the ground, it snapped at him; he slammed the rifle butt at its head, breaking its jaw. He landed awkwardly and almost tripped over the Insectoid Richard had injured. It lunged at him, but a bullet ended its attack.

Three Insectoids that had been dragged into the hole by the falling carriage appeared over the edge. Talbot kicked one back into the hole as the other two leaped at him. A scream rang out. One of the creatures splattered against the wall. Talbot clubbed the other with the rifle. It dropped to the floor, landing half over the edge. As it scrambled back up, Talbot stamped on its head. Its hard head-shell split. Blood and brain seeped from the cracks.

Talbot glanced up at Richard, who panted heavily, a metal bar in his hand dripping Insectoid blood. Talbot nodded. "Thanks."

"You're welcome, and so is the light and rifle." Richard smiled and turned around.

The remaining Insectoids rushed after the fleeing men.

Bathed in orange glow, the two men peered through the windows when they passed. Their gazes picked out a row of transparent containers along one wall that emitted the light. Inside each were dark, indistinct forms.

Richard almost wept in relief when he saw the open door a short distance beyond the windows. He halted outside and looked back when a shot rang out. Talbot had killed another Insectoid, but more scurried down the still falling wreckage and along the floor in pursuit. It would be close; they were fast little buggers. He nipped inside the room and held a hand over the door control. As soon as Talbot's form filled the doorway, he pressed the button. Nothing happened. Two more frantic thumps produced the same lack of action. He groaned. The spaceship was toying with them again.

Talbot's eyes scanned the room. Two strides brought him to a metal table. He gripped an end and dragged it towards the door. The objects on top vibrated and rolled off, some fragile items smashing on contact with the floor. Insectoids, their almost primordial features highlighted in the orange glow, scampered past the windows. Richard rushed over and grabbed the other end of the table. Together they upended it and shoved it over the opening just as the creatures arrived. The table rocked when they crashed into it.

"Find something to jam it in place," shouted Talbot.

Richard backed away and cast his eyes around the room. There was nothing suitable. One of the creatures appeared at the window and watched Richard move through the room. When his toe stubbed something, Richard looked down at the warped floor panel. He hooked his fingers under one end and raised it. It was metal, about eighteen inches wide and eight feet long; it might just do the trick. He dragged it over to the door and rested one end against the table. Talbot helped him jam it under the strengthening bar that ran across the middle of the table's underside.

Ready to slam his weight back against the table if it moved, Talbot backed away. Lacking the body mass to dislodge the prop, the creatures' attempts to break down the barricade failed.

For a few moments Richard and Talbot stared through the windows at the wreckage still slipping into the lower levels. Slowly the main bulk settled and loose pieces rolled and slid as they sought new resting positions.

Richard turned away and sat by one of the containers. "I need to rest before we carry on. I don't have the benefit of your army training."

Talbot glanced around the room. "Believe me, none of my training remotely prepared for this."

When Talbot noticed two of the transparent pods along the wall by the door were broken, he walked over and peered inside. Except for the layer of reddish-brown dust that also covered everything in the room, it was empty. The next container was cracked with a small hole near the bottom. He wiped a hand on the surface to clear a patch and peered inside. A jumble of thin bones and tiny skulls he thought matched the Insectoids lay at the bottom of the tank—baby monsters. The next tank in line was intact and full of orange, semi-transparent liquid. He brushed a patch clean and looked inside. Suspended from tubes were Insectoids. Though smaller than those that had chased them—the biggest here was only about ten inches long—they looked no less formidable. He glanced at Richard.

"Are these things inside alive?"

"Probably. We found a room full of specimens and they seemed to be in some sort of induced hibernation. Some escaped when the ship crashed and infested parts of the ship."

Talbot glanced at the broken container absent any bones and then at the door the creatures continued to scratch at. "What is this place?"

"Does it matter?" said Richard. He had given up trying to fathom the reasons for the strange rooms he had passed through. He was just thankful that for the moment nothing was trying to eat them and he could rest. He doubted it would last. He watched Talbot cross the room, examining everything he passed. "If you find any weapons, I get first choice."

"It seems more like a laboratory than a room where you'd find weapons." Talbot walked past the strange pieces of equipment that lined the countertop around two sides of the room, without coming to any conclusions as to their use. The instruments and unusual tools, most of which had sharp or serrated edges, but too unwieldy to use as weapons, reminded him of medical instruments of the type a mortician would use. He turned towards the tapping at the window. An Insectoid drummed on the glass and stared straight at him. Talbot crossed to the window and placed his face close to the creature's ugly head.

Richard climbed to his feet. "It's probably best not to antagonize them."

Talbot looked at him. "Don't worry; I doubt they'll be able to break the window." When he turned back to the window the creature had gone. A loud bang echoed through the room when an Insectoid crashed into the glass. Talbot yelled in surprise as he recoiled. As soon as it dropped from view, another Insectoid slammed into the glass.

Both men stared at the crack that formed and snaked across the window when a third one struck. They backed away and crossed to the door on the far side. Thankfully, it opened and closed again when they had passed through.

Talbot was going to say they were safe now, but thought better of it. He doubted it was true. He was finally becoming aware of the spaceship's ability to throw one surprise after another at those who dared to trespass within.

*****

Sullivan led the men down the ladder and after the elevator doors had been forced apart on the level they needed to access, they stepped through into the darkness and roamed flashlights around the area an exact copy of the level above.

When Ramirez crossed to the central stairwell where the broken spiral staircase above swung slightly with a groan of metal, he noticed the floor sloped down slightly. It was evidence the train wreck had damaged more than just the stairs. He dropped a flare and noticed two of the strange twiggy monsters they had glimpsed earlier move through its devilish glow.

Colbert looked over at the corridor directly opposite the elevator. The armory should be about one hundred feet along it on the right. He glanced back at the elevator shaft, their only known means of exit. It might also provide them with a shortcut to the hangar level if they could climb past the elevator. Then they would be able to avoid the medical facility and the monsters that dwelled there and not waste precious time looking for a route around it.

"It looks clear," called out Sullivan.

Colbert glanced over at Sullivan and the corridor highlighted by his flashlight. "Cleveland, remain here to keep our exit open and protect our backs. The rest of you with me."

"Don't forget to grab me some of those alien weapons," Cleveland called out, as the men headed along the passage.

The SEALs halted at the armory door, which was a little larger than normal. Though the corridor lights were off, the tiny light on the door panel indicated it still had power. After the men had stood back and aimed their weapons at the door, Crowe pressed the button. The door rasped open to reveal a small chamber and six-feet away another door that wouldn't have looked out of place protecting a bank vault. A light flickered on when they entered. While Stedman, Crowe and Sullivan guarded the corridor, Colbert and Ramirez approached the impressive door.

"This could be a problem," stated Ramirez, running a hand over the cold metal.

Colbert had reached the same conclusion. To have come so far, faced so much and lost a good friend, their mission now seemed doomed to failure. He crossed to a small control console on a side wall. With the inclusion of the alien hand-shape recessed into the top, it was obviously a hand scanner and the door could only be opened by those authorized to do so. With nothing to lose, he placed his hand in the larger alien crew size indent. A green light lit up his hand and buzzed for a moment before turning red. The door remained closed. He stepped aside as Ramirez unwrapped a roll of tools taken from his rucksack and watched him begin dismantling the device. The ship was too fragile to risk blowing open the door, though they would have to try if Ramirez failed to jury rig it.

*****

Cleveland turned away from staring down the corridor the men had taken and walked around the room, checking all the other corridor exits were clear of anything creeping up on him. As he passed the open elevator a sound halted him and focused his light and gaze on the dark opening. Though he thought it was probably nothing but his nerves reading danger into an innocent sound, he took a few steps nearer and cocked an ear at the deep shaft. Though the clicking and scratching sounds were faint, they couldn't be ignored. They didn't want to encounter any surprises when it was time to leave. A few more steps brought him to the edge of the long drop. He listened again, but this time heard nothing out of the ordinary. To double-check, he leaned forward and shone his light into the shaft. The beam highlighted the walls descending into the darkness, but nothing else. Something warm, wet and slightly viscous splattered on his hand. The threat of danger tilted his gaze upwards. The Insectoid assassin perched on the wall above dropped. Cleveland lashed out with the rifle but the creature's surprise attack had caught him off guard. It crashed into him and knocked him into the shaft. His head struck the wall with enough force to crack his skull and plunge him into unconsciousness.

The Insectoid abandoned the falling body for the wall and climbed back up.

*****

It took Ramirez almost three minutes of probing and cross-connecting the strange cabling before he hit lucky and the red light turned green. When the door swung silently open, bright white lights flashed on along the room's length and highlighted the racks of impressive alien weapons lining both long walls. The two men entered and let their excited gazes wander over the strange weaponry.

Colbert smiled. "Christmas has arrived early this year."

They walked past the racks and admired the weapons for a few moments before Ramirez selected a type of rifle. He examined the controls briefly before locating the switch to turn it on concealed behind a small sliding cover and powered up the weapon. He turned a dial marked with increasing larger dots to one midrange and aimed the weapon at the door opposite to the one they had entered. A squeeze of the trigger sent a small blue ball of light that grew to a foot across as it flew the length of the room before exploding in a bright flash on the door. "Well, they work. Now all we have to do is decide which ones to take and how many."

Leaving Crowe guarding the corridor, Sullivan and Stedman entered and gazed in amazement at the alien weaponry.

"We'll have to keep our assault rifles as we need the lights," said Stedman, running a hand lovingly over one of the sleek rifles.

Ramirez walked farther along the racks. "I suggest we pick a selection, two rifles each and a couple of the smaller pistol types."

"I agree," said Colbert. "We can't afford to burden ourselves with too many."

While the men each chose their weapons, Colbert again tried to contact Control, but without success. It was time to put operation Phoenix into action. "Ramirez, once you've picked out what you're taking, set the explosives." Colbert walked the room choosing from the types on offer ones he could easily carry.

Stedman opened a metal box and peered inside at the transparent globes set in soft hollowed out compartments. "Commander, I think these might be alien grenades."

Colbert joined Stedman and took the globe he handed him. He stared at the purple haze filling the globe before handing it back. "Leave them. It might be some type of chemical weapon and we could end up gassing ourselves."

Stedman returned the globe carefully to its compartment and closed the lid.

When Sullivan had selected all he could carry comfortably, he swapped places with Crowe in the corridor so the man could choose his own.

When they all had alien weapons—including some for Cleveland—the men left the room.

Colbert approached Ramirez, who was busy connecting thin yellow cables to a timer. "All set, Ramirez?"

"I just need to know what time to set."

"Twenty minutes should give us enough time to get clear. I'd like more, but as we don't know how far away the Russians are, I can't take the risk."

Ramirez set the timer for twenty minutes and started the countdown.

"I think we may have a problem, Commander," said Sullivan when Colbert exited the weapon store. "Stedman called out to Cleveland but he didn't reply."

Colbert glanced along the corridor. "Assume there's a threat and be ready to retaliate, but we can't afford to hang about as in twenty minutes this level won't exist."

The men moved along the corridor with cautious haste and entered the lobby with their weapons and lights sweeping the circular room, but found no sign of Cleveland.

"Cleveland," called out Sullivan in a loud whisper.

As they crossed the room, they searched the floor for blood splatters or any other evidence of what might have happened to Cleveland.

Stedman focused his attention on the elevator and as he drew near his light aimed through the doors picked out a red splash on the shaft wall. "There's blood here."

Colbert joined him and stared at the fresh blood and the dark opening. He glanced at Stedman. "Cover me."

Stedman was joined by the others and they aimed their weapons at the opening. Colbert stood to one side of the elevator and leaned forward so he could peer inside. He sensed movement above and dodged back. Bullets struck the Insectoid that dropped into view. It shot against the far wall of the shaft and dropped from sight.

Colbert checked above the opening to ensure no more were lurking in ambush before peering down the shaft. Though he couldn't see anything, he sensed something was coming. He glanced back at his men. "Anyone have a flare?"

Sullivan fished one from his pocket.

Colbert struck it and dropped it into the shaft.

As it fell its bright red glow highlighted the Insectoids climbing the four sides of the shaft. It was a vision of demons escaping from hell.

"Monsters!" Colbert shouted. He aimed his rifle at the nearest and fired. It screeched and followed the flare to the bottom.

Sullivan and Stedman swapped their assault rifles for alien weapons, switched them on and rushed forward. The balls of light lit up the darkness and picked out the evil faces of the approaching creatures. A light ball punched a neat hole through an Insectoids head before exploding in a bright flash against the shaft wall. The second passed through two creatures before exploding.

Colbert aimed his light up the shaft and focused on the bottom of the elevator and the gap between it and the ladder. He turned to his men. "We're going to climb past the elevator. Ramirez, do you have any explosives left?"

Ramirez nodded. "I kept a little back in case we needed to blast our way through a blockage."

"Set charges on whatever's holding the elevator in place and get ready to blow it when we're all clear."

Sullivan raised his eyebrows skeptically. "Are you sure that's wise with the ship being so unstable?"

"I can't see what other choice we have now we've set the explosives back there. If the collapsing ship doesn't kill us, those monsters definitely will."

Ramirez glanced below as he stepped onto the ladder. The monsters on all four sides of the shaft were a hellish sight. The captain was right; it was worth the risk. He stepped onto the ladder and climbed.

Stedman and Crowe followed him up.

Colbert fired a few shots at the monsters, halting them four levels below, before climbing after Stedman. By pressing their bodies flat against the ladder it was possible for them to squeeze past the elevator.

When Colbert rose above it, he saw his men continuing to climb and Sullivan opening a door a few levels above. He glanced at Ramirez. "All set?"

Ramirez nodded and held up a remote detonator. "Just say the word."

Screeches from below filled the shaft.

When they had all reached the higher door, Colbert nodded to Ramirez. "Blow it."

Ramirez peered down at the creatures that squeezed around the edge of the elevator and pressed the button on the remote.

The small explosions echoed up the shaft. The elevator fell. Monsters screeched as they were crushed or knocked back down the shaft.

After Stedman and Crowe had picked off the couple that had climbed past the elevator, the door was forced shut.

Colbert glanced around the stairwell chamber. "Now all we have to do is find our way back to the exit."

*****

The Russian salvage team had been following the sounds of gunfire when the explosion rumbled through the ship and halted them. All stared along the corridor the sound had originated from.

"It has to be the American salvage team," realized Nikolay. "It wasn't a big explosion, so it might indicate they have just blown a door open."

Brusilov glanced at his chief engineer. "Perhaps the door to the armory?"

Nikolay shrugged.

They continued on and after a few turns entered a corridor tainted with the residue of explosives in the air. Alert for danger, they silently moved forward and stopped at the entrance to the armory.

After hearing no sounds of anyone inside, Brusilov stepped nearer while the others guarded the corridor. When Brusilov's eyes swept along the racks of weapons, his smile faded to dismay on seeing the packs of explosives distributed throughout the room. When he followed the yellow cables to the timer readout that had reached fourteen seconds, he rushed from the room shouting, "Explosives, RUN!"

CHAPTER 25

Cargo salvage

WHILE SOME OF his men followed the bulldozer towing the cargo ship through the tunnel, Joe McNally led the others over to the airlock that led to the cargo bay. The constant delay of opening and closing the two airlock doors would drastically slow down the salvaging of the alien stores. He turned to his electrical wizard. "Kirby, do you think it's possible to have both sets of doors open at the same time?"

Kirby, never one to shy away from a challenge, headed for the control panel. "If the aliens' electrical system is based on the same principle as ours, then it should be simple enough to override the safety controls."

"Okay good, see what you can do. The rest of you come with me."

The five men passed through the airlock into the cargo bay and wandered over to the nearest stack of cargo containers.

The thousands of storage pods stacked in neat rows were all exactly the same size, seven-foot-seven-inch cube whose sides slotted into each other to form a strong rigid structure. Each was labeled with alien text and color-coded with a stripe along each surface and all pods of the same color were grouped together. Access to the contents was via double-doors fastened by a hexagon catch that turned to release the lock.

McNally opened the first one he came to, which was marked with a green stripe. Inside was a neatly folded bundle of some kind of tough plastic similar to Mylar.

"It's a temporary shelter," stated Jason Kendrick.

McNally turned to the man who had spoken. "How could you possibly know that?"

Kendrick pointed at the diagram fixed to the inside of the open door. "That was the clue."

The men examined the small poster. Though the alien text was illegible, the image of a large oblong habitat with rounded edges, an arched roof and what seemed to be solar panels distributed across its surface was understood by all.

Larry Schaefer, the NASA technician assigned to appraise the alien artifacts and assign their salvage priority, pointed at the two labeled storage crate diagrams beside the habitat image.

"It seems three crates are needed to complete a single habitat. Apart from living accommodations, they probably include workshops, science labs and much more—in fact everything the alien crew needed to set up a temporary base until more permanent structures could be built."

Thinking the design might be adaptable to use as their own temporary habitats on far-flung planets they might explore, Schaefer stepped back and ran his eyes over the symbols marking the nearby containers and pointed some out. "We'll take these nine for starters."

While the others moved on down the row, McNally turned to the waiting forklift drivers and pointed out the selected crates. The three forklifts moved towards the indicated crates and started lifting them free.

McNally rejoined his men, who had opened one of the yellow-striped containers.

Schaefer pulled out one of the smaller boxes formed from a rigid type of plastic that filled the internal space snugly. Inside were neatly folded pieces of linen. They opened a selection of the smaller boxes and found items that seemed to be general everyday wares the crew would need to cook, clothe and exist on a strange new world. Though it wasn't the technology they looked for, Schaefer selected six at random to be salvaged and moved on.

McNally sprayed a red circle on the six selected crates and pointed them out to one of the forklift drivers before moving on.

Schaefer gazed at the rows of containers. It would take weeks to search through them all. They had a few hours, a day or two at the most if they were lucky.

As if reading his mind, McNally suggested they split up and each choose a different coloured crate to examine until they found what they searched for—advanced alien technology. Schaefer agreed and the men spread out.

"I think I found what we're looking for," called out Juan Quintero a few moments later.

McNally and Schaefer crossed to the open container marked with a black stripe where Quintero waited and looked into the smaller box he had opened. Set in a foam-type lining were pieces of machinery of various shapes that hinted they might fit together to make a single piece.

Inspired by the find, Schaefer selected another box that was heavier than he expected. He glanced at Quintero. "Give me a hand."

They lifted out the box, laid it on the floor and opened it. Inside were rows of strange tubes dotted with chunky protrusions and what seemed to be a line of lights along the top.

Schaefer resealed the crate. "It's definitely alien technology. We'll concentrate our efforts on salvaging the black containers first and if we get time, a random selection of the rest."

"I'll go inform the forklift drivers." As McNally headed across the room and felt the the increased movements of the iceberg that had him worried, he wondered how long they had before they were forced to evacuate.

After he had informed the drivers to start shifting the black storage pods, McNally crossed to the airlock and noticed both the cargo bay and hangar doors were open.

Molten metal sparks sprayed from the portable welder Kirby was using to fix the doors in place.

"Good job, Kirby," praised McNally, avoiding staring directly at the intense arc light.

Kirby stood from his crouch and pushed the dark welding visor over his head. "That's the last one. I welded all the doors open so if any safety feature kicks in they won't be able to close on us."

"Good idea. With both doors open it'll speed up the salvaging process."

He glanced over at the two forklifts heading back from depositing their loads outside. Ricky Cassidy stood on the step plate of the lead one. Cassidy jumped off before the forklift drove through the airlock and joined McNally. "There are two high cube containers outside waiting to be filled."

McNally nodded. "Did the cargo shuttle make it aboard the ship safely?"

"Yeah, the wind blew it about a bit, but other than that no problem. The others are just tidying up outside and then they'll come and help."

"We could have done with a few more forklifts. There are so many crates we'll never salvage them all."

"Now the two smaller spaceships are safely onboard the ship, everything else is a bonus," said Cassidy.

"I know, but we'll never get this opportunity again and to not be able to save everything, well...you know..."

"Yeah, I know." Cassidy started heading towards the airlock. "But saving as much as we can is all we can do." He entered the cargo bay.

As McNally walked over to the ice tunnel, he glanced at the remaining cargo shuttles. It was a shame they didn't have time to save another one, but those with a higher pay grade than him thought they only needed one and with the time constraint thrust upon them it was thought any other alien technology they could salvage would prove just as important. He pulled out his radio and made his report to the command ship.

CHAPTER 26

Alone Again

RICHARD'S GAZE FOLLOWED the flashlight beam Talbot swept around the dark chamber. Powerless screens atop the many workstations positioned around the room where some of the crew once carried out their allotted tasks had not seen any activity for thousands of years. It was though, surprisingly clean and almost dust free, hinting the air pumped into the room might pass through a filtering process. Strange pieces of machinery that hung from the ceiling with drooping cables attached were as dormant as every other object in the room.

Set around the walls were tall transparent cylinders. Though most were empty, a few contained a fluid that reacted with a blue glow when Talbot's light fell on them, highlighting the hazy shapes of the nightmarish creatures imprisoned inside.

"Another laboratory," stated Talbot as he walked across the room.

Richard glanced back at the door the Insectoids scratched at. Though he believed they were safe he wasn't about to take any chances and had little interest in the room's function. "We need to find an exit."

Talbot had already noticed one and aimed his light at the door on the far side of the room. "Will that one do?"

"Believe me, I'm not fussy." Richard headed for the exit. He pressed the door control and took a few steps back, leaving Talbot alone to face any danger that might present itself.

Talbot shook his head at Richard and stepped through the opening into a small room with walls covered in what seemed to be electrical apparatus of some kind. Levers, yellow coils, cables and tubes covered every surface except the floor.

"Is it safe?" asked Richard, poking his head nervously around the edge of the frame.

"If by safe you mean is it free of monsters, then yes." Talbot took a few steps farther into the room and shone the weapon light along the offshoot of the L-shaped room. A metal ladder led down to a lower level and another ladder on the far wall reached up to a small platform and a door.

"Is that the only exit?"

Talbot, who hadn't heard Richard approach, was surprised he was so close. "I think so."

Richard reached out and pushed the rifle barrel down so the light pierced the darkness of the lower level. "It doesn't look very inviting down there."

Talbot snatched the rifle from Richard's grasp. "Then it matches the rest of this hellish spaceship. If you want you can go back and look for another route, but I'm taking that one."

Going alone wasn't something Richard was going to do without a weapon or a flashlight, so he followed the owner of both down the first ladder.

A quick sweep of the lower level by Talbot who moved towards the far ladder revealed nothing but inanimate pipes and cables. Just as he stepped on the ladder, the ship trembled and rocked slightly. Something metallic clattered to the floor loudly on the upper level behind him. Talbot almost stumbled to the ground when Richard barged him aside and spurted up the ladder.

Talbot shook his head in dismay. If Richard was ever on a sinking ship he would totally ignore the rule of women and children first and probably grab the best lifeboat for himself and leave the others to their doom. Talbot climbed. When he stepped onto the platform he noticed Richard standing by the door with a hand hovering by the control.

"You ready?" Richard asked.

Talbot aimed the weapon loosely at the door and nodded.

Remaining safely to one side, Richard stared at the door that rasped open with a hesitant grind of metal.

Talbot, also focused on the steadily widening gap, peered at the darkness it opened onto and raised the light. He was about to step nearer when a sound halted him; distant thuds on metal at first hardly distinguishable above the constant groaning of the ship.

When Richard noticed Talbot's concerned expression, he whispered, "What is it?"

Talbot took a step nearer the door. The thuds, louder now, came from along the corridor the door opened onto. When something entered the flashlight beam, he raised the weapon to his shoulder and fired. Four shots rang out before the gun emptied.

"Shit!" Talbot cursed. He looked at Richard with fear in his eyes. "Close the damn door."

Dread greeted Richard again as his hand punched the button, but it was too late.

Something leaped through the closing door at Talbot and swiped claws savagely across the man's chest. Talbot screamed. The monster crashed into him and sent them both to the floor. Richard looked on in horror as the monster took a bite out of Talbot's arm that had lashed out in an attempt to knock his attacker off.

Blotting out the man's pain-wracked screams while he took stock of the situation, Richard froze and watched the monster that had its back to him. For the moment, it hadn't noticed him, but it would if he opened the door. He glanced at the weapon that had dropped from Talbot's grasp and lay on the floor on the far side of the monster. Though it was now useless, the flashlight attached to it wasn't. Hardly daring to breathe lest the monster detect the sound, Richard took a cautious step nearer. He would get only one chance. If his hastily concocted plan failed, the monster would soon be enjoying a second course of human flesh.

Timing his footsteps with the grisly sounds of flesh being ripped and devoured and Talbot's pain-filled screams, Richard approached from behind the feeding monster. He froze when the monster stopped chewing and cocked an ear. It raised its head slightly and sniffed the air. As its head turned, Richard rushed forward and lashed out a foot savagely. The blow landed on the monster's back with enough force to send it toppling down to the lower level. It screeched when it fell and thudded onto the floor below.

Surprised his plan had worked so well, Richard scooped up the weapon.

"Help me."

Richard glanced at Talbot and saw the pain etched on the man's face and the pleading look in his eyes. It was obvious from the man's wounds he was seriously injured and without medical attention wouldn't last long. Richard wasn't prepared to risk his life helping someone who had nothing to offer and stood little chance of surviving.

Richard shook his head. "Sorry, Talbot, dragging you through the ship will slow down my escape."

Richard peered over the edge as the monster struggled to its feet. It looked up at him, howled a chilling rumbling growl and jumped onto the ladder. As it climbed, Richard rushed for the door, opened it and slipped through. He punched the button and stared at the monster that appeared at the top of the ladder. Richard gripped the door and tried to slide it shut faster when the monster rushed at him. When its clawed hand poked through the gap, Richard slammed the butt of the rifle down on it. Bone cracked. The monster shrieked and withdrew its claw. The edge of the door slid into its frame.

Though he believed the monster would finish feeding on Talbot before giving chase, buying him some precious time, he wasn't certain. Worried it might open the door and come after him, Richard fled along the corridor. He was on his own again, which came as no surprise. Though he would have preferred Talbot not to have been killed, he wasn't going to waste time mourning the man. Richard had more important things to worry about: his own survival and escape from the ship.

*****

EV1L drifted into the ghostly blue-lit corridor and stared after the distant slaps of the fleeing two-legs' feet on the floor. Whatever it was it moved faster than EV1L could in its current weakened state. It turned its attention briefly to other matters. The spaceship it was trapped within was moving, but the gentle throb of the engine that normally travelled through the superstructure was strangely absent. The constant agonized sounds the ship emitted were a good indication it was under stress. Though EV1L had no idea of the cause, it sensed the ship was dying and it would be advantageous to its continued existence if it wasn't still aboard when the vessel uttered its final death rattle. But first it had to eat. It concentrated its hearing in the opposite direction of the two-legs' flight, but heard nothing to alert him to any nearby prey. He gazed back along the corridor when the two-legs' running footsteps stopped and went to investigate.

*****

After running for about five minutes, Lucy paused and panting heavily gazed back along the corridor. Comforted by the lack of any sounds of the recently freed creature's pursuit, she approached the open door ahead and gazed into the room highlighted by the blue corridor lights. It was another of the crew's quarters that seemed to be distributed all over the ship, perhaps to make it more convenient for certain crew members to be closer to whatever duties they had to perform until their ill-fated voyage had taken a turn for the worse. When she was certain it was free of monsters, she stepped inside. She would have preferred to close the door, but that would plunge the room in unwelcoming darkness. Resting her tired body on one of the chairs at the table against the wall, she placed one of the weapons and the spear down while she examined the other futuristic pistol. If she could find out how the weapons worked, they would help protect her against the spaceship's vicious inhabitants.

Lights came on when she turned a dial. Unsure what would happen when she pulled the trigger, she crossed to the door and aimed the weapon along the corridor. Her finger stretched around the trigger, which was a little awkward as it had been designed for bigger hands than hers, and pulled. A startled yelp sprung from her lips when a small red sphere of bright light shot from the gun and travelled down the corridor until it exploded in a bright flash against the far wall. She turned the dial a couple of clicks and fired again. The yellow ball of intense light grew as it travelled away until it reached a width of about two feet. It too exploded against the far wall. Lucy smiled as her eyes adjusted back to the gloomy interior. Nothing could stand in her way now.

A check of the other weapon revealed it was also operational. The two functioning weapons boosted her confidence, but she still needed a portable light of some type. From her past wanderings through the ship she knew not every corridor or room would be illuminated; light was as essential as a weapon if she was going to survive.

Her gaze around the room rested on the tall cupboards along one side of the room. Though she thought it unlikely, they might contain the alien equivalent to a flashlight; she had nothing to lose. There were no handles but when she pressed one of the doors, it swished open. A light source remained elusive after she had searched the contents, but she did find something that might prove useful—some alien clothing. She held up a type of shirt or jacket. There were no buttons or zips; it was worn by pulling it over your head. She slipped it on and pushed her arms through the sleeves. Though far too large, Lucy thought with a few minor adjustments she could design something that fit better.

She grabbed the spear and after trimming off some sections was about to try it on again, when she spied the toilet and shower compartment. Layers of grime and monster blood covered her like a second skin, and her hair was matted with all manner of foul gunk. The irresistible urge to be clean again drove her decision. She crossed to the shower room and turned the lever she found on the wall. Though only a small amount of cold water dribbled from the large circular showerhead, it was better than nothing.

Lucy poked her head out into the corridor and listened. Only the familiar groans and creaks of the ship disturbed the silence. Though she knew it was risky and reckless—anything could be heading towards her—the seed of cleanliness had been firmly planted and too alluring to resist. She collected a piece of clothing from a cupboard to use as a towel, grabbed one of the alien pistols and went to have a shower.

*****

As Richard fled through the industrial-themed corridor and leaped over the fallen ceiling panels and beams, he kept the flashlight aimed in front to light his way. The lines of cables attached to the walls and those hanging from the ceiling he dodged around reminded him of the tentacles responsible for dragging him into these hell-spawned levels. He shook that particular nightmare away and concentrated on the one he currently experienced. He had lost all sense of direction and had no way of knowing if he was heading for the front or back of the ship or crossing its width. Trusting his luck that had kept him alive thus far, he ignored all side turnings and doors and continued straight ahead.

After rounding a few corners, Richard slowed on sighting a red glow ahead and halted a short distance away. The fearful chill that shivered through his body set his alarm bells tinkling. His eyes scanned the area ahead for movement, but all seemed still. He spun and aimed the flashlight back the way he had come, but it was absent the approaching menace he had imagined creeping up on him.

With his nerves so far on edge they were plummeting down the side of a cliff, Richard approached the eerie red light seeping through a window set in the wall and highlighting the strange objects that littered the floor. They looked like someone's poor attempt at making pottery vases. Smooth concentric ridges ran down the sides of the foot-tall objects that glistened as if they were wet and drooped to the side to reveal dark empty interiors. He was under no illusion that something hadn't grown inside and hatched from every single one.

As he drew closer he noticed other far more worrisome objects. He poked one with a foot. It was stiff but semitransparent. It reminded Richard of shredded snakeskin, but the ghostly forms hinted at by the shredded skins were nothing remotely snake-like. As Richard gingerly stepped through the egg graveyard, his eyes constantly searched for the hatchlings, or worse, what they had now matured into.

He ducked beneath fallen metal beams propped against the buckled walls. The floor creaked with his steps and though he had the feeling it might collapse at any time, he knew he had to keep moving.

A few moments later, the sounds drifting along the debris-strewn corridor from behind slowed Richard's search for salvation. It was the unmistakable sound of approaching monsters and their bloodcurdling screeches indicated they were gaining too fast for him to outrun. He searched for a hiding place, but his choices were limited. He dropped to the floor, lay tight against the wall and pulled a buckled ceiling panel over him.

The three alien creatures that chased the slightly larger creature along the corridor weren't particularly hungry, as they had hunted and eaten many creatures lately that seemed to have suddenly appeared, but their instinct to eat when normally scarce food was available drove their actions.

The cow-sized creature being chased was covered in long brown hair, had six legs, a triangular head, and was an herbivore. It was also terrified. Terror bulged its eyes and sweat matted its long hair. When it had awoken to its strange surroundings, it had found itself surrounded by many species of creatures that looked at each other hungrily and who seemed just as groggy and confused as it was. It had headed for the nearest exit before they had fully recovered and attacked and hadn't stopped looking for the familiar fields it and its herd had roamed through.

Though it had managed to avoid many creatures, it had failed to avoid the three currently chasing it when it had come across them unexpectedly. It was weak, hungry and knew it couldn't run for much longer.

Richard trembled with fear as the monsters approached and groaned when something heavy thundered across the edge of the ceiling panel he hid beneath, crushing his chest, but he forced himself to silence and peered out at the slightly smaller beetle-like creatures rushing past. Though they had hinted similarities to the shredded skins he had happened across earlier, these had evolved into much larger ferocious creatures. A row of small jointed black legs either side of its golden articulated body—a body that humped in the middle and was adorned with ivory spikes—scuttled the five-foot-long creature along at a surprisingly fast rate. Though no eyes were visible, the front flat segment of the creature seemed to be its head and was armed with two curved, stag beetle-like horns that stuck out like pincers and were set either side of a wide flat mouth.

The bovine beast skidded and crashed into the far wall of the turning. It glimpsed those chasing it almost upon it and spurted forward when one leaped.

Its attacker hit the wall, sprung away and landed on the back of the fleeing beast. It raised the front of its body up and stabbed its pincer-horns into the beast's hairy flesh, causing it to howl in pain and stumble. As it slid along the floor the other two arrived and after a few vicious stabs, ended its life.

After remaining still for a few moments and listening to the all too familiar sounds of the monsters distant feeding, Richard carefully lifted the panel aside and climbed to his feet. He stared at the T-junction at the end of the corridor where the sound originated from and slowly approached. When he grew nearer he noticed the staircase set in an alcove on the far side of the T-Junction. Though he had no idea how far he was below the hangar level, he believed his best chance of finding the exit was to head up until he came across something he recognized.

Prepared for a rushed retreat if anything appeared, Richard cautiously approached the turning. He hugged the wall, inched towards the corner and slowly peeked around the edge. The three alien beetles were gathered around a gruesome mass of ripped flesh they fed upon. Unfortunately only one of them had their back to him. If he moved for the stairs he would be seen, chased, caught and eaten. As he turned back to consider his options, he noticed a flash of red light at the end of the left T-junction corridor. Though it was only a brief glimpse, he thought he had noticed a dark form moving nearer. When a yellow flash erupted a few moments later and lit up the corridor again, the dark form was definitely nearer.

Richard slowly backed into the darkness of the corridor and pressed his shaking body behind a metal support rib.

*****

The sounds of the hunt EV1L had heard previously and that had distracted it from its search for the two-legged creature, had changed into the unmistakable sounds of feasting—evidence the hunt had been successful. Hopeful it would have the same satisfactory outcome, it turned into the dark corridor that branched off to the right and headed towards the sound of feasting. It stopped each time the two flashes of light penetrated into the corridor from behind and caused the three creatures to shoot wary gazes in its direction. Not realizing they had become the prey, the alien beetles paid the patch of shadow little attention and resumed eating.

*****

Richard warily watched the dark shape drift into view at the T-junction and halt for a few moments before continuing along the corridor. When it had passed by, he moved to the corner and gazed after the shadow demon.

EV1L was upon the feeding creatures before they realized it was there. Its smoky form curled around them and engulfed them all in its dark embrace. Though all three experienced excruciating pain, none were able to scream as their paralyzed bodies became absorbed by their attacker. EV1L writhed in pleasure as their sustenance flowed through it.

Taking advantage of the ghoulish distraction, Richard crossed to the staircase and silently climbed its treads. At the top he stepped off into another corridor he didn't recognize and gazed at the three options open to him. He turned left and fled along the dark corridor spookily highlighted by his nervously held flashlight.

*****

The nutrition EV1L had gained from the three creatures had given it strength but it still wasn't enough to solidify its gaseous form. It turned and headed for the staircase it had heard something climb a few moments before.

*****

Lucy looked and felt like a new woman when she stepped from the room twenty minutes later and aimed the alien pistol each way along the corridor to check it was clear of any threat. She had fashioned the alien jacket into a short dress and used a strip of material for a belt, which she had tucked the spare weapon into. Material wrapped around her feet and ankles held the sections of thick material she had cut into soles in place. Her hair was tied back and though still a little grubby, she felt good and ready for anything the spaceship threw at her.

Lucy placed the spear against the wall at arm's length, aimed the alien pistol at the wall beside the tip and pulled the trigger. The small, red light ball exploded in a bright burst. The cloth wrapped around the end of the spear smoldered before flames grew and spread. Lucy nodded her head in satisfaction and, feeling braver than she had ever felt before, headed along the corridor with the flaming torch lighting her way.

*****

Though Richard saw nothing to explain his latest bout of fear, he sensed something approaching. His suspicions were confirmed when a dark wavering patch of darkness drifted into the beam. The creature from below was on his trail. Richard turned and ran. When the ship trembled yet again, a support beam crashed to the floor behind him. The increased groans and bangs that echoed through the ship did not bode well for its stability. Richard threw caution to the wind and ran even faster. The ship rolled, sending him crashing against the wall; he stumbled, regained his footing and continued on. He rounded a corner and then another and fled up a staircase and along the corridor at the top. When the ship rolled in the other direction and a thundering explosion vibrated through the ship, he swayed off balance into a side room, tripped and smashed his head. The weapon fell from his hands and the flashlight went dark when it struck the floor. Richard's collision with the hard floor also resulted in darkness when the black hood of unconsciousness slipped over him.

*****

In a hurried gait, Sullivan led the SEALs through the ship. They had worked out they were two levels above the route they had taken to reach the spiral staircase, so the plan was to head for the back of the ship to avoid all the obstacles encountered on their outward journey, find a way down to the hangar level and head for the exit.

All felt the increased roll and yaw of the iceberg-entombed spaceship and with it the increased groans and creaks of the protesting ice. When the explosion in the weapon store ripped through the ship they were far enough away to escape the resulting carnage, but heard the resulting crashes as parts of the ship collapsed and felt the vibrations rippling through its rooms and corridors. Though they heard an occasional screech or howl from the spaceship's alien inhabitants, none had intercepted them.

When Sullivan approached a junction, he halted the team, aimed his weapon at the turning ahead and listened to the running footsteps heading towards them. The men raised their rifles. A light flashed on the wall. Shots rang out when something appeared.

Colbert knocked Sullivan's rifle at the ceiling and shouted, "Hold your fire. Monsters don't have flashlights."

"Don't shoot!" shouted a man's voice.

The SEALs stared at Jack and Jane when they cautiously appeared and stared back at them.

Colbert, a little surprised by their sudden appearance, stepped forward. "Who are you and what are you doing here?"

"Believe me, it's not by choice," replied Jane.

"We'll explain later," said Jack, urgently. "The iceberg's growing more unstable by the second and we need to get off this spaceship, now!"

"Tag along with us." Colbert nodded at Sullivan. "Lead on."

With Sullivan leading the desperate band of survivors, they continued their dash through the spaceship.

*****

Brusilov and his men ran back the way they had come and reached the first turning when the timer reached zero. The explosion shook the ship violently and sent a radiating wave of chaos out in a circle from the armory. The Russians were thrown to the floor as the blast wave swept over them with a sound like a monster's furious roar. When it had dissipated they glanced behind at the loud crashes that rolled towards them. Collapsing floors, walls and ceilings rushed ever closer. They jumped to their feet and fled.

Babinski shot an anxious glance back along the corridor as the floor dropped away only a few yards away from his heels. "Faster!" he shouted.

When Alexei spotted the missing patch of floor ahead and the pile of twisted wreckage below, he veered into the open door on his right. The men followed him through and away from the entrance as the floor and ceiling outside collapsed and the wall groaned as it sagged at an angle. When after a few moments the ship settled to its usual gasps of stressed torment, the panting Russians roamed their lights around the dark chamber filled with an ominous aura they all felt.

"Well, unfortunately, I guess that's it," said Nikolay to Brusilov. "Unless we can find another weapon store, our mission has failed."

Brusilov nodded glumly. "To have come so close and to have it ripped from our grasp by the Americans." He turned to Nikolay. "Did you see all that alien weaponry? If we could have grabbed just one..."

Nikolay nodded. "There was nothing we could do. We tried our best."

"I doubt that will carry much weight with our superiors when we inform them we return empty-handed."

"We do have some alien technology. The computers and other technological equipment we found on the engineering deck may soften the blow of our failure to salvage any alien weapons."

Brusilov almost smiled. "I admire your optimism, Nikolay, but when they learn the Americans have the weapons we failed to acquire, it will take a lot more than a few alien computer chips to soften the blow."

"Captain, I think there's a door on the far side," called out Mikhail.

Brusilov joined his comrades in gazing around the room and for the first time sensed the menacing atmosphere that had infected the men. Any of the plethoras of gloom-shrouded areas could be hiding the evil presence their senses believed they had detected. Brusilov swept his flashlight into nearby dark recesses but failed to pinpoint anything that would explain their apprehension. "We cross to the exit. Rozovsky, take point."

Rozovsky moved to the front and led the men forward.

*****

EV1L paused when the thunderous roar shook the walls, ceiling and floor and continued when it had passed. A few moments later, EV1L passed the room without noticing Richard's unconscious form and continued along the corridor towards the distant muffled bangs. When it arrived at a pile of wreckage blocking the corridor it turned into a side room filled with darkness and headed farther into its dark depths. It halted and stared up at the higher level as it listened to the sounds of approaching footsteps filtering through the upper open door. It waited for the creatures making them to arrive.

*****

The force of the explosion rippled through the ship, struck the hull and radiated through the ice. The vibrations reached the large fissure and dived down the crevasse's sheer walls. The ice barely holding the two large pieces together relented to the pressure and splintered. It parted with the sharp crack of a deafening thunderclap that rumbled through the ice.

The men in the hangar and the cargo hold froze as the growling tremor struck the ship and shook it violently. The unsalvaged alien vessels shifted and loose storage pods screeched along the floor. The chaos spread through the spaceship's weakened structure. The transparent pods containing the tall aliens cracked and exploded, sending turquoise liquid and the long dead aliens flying across the room. Metal beams and supports shook free and fell, collapsing walls, ceilings and floors. Alien monsters from all over the ship screeched and howled anxiously at the disturbance.

Outside, one of the men organizing the lifting of a recently filled shipping container was struck by a lump of ice falling from the ice wall and killed instantly. A forklift skewed and skidded across the ice shelf when the iceberg tilted, forcing the driver to abandon the vehicle when it tipped over the edge and splashed into the ocean. The shipping container tethered by one cable linked to the large cargo helicopter slid and for a moment balanced half over the ledge before slipping into the sea. The pilot struggled to control the uneven weight as his vehicle was dragged towards the waves. The co-pilot in the back reached for the button that would detach the cable dragging them to their doom but when the helicopter suddenly tilted to the side, he rolled out of the open door and fell onto the ice ledge. Though bruised by the fall, he wasn't seriously injured. He then saw the helicopter heading straight for him and screamed. The helicopter landed hard on the ice and the co-pilots chest, the skid almost cutting him in two. Blood exploded in a wide arc across the ice. As the helicopter skidded and started leaning over the edge the pilot released his harness and dived out the door. He groaned on striking the ice and turned to watch his helicopter dragged beneath the waves.

*****

The weapons and flashlights held by the anxious Russians heading across the room jerked back and forth, probing dark areas for the threat they sensed was somewhere near. As the room shook and loosened more of its structure to rain down around them, they again dodged the falling debris.

When it settled, Mikhail walked backwards with his weapon shifting from one dark patch to another and stopped when he thought he glimpsed movement. His weapon-light jerked back to the source of his concern and focused on the darkness between rows of foot-wide cables and pipes stretching from the lower level up to the ceiling. His eyes tried unsuccessfully to make sense of the dark shape that seemed even darker than the shadows outside the ring of light.

When Babinski noticed Mikhail had stopped with his attention focused on something back along the path, he walked up to him and followed his line of sight. "What do you see?"

Mikhail turned and grinned nervously at Babinski. "Nada. This damn place is playing havoc with my nerves."

Babinski cast his gaze over the area Mikhail had stared at. He also felt a sense of unexplainable foreboding, but saw nothing to explain it. "Da, mine too."

The two men turned away and went to catch up with the others.

*****

EV1L had watched with interest when lights had pierced the darkness and the creatures holding them had entered the room. If it had a tongue and lips to lick, it would have done so in anticipation of the feast it would soon enjoy. There was more than enough food on offer to bring it to its full strength and then nothing would be able to stop it. Unconcerned by the latest batch of falling debris, it slunk through the darkness nearer to its prey and remained still when one of the creatures turned and bathed it in light. Its form, dark and shapeless, all but indistinguishable from its surroundings, had concealed it from its prey. It was a creature of stealth, an assassin without conscience or remorse for the terrible pain it wrought upon its victims. Its survival was its only concern. When the creatures turned away, it drifted from its place of concealment and moved without sound—and at a speed that had caught many off guard—to claim its next victim.

*****

When the weapon clattered to the floor, startling the anxious men, all turned towards the sound and stared at the rifle. Weapons held in nervous grips scanned the area for danger. Though all sensed a malicious presence and an acrid smell, musty and noxious, none were able to pinpoint its origin.

Brusilov looked at Babinski. "Where's Mikhail?"

Babinski shrugged, his eyes darting all over the place for a clue of what had just happened. "He was right next to me and then...he wasn't."

Sergei picked up Mikhail's rifle. "There's no blood."

"He can't have just disappeared," argued Babinski, gazing back along the path for his missing comrade.

"In this alien hellhole I wouldn't be so sure," stated Rozovsky, who peered over the rail and roamed his light below. "Nothing down there either."

Brusilov glanced at the ceiling. It was also clear.

"Mikhail!" called out Babinski.

There was no reply.

"If he was still alive he'd let us know, somehow," said Nikolay, worriedly.

Sergei turned in a circle, his eyes searching for the menace. "We're being hunted."

When the next man was taken, Babinski noticed something and fired. "It's taken Rozovsky."

Surprise appeared on the men's faces when they looked at where Rozovsky had stood a moment before, but saw no sign of their comrade and, thinking Babinski knew what had taken Rozovsky and where it was, copied him in firing into the darkness.

"Cease fire and keep moving," ordered Brusilov. They couldn't afford to waste their limited ammo by shooting randomly into the darkness hoping a lucky bullet would kill whatever hunted them.

"This is too fucking weird," said Babinski. "How can they disappear without a sound?"

Though Brusilov wondered the exact same thing, he wasn't prepared to waste time debating it. "Let's move."

They rushed through the room and reached the far exit without losing another comrade. Sergei closed the door they had rushed through.

While they rested, their thoughts were preoccupied with their latest losses. Two men lost without more than a fleeting glimpse of what had taken them. What made their disappearances even more eerie was that it had been carried out so silently; neither Mikhail nor Rozovsky had uttered a sound. No screams, no sounds of struggle and no blood to shed light on their fate.

Brusilov approached Babinski. "What did you see when Rozovsky was taken?" If they could learn something about the creature it might help them to defend against it.

Babinski shook his head. "That's the thing, I saw him taken, but I saw nothing. It was as if the dark swallowed him. He was there and then...he just disappeared."

Brusilov found the man's account hard to believe. "You must have noticed something."

Babinski shook his head again. "It was as if Rozovsky turned into a shadow, absorbed by the dark."

"Whatever it was, it's now on the other side of that door," said Nikolay. "So at least we'll hear it enter if it comes after us."

"How can we be sure they are dead," argued Sergei. "There was no blood and no bodies."

Babinski humphed. "I think that's extremely unlikely given all the other murderous monsters we've encountered."

"Dead or alive, there are only four of us left and we can't risk more lives finding out." Brusilov glanced around at the surviving men; all wore fearful expressions and some seemed near to panic. "We have to keep pushing forward. The men we have lost will not be forgotten and we will mourn our lost comrades, that I promise, but not here and not now. That time will come when we return to the Motherland and where we will toast them with the finest vodka, the foulest jokes and the greatest pride. But first we have to get off this damn ship."

Brusilov turned and gazed around their new surroundings. They were on a metal platform that stretched across this end of the wide square room. A large machine with four pistons connected to chunky metal arms rose almost to the ceiling of the straight-edged arched ceiling. Three of the pistons rose up and down with a slick suction sound and a loud hiss at each end of their movement. The forth piston was broken and dangled from its supporting arm. At one end of the machine, a blue light sparked like a bolt of electricity in a glass tube, and small red lights dotted the machine. At the far side of the machine a corrugated circular tube compressed and expanded like bellows with each rise and fall of the pistons.

Brusilov turned to the man standing beside him. "Any idea what that is?"

Nikolay shrugged. "My best guess is its pumping air through the ship, perhaps scrubbing it clean and recycling it."

"Whatever its purpose, it's not going to help us complete our mission," said Sergei, keen to press on so they could leave the ship before more deaths occurred.

When they crossed the walkway and opened the door, a blast of cold air assaulted the men. They pushed through and entered a room filled with whirring fans. Each of the six-foot-wide fans positioned at the end of an opening fed cleaned air into the ducts that snaked through the ship. One fan had a failed bearing and clacked with every wonky rotation. Blasts of cold air forced through the round opening in the wall by the bellows in the previous room whooshed through the room.

The men passed through the chilled room quickly and paused in the corridor the far exit led them to. What they saw wasn't an encouraging sight. Dark stains covered the six sides of the hexagon corridor.

Babinski shone his light at the nearest spatter. "Is that blood?"

Every man was certain that it was. Whatever had been killed here it had been killed by something that might lie ahead, but they couldn't go back, not with the silent shadow killer behind them.

*****

When the spaceship settled to ominous silence and a gentle rocking, McNally checked on any casualties and learning of the loss of the two men and the helicopter, he knew it was time to leave. He was about to contact Starlight Control to let them know, when his radio crackled.

"Control to Salvage team, is everyone okay?" enquired Corporal Norton, who like all others on the bridge, had witnessed the iceberg breaking in two.

"We lost a man outside, a co-pilot and a helicopter, so no, we are not okay. I'm calling a halt to the salvage operation. We've already pushed our luck too far and I'm not willing to risk anymore lives."

Norton glanced at the Admiral, who reluctantly nodded.

"Acknowledged. Sending the remaining helicopters to evacuate your men."

McNally gazed around at his men. Take whatever's ready to load and let's get out of here."

The forklifts already loaded with storage pods, headed for the ice tunnel and the men followed.

As they walked across the hangar, Cassidy nodded at the bulldozer. "Are we taking that?"

McNally glanced at the large machine and shook his head. "Leave it. I'd rather use the little time we have left to save the alien artifacts we have ready than to waste time with something so easily replaceable. Leave it."

When the salvage team had left the spaceship, McNally gazed around the hangar and let his eyes linger on the remaining cargo vessels for a moment before turning away and heading back through the ice tunnel.

*****

The motivation for the one-eyed Hunter's journey towards the rear of the spaceship was freedom. Because the tunnel they had dug through the ice was now blocked, it had decided to again seek the cause of the draft of cold, fresh air that wafted through the ship. It glanced at and ignored the

Clicker corpses the humans had killed and moved down the stairs. It sniffed at the foul stench rising from the open floor hatch it arrived at a short distance later and carried on along the corridor.

When it entered a large room with a layer of mist hugging the floor blown by wind from an unknown source, it slunk across the room in the direction it came from. Wary of the human weapons that spat death from afar, it moved cautiously nearer to the large opening and peered into the next room. Though it detected the lingering scent of humans and their distant voices, none were in its line of vision. It cautiously entered and moved towards the opening where the fresh gusts of air entered. The next room was also empty. It followed the sounds of the humans drifting through the ice tunnel and arrived on the ledge as one of the humans' noisy flying machines rose into the air and headed out over the raging sea. It watched it until it had landed on the distant ship before it turned and headed back into the spaceship it had hoped to escape from.

*****

Sullivan arrived at a staircase and without hesitating led the way along the bone-columned corridor it led to. When they arrived at a junction, they halted briefly while they checked it was clear before taking the route straight ahead.

When Jack reached the turnings he called out, "Stop, you're going the wrong way."

The SEALs halted and Colbert walked back to speak with Jack. "Are you sure?"

"Pretty much." Jack pointed along the corridor leading off to the left. "If there's a right-hand turning along there that leads us to the junction where Haax killed the Hunters, then we'll see their remains and know I'm right. From there it's an easy jaunt to the hangar now there are no insects to worry about."

"I think Jack's right," said Jane, vaguely recognizing the junction route they had taken before.

"That's good enough for me," stated Colbert. "Our guide that led us through the ship before took so many wrong turnings I've no idea which is the correct route back."

Following Jack's directions, Colbert led the team along the corridor.

When they entered the insects' domain, Jane and Jack remembered the last time they passed through and became anxious.

"Are you sure all the insects were killed?" asked Jane, her eyes flitting around the foggy room for any sign of survivors.

"I was told all were gassed," reassured Colbert.

Jane reached out for Jack's hand as they moved through the mist.

"We're here, Commander," called out Sullivan when he spied the cargo bay ahead. They entered the cargo bay, which was now almost half empty. Crates, open and sealed, were scattered about the floor or stacked to one side. Colbert, who had expected the room to be a hive of activity, was surprised by its abandoned state. When they passed through the airlock into the hangar, they found that too was vacant.

Colbert's radio crackled. "SEAL Team Five, are you reading me, over."

Colbert replied, "Commander Colbert here. We have just arrived in the hangar."

"It's great to hear your voice, Commander," replied Corporal Norton. "Was your mission a success?"

"If you mean do we have the merchandise, then yes."

"Well done. I'll arrange extraction, but it's going to be dicey. The storm's hit and it's a big one. How many for retrieval?"

"Six. That includes Jack and Jane."

There was a pause as Norton was surprised by the news. "Acknowledged, six for retrieval. Make your way out to the ice ledge. The helicopter's on its way."

Ben Hammott

CHAPTER 27

Escape

THE RUSSIANS RETRACED their steps back along the corridor, down two levels and paused at a T-junction they recognized. Because they couldn't return the way they had come, they headed in the opposite direction. They followed the corridor, opened the door it led to and stepped into a room with four exits. After a brief consultation, they decided to keep heading towards the front of the spaceship until they believed they were past all the blockages and monsters that prevented them from travelling back the original route. They would then turn right and hopefully arrive at the maintenance room from the opposite direction.

They passed through the selected door into a green, ghostly-lit corridor, different than those journeyed through before. This one had curved walls with matching supports set at intervals along its length. Light was provided by a glowing green transparent tube running through the center of a two-foot-wide tube with sides fashioned from metal mesh that ran along the middle of the curved ceiling.

They rushed along it and stopped after covering only a short distance when the mesh tube started vibrating. They turned towards the squeals that drifted along the corridor and saw the cause. Small creatures, the size of baby rabbits, but with none of their cuteness, rushed along it. Though the tube acted as a cage to keep them confined, the Russians had learned not to take anything for granted in the hell-spawned alien vessel and ran.

Rounding a curve, they reached a section that had all but collapsed. Girders and debris was strewn along its path, but worst of all, sections of the tube cage had broken free and lay on the floor. They jumped over the obstacles and kept running as the creatures poured from the missing section and dropped to the floor.

Brusilov glanced behind. The creatures were gaining. He glanced ahead and spied an opening on the right with its door partially open. "Turn right through the door," he yelled.

Babinski dashed into the room. The first thing he noticed was the amount of debris littering the long tall room. The second was the buckled door would never close. "We need to block the door." He grabbed a metal panel and when the last man entered he slammed it against the door. It only covered the bottom half. Sergei and Brusilov piled pieces of metal against it. Nikolay carried another panel over and as he placed it over the top of the gap, he glimpsed the creatures arriving. The men kept piling scrap and props against the door until the panels were held in place.

The men listened. No sound made by the creatures drifted through the door. No squeals, shrieks or scraping at the barrier.

That the creatures weren't trying to break through the barricade worried Brusilov. He shot his gaze around the huge, disarrayed room. It was too large not to have more than one entrance, and the creatures were so small they could fit through a small gap. He feared they hadn't seen the last of them and urged his men on, "Head across the room. There has to be an exit on the other side."

Leaping, climbing and dodging around the many obstacles, they rushed past ornately carved columns stretching up to the arched ceiling covered in paintings too faded and gloom-shrouded to make out their details. The rolling, trembling ship popped free metal panels and girders that clanged to the floor around them, one narrowly missing Nikolay. The men continually dodged the falling debris as they tried to keep their footing on the violently shaking floor during their rush to the far side. All felt the increased rocking of the ship and all guessed if they didn't get off soon they would never leave.

When they reached the middle of the room, the vibrations softened, giving them time to briefly admire the monument standing proudly upon a raised plinth. It seemed to depict a battle between the crew and another far more monstrous species. The arrays of figures were expertly rendered in frozen brutal acts of killing or being killed.

Shrieks and scampering directed their attention away from the artistic, but gruesome sculpture. The vicious Alien Rabbits rushed towards them and spread out.

Brusilov looked around for a place where they could set up a defense. "Climb on the statue," he shouted. It wasn't ideal, but other options and time to find a better defensive position weren't available.

The men climbed.

The creatures arrived.

As if aware they had their prey trapped, the creatures surrounded the plinth and seemed to be contemplating their best method of attack. As if to test their quarry, a small group climbed towards Babinski.

Sat astride a monster that was in the process of being decapitated by the sword held by an attacker that had two, strange, arrow-like objects protruding from a leg and a shoulder, Babinski shot the first creature, the second pull of the trigger alerted him that he had run out of bullets. As the dead creature dropped, he spun the rifle and smashed it on the nearest creature's head. The remaining attackers split up and came at him from all sides. One clamped its sharp teeth on his shin; another leaped onto his arm and sunk its teeth in as he battered another to the ground. As he kicked one away he grabbed the one on his arm around its neck and squeezed until it snapped. The creature nibbling on his leg received a hard blow from the rifle and fell.

As if learning their prey's weaknesses from the brief attack, the others surged forward en masse and the Russians depleted their final bullets by shooting as many as they could.

*****

On hearing the gunshot, Lucy peered into the open door she had planned to pass and swept her flaming torch around the dark room. Where there were gunshots there were humans—perhaps a rescue team sent aboard the spaceship to find her? Though it had come from the room, it had sounded too far away to have come from inside. When more gunshots erupted, she crossed to where it was loudest. The floor creaked beneath her feet and dropped slightly. She cautiously kneeled and placed her face by the gap in the floor. Flashes of gunfire lit up the darkness far below and highlighted the hoard of creatures attacking a small group of men, whose uniforms indicated them as soldiers. If she could reach them and they survived the attack, she would be saved. She glanced at the pistol in her hand. She could help. She poked the pistol through the opening, but the gap was too small to see past her arm. If she fired blindly she might hit the men that could save her.

She tucked the pistol into her belt, grabbed the edge of the floor panel and pulled. It bent slightly, but not enough for her to get a good shot at the creatures. She pressed her back against the wall and kicked at it. It bent more with each blow. One more would do it. When her foot slammed against the panel, it broke from its mountings and spilled Lucy to the floor. The floor groaned and fell out from beneath her. She grabbed out but her fingers found nothing to halt her fall.

Cables drooping from the ceiling to the wall were directly beneath her. She grabbed at them and hooked an arm over one while watching the flaming torch fall to the floor. When the swaying stopped, she hooked her legs over and looked below. The firing had stopped. The soldiers fought off the creatures using rifles as clubs and some used knives. It wouldn't be good enough against so many. She had to help.

She pulled a pistol from her belt, aimed it at the cable where it met the wall and fired. The light ball melted through the cable before exploding in a bright burst on the wall. Lucy dropped. She aimed the weapon at the creatures and clamped her finger on the trigger. Deadly balls of light shot from the weapon in rapid succession as she roamed it over the mass of small horrors. The lethal light balls grew to about two-feet in diameter by the time they reached the hoard and each one killed many of the creatures compressed together by their numbers.

The cable's swing took Lucy around the side of the statue. She continued firing as she swung in a circle, killing creatures on all sides as the four men continued to fight and shoot surprised and shocked glances at her. When her momentum slowed, Lucy slid down the cable and dropped to the floor. She pulled the remaining weapon out and firing both, ran around the fountain picking off the vermin.

All the men had suffered wounds but they couldn't relax as the creatures' attack was relentless. They leaped, bit and scratched at them from all directions.

Lucy didn't trust her aim to shoot the creatures too close to the men, so when she noticed one of them staring at her, she turned the dial on the weapon and tossed it to him. Brusilov stretched for the weapon and caught it. He nodded his surprised thanks and aimed it at the creature about to take a bite from his thigh. The small red ball of light passed through it and killed another climbing up. He quickly killed all those within his sight and then gazed around at his men. Sergei seemed to be having a hard time on the opposite side.

"Sergei," Brusilov called out.

Sergei grabbed a creature from the air, slammed its face into the statue and glanced at the voice. Brusilov threw something at him, a strange pistol. He smiled as he caught it, slipped his finger over the trigger and started picking off the creatures.

Brusilov climbed down, kicking and stamping on any creature that wandered within range, and crossed to the woman who had magically appeared to save them.

Lucy shot two more creatures with the second pistol and glanced at the approaching man. "I'm worried about hitting someone. Can you kill the creatures near them?"

Brusilov nodded, took the offered weapon and aimed it at the creature that had just leaped at Nikolay. The creature's head vaporized when the small red ball of light struck.

"Nice shot," Lucy commented. "I'm Lucy, by the way."

Brusilov fired three times before answering, "Captain Brusilov."

"You're Russian!" Lucy exclaimed, on recognizing the man's accent.

Brusilov smiled. "My mother will be relieved."

"Sorry, it's just that I thought you were American."

"Sorry to disappoint you." Brusilov stepped to the side and shot two more. He noticed Babinski approach, sharing his gaze between the creatures and the pistol he held. "Babinski, take over for me."

A big grin appeared on Babinski's face when he took the weapon. "Yes, sir, Captain." He started firing.

Nikolay noticed the surviving monsters had grown cautious and then, as if deciding they had lost the battle, turned and scampered away. He climbed down as Babinski fired a few shots after them.

"Oh, that's not fair," moaned Babinski. "I get hold of the alien gun and they run away."

"Life's a bitch," said Sergei, spinning the alien pistol like a cowboy gunslinger on a finger. "I shot many."

"Who's the angel who swung down from the heavens to save us?" asked Babinski, running an appreciative eye over Lucy, who thirstily gulped water from the bottle Brusilov had given her.

Nikolay slapped him on the shoulder. "If only God had given us something to make sounds with so we could communicate with each other, we would be able to find out the answer." He crossed to Sergei and examined the alien weapon as Babinski approached the woman.

Lucy held her hand out to Babinski as he approached. "I'll take that pistol, but you can keep the other one."

Babinski reluctantly relinquished the weapon.

Lucy stuffed it in her belt and took a bite of the Russian's equivalent of a power bar. The sweet calorie-embedded snack was the best thing she had ever tasted.

Nikolay gazed up from the alien weapon. "This is amazing. It's so light, more like a toy than a weapon. I wonder what the power source is."

"There will be plenty of time to ponder that later, when we're off this damn ship." Brusilov turned to Lucy. "Thank you. We are all grateful for your timely entrance, but where did you come from and why are you here?"

Lucy swallowed the final piece of the power bar and briefly explained how she had come to be aboard the spaceship, the finding of the weapons, and her sudden arrival.

The soldiers were stunned.

"I can't believe you survived so long on your own, unarmed, with all the alien monsters roaming about. We are trained men and had lots of firepower until our bullets ran out, but still most of us died," said Babinski.

"I'm not sure numbers are an advantage in this place," Lucy said. "They attract too much attention. Have you seen any of the other scientists?"

"Why would we?" said Nikolay. "Those that survived left days ago."

Lucy, surprised so much time had passed, was about to ask about the survivors, when the spaceship shook again and parts of the walls and ceiling crashed to the floor around them. It seemed like the whole room was about to collapse.

"I suggest you tag along with us, Lucy," said Brusilov.

Lucy smiled. "I was planning on it."

Brusilov glanced around at the men's wounds, but none looked serious enough to prevent them from moving, not that there was any alternative. "Babinski, take the pistol from Nikolay and lead us out of here."

Babinski grinned. "Yes, Captain."

They followed Babinski across the room and exited through the door they found on the far side.

*****

The Hunter watched the humans he had heard approach run across the room and head through the ice tunnel. Though it noticed some had weapons, its desperation to escape from its doomed world forced it to ignore caution and follow after them.

As it neared the end of the tunnel, the ice trembled and pieces fell from the walls. It shot its gaze to the ceiling when a crack rang out and tried to dodge the large patch of falling ice but without avail and was knocked to the ground. By the time the ice stopped falling, it was completely buried.

*****

The howling wind funneled through the tunnel had battered and pushed at the SEALs, Jane and Jack as they rushed for the exit as if it were trying to prevent them from leaving.

When they emerged onto the ice ledge, strong gusts threatened to sweep them off their feet as they looked up at the approaching helicopter. As it drew near a loud crack rang out. They turned to the sound and witnessed a large chunk of ice slip from the cliff above. They dodged to the side out of its path. It struck the ledge and exploded into fragments that shot out in all directions. One piece struck Stedman in the chest and another crashed into the side of Jack's head, dropping him to the ground like he had been poleaxed.

Jane rushed to his aid and knelt beside him. She ignored the blood seeping from the head wound and felt for a pulse. She let out a sigh of relief when she detected one. She nodded to Colbert when he rushed over. "He's alive, but unconscious." She glanced at the men gathered around their injured comrade, who groaned in pain. "Is your man okay?"

"A few broken ribs by the look of it, but he'll be fine. We were lucky." Colbert looked at the helicopter as its rotor wash swept over the ledge: it wasn't the CH-47F but the smaller UH-1Y Venom. "We'll put Stedman on first as he can go in a seat, but we'll have to lie Jack on the floor between us."

Jane nodded. "I'll wait with him." She turned her attention to the cut on his head.

Fearing more ice falls, the pilot balanced the helicopter with one skid on the ledge. The rear side door opened and the co-pilot peered out and shouted, "Hurry! If the wind gets any fiercer we won't be able to land on the ship."

After the SEALs quickly handed the co-pilot the larger alien weapons and he stored them in any space he could find within the cramped cabin, Ramirez and Sullivan carried Stedman onboard and strapped him into a seat.

While Ramirez remained with Stedman, Sullivan helped Colbert lift Jack by the feet and shoulders and carried him over to the helicopter. With the co-pilot and Ramirez's help they laid Jack on the floor between the seats.

Sullivan and Colbert climbed aboard and Colbert held out a hand for Jane. As she reached out a strong gust lifted the helicopter up and over the ledge. Jane was struck by a skid and knocked to the ground as the helicopter swept over her. Just before the rotors touched the ice wall the pilot pulled it away, back over the ledge and into the air.

"Stop," Colbert yelled.

The pilot, who had his headphones on, didn't hear. Colbert grabbed a headset and slipped it on. "We have to go back down—Jane's still on the ice!"

The pilot fought the controls as the increased wind tossed it from side to side and glanced down at the prone unmoving figure on the ice and the chunks of ice breaking off from the unstable ice wall that could collapse at any moment. They had already pushed their luck to its limit and the woman looked dead. "Sorry Commander, if I do there's a good chance we'll all die. My orders are that once the alien weapons are on board, everything else is expendable."

"Including lives," challenged Colbert.

"My orders are very explicit, Commander. Compared to the safety of the alien weapons, *everything* and *everyone* is expendable."

As the pilot guided the helicopter out over the churning sea towards the ship, the others looked down at Jane lying on the ice, but saw no sign of movement.

"The helicopter gave her a good whack..." said the co-pilot, leaving the rest unsaid.

Colbert continued staring at Jane until the windborne snow hid her from view.

*****

The Russians sped through corridors, up and down staircases and once had to retrace their steps and search for another route when they came to a blocked corridor, before arriving back at the maintenance room.

Babinski entered first and swept the alien pistol around the room. Though he was eager to fire the weapon, he was pleased the room was free of monsters. "It's clear."

They crossed to the hole in the hull, climbed out and moved through the ice tunnel. When they emerged from the far end, they saw the strong waves tossing the barge up and down and slamming it against the ice.

Brusilov glanced out at the equally storm-tossed salvage ship, little more than a dark blur amidst the wind-borne snow and sea spray whipped across the ocean. The barge was their only chance to reach it. Thanks to Lucy, their mission hadn't been a complete failure. One alien weapon was better than going home empty handed. He hoped his superiors felt the same way, or he and his men might be holidaying in a gulag for the foreseeable future.

"On the barge, everyone," shouted Brusilov loud enough to be heard above the storm.

No one wasted any time jumping onto the wave-tossed barge.

Nikolay crossed to the wheelhouse and brought the powerful engine to life.

The cables tethering them to the iceberg were disconnected and Nikolay reversed, timing his retreat to a lull in the waves. The passengers held on to anything within reach as the barge was rocked violently by the waves that lifted it before slamming it back down and pouring over the bow.

When Brusilov noticed Lucy shivering, he grabbed a waterproof jacket from the small cabin behind the wheelhouse and placed it around her.

Lucy nodded her thanks, slipped her arms into the overlong sleeves and pulled it tight around her.

Even though Nikolay knew it would be an almost impossible task to transfer from the barge to the Spasatel Kuznetsov in the raging storm, it was their only option. He turned the vessel on a heading for the ship and gazed back at the slowly receding iceberg. Whatever the outcome, it was preferable to remaining inside the doomed spaceship.

Brusilov entered the wheelhouse and grabbed the radio. "Captain Brusilov to the Spasatel Kuznetsov, are you receiving me?"

He received a reply almost immediately. "Captain, you're alive. We had all but given up hope."

Brusilov ignored the man's lapse of protocol and replied, "Drop the over-side netting lee of the wind so we can climb aboard."

"Yes, Captain. Good luck."

As the storm-battered barge approached the equally chaotic dance of the ship, Nikolay shouted to be heard over the wind and the noisy diesel engine that throbbed through the floor. "It's going to be a risky crossing, Captain. I'll bring the barge alongside, but I doubt I'll be able to hold her there for long. As soon as we're close enough you'll have to jump. I'll go around again for those that don't make it the first time."

Brusilov nodded and left the relative shelter of the wheelhouse to explain the boarding plan to the others.

Lucy watched the ship grew closer. She wasn't looking forward to the transfer.

"Will you be okay?" Brusilov asked, leaning close so his words could be heard above the storm.

Lucy nodded. "I think so."

"You will cross with Sergei and Babinski. Watch what they do and copy them. Just make sure you time your leap when the barge has reached the top of its rise or you'll be crushed."

"Thanks," said Lucy, worriedly.

Brusilov smiled. "You'll be okay. Compared with what you've been though lately, this will be easy." He moved away to talk to his men.

Lucy stared back at the ship that seemed to tower above the small barge when they drew near.

Brusilov pointed at the net slung over the side of the ship. "Get ready."

Lucy, Sergei and Babinski lined the side of the barge as it approached the climbing net and were thrown to the deck when a wave smashed the barge into the larger vessel and squealed along its length until they parted. They quickly scrambled to their feet and watched the net draw closer.

Sergei went first. He placed a foot on the side as the boat began to rise and sprung when it reached its peak. Babinski did exactly the same and both clung to the netting. Lucy stared at the net as she geared herself to make the crossing. When the end of the net drew nearer and the barge rose again, she placed a foot on the side and jumped just before it dropped. Her hands clawed at the netting and as soon as they touched they enclosed around it. Her body hit the hull harder than she would have liked, but she had made it.

"See, that wasn't so bad, was it?" called out Babinski, a little way above her.

"Look out!"

Lucy turned. Brusilov had his hands cupped around his mouth, as the barge rose up towards her. She jerked her legs clear as the barge's stern struck the ship and slid by.

Brusilov physically relaxed when he looked back to see everyone was okay and climbing up to the crew waiting by the rail above. He crossed to Nikolay peering from the wheelhouse. "That went smoother than I imagined."

"Let's hope our boarding has the same outcome," replied Nikolay as he steered the barge around for their turn.

"As it is customary for the Captain to be last off the ship, I'll take over."

Nikolay smiled. "That only applies when the ship is sinking. This barge can handle a bit of wind and a few rough waves. Besides, I designed her. She's a stubborn bitch and needs a bit of coaxing to perform the way you want her to and only I have the touch."

Brusilov placed a hand on the man's shoulder. "Okay, Nikolay. I wouldn't want to be accused of interfering with your girl, but as soon as we're at the net, you leave her."

"Don't worry, Captain, I'll be right behind you. She knows this ain't no long term relationship." Nikolay nodded ahead as they approached the ship again. "Better get ready."

Brusilov turned to see the bow of the ship plough through the waves a short distance away. He nodded at Nikolay and went to stand at the side.

Nikolay stared at the approaching ship and coaxed the barge to carry out his bidding. As soon as they were level with the net he would rush for the side as the Captain disembarked and leaped for the net. As the bow of the ship slid by, he sensed eyes upon him. He glanced up at the crew lining the ship's rail, but it wasn't from them. When he glanced around the barge his gaze halted on the slightly raised deck hatch. He sensed a presence In the darkness below and then noticed the eyes peering out at the ship. When the two vessels were practically touching, the blackness seeped out like an escaping oil slick.

Nikolay shot a glance at the Captain leaping for the net. As soon as his foot left the side Nikolay turned the barge away.

Brusilov glanced down when he noticed the barge turn away but saw no sign of Nikolay on the net. He looked at the wheelhouse and saw him still at the controls with his attention focused elsewhere. Brusilov followed the man's gaze to the dark menacing form flowing over the deck towards the rail. It was the thing from the spaceship. His hand grabbed the alien weapon from beneath his jacket and fired at the monster stretching like soft tar for the ship. The monster screamed when the bolt of light passed through it and collapsed half over the rail. It jerked back aboard the boat when a wave struck and shredded its form.

When a second shot burnt away more of its body, it drew itself into one solid shape and looked at Brusilov as he fired again. Prepared this time, EV1L parted its elastic form and the ball of light passed harmlessly through the gap and exploded on the deck.

Those gathered at the rail stared at the dark monstrous form.

Lucy shivered in fright on seeing EV1L again.

Though it looked different now, darker, thicker, and slightly glossy, Babinski recognized it as the thing that had taken Mikhail and Rozovsky. He glanced around the deck and shouted, "Quick, someone, fetch me a rope."

Babinski snatched the rope from the man who brought it to him and turned to the rail. "Nikolay," he shouted as loud as his lungs would bellow.

Nikolay tore his eyes away from the monster and glanced up at the men.

Babinski waved the rope when Nikolay looked up at him, and when the man nodded, Babinski threw the coil and kept tight hold of the other end.

Nikolay caught the rope, lashed it around his waist and ran to the side of the barge.

EV1L saw the movement, avoided another light ball and rushed for the man.

Nikolay jumped onto the low rail and leaped from the barge.

EV1L watched the man disappear beneath the waves and turned back to its attacker. Though the human aimed the weapon at him, it didn't fire. Both of them knew it was now trapped on the vessel moving away from the ship.

Babinski and four other crewmen pulled on the rope.

Nikolay gasped as the freezing water sucked all the heat from his body. Knowing he had only seconds to live, he pulled his steadily resisting body to the surface. Fighting a losing battle against the cold and the waves that threatened to carry him away from the ship, he shivered uncontrollably as he looked up the side of the hull and saw the men looking down at him. The rope yanked him nearer. His freezing hands attempted to grip the taut lifeline, but he couldn't close his fingers. They dropped by his side as blackness overwhelmed him.

Babinski and the men dragged Nikolay through the waves and up the side of the ship. As soon as he reached the top, two men hauled him onto the deck. The medical officer standing by ordered the men to strip off his wet clothes and his naked body was scrubbed with dry towels. After fresh dry ones cocooned his body he was carried below deck to the infirmary.

When Nikolay opened his eyes twenty minutes later, he was in a warm bed.

"Welcome back, comrade."

Nikolay turned his head and saw Brusilov's smiling face. "What happened to that thing?"

"It's trapped aboard the vessel and on a collision course with an iceberg. It won't survive for long."

"I jammed the wheel," Nikolay explained.

"I guessed as much. Now rest. We'll soon be heading back home. Our mission wasn't as successful as I had hoped, but we're not returning empty-handed."

Nikolay nodded, remembering his lost comrades. "I hope the Federation appreciates the sacrifices."

"We'll see. I am sure Moscow's propaganda machine is already working on the public account of our predicted success, but behind closed doors..." he shrugged. "Now get some rest, we're heading home."

Nikolay closed his eyes.

CHAPTER 28

Luck of the Devil

WHEN CONSCIOUSNESS RETURNED to Richard's battered body, his eyes opened to darkness and pain. A hand went to the main source of his discomfort, causing him to grimace from the touch of fingers probing the lump formed on the side of his head for cut skin and blood. They found neither. Satisfied his condition wasn't life-threatening, he sat up and listened. The usual groans, metallic squeals and loud rumbles of the ship welcomed him back. He wondered how long he had been unconscious—not long he thought, or some monster would have found and feasted on him. His hands searched the floor around him for the weapon. Panic threatened to overwhelm him when they failed to find it. He rolled onto his knees and ran his hands over the floor as he moved through the room. A thankful sigh escaped his lips when a hand touched the cold metal of the familiar weapon. He fumbled for the flashlight's switch and, hoping it still worked, flicked it back and forth. Darkness remained. Richard's breathing increased with the sweat of fear that formed on his brow. Darkness meant death. He calmed his breathing and ran his fingers over the flashlight until he found the possible cause for the light's dysfunction. He tightened the loose battery screw cap and blinked from the bright light that invaded the dark room. When his eyes had adjusted, he roamed the light around the crew member's room he had stumbled into.

Richard climbed to his feet and walked over to the bed sealed behind a curved door with a window set in the side. It must be one of the escape pods Jane, Lucy and Jack had come across. He pressed the largest button on the small control panel and the door slid open, activating an automatic light. He looked longingly at the comfortable, ready-made bed inside. A few hours rest seemed like a trip to paradise at the moment, but he turned away. There would be plenty of time to rest when he was off this doomed floating sarcophagus. He crossed to the exit and listened for a few moments before risking lighting up the corridor with the flashlight. Satisfied it was free of anything furnished with teeth and claws, he headed in the same direction he had been going before he was knocked unconscious. He hadn't gone far when what sounded like an explosion reverberated through the ship. Richard sighed. *What now?*

The gentle roll of the ship that caused him to stagger from side to side quickly increased and slammed him against the wall. He crashed to the floor and rolled when the ship tipped him in the opposite direction. Richard grabbed at the edge of a door frame to halt his next roll when the ship tilted back. Something bad was happening.

*****

Jack had regained consciousness shortly after the helicopter landed safely on the container vessel and was being carried to sickbay. When his gaze had failed to alight upon Jane and he was informed of what had happened, he had struggled free from the men trying to calm him and rushed through the ship's corridors. As soon as he had discovered the commander's whereabouts, he went to seek him out.

Jack strode angrily into the pilothouse and confronted Thomson, "What in the hell are you playing at? Jane's still aboard the spaceship."

Thomson glared at Jack, briefly considering having him slapped in irons and regretted those days had long passed. "I'm sorry Jack," he said, his voice unemotional, "but I'm not going to risk anymore men or equipment on a foolhardy rescue mission. The iceberg's about to roll and the storm's increasing by the minute. We need to get moving or we could lose everything."

Jack held back the fist that wanted to smack the overbearing bastard in the face. "Jane's life might be expendable to you, but I'd sacrifice all the alien technology aboard this ship to save her."

"Of that I have no doubt, but that decision is not yours to make." Thomson glanced at the vessel's captain. "Get us out of here."

Captain Ramos shot an apologetic look at Jack before nodding to his first mate.

The man increased the speed of the large vessel and pointed the bow in the direction of the open sea.

Jack glanced out through the window at the two crewmen securing the small helicopter they had recently arrived on. He wouldn't leave without Jane. He rushed from the pilothouse, down the staircase and across the swaying deck.

The two men lashing the helicopter to the deck clamps, let out surprised yelps when they found themselves pushed aside and knocked to the ground.

Jack released the straps, jumped aboard the helicopter and started the engine.

Admiral Thomson and the captain stared at the helicopter as the rotors spun.

"What's that damn fool doing?" yelled Thomson.

Ramos hid his smile from the angry commander. "I thought that was obvious, sir. He's stealing the helicopter and going to rescue his girlfriend."

"If he thinks I'm waiting for him to return, then he's very much mistaken. I'm willing to lose a helicopter and a stupid hothead. It's the alien spaceship and artifacts that are important. Take us home, Captain."

Ramos had little choice but to obey, but he would take his time. If Jack didn't get himself killed, he'd make sure the ship was close enough for him to reach. *Good luck, Jack.*

As one of the deckhands climbed to his feet and dived for the helicopter door, Jack lifted it off the deck. When he rose above the containers shelter, the wind shunted him to the side. Jack quickly compensated and turned the helicopter towards the iceberg. The snow and ice particles beating incessantly against the screen hampered his vision. He glanced down at the angry sea, its tall waves distinguishable by their whitecaps in the gloom of early evening. He was well aware his chances of survival were slim, but he could never forgive himself if he didn't try. Death would be preferable to a lifetime of guilt. Fighting the gusts battering the helicopter, Jack headed for the iceberg.

*****

Pieces of ice rolled down the sides of the pile when it moved. A clawed hand appeared, pressed talons into the ice and dragged the Hunter free. It climbed to its feet, winced from the pain in its back, and headed for the exit.

When Jane awoke, wincing from the pain in her head and noticed no sign of the helicopter, she realized she had been abandoned. Pieces of ice breaking from the ice wall exploded around her and forced her groggily to her feet. Her eyes flicked to the tunnel and stared at the shape she recognized passing through the halogen lights. *Doesn't it ever give up?* She moved over to the shipping container and hid behind it as the one-eyed Hunter padded out of the opening.

The Hunter gazed out to sea. It had missed its chance to escape and now it was trapped. It glanced at the metal container when it slid across the ice and then turned its gaze back to the distant lights of the human ship.

Jane moved along the back of the container as it skewed nearer the ice tunnel and peered out at the Hunter. As her hiding place slid towards the edge of the ice ledge, she had no option than to sprint for the tunnel while the Hunter looked the other way.

The Hunter turned lazily and watched the human flee along the tunnel. It wasn't alone as it thought. It headed back through the tunnel to seek her out.

*****

As Jack neared the iceberg, he peered through the hampering weather, but saw no sign of Jane on the ice ledge. The sea's turbulent, angry swells rocked and pitched the huge expanse of ice and broke away lumps of ice, both large and small, from its towering walls. The shipping container hanging over the ledge slid forward, tipped and sunk beneath the waves. Just as he feared the same thing might have happened to Jane, he glimpsed movement in the tunnel. Though nothing more than a fleeting shadow, it might have been Jane seeking refuge from the storm and falling ice. He lined the helicopter up with the entrance and looked along the tunnel bathed in the bright halogen lights, some of which had fallen over, but the tunnel was empty any movement. Jack coaxed the battered craft nearer. Knowing he had to be certain if Jane was inside or not and the helicopter wouldn't be safe on the ice ledge, he flew into the tunnel.

Jack shot anxious glances at the ice walls zooming by a few feet from the rotor tips as he concentrated on keeping the craft in the middle of the passage. It seemed like an eternity before he emerged into the large hangar and was able to relax his grip upon the controls slightly. He hovered and turned the helicopter as he searched for Jane. When he saw no sign of her, the thought that she might have slipped off the ice into the sea filled him with dread.

His eyes searched the collection of cargo transport spaceships gathered at the far end of the hangar and glimpsed movement. A smile formed when Jane appeared and waved. *She was alive!*

He urged the helicopter a little closer before setting it down on the swaying floor, but when Jane remained by the cargo vessel, he sensed something was wrong. He unstrapped himself from the seat and searched for a weapon. All he found was a flare gun and three flares, so he loaded one cartridge before climbing out.

He looked over at Jane. "What's wrong?"

The one-eyed Hunter stepped into view on top of the cargo ship Jane hid beneath. The Hunter and Jack stared at one another.

Jack raised the flare gun and pulled the trigger.

The flare gun wasn't designed for accuracy and sent the glowing missile streaking across the hangar in a wobbling, slightly curved trajectory. It missed its target by a few feet and exploded in a shower of bright light against the far wall. Jack loaded a fresh cartridge and moved nearer, his eyes never wavering from the threat on top of the cargo ship.

Wary of the weapon it carried, the Hunter watched the human approach.

Jack halted a short distance from the craft and glanced at Jane. "When I fire the next flare, run to the helicopter and don't stop until you're safely inside."

Jane nodded and watched Jack aim the weapon. As soon as the flare shot from the gun she sprinted across the room.

The flare was closer this time, causing the Hunter to dodge aside to avoid it when it skidded along the top of the spacecraft.

When Jane grew level with Jack, he joined her dash for the helicopter and loaded the last flare while he ran.

The Hunter leaped from the cargo ship and pursued the humans across the hangar.

While Jane climbed through the open door and squirmed past the pilot's seat, Jack turned and fired at the approaching monster. Though the flare curved down and bounced across the floor, it was on target. The Hunter swerved to avoid it, stumbled and rolled across the floor. Jack climbed into the helicopter, shut the door and increased power to the idling rotors.

Jane gazed past Jack and through the side window. The Hunter regained its footing and ran towards them. "It's coming."

The iceberg rolled steeply, tipping the helicopter at an angle and causing it to slide across the floor with a piercing, metallic screech. The untethered cargo ships also moved in the same direction. Two crashed into each other before separating. One struck the wall, another headed for the center of the room and the helicopter.

Thrown off balance by the sudden movement, the Hunter staggered to the side, tripped to the floor and gazed at the cargo ship sliding past.

Jack also watched the approaching cargo ship and careful to avoid crashing into the ceiling, he lifted the helicopter off the floor and held it at the same slant as the ship. He coaxed it out of the path of the oncoming alien vessel and turned to bring the tail round; the cargo ship screeched by barely a foot from the tail rotor.

Jane looked at Jack with dread etched on her face. "I think the iceberg's about to flip over."

Jack gave her as reassuring smile as he could muster. "Then I suggest we leave."

As he steered the helicopter towards the exit, the ship leveled off briefly before tipping in the opposite direction, forcing him to constantly adjust the angle of the helicopter to match the ship's new incline.

Jane stared at the tunnel opening now at an angle. In the hangar Jack had room to maneuver; the tunnel would provide no such luxury. She glanced at the man beside her, his face creased with concern. She placed a hand on his arm. "You can do it, Jack."

"A piece of cake," he replied bravely.

Jane glanced around the hangar. The Hunter was on the move again, but the erratically swaying vessel threw it from side to side and slowed it down.

Jack crossed the hangar, hovered in front of the opening that tipped one way and then the other and matched the roll and pitch of the ship. He took a deep breath and propelled the helicopter forward. As they flew through the tunnel, Jack tilted the copter left and right and lowed and raised the forward movement when the ice pitched and yawed.

Jane gripped the seat so hard her fingers hurt.

The Hunter chased the helicopter into the tunnel. Its claws gripped the ice to prevent it sliding from the iceberg's erratic movements and ran along the tunnel walls when it tipped acutely.

The ice tipped to the left, but this time it kept on going. The iceberg was rolling over. Worried the scream that leaped to her lips would distract Jack from his impossible task, Jane clamped a hand over her mouth to stifle it. Sweat beaded on Jack's brow as tipped the helicopter to match the roll of the ice until they were flying at forty-five degrees. Chunks of ice fell from all directions. Some struck the helicopter; others smashed on contact with the walls and floor. Jack blinked away the stinging saltiness of the sweat that ran into his eyes. If he lost concentration even for a second they would both die. He glimpsed the end of the tunnel ahead. Not far now. A lump of ice struck the side of the helicopter and nudged the rotors towards the ice. The tips gouged at the wall, spraying ice plumes into the air. Jack compensated and edged the rotors free. When they shot from the end of the tunnel the wind grabbed the helicopter and swept it towards the rolling iceberg.

*****

When the Hunter emerged from the tunnel running and it saw the helicopter heading nearer, it changed direction slightly. Its legs scrambled for a purchase on the ice as it skewed to the side and as soon as they found a grip, they propelled it towards the helicopter as it started moving away again. When it ran out of ice, it leaped off the ledge with its claws poised to grab one of the helicopters skids. Just as it was about to grab hold, the helicopter pulled away. It shrieked as it plummeted into the cold sea.

*****

When the ship tipped to the other side again and didn't stop, Richard fell and smashed into the opposite wall, which was now the floor of the corridor. The rotation continued, sending Richard sliding down the wall and then across the now upside-down ceiling. He guessed the worst had happened and the large iceberg the ship was trapped in had flipped over. He was just wondering if the ship was now beneath the sea when a cacophony of screeches, growls and scraping of claws indicated he had a more immediate problem to worry about. Fear propelled him unsteadily to his feet and aimed the flashlight at the terrifying sounds. He could have cried at what the light picked out. A group of many different species of monsters rushed along the corridor. It worried Richard that they were not attacking each other, but seemed to have a common goal that had superseded their normal instinct to kill and eat. He didn't imagine, however tasty humans were to these foul creatures, that the thought of feasting on his flesh was responsible. The blast of wind that knocked Richard back a step brought with it a deafening roar. He gazed past the fast approaching hoard of claws and teeth. A wall of water surged violently around the corner and chased the fleeing monsters. For a brief moment Richard froze as his brain processed the latest threat to his life—the ship was sinking and he was trapped onboard. His sense of self-preservation kicked in and spun him around and sent his legs running back along the corridor.

Richard shot a glance behind when the pounding footsteps grew nearer. The monsters were almost upon him. Though he wasn't sure if their instinct to kill had returned, the various sets of vicious jaws snapping at him didn't give him any confidence they wouldn't grab a bite as they stampeded over him. To avoid that happening, Richard dived through the next upside down doorway he passed, scraping his legs painfully along the top of the upside down doorframe. He groaned with pain when his chin struck the floor and screamed when something landed on his back and tumbled over his body. Richard raised his head at the monster crashing into the wall and before it could recover, he jumped to his feet and smashed the rifle butt into its head until it stopped moving.

He turned on hearing the screeches barely detectable above the roar of the approaching water. The creatures rushed by. One tried to claw its way in but the tightly-packed herd carried it away. He rushed for the door control to close it before the flood arrived, but dodged back when another monster appeared in the doorway and snarled at him. As it prepared to leap, the water torrent arrived and swept the monster along the corridor. Water started pouring into the room. Richard waded through the surge almost strong enough to knock him off his feet and pressed the door button, but even when he had pressed it a few times the door failed to close.

His eyes glanced around the room. The bed cubicle was his only hope. He waded over and jumped to press the button now high on the upside-down wall. The interior light lit up as the door swished open. Richard climbed up, fell into the inverted pod and rolled into the control panel, accidentally activating the door control that sealed the enclosure. Kneeling on the mattress fallen to the bottom of the upturned pod, Richard gazed out the window at the two monsters swimming in the rising water. One scratched at the side of the pod and pressed its frightening vicious face against the window before the rising current dragged it away.

Richard switched off the flashlight to conserve its batteries and wondered if the airtight bed pod was also watertight. He pressed his face close to the window, which excited the yet-to-drown monsters outside, and looked down. The water was above the level of the bottom of the door. He checked at the seal around the inside of the door and relaxed a little when he detected no water seeping in. Though he might not drown, he was still trapped and the air wouldn't last forever. Even if it did, he wouldn't.

His gaze fell on the small screen he must have activated when he crashed into the control panel. Though surprised to see the list in English, he stared at one option in particular that gave him hope he might yet survive this hell—*Eject Escape Pod.* As he stabbed a finger at the option, he was thrown against the door when the ship tipped to the side and noticed the water had filled the room. He stared into the eyes of the drowning creature outside the window before turning away and redirecting his attention back at the screen, wondering why the pod hadn't moved. He saw the confirmation screen and reached out to confirm the command.

Outside a door rasped open, the pod jerked into motion and entered the escape pod chute. As it turned lengthwise, Richard stared out at the long tunnel. Hopefully fate would be looking upon him as favorably as she had done on other occasions. Richard fell back when the pod shot forward and sent him tumbling to the nose when it tipped on its end and shot down a hole in the chute floor.

Though worried by the speed the pod travelled, Richard trusted in the alien technology to eject him safely from the sinking ship. His major concern was that if the ship was still encased in ice and not the seawater he hoped, he would be killed, but live or die, he could do no more. He was in Fate's hands now.

*****

Jack brought the helicopter level and added power to combat the strong gusts and pull it clear of the ice. When he had reached a safe distance he spun the helicopter and fascinated by the incredible event, they watched the colossal iceberg roll over.

Almost majestically, the iceberg rose out of the sea. Streams of seawater cascaded down its sheer side as cracks appeared with deep-throated roars that sounded like heavy artillery guns firing off a salvo. Large swathes of ice calved away and crashed into the sea, sending up towering fountains of spray and creating tall angry white waves rolling outwards like mini tsunamis.

As the iceberg rolled onto its side and began sinking, multiple growls of thunder filled the air as splinters crept speedily across its surfaces, splitting the ice into smaller sections that slid free of the entombed spaceship.

As if reaching for the skies in a last ditch attempt to escape the planet, the front of the spaceship rose clear of the ice and, for a few fleeting moments, hung in the air before slipping back into the sea and disappearing below the surface.

"Oh...my...god," said Jane, stunned by what she had just seen. "That was by far the most spectacular thing I have ever witnessed."

Jack nodded. "Mother Nature at her most awesome and impressive best."

"I guess that's it," said Jane, watching the myriad of large and small icebergs drift apart. "It's over. The alien spaceship and the monsters aboard are gone forever."

"It's not something I'm going to mourn. I just hope everyone managed to get out in time." Jack turned the helicopter away and headed for the American ship.

"Jack, are you reading me? Over."

"It's Captain Ramos," said Jack, unable to take his hands off the controls he constantly fought to keep the helicopter level and on course.

Jane grabbed the mic. "Reading you, Captain. Over."

"Jane, is that you?"

"Yes, Jack rescued me. We're returning to the ship."

"That's great news, but before you do, there's another passenger that needs rescuing—well, not actually rescued, but picked up from the Russian salvage ship. Do you have enough fuel?"

Jack glanced at the fuel gauge. It was low, but not dangerously so. He nodded at Jane.

"Fuel is okay. Who do we need to pick up?"

"You already know her. She was on your team when you discovered the spaceship. Miss Lucy Jones."

Jane and Jack both wore confused frowns when they looked at each other.

"That's impossible," Jane argued. "She's not in Antarctica."

"I don't know anything about that, but I just spoke to a female who said her name was Lucy Jones and that she had been trapped aboard the spaceship until she met up with the Russians. She is now on their ship and requested we come and pick her up."

"What do you think?" asked Jane

Jack shook his head. "We know it can't be Lucy as she went with Haax, but someone needs picking up and I'm intrigued why someone is using Lucy's name."

Jane nodded. "Likewise." She spoke into the mic again. "Okay, Captain, if you give us the Russian ship's coordinates, we'll go pick her up."

After the Captain had furnished them with the information, Jane replaced the mic in its holder.

"There's something strange going on here," said Jane. "Whoever this woman is, where did she come from and how did she get aboard the spaceship?"

Jack shrugged. "Maybe Lucy changed her mind and Haax brought her back."

Jane shook her head. "Haax would have dropped her off at the base camp, not put her back aboard the spaceship full of monsters."

Jack glanced out at the dim lights on the horizon. "Well I guess we'll soon find out. There's the Russian ship."

*****

When the large waves caused by the collapsing iceberg dissipated and released their hold on the creature they had swept along, the Hunter gazed back at the ice it had recently vacated to find it was no more. It had been replaced by hundreds of smaller icebergs that offered no salvation from the hostile environment it needed to escape from. When its single good eye scanned the horizon and fell upon the lights of the distant vessel, it started swimming towards it.

It had only reached halfway when the freezing sea began to take effect, and the powerful strokes that propelled it through the rough sea grew sluggish. Aware it would never make it, the Hunter headed for a large chunk of ice and climbed out of the water.

*****

When sensors detected the approaching escape pod, they opened the hull door. Seawater poured through the opening with the fury of a Yellowstone geyser. Richard jumped when the water pounded the pod with a thunderous roar and slowed the pod's momentum slightly. He watched the turbulent water streaming past the window and though apprehensive, he believed the water was a good sign—an indication the spaceship was free of the ice. A few moments later his optimism was proven correct. The pod ejected from the side of the sinking spacecraft and shot through the cold sea before it slowed and rolled as it sought its bouncy level.

Richard stared out of the window at the expanse of sea lit by hazy light filtering down from the surface and highlighting the spaceship heading straight towards him. Richard shook his head in dismay and groaned. Powerless to do anything about it, he watched the spaceship grow larger in the window and then noticed the yawning opening of the hangar bay he headed towards. He would soon be back inside the ship.

As the nose of the pod slipped through the opening, a large yellow shape appeared out of the gloom. The bulldozer struck the pod and pushed it back through the hangar door. It rolled along its large blade and was caught by the water pressure pushed ahead of the spaceship and nudged free from the bulldozer's blade. The pod rolled and bounced along the hull of the spaceship, each bang as loud as a car crash within the confines of the pod. Dents appeared alarmingly in its surface. All it would take was one small fracture to allow the sea to pour in and he would drown. Though Richard had no idea if the pod was deep enough to implode from the pressure, the constant groans and creaks it emitted weren't reassuring.

Tumbled about like a sock in a washing machine, all Richard could do was wait until it ended, one way or another. When the pod settled and floated calmly, Richard peered out at the spaceship sliding past. It was the first time he had truly been able to get a measure of its huge size. When he glanced up its length to see how much more of it there was still to come, he noticed an outcropping of the spaceship directly above. A few moments later the two collided. Trapped under the ledge, the escape pod was dragged down with the spaceship.

Richard quickly realized the danger. Even if the pressure didn't implode the pod, if he remained trapped he wouldn't last long. He gazed out of the window to see if there was a way of getting free. The pod was caught under a metal lip on the outcropping hull. To try and knock it free, he raised his body and slammed it hard against the bottom of the pod, but it didn't budge. The pod creaked ominously from the weight of the water pressing against it. Richard slammed his shoulder against the side of the pod again and this time it moved slightly before returning to its original position. He tried again, but harder this time and ignored the pain it caused. As the pod leisurely rolled over the lip, the window cracked loudly. Richard gazed fearfully at the growing fracture as with agonizing slowness the pod rolled around the edge of the outcrop. Spider web cracks continued to slither across the window as Richard willed the pod to rise. Slowly, buoyancy took hold and drove the pod up towards the dim light.

He looked out as the front of the spaceship slid past. When he stared at the curved windows of the strange, bone-shaped bridge, he saw someone inside. From the description the other scientists had given, he recognized it as the dead alien they thought was the captain. The impression was that he was still at the helm and going down with the ship. Richard watched the alien spaceship grow fainter as its final journey took it to the ocean's dark and just as alien depths. When it finally disappeared, he pressed his face to the cold, cracked window and looked up at the grey light drawing ever closer.

The pod torpedoed fully out of the water before splashing back into the choppy waves and settled on its side. After he righted himself from his latest tumble and winced from the fresh batch of bruises, Richard looked through the window; he wasn't out of danger yet. He still had to attract someone's attention to come and rescue him. He smiled. He couldn't believe his latest stroke of good luck—a ship headed straight for him. They must have detected him somehow.

Richard jabbed at the control screen until the side of the bed rose. He shivered when a wave sprayed him with cold water. He cursed his bad decision as water rolled over the side and started filling the pod; he should have waited until the ship was nearer. He waved his arms furiously to ensure his presence had been noticed. The ship continued to head straight for him, but it showed no sign of slowing.

His brow creased with worry when he noticed no crew onboard or at the rail waiting to pull him to safety. He shouted to attract someone's attention, but the wind dragged his shouts away. Starting to think the ship wasn't on a rescue mission and no one had spotted him, Richard knew if that was the case, he would have to save himself— something he had a lot of practice of doing recently. When the ship was almost upon him he noticed it wasn't a ship but a type of barge. The sides were not that high and if he timed his jump correctly he should be able to climb aboard.

The wash from the bow gliding past began pushing the pod away. Aware he would only get one try, Richard climbed onto the pod, ran along its length and jumped. His outstretched hands grabbed at the side of the boat. His body struck the hull hard, adding to his aches and pains, and the freezing sea grabbed at his legs with a numbing coldness he had never experienced before. He hauled his tired body over the side and dropped to the hard deck. Panting heavily, he rubbed circulation back into his frozen limbs. He was safe at last. Free from the spaceship and its alien passengers.

After a few moments, when no crew came to see if he was okay, worry creased Richard's brow as his gaze swept the vessel. There was no sign of any crew. He struggled to his feet and turned to find out who was steering the barge. All he saw in the small wheelhouse was a patch of blackness that seemed to flow out of the door. Richard knew it was the shadow monster from the spaceship. He recoiled in fright and almost fell over the side when a face formed in the black, oil-wet mass and glowing eyes stared at him. The wind rippled the black form like a strong breeze blowing over a still pond.

He tore his gaze away and his eyes desperately swept the churning sea for another vessel that might be able to save him, but the horizon was as bleak and empty as his immediate future. Richard stared at the approaching large block of ice; maybe he could jump onto it to escape the monster. Then what? There was still no chance of rescue and he would soon freeze to death if the wind and waves didn't sweep him into the freezing sea. He gazed over at the remaining part of the giant iceberg that had broken from the piece that had once entombed the ship and that the barge seemed to be on a collision course with. He assumed he would be dead before the two met. He sighed. After all his near death escapades, he was still going to die. He wondered how the monster would do it and if it would be a quick and pain-free death.

He gazed out to sea as he thought of the things he had done. He wasn't a good man, he knew that, but he wasn't bad like a murderer bad. He was just a bit greedy and self-centered. Tears filled his eyes when he sensed the darkness was almost upon him. He wiped away the tears with his cold fingers. He wouldn't die crying. Richard's expression changed from shock to disbelief then from anger to realization and finally to the acceptance of his fate. He was no longer afraid. He turned to face his death head on and stared defiantly at the darkness that had formed into a large wolf-like creature that slowly padded towards him. Death moved slowly, purposefully.

When something from out of the corner of his eye caught his attention, Richard glanced in that direction. Distant faint lights pierced the gloom. It was unmistakably a large ship. He directed his stare to the searchlight stretching out from something in the sky approaching the ship—a helicopter. His mind flicked through different scenarios. Maybe he wouldn't die aboard this boat after all. He turned to face the darkness again and was startled by how close it had come.

Richard held up a hand. "Wait!"

The darkness halted and stared, curiously it seemed, at its victim.

"Can you understand me?" Richard shouted to make certain he was heard above the howling wind and crashing waves. Though the darkness made no response, it remained a short distance away. Whether it was or not, Richard chose this to be a good sign and continued voicing his plan with added arm movements to help the thing understand. "We are both stuck on this boat and will perish if we stay here, but I can help you." He pointed at the lights of the distant vessel. "I can take you to that ship." He pointed at the frightening dark form and then the distant vessel to hopefully enforce the meaning of his words. "There are lots of humans onboard you can kill and eat, or whatever it is you do with your victims. All I ask in return is you *don't* kill me."

EV1L stared across the ocean at the lights of the vessel for a few moments as if contemplating its victim's request. The creature wanted to go to the water vessel. If it could sneak aboard and hide until it arrived at another land, it would survive. It could also snack on others of the species type it had seen onboard to keep its strength up. EV1L returned its scary gaze back upon Richard as it changed form, rising up into a human shape, like a golem formed of black, greasy wet clay, and nodded its malevolent head.

Giving the black golem, that seemed to have understood and accepted the deal, as wide a berth as the width of the barge would allow, Richard anxiously rushed to the stern and into the small wheelhouse. He ran his eyes over the sparse controls. It seemed simple enough, a throttle and a steering wheel. He powered down the vessel and grabbed the wheel, but it wouldn't turn. A frantic search revealed the pin that held it in place. He freed it and pushed the throttle forward halfway while turning the barge until the bow was lined up with the distant ship.

EV1L watched Richard's every move until it was satisfied they were heading for the ship and then moved to the bow and stared out at the approaching vessel.

Though frightened by the proximity of the boat's only other passenger, Richard relaxed slightly when it stopped staring at him and turned away. Death didn't seem so imminent now and he was hopeful he might actually survive this ordeal.

Though Richard was naive at times, he wasn't stupid and knew by the barge being set adrift with the dark phantom as its only passenger, the ship's crew was probably aware of its presence and would take steps to prevent it boarding their vessel. Though he had no idea of what actions they would take, he imagined his life would bear little consideration with their preventative measures. He would have to think of a plan whereby he could be saved without seeming to endanger those on the ship.

As he grew nearer to the vessel he was able to read its name, Spasatel Kuznetsov. It was Russian, not the American ship he had expected. That didn't bode well for his survival; the Russians would care even less about his life than the Americans or British. He needed a good and convincing plan if he was going to live through this. He gazed back at the dark form still focused on the approaching ship and wondered what its plans were. Whatever the unfathomable thoughts of the dark menace, Richard was confident pain and death to others played a prominent role and he didn't trust it not to include him in its killing spree when they were onboard. He looked across the waves at the helicopter drawing nearer to the large ship. He didn't have much time. It was his only means to escape from the dark presence.

As his eyes desperately scanned the ship for a solution that would get him safely aboard, an idea formed that would result in the death of the dark golem and hopefully his survival. Though he saw a few Russians moving about the rolling deck, none looked in his direction. Richard altered course slightly to keep the bow pointed at the Russian vessel and flashed the deck lights on and off in the hope of attracting someone's attention.

*****

Showered and dressed in borrowed clothes a few sizes too large, Lucy exited the cabin she had been allowed to use. She placed her hands against the walls to steady herself against the rolling movements of the vessel as she headed along the corridor towards the galley. Though she had grabbed a quick snack before her shower, she was still famished. Now she had washed away every remnant of the alien grime, she felt like normality was beginning to return to her life that had been anything but recently.

Babinski was tucking into his second helping of food when Lucy entered the galley. He smiled at her change of appearance. "You look better."

"I am thanks." Her mouth watered at the sight and smell of food the men were eagerly consuming at the tables spaced around the room.

Babinski indicated the empty chair beside him. "Come, sit and eat."

Lucy gratefully took him up on his offer.

Babinski turned towards the man behind the counter of the galley kitchen. "A bowl of food for the lady, Gresol."

Gresol brought it over, placed it in front of Lucy with a smile and glared at Babinski. "I don't mind doing it for our pretty guest, but I'm a cook not your personal waiter, so next time you want something, get off your lazy arse and fetch it yourself."

Babinski smiled at the man. "And I was hoping for a private massage later."

Gresol rolled his eyes and returned to his kitchen.

Lucy wolfed down the hot food, a type of meat stew with vegetables.

A man popped his head into the galley. "Lucy, there's an American helicopter on the way to pick you up."

Unable to answer with her mouth full of food, Lucy nodded at the man.

"I'll bring her up," volunteered Babinski. "What's the ETA?"

"It's already approaching off the port bow, so a few minutes."

Lucy placed the spoon in the bowl and let out a satisfied sigh. "I'm ready."

Babinski found Lucy a waterproof jacket and led her out of the galley.

*****

Ivan Chersky glanced at Brusilov when he entered the bridge. "The American helicopter is on its way, Captain, ETA six minutes, but there's something else approaching from the opposite direction."

Brusilov crossed to the radar and peered at the unexpected blip moving through the slower moving blips that formed the newly created iceberg field.

"I think it's the barge, Captain," said Chersky.

Brusilov glanced out across the sea in the direction of the detected blip and noticed a light flashing. He took a pair of binoculars from their place on the wall and walked out onto the small deck surrounding the front of the bridge. Ignoring the wind and snow that whipped around him, he placed the binoculars to his eyes and focused on the flashing lights. He was surprised to see Chersky proved correct; the barge headed straight for them. At first he blamed the wind and waves for altering its course, but as it drew nearer he saw a man leaning out of the wheelhouse waving. He wondered where he had come from, how he had gotten aboard the barge and what had happened to the evil menace; it couldn't still be aboard if the man was still alive. Brusilov swept the binoculars over the length of the deck and was shocked when he spied the dark form standing near the bow with its eyes focused on his ship. Though confused as to why it hadn't killed the man piloting the barge, he was well aware of the danger the dark entity presented if it managed to board the ship. He returned to the bridge, grabbed the radio, reset the frequency and pressed the talk button.

*****

Richard stopped waving at the Russian ship and turned when a voice crackled behind him.

"This is Captain Brusilov from the Russian vessel the Spasatel Kuznetsov communicating with the man piloting the barge heading for my ship. I order you to turn away and keep a safe distance. If you approach you will be blown from the water."

Richard found the radio hanging on the back wall and pressed the talk button. "Captain Brusilov, this is Richard Whorley speaking from the barge. I am a British scientist working with the American salvage team and any aggression levied against me will likely be looked upon as an act of war. I am in trouble and need rescuing. This is an SOS. I repeat—this is an SOS." He lifted his finger and waited.

"Mr. Whorley, you are endangering everyone aboard this vessel by bringing that alien to us and I am within my rights to prevent that from happening. Approach any closer and you will be blown from the water and destroyed."

Richard scanned the ship and saw no sign of any weapons capable of blowing him out of the water. It seemed like a type of work or salvage vessel and definitely not a warship. It was a bluff. Richard looked back across the deck. The dark golem watched him and no doubt grew suspicious. "If I stop or alter course I'm as good as dead anyway, so I have nothing to lose, but I have an idea that may save us all. Do you have any explosives?"

Brusilov, though confused by the man's question, nevertheless answered, "What if we do and why do you ask?"

"I'll explain in a minute. What reach does your crane have?"

Brusilov glanced out at the crane, wondering what the Englishman's plan was. "Twenty-six meters, why?"

"If you extend the jib over the side and lower the cable with an explosive device on the end, I will make sure it destroys the alien and then use the crane to escape from the barge before it explodes. It's a win, win for everyone."

Brusilov raised his eyebrows; he was impressed. The man was obviously capable of thinking on his feet and had somehow managed to convince the black demon to spare his life. "I'll get back to you." He placed the radio down and picked up the internal telephone. "Sergei Antonoff, report to the bridge immediately."

"I thought I recognized the name," stated Chersky, picking up the Russian newspaper he had been reading earlier. "Richard Whorley is one of the scientists that first discovered the spaceship." He handed the newspaper to Brusilov and pointed out the article.

Brusilov stared at Richard's smiling face. "I wonder what he's doing back here." He turned when Sergei entered.

"Captain," said Sergei.

Brusilov quickly explained Richard's plan to kill the black phantom.

"What do you think, Sergei, will it work and do we have enough explosives to fashion a bomb powerful enough to destroy the barge and everything onboard?"

Sergei rubbed the stubble on his chin. "It's a crazy plan, Captain, but we have the explosives and it could work and put an end to that black devil. The only other option is to wait until the barge comes close enough and then throw the bomb onboard, but things could go wrong. A bad shot would toss it into the ocean or the explosion might damage the ship if it's too close. A distance of twenty-six meters shouldn't cause us any damage and even better if the man aboard could steer the barge away at the last moment so it heads away from us."

Brusilov nodded. "It's putting a lot of faith in the Englishman's capabilities." He tapped Richard's newspaper image. "But he does seem to have the uncanny ability to survive. Let's go along with his plan for the moment and I'll get a backup plan ready in case it starts going wrong. Whatever happens, we can't let that alien get aboard this ship."

"I agree, Captain. I'll see to the preparations." Sergei left the bridge.

Not altogether certain the Russian captain would go along with his plan, Richard stared out worriedly at the ship drawing steadily closer and jumped when the captain's voice came over the radio.

"Richard, I have decided to try your idea. Preparations are being made, but any mishap on your part and we will destroy the barge whether you are onboard or not," warned Brusilov.

"Understood Captain."

"Good luck, and turn the barge away from the ship before you disembark."

"I will try my best." Richard hung the radio up and noticed the creature had moved nearer. He smiled nervously and held up a thumb to try and convey everything was okay.

EV1L stared at Richard suspiciously, but as the vessel continued to head for the larger ship, it defrayed from taking any action. At the first sign of deceit it would pounce and kill him.

*****

Sergei hung the strap holding the bundle of explosives together over the crane's hook and set the timer for twenty seconds. All the Englishman had to do was press the red button to set the countdown in motion and lob it at the alien. He gave the signal to the crane operator that he had finished and watched the swaying bomb rise. The crane turned to the side of the ship and extended the boom out over the ocean to its full reach.

Sergei walked past the group of men armed with assault rifles and grenades concealed behind a shipping container to hide their presence from the alien and ready to rush forward if required. If the Englishman failed this was their last line of defense. He joined Brusilov at the rail staring out at the approaching barge and noticed the captain had collected the alien pistol from his cabin.

Brusilov glanced over at the bomb swinging from the crane's cable. "It's all up to the Englishman now."

Richard watched the crane swing out and adjusted course slightly to align with it. He had noticed the alien glance at the crane, but it seemed to pay it little interest. Aware speed would be the only thing that would save him, he had gone over the steps in his mind until he had everything worked out. When the bow of the barge was almost level with the hook dangling too high for the evil golem to reach, he turned the vessel sideways to the ship and inserted the pin to hold it on a course away from the Spasatel Kuznetsov. He rushed from the wheelhouse and climbed onto its roof as the hook lowered and came nearer. He grabbed it, unhooked the bomb, pressed the timer activation button and threw it at the alien rushing towards him. It sunk into its chest when it struck. Richard grabbed the cable, placed a foot in the crook of the hook, and let the boat's momentum drag him off the wheelhouse roof and swing him out over the cold turbulent sea.

EV1L reacted as soon it noticed the human move. It rushed forward but stopped when something struck its chest and sunk into its soft oily form. Strands, black and treacle thick, stretched out from its body when it tried tugging it free.

*****

As the helicopter approached the Spasatel Kuznetsov and Jack noticed the waves tossing the Russian vessel erratically, he knew it was going to be impossible to land safely. He glanced at Jane sitting beside him. "I'll have to do a fly around to find a safe place to hover so our passenger can climb onboard."

Jane nodded and looked down at the angry sea worriedly; if they ditched they wouldn't last long.

Jack brought the helicopter lower and flew around the ship. The helipad presently occupied by the large Halo helicopter counted out the stern as a pickup point. As he rounded the ship something flew through the air towards them.

Jane screamed in surprise.

Jack dodged the helicopter clear.

Jane stared at the man swinging from the end of the crane, who smiled at her. "I don't believe it! It's Richard."

When Jack had leveled off, he looked at the man swinging on the end of the cable, and grinned. "You have to give it to Richard. He never fails to make a surprising entrance."

"But what's he doing here and why is he hanging on the end of a crane?"

Jack shook his head. "Who can fathom why the man does these crazy things?"

Jack noticed two men at the ship's rail waving their arms at him and pointing at the black form on the barge he was about to fly over. He glanced at the evil black shape wrestling with something on its chest, and noticed the red blinking countdown on the object. He jerked the helicopter away sharply and increased power as an explosion lit up the sky. Pieces of metal debris ricocheted off the craft.

*****

Richard hung on as the crane jib swept him away from the barge and the imminent explosion. He heard a loud thrum, turned and gazed at the helicopter rotors heading straight for him and sucked in his chest when they ripped his jacket before pulling clear. He recovered from the fright and couldn't resist grinning at the helicopters occupants when he recognized them. As the crane carried him over the ship, the explosion rang out. He dropped to the deck and sheltered behind a large crate to avoid the pieces of metal clattering to the ground around him. When they had stopped, he went over to the captain standing by the rail and stared down at the sinking wreck of the barge. There was no sign of the black demon.

"Mission accomplished, Captain."

Slightly surprised by the man's relaxed demeanor after such a harrowing ordeal, Brusilov and Sergei looked at him.

Richard smiled. "Now, as much as I would like to stay and accept your no-doubt generous hospitality for saving your lives, I need to get aboard that helicopter."

"Richard!"

Richard turned to the voice, flicked back a clot of gunk-congealed hair and smiled. "Lucy! Well, this is turning out to be a day of surprises. Jane and Jack are around here somewhere in a helicopter, which I assume is here to pick you up."

Lucy took in Richard's filthy, disheveled state and nodded. "I thought you left the spaceship ages ago."

"I did, but the Americans needed my help. But what about you? The last time I saw you, you headed into space with Haax. Didn't you like it?"

Confusion appeared on Lucy's face. "I've no idea what you are on about. Who is Haax?"

Babinski joined them and looked at the approaching helicopter and then at Richard, wondering how he had gotten aboard.

The helicopter appeared alongside the ship and the back door slid open as it edged nearer to the rail. Jane leaned out, showed surprise at recognizing Lucy, and shouted, "Quick, get onboard, Jack can't hold it here for long."

Lucy crossed to the captain. "Thank you for your help Captain, and please thank your crew for me." She gave him a quick hug and slipped the second alien pistol into his hand. "From what you told me, the Americans already have enough alien weapons, so they won't miss this one."

Brusilov nodded. "Thank you, Lucy, you are an amazing woman and I wish you a safe journey and a long life."

Richard, impatient as always and keen to get off the ship, grabbed Lucy's hand and pulled her towards the helicopter.

Pounded by the rotors downdraught, Lucy climbed over the rail. Richard looked worriedly at the two-foot gap between the ship and the helicopter, and the drop into the ocean below as it raised and lowered with the ship's movements. It would just be his luck to fall and drown when he was so close to reaching safety.

When Lucy noticed Richard's worried expression, she grabbed his shoulder and shouted to be heard above the deafening thrum of the helicopter "Time your jump when the ship is at the top of its rise and you'll be fine."

Richard nodded.

When the ship reached the top of its peak and began to drop, Lucy pushed off from the rail and dived through the door of the helicopter. Jane grabbed her and pulled her inside.

When the ship rose and dropped again, Richard jumped for the opening and slipped when a strong gust sent the helicopter speeding towards the tall crane. Someone grabbed his arm and pulled him inside as Jack quickly compensated and steered the helicopter clear.

Jane grabbed the door handle, nodded her thanks to the Russians as the helicopter swooped away and closed the door.

Brusilov, Sergei, Babinski and the other Russians on the deck watched the helicopter grow distant. Brusilov turned away and gazed at the scattered wreckage from the barge littering the deck.

"Well, that's it, thank God. All of the aliens are dead now. Babinski, have the men clear off the wreckage and we'll head home.

*****

Richard nodded at Jane. "Thanks for saving me, back there."

Jane huffed as she wiped clean the foul stains transferred from Richard's filthy clothes to her hands. "I would say you're welcome, but I'm not sure you are."

Richard smiled. "We do tend meet under the strangest circumstances lately. I came to help the Americans, but what are you and Jack doing here?"

Jane smiled and threw Richard's line back at him that he had used when he surprised them in the ice cavern, "You didn't think I'd let you have all the fun, did you?"

Richard groaned.

Jane turned to Lucy. "You didn't like outer space then?"

"Richard asked a similar thing, but I have no idea what you are both on about. The last thing I remember is we were running through the spaceship and then I awoke to find myself locked in a room and practically naked."

"Someone took your clothes," said Richard, picturing Lucy in her underwear and liking the view.

She eyed Richard suspiciously. "Well I certainly didn't take them off."

Richard smirked. "As much as I would have liked to see you so scantily dressed, it wasn't me."

"You fell and banged your head, Lucy," Jane explained. "You were unconscious and we all would have bccn killcd if we carried you, so we hid you in the room—fully clothed I might add—and planned to come back for you when we had escaped from the monsters chasing us."

"But you never did," stated Lucy. "Thanks."

"But we did. We came back and you walked out of the room. That's when Haax, a small friendly alien, turned up and saved us. We used his scout ship to escape and he took us to base camp."

"And then you went with him into space," added Richard.

Lucy shook her head. "Well obviously I didn't, because I'm here."

"But if it wasn't you, then who was it?"

Lucy shrugged.

Fighting the strong gusts that shoved the helicopter to the side and threatened to ditch them into the ocean's cold embrace, Jack turned towards the American ship. As they flew over the expanse of drifting ice, his passengers joined him in staring down at the small drifting icebergs that had for thousands of years entombed the alien spaceship that now rested on the seabed far below.

CHAPTER 29

It Ends

AS THE STARLIGHT skirted the edge of the ice field created by the breaking up of the iceberg, the Hunter clung to the small wave-tossed chunk of ice with its eyes focused upon the approaching ship. When it worked out the vessel would pass by too far away for it to reach, it dived into the sea and swam to another piece of ice directly in its path. It climbed to the top and watched the vessel glide nearer.

Crewman Graham Walker, the man ordered to take position on the bow with a radio and report any stray lumps of ice in the ship's path large enough to damage it, gazed out at the field of mini-icebergs. Like most aboard the Starlight, he had witnessed the spectacular breakup of the enormous iceberg and the huge alien spaceship rising majestically from the sea before it started on its final journey to the cold, dark seabed. He diverted his gaze to the small iceberg the wind and waves drove towards the ship. Though the size of a bus, it posed no threat to the ship even if it struck, but the bow wash would steer it clear like the others. He fished a packet of cigarettes from a pocket of his warm padded jacket, slipped one out and turned away from the wind to light it. As the lighter's flame burst into life, something grabbed him from behind and yanked him over the rail. He screamed as he fell and grunted with pain when he struck the ice and slid down its side into the cold embrace of the ocean.

Lieutenant Miller, the CO of the first watch team, gazed past the tarpaulin-shrouded form of the impressive alien scout ship, and cocked an ear to the wind. Though he thought he had heard someone scream, the wind and rolling ship created so many sounds it was difficult to hear anything over the creaks, groans and the flapping of the covers covering the two salvaged alien spaceships. Duty required him to check it out and informed Patterson and Sawyer of his intentions.

"I'm moving to the bow for a scout around."

"Copy that," replied Sawyer. "Roaming to cover your base."

As Miller approached the bow he glanced around for Walker, who twenty minutes earlier had gone to keep a lookout for icebergs, but there was no sign of the man. He stopped when his foot trod on something. He picked up the object and stared at the lighter for a few moments before gazing around the deck. He had learned to trust his instincts over the years and he wasn't going to ignore them now. Something was wrong. When his eyes probed the many dark areas for signs of anything amiss, he noticed movement, no more than a fleeting shadow darting behind a row of shipping containers. Miller flipped the night vision goggles over his eyes and headed towards it.

Admiral Thomson stood on the aft deck gazing around at the flurry of activity. To ensure the safety of the hastily salvaged alien artifacts, he had ordered for them all to be stored below deck. The crew were just lowering the final shipping container into the hold to join the many already filling its cavernous space. He walked forward and gazed below as it was secured to the hold floor and looked at the three soldiers who would guard the invaluable alien technology that included the alien weapons. They had been wrapped, boxed and stored in a container with its door welded shut to ensure their safety. He regretted the SEALs had left shortly after the completion of their mission; they were true professionals. They arrive, do what's needed of them and then fade back into obscurity without waiting around for praise or a pat on the back for a job well done.

Though he was aware of his paranoia regarding the Russians, Thomson did nothing to subdue it and was confident he had covered all the bases unless a Russian submarine appeared and torpedoed them. He doubted the Russian salvage team had the means to sink the ship, but if a small group of trained men managed to get aboard, a few well placed explosives could destroy the alien shuttlecraft—hence his decision for the armed patrols. The President had already congratulated him personally and then the rest of those involved via the ship-wide intercom for their successful salvage mission, and he wasn't going to risk letting his President down by being careless now.

President Conner had also decreed he bring the ship straight to America and not return to New Zealand as originally planned. The nearest American and British battleships were already set on an intercept course to protect the alien artifacts and escort them home.

As the large cargo hold doors began to close, the Admiral cast one last look around the ship. Satisfied everything was in order, he headed for his cabin. He would celebrate his success with a single glass of brandy and one of the large cigars his wife detested the smell of.

*****

Avoiding any humans it detected, the stowaway crept along the deck searching for a safe place to hide until it could escape onto land. When it arrived at the stern it stared at the large doors sliding together and noticing the space below that would shelter it from the cold. It rushed forward and leaped onto the top of a shipping container.

Selby glanced at his watch, still another four hours before his shift ended. The clink of a spoon on a cup cast his gaze across the room to the coffee station set up for them and where Cooper poured out a fresh cup of the steaming black coffee.

Selby yawned as he walked over to grab himself a helping of the caffeine-infused liquid, but paused when he noticed the shadow move over the ground. He turned and gazed up at the hold doors as they met with a thud and then scanned the shipping containers. When he saw the creature diving towards him, he grabbed the rifle hanging from the shoulder strap and opened his mouth to shout a warning.

One of the Hunter's large paws landed on his face and stifled the warning before it could escape from the human's lips. Claws extended and pierced deep into his skin as they thudded to the ground and another claw smoothly snatched the rifle from the air before it clattered to the floor.

Cooper halted the flow of coffee into the mug and lazily turned his head towards the sound. There was no sign of the man he had noticed there earlier. "You want a coffee, Selby?"

"I wouldn't say no," replied Fitch, crossing the room.

Cooper glanced at Fitch before looking back to where he had last seen Selby and activated his helmet mic. "You okay, Selby?" He placed the coffee jug down when the man didn't reply.

Fitch picked up on Cooper's concern. "Maybe he went for a piss?"

Cooper shook his head and slipped his rifle into his hands. "Not without telling us he was leaving he wouldn't." He pressed the talk button on his radio mic. "Lieutenant, we might have a problem in the rear cargo hold. Selby's gone AWOL."

"Copy that, Coop, we're on our way," replied Miller.

Fitch pointed his weapon across the room in the direction Cooper stared. "What is it?"

Cooper shrugged. "I'm not sure, but it might be the Russian saboteurs Thomson was so concerned about. We better go check it out."

Fitch sighed. He thought he had waved danger goodbye when he had watched the spaceship sink beneath the waves. Still, he thought, a little cheerfully, he'd rather face a Russian than one of those alien horrors again. He followed Cooper's slow walk across the room.

*****

Miller had started running as soon as Cooper had informed him of the problem. Though he had no idea if Selby's abandonment of his post was connected to what he had glimpsed or Crewman Walker's disappearance, he didn't like coincidences. "Patterson, Sawyer, switch comms to live and meet me on the starboard side. There's a problem in the rear cargo hold."

Both men copied their replies and rushed starboard.

When all three met, they rushed along the side of the ship towards the stern door that would take them to the steps leading down to the cargo hold.

*****

Cooper and Fitch paused at the small splattering of blood on the floor and followed the trail of drips that led behind the shipping container with their eyes. Cooper signaled for Fitch to go around to the right side while he headed left. Fitch reluctantly nodded and moved away.

Keeping tight to the end of the metal container, Cooper edged towards the corner. When he leaned out and peered around the edge, he came face to face with a monster. Shock silenced his scream as the monster emitted a low, deep growl that sent piss running down his leg. Claws gripped his head and pulled it towards the vicious face and the jaws stretched wide to receive it. The teeth that scraped along his skull seemed to echo inside his head as his cheek, nose and lips were bitten away.

Fitch halted at hearing the strange growl over his headphones. Whatever he had heard, and he was trying hard not to visualize it, he knew it hadn't been uttered by a Russian saboteur or anything human. Though he desperately wanted to flee in the opposite direction, his compulsion to help Cooper drove him forward.

When the one-eyed Hunter detected the approach of another human, he placed clawed fingers into Cooper's lipless mouth, pulled the weapon away from the human's grasp and climbed the side of the container.

Cooper experienced terrible pain as he was carried like a grotesque human handbag. He glimpsed Selby's bloody corpse when he was set down beside it on top of the container and the man's weapon placed on his unmoving chest. His terrified gaze flicked to the monster and saw it presently looked elsewhere. His hand slowly reached for the dead man's weapon.

Fitch's head appeared around the far end of the container and gazed along its vacant length. Though he was pleased to see it absent any threat, he worried that there was no sign of Cooper. He cautiously moved along the side.

The Hunter gazed down at the human below and then at the human beside it when it felt him move. The obvious pain and fear registered in the human's eyes caused it no concern, but its hand reaching for the weapon moved it to action. A single talon dragged across the human's throat ended the threat. It slipped its fingers from the dead human's mouth and gently laid the weapon down before it moved forward and peered over the edge.

Fitch reached the end of the container, but there was still no sign of Cooper. He lent his head nearer the mic and anxiously whispered, "Cooper, where are you?"

The Hunter leaned over the side of the container and drew back a claw to swipe and kill.

As Fitch pondered what he should do, he stepped farther into the room.

The Hunter's claw swiped nothing but air.

Fitch felt the breeze waft past his cheek and turned. The shock of seeing the monster squeezed his finger resting on the trigger. Bullets ricocheted harmlessly off the container. Fitch turned and ran. The Hunter jumped to the floor and gave chase. Without stopping, Fitch aimed the weapon behind and fired a few panicked shots at the monster. A lucky bullet stuck its leg; it was only a graze but the impact sent the Hunter stumbling to the ground. Fitch reached the door as the Hunter recovered and ran for him. He opened the door, stepped through and pulled it shut. A claw appeared around the edge of the door and yanked it from his grasp. The Hunter growled at him savagely. Fitch fled along the corridor.

Miller reached the bottom of the enclosed staircase first and saw the Hunter by the door. As his gunfire echoed through the cavernous room and bullets pinged off the metal walls around it, the Hunter bounded through the opening.

Miller, Sawyer and Patterson rushed across the room in pursuit.

*****

Fitch shot a glance behind as he rushed up a staircase and saw the monster arrive at the bottom. He dashed along the corridor at the top and when someone stepped into the corridor, shouted, "Get back in the room and close the door."

The puzzlement that had creased crewman Davis's face when the man shouted at him changed to fear when he glimpsed the monster. He disappeared back into his room and the door clanged shut.

Years sat staring at a computer screen had taken their toll on Fitch. Panting heavily, he regretted his lax fitness training when he realized he wouldn't be able to keep ahead of the monster for much longer. He passed the first door leading into the galley and glanced through the window panels that formed the top half of the galley wall. Some of the crew sat at tables eating and chatting casually. A man with a forkful of food halfway to his mouth looked at Fitch and on recognizing him, nodded. A shocked yell brought the various conversations to an end and faces swiveled to the monster in the corridor. The monster's footsteps pounding on the floor grew swiftly closer. To avoid the agonizing death that was about to be upon him, Fitch dodged into the second galley door and shouted, "RUN!"

Chairs tipped, tables screeched across the tiles and plates, food and cutlery crashed to the floor as a mad dash ensued for the far door.

The Hunter swiped out a claw at Fitch as it skidded past, but only succeed in raking claws across the doorframe and breaking off a talon. It changed direction as it skidded and headed for the opening as shots rang out.

*****

Miller, Patterson and Sawyer rushed up the stairs and along the corridor.

When Colbert thought he had a good shot at the monster racing ahead, he raised the rifle and pulled the trigger. His two shots missed when the Hunter unexpectedly skidded to a halt and dived into the galley. When people poured into the corridor he knew he had missed his chance.

To avoid the path of scattered and fallen chairs that blocked his route to the far door, Fitch jumped onto the first of the long line of tables positioned against the corridor wall and rushed along them.

The Hunter entered and ignored the humans scrambling from the room; it needed to catch the one with the weapon. Its plan to hide and emerge when land was reached had failed, but it had noticed very few of the humans had weapons, so if it could kill those that did, perhaps the remaining humans would leave it alone. If they didn't it would have to kill them all. It jumped onto the table and bounded after the human with the weapon.

Fitch stared ahead at the doorway jammed with people and then behind at the monster that would soon have him in its clutches. He shot out the next window and dived through. The rifle strap caught on a shard of glass protruding from the frame and pulled the weapon from his grasp. He struck the wall and collapsed to the floor.

As soon as the human jumped through the window, the Hunter dived through the nearest pane of glass.

As Fitch climbed to his feet, the Hunter appeared in an explosion of glass and smashed into the wall. He glanced at the people filling the corridor behind and knew he couldn't lead the monster towards them. He rushed at the Hunter as it tumbled to the floor and jumped over it. His feet hit the floor running.

The Hunter glanced at the people running away and noticed the armed men pushing through the throng. It wouldn't stand a chance within the confines of the corridor. It climbed to its feet and rushed after the running human.

*****

Thomson sat at his desk in his cabin with a glass of brandy in one hand, a lit cigar curling thick pungent smoke in the other and a satisfied smile on his lips. Life was good. He was about to take another puff of the fine cigar when distant gunshots halted it a hairsbreadth from his lips. His head spun to the door. "Russians!"

The cigar was dropped in the ashtray and the glass slammed on the desk. He rose from the comfortable padded chair, crossed to his wall safe, dialed the combination and pulled out his pistol. He released the safety, pumped a bullet into the chamber and strode from the room.

*****

As the container ship grew closer, Jack wondered how he was going to land on the heaving vessel that rocked and rolled just as erratically as the Russian vessel. One thing he did know was that it would be a rough landing.

"Buckle up tight folks—it's going to be a bumpy ride."

"I'm used to your bad piloting," said Richard.

"Nice to see you again also, Richard, and you still owe me a new airplane."

Richard snorted. "Blow me."

Jack maneuvered the helicopter above the deck and timing his descent with the falling of the ship, he lowered the craft in the area between empty container stacks set around the edges of the ship as a wall to protect the valuable alien spaceships. As the helicopter approached the deck, a strong gust swept it to the side. It smashed into a container and dropped. The rotors sheared off and shot through the air as the helicopter crashed to the ground and settled on damaged skids.

Jack glanced worriedly at his passengers. "All okay?"

Lucy nodded.

"I think so," said Jane, unbuckling her harness.

"That's the last time I get in a vehicle Jack's in control of," stated Richard, adamantly.

Jack glared at him. "I hope that's a promise, because the only time I crash is when you're a passenger. You're a damn jinx."

"Well I definitely wasn't to blame this time."

"So you admit you were before?"

Richard smiled at Jack. "I'm admitting nothing."

"Now, now, boys, we are all safe, so no harm's done," said Jane.

"Tell that to Admiral Thomson when he sees what I've done to his helicopter."

They exited the mangled craft and looked around the deck that rolled and heaved with each wave striking the large vessel.

"Strange that no one came to see if we're okay," said Jane.

"Would you venture out in this weather unless you had to?" said Jack, pulling his jacket tighter together. "Thomson's probably pissed at me for taking the helicopter and forbade anyone to come to our aid."

Jane grabbed his hand. "If he gives you any verbal, he'll have me to deal with. If you hadn't rescued me I'd be dead."

Lucy rolled her eyes. "Before you two start kissing, let's get inside somewhere warm." The oversized jacket the Russians lent her might be waterproof, but it did little to keep out the cold.

Jack thought about securing the helicopter, but it was already a wreck and jammed against the container, so he hunkered against the cold wind and followed the others towards the nearest door. A cup of hot coffee to chase away the chill sounded like heaven to him at the moment.

Richard reached the door ahead of the others and pulled it open.

*****

Fitch glanced behind when the monster's footsteps started up again and looked at the sliver of glass he noticed sticking from his thigh. Though blood seeped from the wound, he felt no pain. He assumed that would come—if he lived long enough—when the adrenaline pumping though his body subsided. When Admiral Thomson suddenly stepped into the corridor and aimed the large pistol straight at him, he almost stumbled into the wall.

Thomson looked along the corridor he judged was the direction the gunshots had come from. The man running towards him, who wore a mask of fear, was obviously fleeing from something. The Russians must be close.

"Get on the ground!" Thomson shouted.

Careful not to hammer the glass dagger in any farther, Fitch dived to the floor.

To his credit, the Admiral recovered surprisingly quickly from the shock of realizing the Russians were not the current threat and focused the weapon on the fast approaching monster. When the first shot echoed along the corridor, the Hunter leaped to the side to avoid the large caliber bullet. It sped harmlessly past and struck a man farther along the corridor in the center of his back. He toppled to the floor with his spine cut in two.

The Hunter avoided the second bullet by leaping onto the wall and sprung across to the opposite side and over Fitch hugging the floor like it was his mother.

The third bullet Thomson fired struck the ceiling when the Hunter crashed into him and savagely raked its talons over his face and body as they both fell. The Hunter abandoned Thomson's blood-soaked corpse when it struck the floor and bounded along the corridor. As it approached the door at the far end, cold air whooshed along the corridor when it opened.

Though Richard's mouth opened to let forth a terrified scream, it was cut off by the Hunter's clawed hand that gripped him tightly around the throat and propelled him backwards.

Lucy, who was directly behind Richard, had more time. Her scream was carried away by the wind as she recoiled from the monster that had suddenly appeared.

Jane stumbled when Lucy collided with her and fell backwards.

Jack reached out and caught Jane before she hit the ground and stared at Richard's terrified expression as the monster carried him past.

Jane stared in horror at the one-eyed Hunter as gunshots followed in its wake from the men that rushed from the doorway.

The monster turned, snarled and threw Richard at them before fleeing.

Gasping for breath from the released chokehold, Richard flew through the air, but his flight ended abruptly and painfully when the men dodged aside, and he crashed forcefully into the wall. He screamed as his leg and arm snapped from the collision and screamed again when his damaged limbs struck the deck. Mercifully, the blackness of unconsciousness swept away his pain.

Miller glanced at the three unexpected arrivals as he halted, pulled out his pistol and held it out to Jack. "Do you know how to use this?"

Jack, still dazed by what had just happened, took the weapon and nodded.

"We're going to drive the monster to front of the ship and kill it, but if it gets past us, don't let it get back inside."

"I'll do my best," said Jack, glancing at Richard's crumpled form. "What about him?"

"Leave him. He can be tended to later when the monster's been dealt with." Miller turned to the two women. "Get inside and head for the bridge. Tell the captain about the monster and to ensure everyone remains inside and to turn on all deck lights. If that thing gets back inside again, I'm not sure anyone will survive the onslaught." Miller rejoined his men and they moved away.

Jane and Lucy were still recovering from the shock of the Hunter's sudden appearance when Jack herded them towards the open door. He pushed them inside and went to close the door, but Jane grabbed it. "What are you doing, Jack?"

"I've got to stay here."

Jane squeezed through the gap. "If you're staying, I am too. Lucy can tell the captain."

Jack knew to argue would only waste time and relented. He glanced at Lucy. "Are you okay going on your own?"

"Alone is something I'm used to lately. Good luck you two." Lucy pulled the door shut and turned the locking mechanism before rushing away to seek out the route to the bridge.

Jack grabbed Jane's hand and together they roamed their eyes across the deck.

*****

Miller, Sawyer and Patterson paused and roamed their weapons across the deck.

"If we can drive it to the bow, it'll have nowhere to go," said Miller.

The two men nodded and spread out with their weapons raised and moved forwards.

Miller moved over to the crashed helicopter, which explained how the new arrivals had gotten onboard, and after checking the monster wasn't hiding inside, moved on.

Sawyer moved past the shipping containers stacked along the port side and peered around the edge of the last one. His eyes roamed the area but detected no sign of the Hunter.

Fighting against the rocking motion the ship, Patterson moved cautiously along the starboard side. As he approached the end of the shipping container, the light ahead went dark. He flipped the night-vision goggles over his eyes and edged forward. When his boots crunched on broken glass, he paused and glanced up at the broken light and knew the Hunter was responsible and somewhere nearby.

"I have a broken light on the starboard side," Patterson whispered into his helmet mic.

"Nothing portside, so I'll head towards you," said Sawyer.

Patterson roamed the goggles around the deck bathed in the NVGs' ghostly green light. The constant creaks of metal the ship and the containers emitted and the windblown snow and spray that howled around him made it difficult to hear and visualize everything clearly. With his senses on high alert and his eyes and weapon sweeping across every possible hiding place the monster might have concealed itself, he moved forward.

*****

The Hunter ignored the cold spray that washed over it from below and blinked the snow from its one good eye as it watched the human pass by less than a yard away. It slowly climbed over the rail it hung from and stepped silently onto the deck. Two steps brought it behind the human. A claw reached over the man's head, grabbed the helmet and yanked it back. The human's exposed throat gushed blood when its claws raked deep gouges through the soft flesh.

As Patterson died, his finger squeezed the trigger.

Sawyer dived behind the forward anchor-winch housing to escape the bullets that sprayed around him. He peered out when they stopped and glimpsed movement in the shadows shrouding the deck. He flipped down his NVGs and saw Stedman's motionless body and the rapidly cooling pool of blood around the man's head, but no sign of the Hunter responsible for the slaughter.

He leaned into his mic and, keeping his emotions under control, whispered, "Patterson's down. It's on the starboard side."

"Copy," Miller replied. "I'm moving around to cut off its retreat. Hold your position and I'll drive it towards you."

Sawyer focused his weapon on the starboard side and waited.

Miller rushed back past the crashed helicopter and around the side of the starboard container stacks. As he moved along he sensed danger and looked up. Though he saw nothing, he was certain he had heard something moving along the top of the containers. It could only be the Hunter trying to get behind them.

Miller shouldered his rifle and informed Sawyer, "It's moving along the top of the containers. I'm going up while you move to the back and cut it off."

"Copy that," replied Sawyer and rushed for the stern.

Miller climbed up to the top of the doubled-stacked containers and when he cautiously peered over the edge he came face-to-face with the snarling monster. Its evil gaping mouth darted at his head. Miller dodged to the side, slipped and fell. He landed awkwardly, twisting his ankle, and stumbled against the rail, pain shooting up his spine from the impact. He grabbed at his rifle when the monster landed beside him. The Hunter snarled menacingly and lashed out a claw that sent the weapon flying over the side into the sea. Miller instinctively reached for his pistol that wasn't there as he had given it to Jack and grabbed for his knife instead. Pain rippled up his spine as he retreated from the advancing monster.

The Hunter glanced at the knife Miller held threateningly and seemed to smile as it held up a claw and flexed its talons. It had a handful of sharp blades.

Miller spoke into his mic, "Sawyer, I could do with your help here. I've lost my weapon."

Sawyer increased his speed on hearing Miller's plea that wouldn't have been made if he wasn't desperate. As he rushed through a gap between the containers and into an open area, he snapped his eyes closed as the ship's main deck lights flooded the area. Increased in intensity by the NVGs still over his eyes, the light stabbed painfully into his retinas. He swiped the NVGs up, but temporarily blinded he failed to see the angled support beam of the quick-launch lifeboat structure pointed steeply over the side of the ship he ran towards. His head struck with such force his legs shot out from beneath him and he slammed to the deck.

*****

Jack's eyes constantly roamed the deck for signs of the one-eyed Hunter. When he glimpsed movement the weapon focused on it and he barely held his finger back from squeezing the trigger when he saw the soldier appear. As he relaxed, light flooded the deck and the man crashed to the ground. He and Jane rushed over and knelt beside him.

Sawyer, dazed from the blow, opened his eyes and looked at the face waving hazily in his blurred vision. "Miller's in trouble...starboard side...lost his weapon." He pushed Jack away. "Go help him."

Worried about leaving her, Jack glanced at Jane.

Jane grabbed Sawyer's rifle. "Go Jack, I'll be fine."

Though reluctant to leave Jane with the monster somewhere nearby, he figured she could handle herself and Miller might be in need of urgent assistance. He dashed away to find him.

*****

Miller backed into a metal support column and held the knife ready to fend off his attacker. The Hunter rushed at the human and barely registered the pain from the slash along its arm from the human's knife. It gripped the man's knife hand and bent it back with a loud crack of bone. Miller groaned in pain and dropped the knife when his arm snapped like a twig from the monster's strength. A hot wave of nausea swept over him as he staggered to the side and collapsed to the floor. He grabbed at his fallen knife with his good arm, but a kick from the monster sent it over the side. The Hunter moved in for the kill with its clawed limbs either side of his pain-wracked body. Its tongue slithered over teeth prepared to rip his flesh. Miller tried one last move and kicked his good foot as hard as he could into the monsters groin area. The Hunter howled and then snarled as it moved its angry snout closer. It stared straight into his eyes and sniffed his face before widening its jaws and moving its head back slightly. Miller knew it was all over.

Three shots rang out.

The Hunter jerked from each bullet that struck. It twisted around, snarled at the human responsible for the pain, and sprung towards him.

Jack forced aside the screaming urge to flee from the terrifying form of the Hunter rushing at him and aimed the gun at the monster's ferocious face and repeatedly pulled the trigger until it ran out of bullets.

Though wounded the Hunter sprung from side-to-side and avoided all but two of the bullets. It landed on the deck when the weapon made a different sound and the bullets stopped. It loped with intended malice towards the defenseless human. Jack slowly backed away. The Hunter sprung with its claws outstretched to grasp its prey.

Gunshots rang out. Blood pumped from the row of bullet holes that peppered the Hunter's side and sent it flying to the ground. The momentum of the fall sent it tumbling across the water-slick deck, stopping a few inches away from

Jack with its back legs dangling over the edge. Jack placed a foot on its head and pushed. The monster stared at Jack as it slithered over the edge. Its claws failing to find purchase screeched along the metal deck until dropped from sight and splashed into the cold sea. Jack grabbed the rail for support as the adrenaline rush subsided and looked at Miller, who sat up and looked back at him. The two men nodded at each other. It was over.

Richard had regained consciousness to the sound of gunfire and had watched the Hunter's demise. He looked at his arm bent at an impossible angle, the bloody splintered bone protruding from his leg, and even though shock barely dulled the pain, he smiled. He had survived.

"Are you okay, Jack?" enquired Jane, as she rushed over. She let Sawyer's weapon clatter to the ground and held Jack's arm.

Jack smiled at her. "Thanks to you I am. Will you marry me?"

Jane looked at him in shock. "What?"

"Will you marry me? I don't have a ring yet, but I promise I'll buy you a nice one."

Jane glanced around the ship at the wounded and the carnage. "Your idea of a romantic setting needs some work, but yes, Jack, I will."

They kissed.

"Before you two starting planning the wedding, I could do with some help here," called out Miller, using the rail to pull himself upright.

"And me," called out Ramirez, who had dragged himself across the deck to find out the fate of his friend.

"Don't worry about me," called out Richard, raising his good arm weakly. "I'm not one to complain." He flashed them all a broad smile.

Jane looked at the man who excelled in complaining. "That knock on the head must have caused some serious damage."

Jack smiled and gave Jane a peck on the lips. "Come on, let's round up the wounded and then we can find somewhere private to relax."

*****

The oily black splotches on the side of the Spasatel Kuznetsov, gone unnoticed by the Russian crew, resisted the lashing waves' attempts to pull them into its cold depths, slithered across the cold steel hull and oozed together like puddles of mercury. When all had become one, the small, black, greasy blob—a mere fraction of its former self—crawled up the side of the ship, onto the deck and looked for somewhere it could conceal itself.

#
EPILOGUE

After everyone aboard the American vessel had recovered from the shock of the carnage, the remainder of the Starlight's voyage to America was uneventful. Its precious cargo was unloaded at Norfolk Naval Shipyard in Portsmouth, Virginia, and under the cover of darkness transported to a secret location.

Jane, Jack, Lucy and Richard were returned to England, and three months later Jane and Jack were married.

Though the conspiracy diehards claimed a second Roswell cover-up had been instigated by the American government to hide the truth and that the Antarctic spaceship and the alien monsters were real, a series of photographs, YouTube videos and various blog articles that appeared on the Internet over the coming weeks shed uncertainty on the validity of Richard's sensational story.

Richard's plan to profit from his experiences in the Antarctic petered away with the loss of Little Lucifer, the only substantial proof he had his story was real. Clinton Smythe stopped returning his phone calls, and Richard's pleas for the others who had witnessed some of the events to corroborate his stories fell on deaf ears. Unable to stand the continuous ridicule he received in public and at the speaking engagements he personally set up, Richard shunned publicity and once more slipped into obscurity.

As the Spasatel Kuznetsov pulled into port, a large black car pulled alongside the wharf. When the ship had been moored and the gangplank lowered, two men climbed out of the car and boarded the vessel. Captain Brusilov met them at the top and placed the two alien weapons in the metal suitcase handcuffed to one of the men's wrist. As they turned away without a word and headed for the gangplank, a small black blob slithered unseen onto the suitcase-carrying man's shoe.

Brusilov watched the men until they had climbed back into their car and driven away, and then returned to his cabin to wait for those to arrive who would debrief him and the crew before it was decided if their mission had been a success or a failure. The outcome of that decision would determine if they received praise or punishment.

After a long drive the car turned onto a small road that stretched across the cold Siberian tundra, passed through the first of five checkpoints stationed with armed guards along the road's fifty-mile route and continued on its journey. At the road's end, the driver steered the car through the gates of the security-fenced compound and pulled to a stop alongside an unassuming agricultural building. The man with the suitcase climbed out, shivered from the biting wind that assaulted him and crossed hurriedly to the door. He stared briefly at the camera focused on him until a buzzing signalled the unlocking of the door. He entered, crossed the vacant dusty room and stepped into a small chamber. Once the door was closed, the elevator carried him deep below ground.

The man stepped out of the elevator, walked along the drab gray-painted corridor and passed through the final security check. He entered a modern room where a group of white-clad scientists waited, placed the suitcase on the table they were gathered around and unlocked it. The scientists stared excitedly at the alien weapons before one of them removed them from the case. As the other scientists huddled round the weapons and the man closed the suitcase, the black blob slid from the man's shoe and slithered across the room to hide in the shadows until EV1L had decided on its next move.

Note from author

I hope you found Ice Rift - Salvage an exciting and enjoyable read.

I welcome your feedback good and bad, as it helps me to improve my writing, and I would appreciate it if you left a review on Amazon or your place of purchase showing your enjoyment of my book. It doesn't have to be a long review, a few words will suffice.

If you would like to be added to my mailing list to receive notifications of my new books, receive limited free advance review copies and the occasional free book, send feedback or just to drop me a line, please contact me at: **benhammott@gmail.com**

Your details will not be shared with anyone and can be removed at any time by contacting me via the above email address requesting your removal.

Details of all my books can be found at **benhammottbooks.com**

If you have any questions or comments about this book, or any of my other publications, please contact me at **benhammott@gmail.com**

As always, thank you for your continued support.

Ben Hammott

Coming Soon

Spore (Working title)

THE 13TH TREASURE SHIP

RETURN TO CASTLE DRACULA

BEACON 666

SPACEWRECK

THE GOBLINS CURSE - DEAD DRAGONS GOLD 2

LOST PYRATE TREASURE - BUTLER CRONICLES

2

OTHER BOOKS BY AUTHOR

EL DORADO Book 1: Search for the Lost City - An Unexpected Adventure
EL DORADO - Book 2: Fabled Lost Treasure - The Secret City

One of the world's most legendary and elusive treasures, sought after for centuries. . .
An ancient mystery.
A Lost Treasure.
A Hidden City.
An impossible location.
An unimaginable adventure.

Included in Aztec and Mayan legends, Conquistadors had heard rumours of its existence when exploring the New World, but never found it.

During World War 2, Nazi inspired archaeologists were convinced they had pinpointed its location. They packed a U-Boat with supplies and set a course for the Amazon Jungle. They disappeared!

Many adventurers eager to claim the legendary gold as their own entered one of the most inhospitable places on earth, the Amazon Jungle. Most were never seen again!

And yet the exact location of El Dorado and its fantastic hoard of Mayan, Aztec and Inca treasure so many have dreamed of finding, remains a mystery. Any who may have stumbled upon it never returned to tell the tale.

It was as if someone, or something, was protecting it...

Ben Hammott

SOLOMON'S TREASURE 1

BEGINNINGS: A Hunt for Treasure

and

SOLOMON'S TREASURE 2

THE PRIEST'S SECRET

(The Tomb, the Temple, the Treasure Book 1 and 2)

An ancient mystery, a lost treasure and the search for the most sought after relics in all antiquity.

The Tomb, the Temple, the Treasure series, has become an international best seller.

An exciting archaeological thriller spanning more than 2000 years. Beginning with the construction of Solomon's Temple, the Fall of Jerusalem, the creation of the Copper Scrolls and the forming of the Knights Templar and their mysterious tunnelling under the Temple Mount. The story then takes us into the trap-riddled catacombs beneath Rosslyn Chapel, on to Rennes-le-Chateau, into the Tomb, Jerusalem and its secret tunnels and beyond.

"This is one of the most exciting novels I've read in years."

"Hammott's writing is solid and the premise intriguing. An entertaining quest filled action adventure."

"...a terrific book with a likable protagonist, skilled plotting and interesting characters. This gripping quest for lost artifacts mystery had me hooked from the first chapter."

*****

An Insatiable Thirst for Murder

Serial Killer Henry Holmes

STORY OF AMERICA'S FIRST DOCUMENTED SERIAL KILLER. (Fiction)

This book contains the shocking dramatization of real events carried out by the serial killer, Henry Howard Holmes.

America's first documented serial killer, Henry Howard Holmes, holds a dubious and ghastly record that few serial killers in history have surpassed. The 19th century killer is thought to have committed over 200 murders, but, for unexplained reasons, appears to have been overlooked by many true crime enthusiasts. Set partly in the era when "Jack the Ripper" was terrorizing the foggy streets of London with his gruesome slayings in the 19th century, Holmes was committing his nefarious crimes in America, undetected.

*****

Also available is the best non-fiction account of Holmes Crimes, frauds, capture and trial:

The Hunt for H. H. Holmes and Trial of America's First Serial Killer

Holmes Pitezel Case - History of the Greatest Crime of the Century and the Search for the Missing Pitezel Children by Frank P. Geyer 1896.

(Illustrated - complete and unabridged) 4 Books in 1 Edition includes Holmes prison confessions.

Detective Frank Geyer, the author of the above book, was the man responsible for bringing H. H. Holmes to justice and revealing some of his atrocious crimes.

*****

The Lost Inheritance Mystery

(The Butler Chronicles Book 1)

A Victorian mystery adventure revolving around the search for a lost inheritance worth millions.

The two rival miserly Drooge brothers, a butler, a murderous hunchback, a shadowy assassin, a fashion senseless burglar, a beast named Diablo, strange henchmen, an actor who once had a standing ovation, and many more oddball characters, all conspire in ways you couldn't possibly imagine to steal two paintings that contain clues to the long lost inheritance of Jacobus Drooge.

This is a complete stand-alone adventure with no sudden ending or cliffhanger.

*****

Dead Dragons Gold - Book 1

A Gathering of Dwarfs

Not every Fairy Tale ends happily for all...

A dauntless young hero.

An impossible quest.

A Hunt for Dead Dragons Gold.

"A dark fantasy tale interjected with humour interwoven in an original plot that will change your view of Snow White's seven dwarfs."

"If you like your fantasy stories full of originality and humour, this is the book for you and one for Pratchett fans of all ages. Highly recommended."

-

Ben Hammott's books are available from your Amazon store in eBook and paperback formats.

Information about Ben Hammott's books can be found at **www.benhammottbooks.com**

Made in the USA
Middletown, DE
09 March 2019